KAREN ROBARDS

Delacorte Press

Published by
Delacorte Press
Bantam Doubleday Dell Publishing Group, Inc.
666 Fifth Avenue
New York, New York 10103

ISBN 0-385-30836-1

Manufactured in the United States of America

This book is dedicated to my sister Lee, who once again inspired me. And, as always, it is also dedicated with much love to the men in my life —my husband, Doug, and my sons, Peter and Chris.

*E*ver since that nightmarish dawn, Rachel Grant had not been able to abide the scent of summersweet. It was ironic that at this of all possible moments the smell seemed to be practically smothering her.

She stood on the sweltering asphalt in front of the Greyhound bus station, waiting to welcome Johnny Harris home. Johnny Harris, the bad boy to whom she had tried to teach high school English all those years ago. Johnny Harris, the swaggering son of the local no-good, whom the whole town had expected to turn out just like his dad but who had in fact turned out to be far worse.

Johnny Harris, convicted of murdering and accused of raping a seventeen-year-old high school cheerleader eleven years before.

Today, with her help, Johnny Harris was coming home.

The sound of the bus engine reached her before the vehicle itself came into view. Rachel tensed, glancing nervously around to see who might be watching. Bob Gibson, the ticket agent, was nothing more than a blur behind the plate-glass window that fronted the converted gas station that served Tylerville as a bus depot. Jeff Skaggs, who'd graduated from high school this past May and now worked at the 7-Eleven, was dropping coins into the Coke machine at the side of the building. Just beyond his parked pickup truck she discovered the summersweet bush with its shiny bright green leaves and spikes of white flowers.

Identifying a very real source for the smell made Rachel feel a little better. Still, the coincidence was eerie. Marybeth Edwards's bloody corpse had been found beside a summersweet bush eleven years ago almost to the day in the midst of a heat wave much like the one Tylerville was presently experiencing. A shower of blossoms, apparently dislodged in her struggle with her assailant, had covered the girl's body. The sweet scent of the flowers had almost masked the more pungent odor of blood. Then as now, it had been late August, and as hot as the inside of a pizza oven. Rachel, on her way to Tylerville High to get her classroom in order for the coming year, had been one of the first on the scene. The horror of the sight had never left her.

Neither had her certainty that Johnny Harris, who'd been notoriously sweet on the pretty blonde, had not killed her. He had been seeing Marybeth on the sly, against her parents' orders, and when she was found dead with his semen inside her body, the case had seemed open and shut. He'd been arrested within a week of the murder, tried, and subsequently convicted of murder, on the theory that Marybeth had told him that night that she meant to stop seeing him. The rape charge was dismissed. There had been too many people, like Rachel, who knew exactly what kind of relationship Marybeth had had with Johnny. She'd been sure that the boy she knew could not have committed so heinous a crime. She'd always been convinced that the only crime of which he was guilty was simply being Johnny Harris.

Now she only prayed she was right.

With a swoosh of tires and a squeal of brakes, the bus pulled into the station and stopped. The door opened. Rachel watched the empty spot, her fingers tightening around the strap of her summer purse. The heels of her neat white pumps sank into the asphalt as her body tensed in anticipation.

Then there he was, in the doorway. Johnny Harris. He wore scuffed brown cowboy boots and beat-up jeans and a white cotton T-shirt. His shoulders were wide enough to stretch the knit shirt taut across them. His biceps bulged with muscle, and his skin was surprisingly tan. He was thin. No, that wasn't the right word—*lean* was the one she wanted. Lean and hard and tough as leather. His hair was the same color, coal black, as it had always been, though it was longer than he used to wear it, almost touching his shoulders, and wavy. His face was the same—she would have recognized him anywhere once she looked into it, although several days' worth of stubble blurred the lines of his jaw and chin. The sullenly handsome boy she remembered was still sullen, still handsome, but no longer a boy. He had matured into a dangerous-looking man.

It occurred to her with a sense of shock that Johnny Harris was now almost thirty years old. If she had ever known anything about him, she no longer did.

He had spent the last ten years of his life in federal prison.

He stepped down onto the asphalt, glanced around. Rachel, who had been standing off to one side, gave herself a mental shake and started forward. Her heels caught in the tiny craters they had created in the pavement, and she stumbled. When she recovered her balance, his eyes were on her.

"Miss Grant." He didn't smile as he gave her a thorough once-over. The look was almost offensive in its bold assessment of her femininity, and it threw her mentally off stride. It was not the kind of look that she as a teacher expected to receive from a male student, or former student, for that matter. Respect was not in it.

"J-Johnny. Welcome home." It seemed absurd to address this hard-faced man as she would have addressed the high school boy, but his name came automatically to her lips, just as, apparently, he had also slipped by force of habit into the remembered form of addressing her.

"Home." His lips thinned as he glanced around. "Yeah, right."

Following his gaze, she saw that Jeff Skaggs, eyes wide and Coke can suspended halfway to his mouth, was gaping at the pair of them. The news of Johnny Harris's return would be all over Tylerville by suppertime, Rachel knew. Idell Skaggs, Jeff's mother, was the biggest gossip in town. Not that Rachel had ever thought to keep Johnny's return a secret. There were no secrets in Tylerville, Kentucky, at least not for long. Everyone knew everyone else's business. Still, she had hoped to give him a chance to arrive and get himself reoriented a little before the inevitable storm of protest broke out. If certain segments of the population had known in advance that Johnny Harris was coming back to Tylerville, they would have raised heaven and earth to keep him out.

Now they knew, or very soon would know, but it was too late for them to do anything about it. There was going to be a huge outcry, and much of it was going to be directed at her. But she had known that ever since she had read his letter asking for a job so that he could win parole and she had written back to say yes.

She hated controversy. She especially hated to be at the center of a controversy. But she had felt strongly that the boy she remembered deserved a better shake than he'd gotten. She still felt that way.

Only the tall, surly-looking stranger beside her was not the boy she remembered. That nearly insulting glance proved it, if anything more than his altered appearance were needed.

The driver stepped down, turned to open up the belly of the bus. Rachel took a firm grip on her composure.

"We'd better get your things."

He laughed. It was a sound of derision rather than amusement. "Miss Grant, I'm holdin' 'em."

A stained canvas duffel bag that he'd been dangling over one shoulder was swung around for her inspection.

"Oh. Well then, shall we go?"

He said nothing. She turned to lead the way to her car, feeling oddly disconcerted. Of course she had not really expected the eighteen-year-old boy she had taught to step off the bus, but she had not been prepared for the man, either.

More fool, she.

Trying not to panic, Rachel reached her car, a blue Maxima, opened the door, and glanced over her shoulder just in time to catch Johnny Harris flipping Jeff Skaggs the bird. The sight of that long middle finger pointed obscenely skyward was all she needed to confirm her suspicion that where Johnny Harris was concerned, she just might have bitten off more than she could chew.

"Was that really necessary?" she asked in a low voice as he approached.

"Yep."

He walked around the car, opened the rear door, threw in his duffel bag, then slid into the front passenger seat. Rachel was left with nothing to do but get in herself.

She did. It was amazing how small her usually roomy Maxima seemed now that Johnny Harris was in the bucket seat beside her. His shoulders were broader than the gray plush seatback, so broad that they seemed to infringe on her space. His legs, too long to stretch out, sprawled apart. One jean-clad knee rested against the gear console between the seats. His proximity made her uncomfortable. He turned his head in her direction, and his eyes (they were a deep, smoky blue—funny she hadn't remembered that) moved over her again. This time there was no mistaking the nature of his glance.

"Put your seat belt on, please. It's the law." Rachel had to fight an urge to hunch her shoulders forward to shield her breasts from his view. She was not usually ill at ease with men. In fact, for the last several years, she had tended to scarcely notice them. Once, long ago, her foolish heart had loved madly, as she had always expected to love a man. He had taken all the love she had had to give, and all the mindless young passion, too, and dismissed it as a gift of little value. She'd survived but in the process she had learned that it was safer to shut men out.

But there was no shutting out Johnny Harris. His eyes—no, she was not imagining it—lingered on her breasts. Instinctively, Rachel glanced down at herself. Her sleeveless dress of white cotton knit with bold purple hydrangeas splashed across it had a high, round neckline and a skirt that swept her ankles when she walked. It flattered her slender figure while being both ladylike and modest. There was nothing about the way she was dressed to provoke that disturbing glance. Still, with his eyes on her like that, she felt hideously exposed, almost naked, and she didn't like the feeling one bit. Ignoring his behavior took an effort, but she could think of no other way to handle it, so ignore it she did.

"We sure wouldn't want to break the law, now would we?"

If there was a jeer hidden somewhere in his words, and Rachel strongly suspected there was, at least he pulled the seat belt around himself and fastened it. No longer feeling his gaze on her person was a palpable relief.

By this time, Rachel was so rattled that her fingers shook as she inserted the key into the ignition. It took three tries before the key went home and the engine turned over. Hot air blasted out of the wide-open air conditioner vents, nearly choking her. Fumbling for the buttons, she rolled down the passenger side window and her own. The air outside was no cooler, and she could feel beads of sweat forming on her forehead.

"It's hot, isn't it?" A good, safe topic of conversation, she thought.

He grunted.

So much for that. She shifted gears, lifted her foot off the brake, and pressed down on the gas. But instead of driving forward out of the lot, the Maxima shot backward. It was brought to a jarring halt by a telephone pole that sprouted from the grassy strip separating the bus depot from Callie's Laundromat next door.

Apparently she had put the transmission into reverse by mistake. Rachel swore silently.

For a moment after the impact neither of them moved. Rachel was still recovering her presence of mind when Johnny slewed around in his seat to survey the damage.

"Next time, try drive," he said.

Rachel said nothing. What was there to say? She put the car into drive and pulled away. If she had a dented bumper, which she probably had, examining it could wait until Johnny Harris was out of her car.

"Am I making you nervous, Miss Grant?" her passenger asked as Rachel somehow managed to pull out onto the two-lane road that bisected the town without hitting any oncoming traffic. The humid air rushing through the windows whipped strands of her usually smooth, chin-length brown bob in front of her eyes, making it difficult to see where she was going. Distractedly, she pushed her hair back from her face and held the foremost sections at her crown with one hand. Coping with Johnny Harris while at the same time trying to drive only *seemed* like mutually exclusive activities, she told herself. With a little concentration, she could surely manage both.

"Of course not," she said, and forced a smile. She had not taught high school for thirteen years for nothing. Keeping her cool in the face of constant chaos and occasional disaster was second nature to her by now.

"You sure? You look like you're wondering whether I'm about to jump your bones."

"Wh-what?" Rachel was so taken aback that she could scarcely get the word out. The hand that had been holding her hair out of her face dropped to the steering wheel as she shot him a shocked glance. She knew what the expression meant, of course. It was teenage slang for "have sex with you." But she couldn't believe that he would actually address such a remark to her. She was five years his senior, and even in her youth had been nobody's idea of a boy-toy. Besides, she had been his teacher, for goodness' sake, and was trying her level best to be his friend now.

Although being Johnny Harris's friend was turning out to be altogether more difficult than she had anticipated.

"After all, it's been ten years since I've had the pleasure of a woman's—oh, sorry, in your case I guess I should say a *lady's*—company. You might be worried that I'm kinda horny."

"What?" This time it was more a gasp than a question as she stared at him in disbelief.

"Damnation, woman, watch the road!" The unexpected roar made Rachel jump to obey, even as his hand shot out to grab and jerk the steering wheel. A heavily laden coal truck thundered past, causing the small car to shiver.

"You nearly got us killed! Jesus H. Christ!"

Heat and tension combined to make Rachel nauseous. She pushed the buttons that rolled up the windows. The flow from the vents was now blessedly cool. For a moment she enjoyed the feel of the chilled air on her overheated face.

"For God's sake, who the hell taught you how to drive? You're a menace!"

When she didn't reply, he slumped back into his seat. His hands, which were clenched into fists in his lap, were the only outward sign of tension he betrayed. That, and the way his eyes were now fastened on the road.

At least she had found a solution to the problem of warding off his lewd glances. But ignoring the issue was probably a mistake. The only way she or anyone else had ever been able to deal with the youthful Johnny Harris was to stand up to him. If he thought he could walk all over someone, he did.

"You can't talk to me that way," she said into the tense silence. "I won't allow it."

Both her hands grasped the steering wheel as she spoke, and she kept her eyes fixed firmly on the road. Stay cool, calm, and collected, she told herself. That was the way to handle him. Unfortunately, the bus depot was on the other side of town from their destination, which was still some ten minutes away. Traffic on this Thursday afternoon was surprisingly heavy. Even under the best of conditions she had a regrettable tendency to let her mind wander from the road. She was always building castles in the air, to use her mother's exasperated description, instead of keeping her feet planted firmly on the ground and her mind affixed to her business. As a result, she had suffered untold numbers of fender benders.

These were not the best of conditions.

"What way? Oh, you mean the part about my being horny? I was just trying to reassure you. You don't have to worry about being attacked or anything. At least, not by me."

This innocent-sounding statement was accompanied by another sliding glance that made no effort to disguise its purpose: a blatant appraisal of her body. It was almost as if he were deliberately trying to make her uneasy in his presence, though if he was, Rachel couldn't imagine why. At this point, she was just about the only ally he had left in town, if not in the world.

"Are you determined to make things difficult for yourself, Johnny?" she asked quietly.

His eyes narrowed. "Don't come all teacherish with me, Miss Grant. I'm not in high school anymore."

"Your manners were better then."

"So were my prospects. They've both gone to hell since, and you know what? I don't give a big goddamn."

That shut her up, as it was no doubt meant to.

In silence they passed the Wal-Mart, the Burger King, the Kroger, and the cluster of antique shops that had sprung up on the corner of Vine and Main. With their destination now near at hand, Rachel began to relax a little. Just a few more minutes, and she would be rid of him. She concentrated on pulling without mishap into the parking lot at the rear of Grant Hardware, which her grandfather had founded just after the turn of the century and which she now oversaw.

"There's an apartment over the store. It's yours. Just go around to the side and up the stairs." Rachel stopped the car and put the transmission into park as she spoke. Reaching into the door pocket beside her, she handed him a single key dangling from a round metal ring.

"Here's the key. The rent will be deducted from your paycheck each week. As I told you in my letter, the hours are from eight in the morning till six at night, with an hour for lunch, Monday through Saturday. I expect you to be on the job at eight in the morning."

"I'll be there."

"Good."

Still he sat, the key dangling from his fingers, looking at her with an expression she couldn't decipher.

"Why'd you offer me a job, anyway? Aren't you just a little bit afraid of a man who'd rape and kill a teenage girl?"

"We both know that you were innocent of raping Marybeth Edwards," Rachel replied crisply, though such plain speaking caused her hands to close tightly around the steering wheel. "I, for one, am perfectly willing to believe that the two of you had consensual sex, just as you claimed. And that she was alive when you left her. Now, would you please get out of my car? I have things to do."

To Rachel's secret relief, he opened the door and slid out without another word. How she would have ejected him had he proved difficult, she couldn't imagine. Putting her foot on the brake, she carefully moved the gearshift down to drive. When she looked up again he was beside her, his arm resting on the roof of the car as he pecked with one finger on her window.

Lips compressing, Rachel pushed the button that rolled the window down. The heat assaulted her anew.

"There's something I gotta tell you," he said in a confidential tone as he leaned toward her. His face was close to hers, too close. He was making her uncomfortable again, as he no doubt intended.

That notion stiffened her spine.

"What?" she all but snapped.

"I had a major case of the hots for you when I was in high school. I still do."

Rachel's mouth dropped open in shock. He grinned at her cockily and straightened.

It was only as she watched him saunter away that she realized her mouth was agape. She closed it with a snap.

2

———————

From the driver's seat of a nondescript tan car that had pulled to the curb a little way up the road from the hardware store, an unnoticed observer watched them with an unwavering gaze. The watcher's eyes were faintly glassy as they drank in every detail of the man walking with slow arrogance across the parking lot and around the corner out of sight. The blue Maxima reversed with a squeal of tires and pulled out into the street far too fast, then drove off heading away from where the parked car waited. But the watcher hardly noticed.

He was back. Johnny Harris was back. The watcher had been waiting—oh, it seemed like forever—for this moment. The rumors had been true for once, though the watcher had scarcely dared believe them until *he* stepped off that bus and into view.

Johnny Harris. He was home at last, and now it was time to finish what had been started eleven years ago.

The watcher smiled with anticipation.

3

"*D*id you hear? Idell says her boy saw Rachel Grant meeting some-body at the bus depot this afternoon, and you'll never for the life of you guess who!"

"Who?"

"Johnny Harris."

"Johnny Harris! Why, he's in prison! Idell must've got it wrong."

"No, she swears that's what Jeff told her. He must've got out on parole or something."

"Do they do that, for murder?"

"I guess. Anyhow, Idell says Jeff saw him, big as life, with Rachel Grant. Can you believe it?"

"No!"

"It's true, Mrs. Ashton," Rachel interrupted the conversation. "Johnny Harris is out on parole, and he's going to be working at Grant Hardware." Still shaken from her encounter with the aforesaid Johnny Harris, Rachel had a hard time summoning up a serene smile to show to her neighbors, though in the end she managed it. This was, at one and the same time, both the best and worst thing about Tylerville: there was no escaping being the recipient of other folks' views about what was going on in your life. The two chatting women were in the checkout lane at the Kroger's, so busy with their gossip that they hadn't noticed her in the next lane over. Mrs. Ashton was sixtyish, a friend of Rachel's mother, and the recipient of the news. Pam Collier was younger, perhaps forty-five, with a terror of a sixteen-year-old son who would, in all likelihood, be in Rachel's class the coming fall. Rachel would have thought that with such a hellion of her own, Pam might be slightly sympathetic to Johnny's plight, but apparently she was not.

"Oh, Rachel, what about the Edwardses? They'll just die when they hear." Mrs. Ashton's distress for the slain girl's family was plain in her eyes.

"I'm sorry for them, you know I am," Rachel said, "but I never did think Johnny Harris killed Marybeth Edwards, and I still don't. I taught him in high school, remember, and he wasn't a bad boy. At least, not *that* bad." Conscience forced her to amend that last sentence. Johnny Harris had been bad, in a lip-curling, back-talking, black-leather-jacket kind of way guaranteed to set up the backs of the decent folks of Tylerville. He got drunk, he got in fights, he smashed lights and windows, he cursed people out, and he rode a motorcycle. The kids he had associated with were mostly trash like himself, and if talk were believed, he and his crowd had done some wild partying the likes of which had not been seen in Tylerville before or since. He'd been in almost constant trouble in school and out, and his smart mouth had not helped his reputation any. But his saving grace, in Rachel's eyes, was that he had liked to read. In fact, that was what had first caused her to think he might be different from what he seemed.

She'd been hall monitor one day in the fall of her first semester of teaching, when she was just about to turn twenty-two, and she'd seen sixteen-year-old Johnny Harris swagger out the side door of the school as if he had every right in the world to do so. She followed him, suspecting he meant to sneak a cigarette or worse, and discovered him finally in the parking lot, stretched out in the back seat of some other student's car. Alone, his high-top sneakers with the hole in the left sole sticking out the window, his long legs crossed at the ankles, one arm bent behind his head for a pillow. An open book had been propped on his sweatshirted chest.

Her astonishment had nearly matched his belligerence upon being discovered.

"All those Harrises are bad—every last one! Why, you remember when Buck Harris claimed to have got religion and started calling himself a minister, then set up his own church and collected no telling how much in donations for it, saying as how the money was going to go to feed starving children in Appalachia? And he went and spent that money himself, gamblin' and drinkin' and livin' high? He went to jail for near a year for that, and that isn't the worst thing he's done. Not by a long shot, probably, if the truth were known." Mrs. Ashton was tight-lipped at the memory.

Rachel wondered if perhaps she were one of those who had contributed to Buck Harris's "church." It was well known around town that only the more gullible residents had fallen for that one. After all, who in his or her right mind would trust Buck Harris? She said mildly, "You can't blame Johnny for something his brother did."

"Hmmph!" said Mrs. Ashton, clearly unconvinced.

Rachel saw with relief that Betty Nichols, the checkout clerk, was busy stuffing her groceries into two brown paper bags even as the girl listened to the gossip wide-eyed. Blood pounding in Rachel's temples signaled the impending onset of a headache. She'd been prone to them for years now, ever since she had figured out that she was never going to get away from Tylerville. Not ever. Bonds of love and duty had closed around her, and now held her fast as securely as iron chains. She had accepted that, was resigned to it, and even felt a certain grim humor at her fate. She, who had always dreamed of flying high and far into a very different sort of life, had had her wings summarily clipped. That fateful summer eleven years ago could count her, too, as one of its victims.

Her life was now solidly set on the track it would doubtless travel for the next fifty years: that of a small-town schoolteacher. It was her calling to undertake the often-Herculean task of prying open the minds of Tylerville's youth, to acquaint them with the power and beauty of words. At first the prospect had excited her. But over the years she had come to realize that delving for the requisite spark of imagination and creativity in the brains of those she taught was as unrewarding a task as searching through an ocean bed full of oysters for the occasional pearl. Only the infrequent successes made it a job worth doing.

Johnny Harris had been one such success. Perhaps, even, her least likely one.

At the thought of him, her headache came on in earnest. Wincing, she fumbled in her purse for her checkbook, the faster to make her escape from the grocery store. What she did not need, at the moment, was the stress of having to defend Johnny Harris (who, however innocent of murder he might be, was not the boy she remembered) to anyone before she was comfortable with what he had become herself. Just at that moment, what she most craved was ten minutes alone. Mrs. Ashton's groceries were already being loaded into a cart, and Pam Collier's last few items were being passed over the computerized price reader. The catechism would not last much longer, thank heaven. In just minutes she should be able to escape.

"Sue Ann Harris was nothing but a little slut, if you'll excuse my French. Now she's living up in Detroit, and I hear she's one of those welfare mothers with three kids by three different men. And she never married any of 'em, either."

"You don't say!" Mrs. Ashton shook her head.

Pam nodded. "That's what I hear. And everybody knows that Grady Harris was the biggest drug dealer in the state when he drowned three years ago. And he wouldn't have drowned if he hadn't been high on some kind of dope."

Rachel took a deep, calming breath. Her head throbbed, but she ignored the pain. "What I heard was that he and some friends had been partying on a boat, and he fell overboard and hit his head. If he'd been doing anything but drinking bourbon, then it's more than anybody ever proved. And if drinking bourbon's a crime, there sure are a lot of criminals around these parts." Despite her own very recently renewed misgivings about at least one of the Harris siblings, Rachel felt obliged to point out the facts, much good might it do. Like everyone else in town, she was aware of the gossip. What neither she nor anyone else knew was how much of it was actually true. Not that that stopped anyone from repeating it, of course. Gossip was the lifeblood of Tylerville. Silence it, and she suspected that a good portion of the population might actually expire.

Though if she faced the issue squarely, she would have to admit that there was more than a grain of truth in what Pam and Mrs. Ashton said. As a group, the Harrises were not Tylerville's most desirable citizens. Rachel wasn't disputing that. All she wanted to do was offer a second chance to a boy—no, a man now—whom she felt deserved one. She was not trying to promote Johnny Harris to sainthood. She merely felt that, as far as the murder of Marybeth Edwards was concerned, he had gotten a bum rap.

"Willie Harris has kids all over the place, too. Even some of 'em in Perrytown are his, is what I hear." Pam's voice dropped as she related this last tidbit. To understand its significance, one would have to know that Perrytown was the black enclave just on the outskirts of town. While integration was the law and nearly everyone in Tylerville was a vocal opponent of racism of any stripe, the reality was that most of the blacks lived together in their own small community.

"Oh, I don't believe that!" Even Mrs. Ashton sounded shocked at this slander on Johnny's father.

"That's what I hear."

"That'll be thirty-seven sixty-two, Miss Grant."

"What?"

Betty Nichols patiently repeated the total. Recalled with relief to the business at hand, Rachel hastily wrote a check and passed it over. Everyone in Tylerville knew everyone else. Betty was a former student of hers, so there was no need for a driver's license or anything like that. The whole town knew that the Grants' checks were good as gold, just as the whole town would have refused to accept one from any of the Harrises.

That was life in Tylerville.

"'Bye, Mrs. Ashton. 'Bye, Pam." Rachel caught a bag up in each arm and headed for the parking lot.

"Wait, Rachel!" Mrs. Ashton called after her. Pam called something, too, but by then Rachel was through the automatic door and didn't hear what it was. Not that she was sorry.

Driving toward home, head pounding, Rachel decided that she'd never felt so wrung out in her life. Maybe it was the heat. Or maybe it was the strain of championing Johnny Harris.

Her purse rested on the passenger seat. Pulling it toward her and groping inside it with one hand, she found the tin of aspirin that she always carried with her. Opening the small metal container without running off the road was quite a trick, but she managed it and swallowed two tablets dry.

" 'This is my letter to the world / that never wrote to me. . . .' "

Emily Dickinson's words flitted into Rachel's mind. She had always loved poetry, and that line had lately seemed to her an apt summation of her existence. To her, it symbolized a yearning soul locked tight into the humdrum everydayness of an ordinary life. Like Emily Dickinson, Rachel lately found herself wanting more, though just what it was she longed for she couldn't have said. Often she felt almost achingly alone despite the fact that she had never lacked for friends or company. But no one she knew was the rarest of all creatures—a kindred spirit.

Over the years, she had come to realize the she did not quite fit in in Tylerville. She was different from her family, different from her neighbors, different from her co-workers and students. She read everything she could get her hands on—novels and plays, biographies and poetry. Newspapers, magazines, cereal boxes—anything. Her mother and sister read cookbooks and fashion magazines. Her father read *Business Week* and *Sports Illustrated.* She was content in her own company for hours on end. Given the choice, she even preferred to be alone. They were unhappy without a busy social calendar. She even wrote poetry herself and dreamed that one day it might actually be published.

Her family laughed indulgently at her scribbles.

Yet she loved them and they her.

Sometimes she reminded herself of the ungainly baby swan in the story of the ugly duckling. No matter how hard she tried to be like the others—and she had tried, over the years—she just couldn't do it. Finally she had learned just to simply pretend she was like them. It made life easier, and it wasn't difficult. All she had to do was keep to herself about eighty percent of what she thought and felt.

Pulling in between the large stone pillars that marked the entrance to the 250-acre farm called Walnut Grove, which had been home to the Grant family for generations, Rachel felt the worst of the tension begin to seep from her body. The pounding in her temples eased, for which she was thankful. Coming home always had a soothing effect on her. She loved the rambling, century-old house in which she'd grown up. She loved the long driveway, only paved within the last ten years, that meandered through towering oaks and maples. She loved the flowering dogwood and redbud trees that made the place a wonderland of beauty in the spring, the peach trees that grew out back and provided fruit, and the walnut trees that littered the driveway and yard with hard green balls in the autumn and gave nuts for munching in the winter. She loved the sight of the few horses they kept nowadays cropping grass in the wood-fenced fields beyond the house. She loved the barn that her granddaddy and his father-in-law had built, and every one of the three ponds, and the woods that took most of the back field. She loved the old-fashioned porte cochere that extended from the side of the house, beneath which she customarily parked her car. She loved the soft white paint that had chipped here and there to show the rose-pink of the bricks of which the house was built, and the red color of the tin roof that formed peaks and gables three and a half stories above the ground. She loved the wide veranda with its fat white columns that graced the front of the house, and the stone path and terrace that led to the rear. She followed that path with her arms full of groceries, allowing the sights and smells and sounds of the place to soothe her jangled nerves. As always, it was good to be home.

"Did you get the pork chops? You know your daddy said he wanted pork chops." Elisabeth Grant, Rachel's mother, met her at the kitchen door, her voice fretful as it often was nowadays. Barely five feet tall and weighing maybe ninety pounds, Elisabeth's physical legacy to her daughter was her build. Other than that, there was little outward resemblance. Elisabeth's hair, which was short and curly, had once been naturally black, and now was artificially so. Her skin was paper-thin, olive in tone and wrinkled from years of lying in the sun, but her makeup was exquisitely applied and compensated for a good deal. Even when she had no plans other than to remain at home, Elisabeth was always perfectly groomed. Today's attire was an emerald-green linen shirtwaist dress with tasteful gold jewelry and matching pumps. Elisabeth had once been a beauty, and traces of it still showed. No beauty herself, Rachel had always felt she had disappointed her mother in that regard. Her coloring and features more closely resembled her father's.

"Yes, Mother, I did." Rachel surrendered the groceries to Tilda, who sidestepped Elisabeth to receive them. Tilda, comfortably plump in the stretch pants and trendy oversize T-shirt she wore in defiance of her fifty-two years, had been the Grants' housekeeper for as long as Rachel could remember. She and her husband J.D., who did general work about the place, were almost family, though they did return to their small frame house in Perrytown each night.

"I would have gone to the store, Mrs. Grant, if you'd told me you needed something." Tilda's voice was slightly reproachful as she carried her double burden over to the long counter beside the sink. Rachel was her baby, or rather one of her babies as she had six of her own, and she didn't like her babies being imposed upon, as she would have put it, by anybody. Not even by Rachel's own mother.

"You know I needed you here today to help J.D. with Stan, Tilda. The way he is now, I'm just not strong enough to do anything with him."

"He must be having a good day if he asked for pork chops." Rachel filched a banana from the bag Tilda was emptying and peeled back the skin. Stan was her beloved father, past seventy now though it was hard to believe. He suffered from Alzheimer's, which had, over the course of the last eight years, robbed him of both mobility and, to a large degree, reason. Only occasionally now would he emerge from the fog of incoherence in which he dwelled to recognize one of them, or even to talk at all.

"He is. Why, he knew me this morning. He even asked where Becky had been hiding herself. Of course, he's completely forgotten that she's married and has the girls." Elisabeth bent to extract the big iron skillet from the cabinet beside the stove.

Becky was Rachel's younger sister, who lived in Louisville with her husband, Michael Hennessey, and their three small daughters. She was their mother's spitting image, physically and in personality, too. And that, Rachel imagined, was why she was also their mother's favorite. Elisabeth understood Becky clear down to her toes. Becky had been first a cheerleader, then prom queen, then homecoming queen, and she and Elisabeth shared a keen interest in clothes and men. Rachel, on the other hand, always had her nose in a book and her head in the clouds. A dreamer, Elisabeth had termed her, and the description was not necessarily a compliment. Elisabeth's partiality no longer bothered Rachel, though it had been a secret and carefully hidden hurt while she and her sister were growing up. But as the pair of them had grown older, Rachel took on the role of Daddy's girl, joining Stan on jaunts about town and on his favorite fishing trips and exerting herself to learn all she could about the hardware business to please him. *He* didn't care if she wasn't a beauty, or get upset if she occasionally got so caught up in a book that she forgot to watch the stove and let supper burn. That special relationship with her father became very precious to her over time, and as it did, Becky's closeness to their mother had ceased to wound Rachel.

"Did that Harris boy come?" Elisabeth's voice was full of disapproval as she opened the package of pork chops that Tilda had placed on the counter. Rachel, who now handled nearly everything to do with the store, had not consulted with her mother before offering Johnny Harris a job. Indeed, she had told her mother what she had done only the day before, when she could avoid it no longer. As Rachel had expected, Elisabeth had been horrified at the mere idea of Johnny Harris returning to Tylerville. As for employing him, why, she would sooner hire the devil himself, she said. She was coldly furious with her daughter over it. Rachel knew that in punishment she would suffer subtle jabs, such as the one about her father asking for Becky rather than herself, for days.

"Yes, Mother, he did." Rachel took a large bite out of the banana, found she no longer fancied it, and threw it, half eaten, away. "He's very grateful to us for offering him the job." And that was a fib if ever she'd told one.

Her mother sniffed. "*We* didn't offer him a job. *I* never would have done any such thing. It's all your doing, missy, and it's you alone who will bear the consequences. He'll attack some girl, mark my words, or do something else dreadful. He always was that type."

"I think he'll do just fine, Mother. Tilda, where's Daddy?"

"He's up in the ballroom. J.D.'s got him one of those Elvis tapes he likes, and they're up there listening to it."

"Thanks, Tilda. I think I'll run up and see him. Call me if you need any help, Mother."

"You know I don't need any help cooking." Elisabeth's cooking ability was her pride and joy. Rachel's offer had been more in the nature of riposte for her mother's earlier jab than anything else.

"I know, Mother." Rachel's voice gentled, and she smiled at her mother before she left the kitchen and turned left, climbing the narrow backstairs. Her relationship with Elisabeth had always been as much prickles as hugs, but still she loved her. It was hard on her mother, the fate that had befallen Stan. More even than she loved Becky, Elisabeth loved her husband.

Well before she reached the third floor, Rachel could hear the rollicking strains of "Hound Dog." The ballroom, which was a grand name for what was in essence a large glassed-in sleeping porch that took up about half of the top of the house, was devoid of furnishings and had a hardwood floor without the noise-deadening oriental carpets that warmed the rooms below. Sound was amplified by the room's bareness. Despite herself—she had never been a big Elvis fan—Rachel found herself bopping to the beat as she walked along the upstairs hall. The song was infectious. Stan had always loved Elvis and had mourned as if at losing a family member when he died.

The door to the elevator, which they had had installed for Stan and his wheelchair, stood open as she passed it. Later it would take Stan and J.D. down to the first floor, where he would eat and be wheeled outside for his daily walk. Still later, it would bring him back to the second floor to be bathed, given his sleeping prescription, and put to bed. Such was the unremitting routine of his days. Whenever she thought of her vigorous father being reduced to such never-ending monotony, Rachel wanted to weep. So she tried not to think about it.

Just as she had expected as she turned the corner to enter the ballroom, Rachel found that her father was seated in his wheelchair, eyes closed, nodding his head in time to the music. Listening to Elvis's songs was one of the few pleasures that remained to him. They managed to reach him when nothing else could.

J.D. sat cross-legged on the floor beside Stan, his belly protruding hugely over the waistband of his gray work pants, his lighter gray shirt unbuttoned to reveal the white undershirt beneath. Darker skinned than his wife, he was also more ebullient, with a ready smile for anyone who passed his way. He hummed along with the music, his gnarled fingers drumming a beat on the polished floor. Rachel must have made some sound, because he looked up, grinning when he saw her. Rachel waved at him. Any attempt at speech was almost certainly doomed given the volume of the music.

She crossed to her father and touched his hand.

"Hello, Daddy."

He didn't open his eyes, didn't even seem aware of her presence or of her fingers resting on his. Rachel kept them there for a minute, then removed them, sighing. Not that she had expected any other response. These days it was enough for her to see him, to know that he was comfortable and well cared for.

Attending to his physical needs was all she or anyone else could do. At least they'd managed to keep him at home. Without J.D., who alone could handle him when he became unruly, and without Tilda to help, they would have had to put him in a nursing home.

Rachel cringed at the mere idea, although Dr. Johnson, Stan's physician, had warned that institutionalization might yet become necessary as the disease progressed through its last stages. Elisabeth could not even consider the prospect without hysterical tears. They had been married forty-one years.

Stan had once been a big man, over six feet two and about two hundred twenty pounds. He was still physically large, but his illness seemed to be shrinking him. Or perhaps, now that he depended on her instead of the other way around, it was Rachel's perception of his size that had changed. In any case, she felt a fierce, protective love as she looked down at the few silvery strands of hair that made a poor job of covering his scalp. Aging was never a pleasant prospect, but this disease that took the soul before the body was a hideous thing.

"I'll be here as long as you need me, Daddy," Rachel promised silently, and her hand tightened over his.

"Hound Dog" changed to "Love Me Tender," and at the sweet, sad notes Rachel felt tears threaten. Ridiculous. The only thing crying would do was give her a stuffy nose. Blinking the moisture back, she patted her father's hand one last time, waved at J.D. again, and turned away. She would change clothes before going downstairs. If her mother was making her famous southern-fried pork chops, a time-consuming process, Rachel had plenty of time to get her thoughts in order before they sat down to eat.

Rachel could faintly hear strains of "Heartbreak Hotel" as she slid into a pair of blue and green plaid shorts and a bright green polo shirt. A pair of white socks and sneakers completed her outfit. Running a brush through her hair and then fluffing it out with her hand, Rachel surveyed herself in the mirror. For the first time in a long time, she realized, she was really seeing herself instead of just spot-checking her hair and makeup. Then she realized why. Unable to avoid the specter of Johnny Harris any longer, she was subconsciously trying to view herself through his eyes.

"I had a major case of the hots for you in high school. I still do." Unbidden, Johnny's words popped to the forefront of her mind. Rachel's hand clenched around the brush she still held. Surely he had not meant it. He was just trying to make her uncomfortable for some reason she couldn't fathom. Certainly she was not the kind of woman who ordinarily filled men with lust. That was one reason she had been so dazzled by Michael. Handsome, brilliant Michael—in love with her. Even at the time, she'd had trouble believing it.

A pang of remembered pain made Rachel grimace. It had been so long ago since he had given her up with a kiss on the cheek and a line about how they were not really suited after all, were they? Her heart had broken, but he hadn't seemed to realize, or care. She hardly ever thought of Michael anymore. Not, at least, in connection with herself. He was no longer hers to think about. He was Becky's now. Becky's husband.

Her thoughts slid away, to a subject that was more immediately troublesome. The notion that she might have inspired a case of the "hots" in a teenage Johnny Harris, who'd been quite a stud, to borrow from her students' idiom again—well, it was quite simply laughable.

She simply wasn't the type.

She was thirty-four, almost thirty-five years old, though she supposed she didn't look it. A lifelong aversion to the sun because she always burned instead of tanned had left her unwrinkled except for a few lines around her eyes. Her figure was slender, but that was the only point in its favor. Most thirteen-year-old girls had curves she might envy. Her best-kept secret was that she could, and often did, buy her clothes in the preadolescent boys' department of Grumer's, the local department store. Her hair was plain medium brown, cut chin length and turned under at the ends to frame a face that was passably pretty, with its delicate even features and oval shape, but rather colorless. Certainly it fell far short of beauty. Her eyes were large and well shaped, with a thick sweep of dark brown lashes, but they were of an ordinary shade of hazel that would mesmerize no man. "Cute" was how she had most often heard herself described. Even Rob, the man she'd been desultorily dating for the better part of the past two years, had called her that.

Rachel hated to be called cute. It was a word for toddlers and puppies, not grown women. Even if it was accurate, she considered the description mildly insulting. But of course Rob had no way of knowing that, and she hadn't told him. He was a nice man, and he had only meant to compliment her. He had a good income—he was a pharmacist and owned his own drugstore—and nice manners, and he was reasonably good-looking. She was sure that he would be a good father. And she was starting to want kids.

It was time she married. If Michael's defection had killed an elusive something inside her, well, such was life. She did not delude herself that she was the only woman who had ever been dumped. Her broken heart had long since healed. Certainly she no longer ached for Michael. Age had given her the wisdom and determination necessary to make a marriage work. If she was hesitating because she remembered the fiery excitement of her passion for Michael and found it lacking in her relationship with Rob, she had only to remind herself that she was no longer the naive, starry-eyed girl who had loved with a whole heart and unbounded confidence in her future happiness. She had grown up and wised up.

"Rachel! Rachel, come down here this minute!"

For her mother to yell up the stairs like that was unusual enough to snap Rachel to attention. Turning away from the mirror, she opened her door and hurried toward the kitchen. Elisabeth stood at the bottom of the stairs, a long-tined fork clutched in one hand. From her expression Rachel could tell she was upset.

"There was a call for you," she said before Rachel could ask what the matter was. "It was Ben from the store. He said you'd better come down right away. The police are there. There's been some trouble with that Johnny Harris."

4

Two police cars were parked in front of the hardware store. A half-dozen or so bystanders milled around outside, kept from entering by a uniformed officer. That officer was Linda Howlett, Rachel saw as she got out of the car, whose younger sister had been in Rachel's class two years before. Linda spotted Rachel and waved her on past, and Rachel hurried into the store. The scene that greeted her was so appalling that, just inside the entrance, it momentarily stopped her cold.

Two men were sprawled on the floor, one prone, one supine, and three uniformed officers were crouching over them. Greg Skaggs, son of Idell and older brother of Jeff, had joined the Tylerville police force just the year before. One of his knees was pressed into the center of a broad, white T-shirted back, while his drawn pistol was nuzzled into a head of unruly black hair. Another officer, Kerry Yates, was kneeling as he held the prone man's arm twisted up hard behind his back. Rachel needed no more than a glance to identify Johnny Harris as the man being thus detained. A few feet beyond him, the identity of the other downed man was more problematic. Chief Jim Wheatley bent over him, his posture indicating that he perceived little threat as he pressed two fingers to the pulse in the man's throat. Behind the counter, Olivia Tompkins, the nineteen-year-old who worked in the store part time, watched, her heavily mascaraed eyes huge. Ben Zeigler, the store manager, emerged from a rear stockroom as Rachel hesitated. Clearly none of them were as yet aware of her presence, and Ben, perhaps blinded by the late afternoon glare that was pouring in through the windows, did not immediately see her standing there.

"Mrs. Grant said Rachel's on her way," Ben said to Chief Wheatley.

"Good."

"Get the hell off me, asshole! You're breaking my goddamned arm."
The snarl came from Johnny, who made an abortive movement to free
himself that was halted by a hard jerk on his twisted arm. He responded
with language so filthy, it made Rachel blink. It occurred to her then that
however innocent Johnny might have been when he was tried and convicted, prison might have changed him so that he was now truly a threat
to decent society. Certainly he had been less than a gentleman with her
earlier. Whatever had gotten him into the position he now occupied must
have been dreadful to merit such a reaction on the part of Tylerville's
usually laid-back police force.

"Keep fightin', scumbag, and I might just get to blow a hole through
your thick skull yet today."

This threat, drawled by Greg Skaggs, roused Rachel from her momentary disbelief. Whatever Johnny was or was not, she was not going to
watch him get shot before her eyes.

"What in the name of heaven is going on here?" she demanded,
stepping forward.

Chief Wheatley, his officers, Ben, and Olivia all looked up at the
same time.

"Rachel, there just wasn't anything I could do!" Olivia wailed. "I
was already real nervous because that Johnny Harris had come into the
store when Ben had promised me that he never would while I was here,
and then Mr. Edwards came in and I just knew there'd be trouble, and
there was! There was an awful fight, with them tumblin' all over the place
and chokin' and punchin' each other, and I called the police, and a good
thing, too! That Johnny Harris smashed Mr. Edwards in the throat with
his fist and knocked him unconscious. It's a wonder it didn't kill him!"

"Apparently Carl heard that Harris was here. He came looking for
him, and he found him. I told you that hiring Harris was a mistake, and
you see how right I was. He hasn't been here more than a couple of
hours, and look what's happened." Ben gestured to the group on the
ground. "They tore the heck out of the store, fighting. Look at this
mess!"

Rachel looked. Paint cans, brushes, rollers, and color charts littered
the floor from an overturned display. One can had burst open, spilling
bright scarlet enamel across the black and white tile. A plastic bin that
had once contained a huge assortment of nuts and bolts lay on its side, its
contents scattered everywhere. Wild birdseed that had been stored in a
large metal trash can made a gritty carpet underfoot. The can itself, now

badly dented, rested against the foot of the wooden counter. From the look of it, it had been thrown at someone.

"You should've checked with me before you did anything so all-fired foolish as giving Harris a job, Rachel," said Chief Wheatley. "Anyone with a lick of sense would have foreseen that the Edwards boys would be after him the minute he hit town. Hell, I can't blame 'em, though I'll uphold the law as I'm bound. It ain't right that Carl here's sister's dead and her killer is runnin' around loose, back in our town." As he spoke, the chief straightened away from the second downed man, whom Rachel now recognized as Marybeth Edwards's older brother Carl.

"Could you get off him, please?" Rachel said very quietly to Greg Skaggs, indicating Johnny. Clearly these men were prejudiced against him and would not have the slightest qualm about doing him an injury. She had believed in him all these years in the teeth of overwhelming public opinion, and she wasn't going to abandon him now just because he was not the peach-fuzz-faced boy she had idiotically been expecting. "I hardly think any of us are in danger from him with so many armed policemen around. He doesn't have a gun, does he?"

"Far's I can tell, he's unarmed." Kerry Yates, having just completed a quick frisking of the prisoner, spoke grudgingly to Chief Wheatley.

"Get the hell off me, asshole!"

"Shut your mouth, boy, or you'll end up back in jail quicker than a sneeze," Chief Wheatley said, his voice a low growl.

"Fuck you." Johnny's reply made Rachel wince. Greg Skaggs rapped the black head with his pistol a little harder than was necessary for a mere warning. Kerry Yates yanked the arm he was holding a little higher and grinned. Johnny grunted with pain. Watching, Rachel saw red.

"Let him up!" Rachel raised her voice, something she rarely did. Chief Wheatley looked at her, looked at his men, hesitated, then nodded.

"Let him up," he said. Then, to Johnny as he jerked his arm away from Kerry Yates's loosened grip, he added, "You behave yourself, boy, or you'll be back on the floor before you can wipe your nose."

"Get up then," Greg Skaggs said, and eased back away from his erstwhile prisoner before standing. He did not return his gun to its holster but kept it ready in his hand.

Johnny's reply as he got to his feet and turned to face them was offensive enough to make Rachel excuse the sudden tension in the officers' stances. He stood balanced on the balls of his feet, his fists clenched at his sides as if he expected to be attacked at any minute, his face white and smeared with blood, his eyes glittering with rage.

"I'll run into you one day when you're not wearing a uniform, kid," he said to Greg Skaggs. "Then we'll see how tough you are."

"That sounds like a threat to me." Chief Wheatley's voice had a warning edge to it.

"You hush," Rachel said fiercely to Johnny, and walked right up and tapped him in the center of his chest with an admonitory forefinger. Without any real reason other than gut instinct, she was suddenly, fiercely, one hundred percent on his side. He glanced down at her, jaw tight, eyes hard, but, silenced by the look she gave him, he said nothing more. Rachel pivoted in front of him, standing between him and the others like a shield. The absurdity of her protecting him, when the top of her head didn't quite reach his shoulder and she was perhaps half his weight, was lost on her at the moment. The injustice of the situation inflamed her. What had he done, after all, that Carl Edwards had not done, too, except be Johnny Harris?

On the floor, Carl Edwards moaned, stirred, and sat up, rubbing the back of his head. He glanced around, saw Johnny, and his face contorted.

"You son of a bitch," he snarled. "I'll get you, see if I don't. You murderer—you think you can kill my sister and get away with it?"

"That's enough, Carl," Chief Wheatley said sharply, going over to catch him by one arm and haul him to his feet. "You want to press charges against Harris for assault?"

"Hell, yes, I—"

"To be fair, Edwards threw the first punch," Ben interrupted, his tone reluctant.

"See there?" Rachel looked triumphantly at Chief Wheatley. "Why don't you ask Johnny if he wants to press charges against Carl? That's only fair."

"Rachel—" Chief Wheatley sounded harassed.

"I don't," Johnny said abruptly from behind her.

"Don't do me any favors, you bastard!" Carl Edwards rasped. "I'm gonna cut you up just like you did Marybeth. Remember how pretty she was, Harris? She wasn't pretty after you got through with her, was she? You scum—how could you do that to her? She was just seventeen years old!"

"Now that sounds like a threat to me," Rachel said, but the measure of satisfaction afforded her by the reversal was erased by the sudden, pitiable collapse of Carl Edwards's face.

"Come on, Carl, let me take you on home," Chief Wheatley said quietly as Carl gasped with emotion and tears started coursing down his face. Rachel felt her heart contract with pity for him. It must have been unimaginably hard to lose a sister in such a horrible way—but nevertheless, she was on Johnny's side.

"You tell him not to come back in here, Chief. I'll press charges for trespassing against him if he does," Rachel said clearly as Chief Wheatley, his men following, escorted a sobbing Carl Edwards toward the door.

"God, Rachel, don't you have any compassion at all for him? Edwards loved his little sister. You gotta feel sympathy for him." Ben sounded aghast at this cold-hearted threat.

"I do feel sympathy for him." She turned to look at Johnny. Blood from a split lower lip was smeared all along the left side of his face. A liberal amount stained the once white T-shirt. Outside, the sound of cars pulling away told her that the police had left. The store was once again open for business.

"Olivia, get back to work, please. Ben, is the inventory done? I'll want to go over it with you first thing tomorrow morning, so you'd best be finishing it up if it's not." Behind her, the tinkling bell that announced the opening of the door told Rachel that a customer, probably one of the curiosity-seekers who had gathered outside, had entered.

"Can I help you?" Ben asked smoothly, moving toward the newcomer. Rachel didn't even look around.

"You come with me," she said to Johnny, her voice crisp with authority. Crooking her finger at him imperiously, she started toward the stockroom door. From there, a small staircase led up to his apartment, where they could be private. Without looking behind her to see if he followed, she knew that he did. Her sixth sense where Johnny Harris was concerned was proving to be disturbingly acute.

5

"*L*et me get you some ice for your mouth."

The furnished apartment's galley-type kitchen was complete, down to a refrigerator with an ice-maker. Rachel found a dish towel in the drawer beside the sink, opened the freezer compartment to scoop up a handful of ice cubes, wrapped them in the towel, and wet the knobby bundle. Then she handed it to Johnny, who leaned against the counter by the stove. He accepted the ice pack without a word and pressed it to his swollen lip. Judging from his slight wince, the sensation brought more pain than relief.

"All right, suppose you tell me what happened."

"What are you, my parole officer?"

The smart-alecky drawl was vintage Johnny Harris. Absurdly, Rachel found his surliness reassuring. It meant that something of the boy she remembered was left in the man after all.

Rachel met his eyes for a long, unwavering look. "I'm your boss, remember? Your employer. You just had a fight with a customer in my store. I think I'm entitled to some explanation."

"Before you decide whether or not to can me?"

"Exactly."

His eyes narrowed. Rachel folded her arms across her chest and waited. For a long pause neither of them gave an inch.

Johnny shrugged. "You want the truth? Edwards attacked me. I defended myself. You can believe it or not."

"I believe it."

Now that he had lowered himself to explain, however tersely, he sounded hostile, which was just the attitude that Rachel had expected him to take. The tension in her spine relaxed a little. No matter how much he had changed outwardly, the person inside the hard-as-nails exterior seemed essentially the same.

At her profession of faith, his jaw tightened, and he tossed the ice pack onto the counter. The cloth untwisted. Ice spilled out with a clatter. Rachel tsk-ed in disapproval and was instinctively scooping the ice toward the sink when her attention was caught by his sudden movement. Without warning, he caught the sides of his T-shirt in both hands and dragged it up over his head. Frowning and turning instinctively to face him, Rachel found herself eyeballing a masculine chest that was gorgeous enough to make her catch her breath.

Whatever else he'd done in prison, clearly he had found time to work out. His pectorals were sharply defined, his abdomen flat and ridged with muscle. His upper arms bulged. His waist was narrow compared with the corded width of his shoulders, and the center of his chest was covered with a triangle of silky-looking black hair.

Wow, was the thought that ricocheted through her stunned brain.

The shirt came all the way off and was wadded in one hand. He looked at her, the glint in his eyes wicked. Clearly he meant to discompose her. For her, the trick was not to let him know that he had succeeded. She had to regain her presence of mind—quickly.

"What are you doing?" If her voice was calm, she owed it to the unflappability engendered by years of teaching budding hoodlums.

"Changing my shirt. What did you think I was doing? That I was going to jump your bones right here and now, teacher?" He took a deliberate step toward her until his chest was just inches away from her face. Rachel had to look up, way up, past swirls of black chest hair and broad shoulders and a strong, stubbled chin to meet his eyes. They were narrowed, the pupils slightly dilated, the irises a deep, smoldering blue.

"Were you hoping?" he asked, his voice husky, the question no louder than a silky whisper.

For an instant—no longer—Rachel's blood seemed to cease its flow. He was scaring her, there was no doubt about it. What restored her to sanity after a lightning plunge into icy doubt was the absolute certainty that he was coming on to her with the intent of scaring her. He was like a child who, told by everyone he was bad, was determined to prove them right.

This insight gave her the courage to stand her ground.

"In your dreams," she said with a snort, and turning away, continued scooping chunks of melting ice into the sink as if she had not a worry in the world.

For a moment he was silent, watching her. Rachel got the feeling that he was nonplussed. But if he meant to play Big Bad Wolf to her Little Red Riding Hood, then he was destined to disappointment. She had not the slightest intention of turning tail and running away from him, ever. Early in her career, she had learned that the biggest mistake anyone in a position of authority can make is to show even the faintest suggestion of fear to those whom they wish to lead.

"Still the same Miss Grant, I see," he said finally, and some of the hardness left his eyes and his mouth. "You always did have an answer for everything."

"Not everything." She glanced up at him with the beginnings of a smile.

"Close enough."

With that, he turned and left the kitchen's narrow corridor. Reaction set in, and for an instant Rachel went limp with relief. Leaning against the counter, feeling as if it might be some time before she had the psychic energy to stand up again on her own two feet, Rachel watched him go. That was a mistake. The sheer amount of sex appeal he exuded was unbelievable. Black wavy hair just touching wide, bronzed shoulders, a broad, muscular back, tight jeans hugging to-die-for buns, long legs swaggering on high-heeled cowboy boots: the sight of him doing nothing more suggestive than walking away from her made her loins clench.

The intense physicality of her reaction stunned her. Though far from promiscuous, she was no stranger to sex. There had been Michael, of course, but while she had been madly in love with him, she had also been young and nervous, and their encounters had left her with the feeling that poets had grossly exaggerated the pleasures of physical intimacy. Over the ensuing years there had been two other men who had wanted to marry her. Both had read only the Sunday newspaper, and both had been quite content to pass the rest of their days doing exactly what they had always done. She could envision spending her life with neither of them. The magic was simply not there.

It was only as she passed thirty that she had realized that to have the family she wanted, she might have to do without magic. She was now prepared to settle for a good solid friendship with her mate, like the friendship she believed she was developing with Rob. He would run his drugstore and read the Sunday newspaper and perhaps *Business Week.* She would have a whole inner life of which he would know nothing. But perhaps most marriages were like that. With that in mind, she had let Rob make love to her some half-dozen times, and she had enjoyed their encounters. But their coupling was something less than feverish, and never, even in their most intimate moments, had she felt heat like that which enveloped her now.

Good God, what was wrong with her? The mere sight of Johnny Harris without a shirt was making her ache.

Surely she, at the ripe old age of thirty-four, was not in danger of turning into a Johnny Harris groupie, as the *Tylerville Times* had termed the half-dozen or so young girls who had turned up every day without fail at his trial. She would never have suspected that his bad-boy persona might appeal to her, too.

Although in her case she guessed that the appeal stemmed less from his persona than from his body. Though she wouldn't previously have suspected it, she supposed that she, like most women, was far from immune to a magnificent masculine physique.

Her reaction, therefore, was perfectly normal, even something that might have been expected. Certainly she had no reason to feel embarrassed by it—particularly since no one except herself need ever know about it.

What she had to do was keep her libido firmly in check. Johnny Harris was not a man any woman of sense would want to get involved with.

The creak of aging wood beneath the carpeted hall floor warned Rachel of his return. She was suddenly very busy wringing out and hanging up the towel. As he appeared in the doorway, all but blocking it, she saw that he had indeed changed his shirt for another just like it and washed the blood from his face.

"What I want to know is, what were you doing in the store in the first place? You had no reason to be there until morning." Still faintly rattled, afraid that he might discern something of the effect he had had on her, she cast him the merest glance, busying herself with wiping down the counter with a paper towel.

"I remembered that Grant's used to sell snacks, and I was aiming to buy a bag of potato chips and a Coke for supper." Having apparently decided to abandon his attempts to frighten her for the time being, his reply was nonchalant.

"You should've gone down to the Clock for a meal." The Clock was a cozy, family-style restaurant run by Mel and Jane Morris. It was about two miles away, at the other end of the downtown area, but he could have walked easily enough. Most of Tylerville ate there at least once a month. The food was good and plentiful, and the prices were cheap. Then it occurred to Rachel that perhaps he didn't have the money to cover even a meal at the Clock, and she felt ashamed of her own lack of foresight. She should have offered to pay him a week's wages in advance, but until this moment it hadn't even occurred to her.

"I did. The old bat at the door told me that they were full up."

Rachel looked up then, frowning. "Full up? But they're never—" Comprehension dawned in a flash.

"They weren't tonight, either. I could see four empty tables from where I stood. I guess they don't want to serve 'my kind' in there." There was an edge to his voice.

"I'm sure . . . ," she began, uncomfortable but hoping to try to ease what she suspected was the humiliation he'd suffered.

"I'm sure, too. Sure that Tylerville doesn't change." He stepped back, clearing the kitchen doorway. "You'd better be on your way. We wouldn't want to give Miz Skaggs or the rest of 'em reason to talk. Think of the scandal: that nice Rachel Grant went upstairs with that Harris boy and didn't come back down for a whole"—here he glanced at his watch —"a whole half-hour."

But this time the leering smile that twisted his mouth went right over her head.

"You're coming with me," she said, crumpling up the paper towel and heading past the small dinette set in the end of the great room nearest the kitchen, toward the apartment's rear door. As she passed him she beckoned imperiously. "Come on."

"Where?" When she reached the door and turned back to face him, a hand on the knob, she saw he hadn't budged.

"We're going back to the Clock, and we're going to eat. They're not going to get away with treating you like that."

Johnny simply looked at her for a moment. Then he shook his head. "I don't need you to fight my battles for me."

"You need somebody to. You don't seem to me like you're doing any too well on your own." Her voice was tart.

For a long, pregnant pause, their gazes locked. Then Johnny shrugged, capitulating.

"Sure. Why not? I could eat."

"So could I." For an instant the vision of her mother's painstakingly prepared pork chops danced in her mind's eye. Elisabeth would be put out if Rachel passed up that meal in favor of the Clock, but on the other hand, Elisabeth's reception of Johnny at Walnut Grove would likely be far more dramatic than the Clock's snub. She could not take him home to supper, and she was determined to see him fed. It was equally important that the townspeople not be allowed to treat him as a pariah. If she could help it, they would not.

When Rachel descended the stairs, Johnny was behind her. As her car was parked out front, she saw little alternative to heading through the hardware store. She felt herself tensing at the prospect, but she kept her head high and tried to look as confident as she wished she felt. Sure enough, the store was busy—busier than it normally was on a Thursday right at six o'clock closing time. Clearly, word of the previous hour's altercation had spread. As she left the stockroom and made for the door, Johnny sauntering behind her as if he owned the place, Rachel was conscious of every eye in the vicinity on the pair of them. Friends she acknowledged with an offhand wave. The merely curious she ignored.

"Miss Grant, your mother called. She said to tell you supper's almost ready, so you should hurry on home." Olivia's high-pitched voice followed her across the floor.

"Thank you, Olivia. Would you call her back for me and tell her I won't be home, please? Johnny and I are going to eat at the Clock."

There. Now everybody in the store knew. The whole town would know in a matter of hours. The gossips would buzz; her mother would have a conniption. Rachel supposed that taking Johnny Harris to supper at the most popular restaurant in town and publicly announcing that she meant to do so was the modern equivalent of throwing down the gauntlet.

Which was exactly what she felt she was doing.

Dead silence greeted her announcement. Rachel waved cheerfully in the general direction of the counter, reached the door, opened it, and stepped out into the fading heat of the late summer evening.

"You like living dangerously, don't you?" For the first time since she had met him at the bus depot, Johnny was actually smiling. It wasn't a broad smile, more a slight curve of his lips. If it hadn't been for the amused glint in his eyes, she would have half-thought she was imagining the whole thing.

"I dislike injustice," she said briskly, and got into her car.

6

$\mathcal{M}$inutes later, when they entered the Clock, Rachel saw at a glance that the restaurant, while busy, was nowhere near filled to capacity. As Jane Morris, a plump, cheerful-looking woman in her early sixties, approached, Rachel smiled at her.

"Why, Rachel, it's good to see you!" Jane glanced beyond Rachel's shoulder to where Johnny Harris loomed, tall, dark, and disreputable, and her welcoming smile faltered.

"It's good to see you, too, Jane. How's Mel doing?" Jane's husband had broken his ankle some two months before, and his recovery had been slow and uneven. He still limped badly and used a cane.

"So-so. At our age, healing a fracture's not so easy." Jane had recovered from her obvious surprise at the identity of her friend's escort. Only her determined focus on Rachel revealed her dismay.

With a wide smile, Rachel decided to take the bull by the horns.

"You remember Johnny Harris, don't you?" Which was a ridiculous question, of course. Everybody in Tylerville knew everybody else from birth on, and Johnny Harris was easily the town's most notorious native son. "He's working for us at the store now, you know. I used to teach him in high school."

Unspoken between the three of them lay the word *before*. Before Marybeth Edwards had been found with thirteen stab wounds in her body.

"Johnny, of course you know Jane Morris." Still smiling, Rachel reached out and curled her hand around Johnny's hard-muscled upper arm, urging him forward until he stood beside her. Not by so much as the blink of an eyelash did any of the trio betray the slightest awareness that this was Johnny's second visit to the restaurant that evening.

Jane eyed him up and down, from the overlong hair to the scuffed boots, in a single disapproving glance.

"Miz Morris." If Johnny's acknowledgment was terse, it was more than matched by the nod Jane bestowed on him.

Once more into the breach, Rachel thought with slightly hysterical humor. "So what's your special tonight, Jane? I'm hoping for meatloaf."

"You're in luck, then." Jane's demeanor thawed as she focused once again on Rachel. "Meatloaf and mashed potatoes it is. You want iced tea?"

She was leading them to a table in the back as she spoke. Victory, just as Rachel had expected. When Jane turned to walk away, beckoning them to follow, she had felt an easing in the tight muscles of Johnny's forearm before she released it. Apparently he had not felt as confident of the outcome of the confrontation as she had.

But she supposed that, by virtue of simply being Johnny Harris, he was used to rejection.

"Glenda," Jane called to a pink-uniformed waitress as they reached their destination. "Rachel here'll have iced tea and the meatloaf." Her eyes slid to Johnny, who, like Rachel, was settling into a seat. "What about you?"

If there was a certain hardness to her tone, at least she had spoken directly to him, which in Rachel's eyes was a huge first step. It was not in Jane to snub someone without reason once she had been brought to acknowledge them.

"I'll have the same."

"Make that two," Jane called to Glenda, then smiled at Rachel. "Tell your mama I said hi."

"I will," Rachel promised. Drawn by the arrival of more customers, Jane hurried away.

"Here's your drinks. Food'll be up in a minute." Glenda removed two tall, wet glasses from a tray and placed them on the table. Then, apparently seeing Johnny for the first time, her eyes widened.

"Why, Johnny Harris! What're you doin' out of jail?"

Rachel winced. Johnny took a sip of his tea, then smiled at the woman.

"You should've known they'd be letting me go eventually. You been waitin'?"

Glenda giggled. "Hell, I got four kids now. Cain't hardly call that waitin'."

"No, you can't."

It was clear to Rachel that these two had once known each other rather well. She knew who Glenda was, now that she thought about it. By birth she was one of the Wrights, who were considered trash just like the Harrises. Rachel hadn't placed her right off because Glenda had never gotten as far as high school. With her bottle-blond, perm-frizzed hair and the web of wrinkles around her eyes, she looked older than Johnny, but Rachel realized that they must be about the same age.

"I saw your dad yesterday. He didn't say nothin' about your comin' home."

Johnny shrugged and took another sip of tea.

"Glenda! Can you get these people their drinks?" Jane sounded harassed.

"Sure, Miz Morris! Good to see you, Johnny. You take care."

"You too, Glenda."

"It's obvious *she's* glad to see you," Rachel observed blandly after a moment's awkward silence.

Johnny's mouth twitched into an involuntary half-smile as his eyes met Rachel's. "Yeah. There'll be a few."

Glenda was back with heaping plates of food, which she set down on the table with a snap. "Need ketchup?"

"Yeah."

"No." They spoke at the same time. Rachel looked at Johnny, then nodded in the direction of the waitress. She needn't have bothered. Glenda was already setting the catsup bottle on the table before hurrying off to take care of her other customers.

"Hey, it kills the taste," Johnny said in response to the look on Rachel's face as he reached for the bottle, uncapped it, and dumped what looked like half its contents onto his meatloaf and mashed potatoes. Mildly revolted, Rachel nodded, then glanced away as he started to shovel the food down. His table manners were not the best she had ever seen.

Then conscience overcame her. He had not, after all, spent the last ten years in a school for manners. And before that, considering his background, she doubted that he had had much opportunity to learn the niceties of wielding knife and fork and napkin.

"Aren't you going to eat?" He managed the question between mouthfuls.

"I'm really not all that hungry." She had taken no more than three bites of her meal. Feeling slightly self-conscious, she glanced around to see if the other diners had noticed Johnny's assault on his food.

There was a moment of charged silence, unbroken even by the clink of his fork against his plate or the sound of his food being chewed.

The silence drew Rachel's attention. She glanced at him. He was staring at her narrow-eyed, his well-loaded fork suspended in his hand. There was a tiny smear of catsup at the corner of his mouth. Her eyes focused on that, and something in her expression must have conveyed her distaste to him because his mouth twisted violently. He put his fork down with a clatter as the tines struck the china plate, snatched up the napkin that had never been unfolded from its neat triangle, and swiped it across his face with a savagery more eloquent than an outburst of swear words would have been.

"Am I embarrassing you, teacher?"

Taken aback, Rachel stuttered, "N-no."

"You're lying."

"More tea?" Glenda was beside them with a big yellow plastic pitcher beaded with moisture.

"No, we're done. Just give us the check, please." Johnny managed a crooked smile for Glenda, but the glint in his eyes as they swept over his dinner companion told Rachel that he was furious.

"Pay up at the front." Glenda fished through the half-dozen or so checks that stuck partway out of her skirt pocket, extracted one, and placed it on the table in front of Johnny. Then she smiled at him. "Come see me when you get a chance," she said softly. "Me and the kids live out at Appleby Estates—you remember it, don't you? That trailer park down by the river? My husband and me—we're split up. Guess we'll be gettin' a divorce. When one of us can afford to pay for it."

"I'm sorry to hear that," Johnny said.

"Yeah."

"Glenda! These people need tea!"

"Gotta go," Glenda said resignedly, and hurried away with her pitcher to answer Jane's call.

"Give me that," Rachel said under her breath as Johnny picked up the check and studied it. Hostility emanated from him in waves.

"Oh, right. Add insult to injury, why don't you?" His voice was almost pleasant, but his eyes as they met hers were far from that.

"Don't be silly. You don't have any money, and—"

"You do?" he finished for her, too politely.

Rachel sighed. "Look, Johnny, I'm sorry if I hurt your feelings. It's just—I'm not a big ketchup lover, and the sight of that lovely food being smothered in the stuff kind of got to me. It was rude of me to let you see how I felt, and I apologize for that. But that's no reason for you to be ridiculous." The expression on his face shut her up. Clearly her words were not appeasing his anger. Perhaps he would feel humiliated if she paid the check instead of him. After all, he was a man, and men were silly about some things. Opening her purse, she fished in the side pocket and came up with a twenty-dollar bill, which she passed across the table to him in as unobtrusive a manner as possible. "All right, all right. You win. Here, you pay."

The way he looked at the twenty, someone might have assumed that it was a snake getting ready to bite him.

"I pay, all right. With *my* money." He stood up, taking the check with him. Thrusting a hand into his pocket, he pulled forth a couple of crumpled dollar bills, which he put down on the table with a slap before heading toward the cash register. Rebuked into silence, Rachel was left with nothing to do but retrieve her twenty and follow.

One by one, heads turned as he passed, and in only a couple of seconds it seemed as if every eye in the place were on him. Rachel, trailing some little way behind, was in a perfect position to observe the reactions of her fellow citizens to Johnny Harris.

"Isn't that—?"

"Oh, my land, it is!"

"What's he doing here?"

"I heard he got parole because the Grants offered him a job in their hardware store."

"Elisabeth never did any such thing!"

"Not Elisabeth, Rachel. Look, there she is with him. Can you believe it? Oh, hi, Rachel!"

This last was said in a much louder tone as Rachel turned her eyes on the speaker. Rachel responded to the greeting with a tight smile and a small wave. She'd known nearly everyone in the restaurant her entire life, but that wouldn't keep them from stripping her flesh from her bones with their tongues, she knew.

"Hope everything was all right?" Jane, having bustled up to the cash register, sounded slightly friendlier as she took Johnny's money. He handed her a twenty. Where had he come by any cash? Rachel had heard the state paid convicts for working while they were in prison, but the wage was something like ten cents an hour. He'd been in there for ten years, so at forty hours a week that came to . . .

She was still trying to arrive at the approximate sum when Jane handed him his change and he stalked on out the door.

With a quick smile at Jane, Rachel followed.

He was already in the parking lot heading for her car by the time she caught up with him, his long legs eating up the short distance. That he was still furious was obvious enough to the most casual observer, Rachel thought, casting him a reproving glance over the roof as she unlocked the car and got in. He slid in beside her, jaw tight, eyes hard. Rachel's lips pursed.

"You're acting like a child in a tantrum," she told him as she edged the transmission into reverse.

"Oh, yeah?" His eyes took on an unpleasant glitter. "Well, you're acting like a damned rich-bitch snob. Sorry if my manners don't suit you, Miss High and Mighty."

"Your attitude suits me even less than your manners," Rachel snapped, goaded. "And don't you swear at me! You might try showing a little gratitude."

"You'd like that, wouldn't you? For me to be grateful. Should I kiss your feet or your ass, teacher?"

"You," Rachel said fiercely, "can go straight to hell!"

With that, she stepped on the gas. The car shot backward.

"If you're not careful, we'll both end up there. Keep your mind on what you're doing, for God's sake," he said through his teeth as she screeched on the brakes, the rear bumper a scant few inches from a solid brick wall. "My life may not seem like it's worth much to you, but I sure as hell don't want to end it in a car wreck."

Rachel had to fight an urge to hit the gas hard just to teach him a lesson. Her jaw now set as obstinately as his, she concentrated on her driving and got them to the store without any mishaps more serious than a run-over curb.

When they pulled into the deserted parking lot behind Grant's Hardware just minutes later, neither of them had said so much as another word. Rachel suspected she owed Johnny's forbearance to his healthy fear of her driving. She took a deep breath. If he was being childish with his lowered brows and scowling mouth, well then, honesty forced her to admit that so was she.

"Now then," she said as she put the transmission in park and turned to look at him, "suppose we talk this out."

"Suppose we don't." He reached for the handle, opened the door, and got out without another word. Freshly affronted, Rachel winced at the volume of the slam. As she watched him walk around the front of the car and noted his leanness, conscience overwhelmed her again. Whether she was mad at him or not, the man had to eat. Fumbling with the button, she rolled down her window.

"Johnny?"

He turned his head to look at her, his eyebrows lifting. Rachel beckoned. His expression was forbidding as he approached her side of the car, but Rachel, already fishing in her purse for her checkbook, didn't notice.

"What?" Glancing up, she saw that he was now beside the car. Her fingers touched the cool vinyl of her checkbook. Triumphantly she pulled it out.

"I'm going to pay you your first week's wages in advance." She flipped the checkbook open as she spoke, extracted the pen that she kept neatly tucked into the fold, and began to write.

He leaned over, one forearm resting on the inch or so of window that had not disappeared into the door, his head coming partway through the opening, his other hand reaching for her.

Startled, Rachel shrank back as his arm brushed her breasts, but immediately she realized that his object was not to molest her. His long fingers clamped around her wrist, preventing her from finishing writing his name on the line marked "payee."

"Don't do me any favors," he said harshly, his fingers almost bruising the soft skin at the sides of her wrist as his grip tightened. "I'm not some kind of fucking charity case."

Before Rachel could reply, before she could even think of a reply, he made an inarticulate sound under his breath that drew her gaze to his. For a second, the longest second that she ever remembered living through, Rachel held her breath at what she saw as his eyes moved over her face. His lips parted as if he would say something else, then they abruptly clamped shut. His eyes went as blank as if a curtain had fallen behind them. Without so much as a tug on her part to free herself, he removed his hand from her wrist and straightened, turning away.

As she watched him walk away, Rachel was suddenly frighteningly conscious of the accelerated beating of her heart.

7

*H*e heard the unmistakable sound of a car approaching behind him. Johnny didn't bother to look or stick out a thumb. Who in his right mind, here in Tylerville, would give him a ride? No one, that was who. He was Johnny Harris, murderer. People gave him a wider berth than a dead skunk.

Hell, he couldn't even eat right. The memory of his humiliation over supper made him grit his teeth. He'd always eaten with the object of getting his food down before somebody else got to it. Manners and napkins and all that stuff had never been important. But they were important to *her*. So, damn it, he would learn to do it right. It gnawed at him, being made to look small in Rachel Grant's eyes. It bothered him, too, that she had tried to give him money. An advance on his salary, she'd called it. He called it charity, and the idea of being the recipient of it burned him up.

A new-looking red pickup whooshed past, its bright color gleaming through the deepening twilight. For a moment Johnny looked after it almost enviously. There'd been a man and a woman and a little girl and a little boy wedged into that cab. A family. He'd always imagined having a family like that. Hell, in those years in prison he'd imagined all kinds of things—imagining was what had kept him sane.

But this was here and now, reality. He was plodding along the side of a crumbling blacktop road that led through the poorest section of the county. Tumbledown frame farmhouses with yards full of junk were interspersed with one-story shacks with yards full of more junk. Kids, barefoot and dirty, played in waist-high weeds. Fat women in house dresses sat, bare knees apart, staring at him from rickety porches. Scrawny men in tank-style undershirts scratched their armpits and eyed him as he passed. Skinny, mangy dogs of no identifiable breed rushed toward him, barking.

Welcome home.

As awful as it was, he was a part of this place, and it was a part of him. He had once been one of those kids playing, as filthy and undernourished looking as they. His mom had been every bit as fat and slovenly as the women he shrank from now. His dad had been a mean son of a bitch, quick with fists and curses, and he'd worn only an undershirt every day he'd been at home. Probably, judging from the holes and stains that had always decorated it, the same one.

These were his people. Their experience of life was his. Their bad blood was in his genes.

Once, he'd hoped to escape.

Once. Hell, once he'd hoped for a lot of things.

It was a one-story frame house, every bit as ramshackle as the worst of those he'd passed, atop a small knoll. A gravel driveway led up to it. Two rusted-out pickup trucks were parked in the drive, one, having lost its tires, propped on cement blocks. Chickens scratched in the yard. Through the open front door he could see the flicker of a television.

Someone was home. Johnny didn't know whether to be glad or sorry.

He walked up the driveway, stepped onto the porch, and looked through the screen door with its innumerable small holes and tears.

A man lay on a sagging couch watching TV. An old man, grizzled and thin, in a raggedy, stained, tank-style undershirt, nursing a bottle of cheap beer.

The sight made Johnny's throat close.

Home. For better or worse, he was home.

He opened the door and walked in.

Willie Harris glanced up at him, appearing momentarily startled at the intrusion. Then recognition narrowed his eyes.

"You," he said in a voice heavy with contempt. "I knew you'd turn up sooner or later, just like a damned bad penny. Get out of the way—you're blockin' the TV."

"Hello, Dad," Johnny said softly, not moving.

"I said move your ass!"

Johnny moved. Not because he was afraid of his father or his fists any longer, but because he wanted to see the rest of the house, see what had changed. He walked into the small kitchen with its chipped white enamel counters and the card table around which they'd always eaten—when there'd been something to eat. If it wasn't the same card table—

could something so flimsy have lasted so long?—the one there now was its twin, down to the chunk missing from the center of the top. Dirty dishes were piled beside the sink, as always, only now there were just a few of them. The same pink-flowered curtains, limper and dingier than ever, hung from the same sagging yellowed rod over the sink.

There were two tiny bedrooms and a minuscule, barely functional bathroom off the hall, just as there had always been. Johnny glanced into each, wondering if the double mattress that rested on the floor in the smaller of the two bedrooms was the same one on which he and Buck and Grady had always slept. Sue Ann, being the only girl, had had the living-room couch to herself. His parents had shared the bed in the other bedroom, until his mother had taken off for Chicago with some guy. Then his father had slept in there with whichever slut he'd been humping at the time. Sometimes one or the other of the boys—usually Buck—had humped her, too.

Home.

He stepped back into the living room and switched off the TV.

"Damn you!" his father said, his face contorting with anger as he set the beer bottle down on the floor and sat up.

"How you been, Dad?" Johnny sat down at the end of the couch just made vacant by the removal of Willie's bare feet and kept his father from getting up to turn the television back on by gently grasping his arm.

The beery, aged smell of the old man assaulted him.

"Goddamn you, get your goddamned hand off my arm!" Willie tried to jerk his arm free, without success. Johnny smiled at him and tightened his grip. Not enough to hurt, but just enough to warn. Things had changed, and he was no longer going to put up with a fist to the mouth or the stomach whenever his old man felt like lashing out.

"You living here alone now?"

"What the hell business is it of yourn? You're sure as hell not movin' in!"

Ten years of absence, during which Willie had never written, called, or visited his son, had softened Johnny's memories of the old fart. He'd actually hoped that his father might be glad to see him.

"I don't want to move in. I've got an apartment in town. I just came out to see how you are."

"I was a hell of a lot better before you showed up."

Nothing had changed. Hell, did anything ever change around this town?

"You heard from Buck or Sue Ann lately?"

Willie snorted. "What, do you think this is the goddamned Waltons or somethin'? No, I ain't heard from them. Don't care to, neither. Just like I don't care to hear from you."

That hurt. It shouldn't have, but it did.

Johnny thought about just getting up, walking out the door, and never coming back. He never had to see the old bastard again.

But he couldn't let it alone. One thing he'd learned in prison was the value of things, of people. Of relationships. Most people had them without even trying. He wanted some relationships in his life.

"Look, Dad," he said quietly. "You hate me and I hate you, right? That's the way it's always been. But it doesn't have to be like that anymore. We can change it. There are too many people in this world who don't have anybody. You want to die alone, have nobody grievin' at your funeral? Hell, I don't! We're family, man. Blood. Can't you see that?"

His father stared at him for a minute. Then he reached down for his beer and took a long pull. Watching him, Johnny felt hope aching inside him. Maybe, just maybe, they could start anew.

Willie put the bottle down and wiped his mouth on the back of his hand.

"Hell, sounds like prison turned you into a damned pansy. Must've been all those peckers drillin' you, made you into a damned cryin' woman. I got no time for you. Get out of my house."

For a moment Johnny battled the almost irresistible urge to smash his fist into his father's leering face. Then, controlling himself, he dropped the scrawny arm he held and stood up.

"I hope you rot in hell, old man," he said unemotionally, then turned on his heel and walked out.

The banging of the screen door behind him was the only answer he got.

He walked around the side of the house past the pickup trucks and up the drive a little way to where the shed had once been. It still stood there, listing some to one side just as it always had. From the hen perched in a glassless window and the sounds from inside, he saw it was now used as a chicken coop.

He ducked his head through the low door and went inside.

It was still there. He'd hardly dared to hope, but there it was. It was covered with chicken shit, the tires were rotted to ribbons, and a hole was pecked in the vinyl seat so that the foam rubber showed through. But it leaned against the far wall just where he'd left it: his motorcycle.

God, he'd been proud of that thing! A Yamaha 750, cherry red and silver, bought with his own money earned doing odd jobs around town and cherished like a good-looking girl. When they'd come to arrest him, he'd parked it in the shed, little knowing that it would be almost eleven years before he made it back. Didn't look as if it had been touched except by chickens in all that time.

As far as actual usage was concerned, it was still practically brand new. New tires, maybe a tuneup, and it should run as well as it ever had. He would no longer have to depend on his feet or Rachel Grant to get him around. He'd have wheels.

There was something empowering about having wheels. He'd felt less a man without them.

A low growl from somewhere behind him made Johnny glance over his shoulder. A dog stood in the doorway, huge, stiff-legged, hackles up, teeth bared. The sound that emanated from its throat was a threat.

Moving slowly, Johnny turned to face it. It was dark outside now, and darker yet in the shed. Faint moonlight silhouetted the animal's body. A mangy cur like all the other mangy curs, a little bigger than most. Underfed, bred for meanness, probably dangerous.

They'd always had a dog like that. Big and ugly and full of hate, and no wonder. Willie would kick it and tease it and chain it and starve it to make it mean. As mean as the old man himself.

Only this dog wasn't chained.

The growl deepened, intensified. The animal's head lowered menacingly. Johnny felt his muscles tense in anticipation of an attack. Glancing around, he sought for something, a chunk of wood or anything, with which to smash the creature when it leaped.

But it didn't leap. Instead, after another rumbling growl, its head came up, and it seemed to sniff the air. A chicken fluttered and squawked off to the right, but the animal never so much as twitched an ear in the direction of the distraction. Instead it seemed to be staring intently at Johnny.

Struck by its attitude, almost as curious now as he was afraid, Johnny stared back. As his eyes traveled over the tawny pelt, absorbing such details as the shape of the head and ears and the thickness and length of the tail, an incredible possibility occurred to him.

The dog whined softly.

"Wolf?" It couldn't be. The dog had been four years old when he'd been arrested. That would make him—fifteen now. An incredibly advanced age for a mongrel for whom mistreatment had been the norm.

"Wolf, is that you?" He'd loved the damned dog, as stupid as that sounded. The pup had been one of a litter borne by a stray who'd taken up residence in the rotting, abandoned barn that had stood in a nearby field. With his brothers and friends, Johnny had thrown rocks at the bitch and her whelps, but at night he'd sneaked back over with pans full of food scraps. The bitch had never lost her wariness of him, but the pups had, particularly the largest one, who took to him like a duckling to its mother. One day, when the pups were about seven weeks old, he found the mother lying dead out by the road. Not knowing what else to do with them, he fetched the pups home. He should have known better. His father had promptly tossed four of the five squirming, licking little creatures into the back of his truck and driven them off to dump them God knew where. The fifth, Wolf, had been allowed to stay because of his size and because Willie thought that he had the makings of a good watchdog. Despite Johnny's protests, Willie had immediately chained Wolf and set about making him mean. Though Johnny had tried to protect the dog, his father had succeeded with him, to the extent that Johnny was about the only person in the world the animal had ever had any use for.

Sometimes, in prison, when he'd been lying awake at night staring at the bunk over his head, Johnny had thought that he missed Wolf most of all.

Wasn't that a damned sad commentary on his life?

The dog whined again. Knowing he was being ridiculous, that he was liable to lose the hand at the wrist when the animal charged, Johnny nonetheless took a step forward, holding out his fingers for sniffing.

"Wolf? Come here, boy."

Incredibly, the huge animal sank to its belly and slunk forward, behaving as if it wanted to believe but feared a cruel trick. Johnny dropped to his knees to greet it, his hands reaching out, burrowing in the coarse hide, stroking and scratching as the dog whined and licked and pawed him and butted him with its head.

"Ah, Wolf," he said as he accepted the truth at last, that this one thing that he had loved had been spared in order to greet him. Then, as the big head snuggled into his lap, he wrapped his arms around the dog's thick neck and buried his face against the animal's side.

For the first time in eleven years, he wept.

8

"**R**achel, we got a problem."

So what else was new? Rachel thought wearily as she shifted the kitchen phone to her other ear. In the forty-eight hours that had passed since Johnny Harris's return to Tylerville, her life had been filled to bursting with problems, all directly attributable to him. Just as this one would be, as sure as God made little green apples.

"What is it, Ben?"

"You know that bunch of kids we've had our eyes on? I finally caught one of 'em shoplifting. Only Harris won't let me call the police."

"What? Why not?"

"I guess because, as a criminal himself, he has sympathy for other criminals. How the heck should I know? All he'll say is that if I call the police, he'll kick my—well, I won't repeat it."

"Oh, lord."

"I tell you, Rachel, I don't think I can take this guy much longer. He's a real pain in the butt."

"Put him on the phone. I'll talk to him. No, on second thought, I'll come down to the store. Just try to keep the shoplifter there till I arrive, will you?"

"I'll try. But Rachel—"

"Talk to me about it when I get there, Ben."

Rachel hung up the phone. Unfortunately, her mother, who stood at the stove making her daddy's favorite hot-water cornbread in a bid to tempt his failing appetite, had heard every word of her side of the conversation. That was obvious from the moment she turned around and saw unmistakable signs of tension in Elisabeth's expression.

"You never will listen to me, will you, Rachel? I told you from the get-go that you were making a big mistake offering that boy a job. How you came to be so headstrong I can't imagine. Why, I can scarcely hold my head up in town, what with what my friends are saying about you befriending that boy. As for having to try to come up with some explanation for Verna Edwards when she called me in tears—"

"I know it's hard on you, mother, and I'm sorry. I'm sorry for Mrs. Edwards, too. But I don't believe Johnny killed Marybeth. He—"

"Johnny?" Elisabeth stiffened alarmingly. Her posture reminded Rachel of a hunting dog that has suddenly scented rabbit. "Rachel, there's nothing to this talk about you and that boy, is there? I hope I know my own daughter better than to think you'd fool around with trash like that, particularly as he is a *convict*, Rachel, and years younger than you to boot, and—"

"I hope you do, too, Mother," Rachel said gently, and fled.

It was late Saturday afternoon. Rob was supposed to pick her up at her house in an hour. Thank goodness she had already done her hair and makeup, Rachel reflected as she ran up the stairs. She had only to pull on her dress—a short, figure-hugging garnet red knit with a scooped neckline and tiny puffed sleeves—struggle into sheer black pantyhose, step into her black pumps, and clip on a pair of black button earrings, and she was ready.

Quickly pulling a brush through her hair to the tune of "Jailhouse Rock" drifting down from the third floor, Rachel checked her appearance one last time in the mirror. Exiting her bedroom, she ran into Tilda, piles of clean, folded sheets in her arms.

"Woo! Don't you look nice?" Tilda nodded with admiration as she surveyed Rachel from head to toe. "You goin' out with that handsome pharmacist?"

"Yes."

"Thought so. You're wearin' your red lipstick. Us women know about red lipstick, don't we?"

"It matches my dress, Tilda," Rachel said primly, but at Tilda's droll look she had to grin. With a wave she left the other woman, running with as light a step as she could manage down the stairs. She was out of luck. Elisabeth awaited her at the front door.

"Don't you be too late, Rachel. You know how I worry about you girls. Especially now that that boy is back in town."

Rachel stifled an urge to remind her mother that she was thirty-four years old and a perfectly competent adult capable of deciding when to come home.

"I won't be late, Mother."

Had she ever been late? Rachel reflected wryly as she drove through the stone gates and headed toward town. All her life, she'd been the very model of the dutiful daughter, much good had it ever done her. Becky had been the one who had gone to every dance and party, staying out late with one boy after another and coming home drunk on more than one occasion, to their mother's dismay. Quieter and less popular than her younger sister, Rachel had been content to spend her nights at home with a book. "You'll dream your life away!" Elisabeth had warned her, but at the time Rachel had had no suspicion that her mother's words might actually prove true.

When the time had come, Rachel had gone away to college, though not too far away. Her good grades had enabled her to get into Vanderbilt, which was about a three-hour drive from Tylerville. But Nashville, where Vandy was located, was light years away from Tylerville in outlook and opportunity. Nashville had excited her, and she had been a little sorry to return home upon graduation, teaching certificate in hand, to take on the job of educating Tylerville's youth. Not that she meant to remain a high school teacher forever. She had been absolutely sure that life had something wonderful in store for her.

Then had come that fateful summer—the long, smoldering summer of eleven years ago, when there must have been some sort of astrological cataclysm to cause so many disastrous events. She had returned to Vandy to take some graduate courses, with the thought that she might get her master's degree at some point in the future. One afternoon she had been walking along a brick path that cut across campus with her head in the clouds as usual. She'd been mentally composing a poem for her writing class assignment when a runner had knelt in front of her to tie his shoe. She hadn't noticed, of course, and had tripped over him and fallen headlong. He had picked her up, full of apologies, and she had been instantly smitten with his dark good looks. For the rest of the summer they'd been inseparable. Rachel had fallen in love. She'd been so happy when she'd brought him home to meet her family. They had talked of marriage, and she had expected to make the engagement official during that summer's-end visit.

But Michael had taken one look at lovely, vivacious Becky and tumbled head over heels. Rachel could do nothing but watch with growing agony as the only man she had ever loved was charmed effortlessly away. Not that Becky had meant to hurt her. Rachel knew that. It was just that Becky, being Becky, had never considered the matter from Rachel's point of view. Like her older sister, Becky had fallen madly in love with Michael on sight. They had been engaged within a month, married within three. Rachel had stepped aside with outward grace, even acting as Becky's maid of honor. But had it not been for the distraction of Marybeth Edwards's murder at about the same time, Rachel thought she might have died from the agony of losing her boyfriend to her sister.

To make things worse, Michael took Becky back to Vandy with him to finish out his third year of law school.

Rachel had never been able to face Nashville again.

So she had stayed home, to the delight of her parents, who had dreaded the thought of losing both daughters at once. It had been a temporary thing, she had thought, maybe a year at most, to give her time to recover her balance. She had gone back to teaching at the high school, and gradually, as months passed, the worst of the pain had gone away. She dedicated herself to her job and her students and waited for the shining bright excitement that had died with Michael's defection to return to her life.

Only it never had. Then her father had been diagnosed with Alzheimer's, and any thought she might have harbored about escaping Tylerville had been put on hold. With Becky married and gone and her mother distraught at the fate facing her husband, she'd been truly needed. Too, she had wanted to spend every available minute with her father while she still could. But sometimes she felt that life was passing her by while she waited for him to die.

And that, she scolded herself, was a terrible thought for a loving daughter to harbor. Now Rachel pushed it right out of her mind and concentrated instead on the evening to come.

Just as he had done for the past two years, Rob was taking her to Heart Beat, the open-air concert designed to benefit the Heart Society that was held the last Saturday in August on the grounds of Tylerville Country Club. In fact, they'd gone to Heart Beat on their first date.

She would have to call Rob from the store and ask him to pick her up there. No—outside the store, so as not to chance Rob having a run-in with Johnny. Rob had already made his views on the subject of Johnny very clear, in a series of four phone calls and one lunch date over the past two days.

Why was life never simple? Rachel thought with a sigh. She had done only what she had felt to be morally right in offering Johnny a second chance, and as a consequence her entire existence had been thrown into turmoil. How much easier it would have been simply not to answer Johnny's terse letter—but, Rachel acknowledged, she could not have lived with herself if she had not. Hadn't someone said once that the seeds of one's own destruction are sown by one's character? That single act of kind-heartedness (or soft-headedness, if Rob was to be believed) was the seed that was destroying the even tenor of her existence. Her life had been smooth up until she had met that bus. Ever since then, she'd had scarcely a peaceful moment.

The fact was that Johnny Harris was trouble, plain and simple. He always had been, and in that if nothing else, he had not changed.

Rachel parked in the lot in back of the store and, squaring her shoulders, went in through the rear door. Olivia was at the cash register, ringing up what looked like a sackful of nails and some woodworking tools for Kay Nelson, a plump, pretty woman of thirty-one who'd been a close friend of Becky's since they'd been in grade school together. Unlike Becky, Kay had never married. She ran a florist's shop and seemed quite content with her single state.

Olivia glanced up, saw Rachel, and indicated the storeroom with a gesture. "Oh, Rachel, they're back there." Rachel nodded. Ben's office was at the back of the storeroom, which seemed a logical place for a shoplifter to be detained.

"Thanks, Olivia." Though Olivia's worried tone would have indicated unmistakably to any intelligent listener that something was amiss, Rachel's reply was offhand. There was no sense in letting the whole world in on what was essentially a store problem. If word of it got out, the current standoff would just provide more grist for the gossip mill, which was already working overtime.

Determined to appear carefree if it killed her, Rachel smiled with deliberate cheerfulness at Kay. "Hello, there. I missed you at church last Sunday. How are you?"

"I'm just fine, Rachel. It was one of those twenty-four-hour bugs. The question is, how are you?" There was more concern in Kay's voice than the courteous question normally invoked, and Rachel understood that Kay had heard about and was commiserating with her over the presence of Johnny Harris in her life. The unspoken sympathy made her want to gnash her teeth, which of course, if she wanted to continue to appear untroubled, she could not do.

"Just fine. Planning on building something?" Nodding at the other woman's purchases, Rachel smilingly changed the subject.

Kay glanced down at the items on the counter and gathered them up almost defensively. "Oh, no, these are for my brother. He's the family carpenter. Have you heard from Becky lately?"

Et tu, Brute, Rachel thought, realizing that like most of their customers over the past two days, Kay must have come to the hardware store out of curiosity. "Last week. She'll be home Thanksgiving, I think, with Michael and the girls."

"I'll have to come see her."

"You do that," Rachel said, and with a wave passed beyond the counter into the storeroom. As she had expected, the door to the manager's office stood ajar. The phone was affixed to the wall at her left, and she paused only long enough to make a quick, quiet call to Howard's Drug Store, which Rob owned. She left a message for him, then hung up. Realizing she could delay the inevitable no longer, she walked toward the open door. On the threshold she paused, surveying the scene before her.

A little boy with shaggy blond hair and a thin, pointy-featured face sat in Ben's big leather chair behind the desk. Johnny was perched on the edge of the desk, talking to the boy, his back to the door. His overlong hair had been gathered into a neat ponytail and secured by a blue rubber band at his nape, and in his T-shirt and jeans he could not have looked more different from the heavy-set, bespectacled Ben, who leaned against the side wall, arms crossed over his chest. Ben's neatly pressed gray trousers, blue-striped shirt, and navy tie were inexpensive but immaculate and served as silent testimony to the way he felt a man should dress in his place of employment. Rachel wondered with an inward sigh if Johnny had chosen to wear the ponytail just to irritate Ben. Probably. It seemed like something Johnny Harris would do.

Closing the door gently behind her, Rachel steeled herself to deal with the problem at hand. Glancing up, she discovered three very different pairs of eyes focused on her. Ben's were transparently relieved, while the expression in Johnny's was more difficult to decipher. She had neither seen nor spoken to him since their unfortunate dinner together. At the memory of the terms on which they had parted, butterflies fluttered in her stomach.

Uncertain of what to expect from him and equally uncertain of the relative degree of her own guilt and anger, Rachel let her gaze skim past his. By default, the boy's eyes were the ones she met: golden brown, thickly lashed, they were ringed with faint shadows and wide with what she took for fear.

"Rachel." Ben came away from the wall, picked up a small plastic alarm clock from the desk, and held it up for her inspection. "This is what he took. Olivia saw him do it, and when I stopped him, I found it hidden down the front of his shirt, just like she said."

"It's a goddamned lie!" Coming from such a little boy—he didn't appear to be more than seven or eight, and he no longer looked in the least afraid—such profanity was shocking. "I never took nothin'!"

"We caught you red-handed, you little thief! There's no way you can deny it!" Ben's voice was tight with anger as he swung around to wave the alarm clock at the boy. "And this isn't the first time, either. You and your friends are always in here stealing something."

"We never took nothin' from you, and you can't prove we did." The small voice was defiant.

"That does it." Ben turned back to shake his head at Rachel. "He's not even remorseful. If we don't call the police, we might as well send out an invitation to every kid in town to come in and steal us blind."

"I told you about calling the police, Zeigler, and I meant it." The quiet warning came from Johnny, who had slid off the desk to join them after whispering something to the boy.

"You don't tell me anything, Harris. You work for me." Ben's hushed rejoinder sounded no less furious for its lack of volume.

"I work for Rachel, not you."

The insolence of Johnny's voice matched the insolence in his eyes as they moved over Ben. Ben bristled. Johnny smiled at him with slow challenge.

"You both work for me," Rachel said sharply. She looked up into Johnny's narrowed gaze. She saw no apology for his behavior at their last parting there—and no anger, either. His use of her given name was not lost on her, but this was not the time to dwell on its portent. "Ben is exactly right: Store policy is to prosecute shoplifters, and this child is one of a gang of boys whom we have suspected of stealing things from us for nearly six months. We finally caught one of them in the act. Why shouldn't we call the police?"

"Because he's nine years old, and he's scared to death. What kind of woman are you, to turn a little kid over to the police?" Reproach was in his voice.

"A businesswoman," Rachel hissed, glancing at the child again. It was a mistake. He did look scared, she decided, as he watched the three adults arguing his fate in undertones, though it was clear he was trying valiantly to hide it. She glared at Johnny even as her heart threatened to overrule her head. He was such a small boy, for all his nasty talk. She wouldn't have guessed he was nine.

Rachel sighed, already knowing that she was not going to call the police. "Let me talk to him a minute. What's his name?"

Ben shrugged. "The little hellion wouldn't even tell us that much."

"Jeremy Watkins. I know his mom." Johnny's answer was abrupt.

"Oh?" Rachel looked at him with eyebrows raised.

"Remember Glenda, the waitress at the Clock?"

"Oh." There was a wealth of meaning in the syllable. So that was why Johnny was championing the boy—for the sake of his mother. For some reason, that notion didn't suit Rachel well at all. Neither did the realization that Johnny had obviously taken the waitress up on her invitation to visit, if he had gotten to know the boy. Unbidden came the memory of his voice drawling, *It's been ten years since I've had the pleasure of a woman's company. You might be worried that I'm kinda horny.* Apparently he had since taken the opportunity to remedy his lack.

"The parents are getting a divorce. It's tough on the kid. Cut him some slack, can't you?"

"Of course, you would condone criminal behavior, Harris. Maybe if someone had refrained from cutting you some slack when you were a child, you wouldn't have ended up in prison." There was no mistaking the venom in Ben's whisper.

"And maybe if someone had rearranged your face when you were a child, you wouldn't have ended up being a sanctimonious dick-head. But we'll never know, will we?"

"Why, you—" Ben's fists clenched, and his face darkened with anger.

"Come on, Zeigler. Anytime." Johnny smiled again, unpleasantly, his eyes bright and clear. It was obvious to Rachel that he was spoiling for a fight, and Ben, from whom she would have expected more restraint, was just as bad. She guessed the only thing holding Ben back was the certainty that the younger, taller, stronger man would wipe the floor with him.

"Damn it, I have had enough!" Rachel hardly ever swore. That they had driven her to it between them increased her fury. "I will not listen to another word of this exchange. Ben, would you kindly go back out to the store? I'm sure Olivia could use some help. As for you"—her eyes flickered up to Johnny's face, their expression boding nothing good—"I'll talk to you in a minute. First I want to deal with this child."

"If you don't press charges against that little brat, I quit." Ben's voice vibrated with anger.

"Good." It was the merest breath of a taunt from Johnny, but Ben didn't appear to hear it. Rachel was able, for the moment at least, to respond with no more than a sidelong glare at Johnny while she did her best to placate her store manager.

"You're being ridiculous, Ben. You've worked here for six years now, and I'm not about to let you quit. But I do reserve the right not to call the police if I don't feel it's warranted. You know as well as I do that we make exceptions to policy all the time."

"If you don't call the police, I quit," he reiterated fiercely. Swinging around, he stalked out of the office.

9

"*A*sshole," Johnny said.

"You shut up." It was all Rachel could do not to shout it. Instead, she shot him a furious glance, turned her back on him, and walked around the desk to confront the boy.

"Jeremy—is that your name?"

He looked up at her, huge eyes dark with suspicion.

"Maybe it is, maybe it ain't."

"You can trust her, Jeremy. She's okay." Johnny was beside her, his voice gentle as he spoke to the boy. Rachel gritted her teeth.

"Would you please let me handle this?" she said, too sweetly. If she said what she really wanted to say to the aggravating son of a gun, in the tone she really wanted to say it, she would scare the child to death.

"Be my guest." Johnny settled back down on the edge of the desk with a gesture that said the problem was all hers.

Ignoring him, Rachel crouched down beside the child so that they were at eye level.

"Jeremy, I know you put the clock in your shirt, and that you and your friends have done things like that before. It probably seems pretty exciting, doesn't it, to take things and not pay for them? You want to see if you can get away with it. But I don't think you realize that what you're doing is stealing. Stealing is wrong, and you can get in big trouble for it. The police will come, and you'll be arrested and have to go before a judge. What happens after that is up to the judge, but I guarantee it isn't any fun." She paused to let her words sink in, then continued. "I'm not calling the police this time, because I think everybody deserves one warning. But if you ever do such a thing again, in here or in any other store, neither I nor anyone else will have a choice. Do you understand me?"

While she talked, his vanilla-wafer eyes had grown suspiciously moist, as though tears lurked just beneath the surface. Hurting for the child, she impulsively leaned forward to put her arms around him. As soon as she touched him, Jeremy shoved her away. Rachel sat back on her bottom, prevented from tumbling all the way over only by Johnny's hand catching her shoulder at the last split second.

"Jeremy!" Johnny said sharply, and stood to help Rachel to her feet. Rachel was already scrambling up. If she hadn't been wearing heels, she wouldn't have toppled over in the first place, she thought with disgust, feeling a fool.

"Are you all right?" Johnny's voice was low, his hand circling her forearm warm and comforting. She looked up to find his face disturbingly close. There was concern for her in his eyes, and it went a long way toward disarming her. The memory of their acrimonious last encounter still rankled, but it was rapidly losing its sting.

"I think I'll live." As she spoke, she brushed a hand down the back of her dress where it had made contact with the floor.

"Here, let me." The concern vanished, replaced by cool deviltry as he ran his hand palm-down over her derriere just as she had herself, though his hand tended to linger where hers had not. Similar though the two gestures were, their effect on her was wildly divergent.

"Stop that!" Rachel was so startled by the intimacy of his touch that she jumped away, and the reprimand was louder and shriller than she had intended. For a moment she feared Ben would come bursting back through the door to her rescue, but to her relief he did not. He must have taken himself off beyond earshot.

"I was just helping you brush away the dust," Johnny said innocently, though his eyes teased her. Red-faced, Rachel gave him a look that should have brought him to his knees with shame. Every single time she was on the verge of congratulating herself for discerning the basic decency behind his arrogant, aggressive, infuriating demeanor, he immediately did something to set her back up again. She began to suspect it was deliberate. Rachel toyed with the thought, then pushed it aside for later consideration as she remembered the presence of the boy. Self-consciously, she turned her gaze on him to discover that he was observing the pair of them with obvious interest.

"Will you promise me that you won't steal anything again, so I don't have to call the police?" Her thoughts were still befuddled by trying to make sense of Johnny Harris, so her voice was perhaps softer and gentler than it should have been to achieve the result she hoped for. She was all too conscious of the man watching her with his wicked smile and damnable sex appeal to be properly stern with the boy.

"You cain't prove nothin'," the child said.

For a moment Rachel was speechless at the ingratitude of the surly response. Then, her mind effectively cleared of all but the matter at hand, she shook her head at the boy. "You're wrong, Jeremy. If Mr. Zeigler, the man who was just in here, and Miss Tompkins, the lady behind the counter, were to go to court and testify against you, we could prove that you tried to steal the clock. But we're hoping not to have to do that, this time. If it happens again . . ."

"It won't happen again. I'll say something to Glenda." Johnny moved to stand beside her. Fortunately for Rachel's peace of mind, Johnny's attention was focused on the child.

"Don't tell my mom." Jeremy's bravado suddenly crumpled. His lower lip quivered, and at last he sounded like the small, scared boy he was. "Please don't tell my mom."

"The way you behaved to Miss Grant here, I don't reckon I have much choice." As intrigued as Rachel was by this discovery of an Achilles' heel to the child's tough-guy facade, Johnny crossed his arms over his chest, his expression severe. Jeremy met his gaze briefly. Then his lids dropped, and he stared at the floor, the very picture of youthful misery.

"If you tell her, she'll cry. She's been cryin' a lot lately. On account of my dad havin' a girlfriend and leavin' us to live with the whore, and us not havin' any money even with Mom workin' all the time. They turned off our lights last week, and it took three days before she was able to pay 'em enough to turn 'em back on again. It got real hot in our trailer with the air conditioner turned off. And the meat spoiled in the freezer, and we couldn't afford to buy no more till yesterday. And the clock by her bed, it's broke and she cain't buy another one 'cause she spent all her extra money for meat, and if she's late to work much, she'll lose her job. Then she'll cry and cry and cry, and we'll prob'ly have to go live with my dad and the whore, and they don't want us, or else we'll all starve."

This tumbled confession pierced Rachel's heart. She crouched again, wanting to hug the child tight but knowing better this time. She touched his blue-jeaned knee, about to tell him that he could have the clock and anything else he wanted. Johnny's hand closing over her shoulder stopped her, and she glanced up at him. He shook his head warningly at her. Rachel, acknowledging the justice of that warning, shut her mouth and removed her hand. To be too soft with the boy now would undo all the good their warnings might have done.

"You don't want to cause your mom any more grief by getting

caught stealing, now do you?" Johnny's voice was stern and gentle at the same time.

Jeremy glanced swiftly up at him. "Cain't nobody prove—" Something in Johnny's expression must have gotten through to him at last, because after a single swift glance at Rachel, he hung his head. "No, sir."

"Good boy. Then nobody will have to say anything to your mom—this time. If there ever is a next time, then we'll tell her, and we'll see she hears about this episode, too. Now you say sorry to Miss Grant and scoot on out of here. There's a door in the back here that you can use so you won't have to see anybody else from the store."

"You mean that man? He don't like me."

Rachel assumed he was referring to Ben.

"No," Johnny answered. "You don't have to see him. Now, what do you say to Miss Grant?"

"Sorry," Jeremy said with another of those quick glances at Rachel. "I won't do it no more."

Then, at a nod from Johnny, Jeremy got up from his seat and bolted past her out the door. For a moment they could hear the sound of sneakered feet pounding over the hardwood floor. The heavy metal delivery door creaked open and banged shut, and Jeremy was gone.

Rachel stood up. She was disconcerted to discover that that put her so close to Johnny that her shoulder was practically touching his chest, and her skirt brushed his jeans. Uncomfortable, she stepped away from him, covering the sudden awkwardness she felt by scooting the desk chair in which the child had been sitting back into its cubbyhole. The faint squeal of its wheels was jarringly loud in the sudden silence.

"Thank you for not calling the police," Johnny said, and she had no choice but to look at him again. There was that gentleness in his eyes again, and anyone who was acquainted only with the swaggering, cock-of-the-walk side of his personality would have found it surprising. But Rachel had always sensed it was there. If things had turned out differently for him, if the circumstances of birth and fate had not conspired against him, he might have been a very nice man. "The kid's going through a hard time."

"If he does it again, I'll have to." In her heart she knew that wild horses couldn't force her to turn that child over to the police after the glimpse he'd given her into his life. It had been all she could do not to beg him to take the clock with him when he ran off.

"If he does it again, I'll personally tan his backside until he can't sit for a week," Johnny said. "That'll make more impression on him than calling the police, believe me."

"I don't believe in spanking children."

He smiled at her. The smoky eyes were suddenly very blue, and their vividness dazzled her. Looking into them for a moment left her feeling as dazed as if she'd stared too long at the sun. "You've got a soft heart, teacher. I knew you wouldn't call the police. Just like I knew, when I asked you for a job, that you wouldn't be able to turn me down."

"Why did you want to come back here, anyway?" The question had been troubling her for the past two days, after the grateful penitent she had imagined herself aiding had never arrived. Instead, the real-life Johnny Harris who had stepped off that bus was as insufferable as ever he'd been as a trouble-making adolescent. His presence had stirred up a hornet's nest of resentment in town, as he must have known it would, and it had turned her life on end. Clearly he had not, as she had supposed, come back to try to make his peace with the community. It seemed more as if he had come back to declare war on it.

His eyes narrowed, and some of the brightness left them. "Because this is my hometown, and I'll be damned if people are going to run me out of it until I'm good and ready to leave."

"If you would just . . ."

"Just what?" A mocking note entered his voice as hers trailed off. Rachel blinked unhappily at him, unable after the recent debacle over his table manners to find the words to tell him that if he would just change his attitude, the townspeople might change theirs.

But it seemed as if he read her thoughts pretty accurately without her having to say a word. His face hardened as he looked down at her. The gentleness was long gone from his eyes. What Rachel was coming to think of as his mask had slipped once again into place. It made her wary.

Without warning, he reached out to grasp her arm, sliding his eyes boldly over her as he turned her for his inspection before she even thought to resist. "I like that dress on you, by the way. It does great things for your ass."

Rachel jerked away, bright color rising into her cheeks, but before she could annihilate him as he deserved, the sound of heavy footsteps outside the door warned her of someone's approach.

It was Rob. Struggling for composure, she managed a smile at him as he entered. Apparently, judging from his sudden frown, her smile left something to be desired.

"Are you okay, Rachel?" he said, his eyes moving from her face to fasten on Johnny with dislike.

"You got here in the nick of time," Johnny said, grinning insolently at him. "I was just about to start ripping off her clothes."

"Why, you—" Rob bristled with hostility.

"Of course I'm okay." Rachel quickly laid a restraining hand on

Rob's arm as she cast Johnny a glare that should have scourged him. Annoyance at Rob's assumption that just being alone with Johnny put her at risk, combined with aggravation at Johnny's behavior, made her voice sharp. "Johnny is teasing. Aren't you?" The faint emphasis she put on the question said that he had better answer in the affirmative if he knew what was good for him.

"Oh, absolutely." But the very way he said it was provocative. Rachel frowned fiercely at him. Why must he go out of his way to make people dislike him?

"Are you ready? We'll be late for the concert." Rob's words were abrupt as he took her hand from where it rested on his arm and entwined his fingers with hers.

Rachel hesitated, glancing from one man to the other. Animosity crackled in the air between them, and clearly such courtesies as reintroducing them would be unwelcome to both. There was such a contrast between them that they would probably have disliked each other on sight, even if neither knew a single thing about the other. Divorced three years before, Rob was forty, well educated, sophisticated in his expensive gray suit and maroon silk tie. His medium height and slight stockiness added to, rather than detracted from, his air of solid, upper-middle-class respectability. His light brown hair was cut short and impeccably styled, and he made no effort to hide the bald spot that was growing at the back of his head. If he was not as handsome as the younger man, or as dangerously appealing, he certainly had more long-term potential. And that, of course, was what mattered to a woman of sense.

"I'm ready," Rachel said, returning the slight pressure of his fingers. "But I need to talk to Johnny for just a minute before I leave. Would you mind very much waiting for me in the store?"

Rob looked down at her with a frown that said he would mind very much indeed. She smiled coaxingly at him.

"Please? It will only take a second, I promise."

He didn't return her smile. Instead, his eyes shot to Johnny in a clear warning.

"I'll wait in the storeroom," he said, with the obvious if unspoken implication that he would be within calling distance if she should need him. Rachel sighed inwardly as he released her hand and walked out the door. Getting respectable Tylerville to regard Johnny with anything but extreme suspicion was an uphill fight.

"I didn't know you had it in you to be so sweetly feminine, teacher." Johnny was smiling, but the jut to his jaw spoke of anything but good humor. " 'Please,' she says, batting those big eyes, and he just melts. Do you sleep with him?"

"One day," Rachel said with precision, "someone is going to shut you up by burying his fist in your smart mouth. I just wish I could be the one to do it."

"Answer the question: Do you?" The smile had faded.

"That's none of your darned business. And if you don't do your best to get along with Ben, I am going to fire you, and without a job they'll cart you straight back to prison. So how do you like them apples, tough · guy?"

Johnny's lip curled at her. "Never make threats you don't mean to carry out. You could no more fire me than you could call the police on that boy."

"Don't count on it." Thoroughly ruffled, Rachel turned her back on the source of her annoyance and started for the door. She could feel his gaze on her, and the notion that he was watching her made her suddenly self-conscious. In her teetering heels, she could not help but sway.

Just as she reached the door, he made an odd sound that caused her to glance back at him, startled.

"Rachel," he said in what was scarcely more than a husky whisper, while his eyes drilled into hers, "don't sleep with him. Sleep with me instead."

Her breath caught for a moment as the words coiled around her like a seductive snake. Only by forcing herself to keep walking was she able to escape.

10

⤳

$\mathcal{T}$he concert, held under a huge tent by the small lake that bisected the club grounds, was a success. Or so Rachel was later told. So busy was she with her thoughts that she heard scarcely a note of it.

The unwanted heat engendered in her by Johnny's words had largely dissipated by the time the well-dressed patrons filed out of their three-hundred-dollar seats. To Mozart and Chopin, her wayward imagination had conjured up sweaty images of what it would be like to sleep with Johnny Harris. It had taken considerable mental effort to banish the shamefully explicit acts that, through no conscious effort on her part, were played out on the screen of her mind. The sudden sexual awareness that had made her breasts swell and her loins quicken was even harder to get rid of. She had managed it to the extent that her body was now only slightly achey, but only by clear-sightedly focusing on things as they were and not as she wished them to be. Johnny Harris as a bed partner was out of the question, however sexy she found him. She had never been promiscuous, and she would never sleep with a man, no matter how temptingly attractive, just to scratch a bodily itch. At her age, with the example of her sister's three girls to lure her, when she thought of a man she should be thinking marriage and babies. Johnny Harris's potential in that area was effectively zilch.

Though she was as convinced as it was humanly possible to be that he had not committed the crime for which he had been sent to prison, the fact remained that he was a convict, as her mother had pointed out. The stigma of that could never be erased. Nor could the town's conviction that he was guilty. Only the revelation of the identity of the real murderer could change that, and Rachel acknowledged that such a denouement was extremely unlikely. After Johnny had been arrested, she had spent much time mentally constructing alternative scenarios to explain Marybeth Edwards's death, with all possible suspects in the lead role of murderer. The fact was, she couldn't imagine anyone she knew committing so dreadful a crime, and each villain she came up with was more improbable than the last. Her preferred theory was that the girl had fallen victim to a killer who happened to be passing through. A serial killer, a nut, someone who preyed on young girls.

But in sleepy Tylerville, that seemed pretty far-fetched, too.

When she replied to his letter, she had been responding to the Johnny Harris she remembered. Her student, one of the few who had responded to books and poetry as she did, no matter how he tried to hide it. Reading of any kind was not macho, and reading poetry was downright sissy. As a teenager such proclivities had embarrassed him to the point that he'd hidden his addiction to the printed page like a secret vice. But sometimes, when she'd come upon him away from his unruly friends, she'd been able to coax him into talking of books and poetry, and from there their conversations had wandered down all manner of paths. Personalities, politics, religion—they had discussed them all. As he had talked, Johnny had grown animated, revealing a side of himself that she thought few others had ever seen.

Something in him had drawn her even then, a glimmer of unusual intelligence and sensitivity that shone like a flickering candle through the mask of sneering toughness that was his everyday wear. Johnny Harris, she had been convinced, was worth exerting herself for. At the time, she had hoped to save him from the life he seemed locked into by birth and grinding poverty. Later, she had wished she could save him from a fate that was far worse.

But wishes did not always, or even very often, come true. His wildness, for which she had reprimanded him more than once in those long ago days, had been as much a factor in his conviction as had any hard evidence, because there'd been very little of that. The most damning piece was that he had been the last person to admit to seeing Marybeth Edwards alive. Against her parents' wishes, the girl had sneaked out to meet him that night. He had admitted it, had even admitted to making love with her in the back seat of her father's Lincoln, which was parked in the driveway. Johnny claimed she had gone in around two A.M., and he had watched her walk toward her back door. He had not seen her enter; instead, he had climbed onto his motorcycle and ridden away.

The next morning, Marybeth Edwards had been found almost a mile away, lying in a ditch by the side of the road, her body covered with blood and summersweet blossoms.

Johnny had sworn, over and over again, that he had not killed her. He had not been believed; he would never be believed. Not by the people of Tylerville.

She could not sleep with him, however much the notion secretly excited her. Even if he had never been convicted of murder, the prospect was unthinkable. She was five years older than he, and he had once been her student. Tylerville would rock with the scandal of it.

Her mother would die.

"You're very quiet tonight," Rob observed in her ear as, an arm around her back, he ushered her along the moonlit path beside the lake. Ahead of them, other couples followed the same route, alternately admiring the luminaries that had been set up to one side of the path and the panorama of bright stars overhead. The night air was warm, the gravel path was crunchy underfoot, and the blurred reflection of the night sky in the placid surface of the lake was lovely enough to soothe even the most agitated of thoughts.

She would put Johnny Harris out of her mind, Rachel resolved firmly, and leaned a little closer against Rob's side.

"I'm just tired, I guess."

"We could always go to my house and, uh—relax."

Rachel knew perfectly well what he was suggesting, and that relaxing had nothing to do with it. Funny, she had once had the same thought as to how their evening together might end. Now the idea lacked appeal. *Sleep with me instead,* she seemed to hear Johnny's whisper on the low moan of the wind, and she shivered in Rob's grasp.

"Cold?"

"No."

"Good." Taking advantage of the shelter provided by a tall northern pine, Rob pulled her off the path into his arms and kissed her mouth. Rachel had to tell herself to relax against him, to encircle his neck with her arms. For the first time, his tongue entering her mouth was an intrusion. Her instinct was to turn her face away.

She had to remind herself that Rob was the future. In a town the size of Tylerville, a better prospect for husband and father would not be found. And she wanted both.

"Hey, you two lovebirds, break it up. I've got an idea."

The voice belonged to Dave Henley, the town dentist, who with his wife Susan had accompanied them to the concert. Dave was Rob's best buddy. Rachel was fond of him and fonder still of Susan, with whom she had been good friends since grade school. She knew that both of them were hoping that she and Rob would make a match of it. They made such a good foursome.

"Bug off, Henley. Can't you see we're busy?" But Rob's voice was good-natured, and he released Rachel. If she was honest with herself, she had to admit that she was relieved by the interruption. She moved away from Rob's side to join Susan, who grinned conspiratorially at her.

"So what's your idea?" Rachel asked Dave, unable to reply to Susan's grin in any way her friend was likely to find satisfactory.

Dave said, "They've just opened up a new place out on Highway Twenty-one. Hurricane O'Shea's, I think the name of it is. They're supposed to have good music and dancing and—"

"Booze," Susan finished, sounding like someone presenting the pièce de résistance. Tylerville was situated in a dry county, which made the lure of liquor nearly irresistible.

"Wow," Rachel responded, laughing at Susan's air of exaggerated eagerness.

"You want to go?" Rob asked, joining Rachel and taking her hand. He was smiling down at her, and she thought for what must have been the hundredth time since she had started going out with him, what an estimable man he was. What kind of fool was she not to snatch him up? Only in books did bells ring and rockets burst and heavenly choruses sing when a woman found Mr. Right. In fact, only in books *was* there a Mr. Right. In real life, most women were happy to settle for Mr. Good Enough.

"Sure, why not?" At least for another hour or two it would keep her from having to decide whether to let Rob take her to bed tonight. Guiltily she realized that, if faced with the choice at that moment, her instincts would all shout no.

The drive out Highway 21 took some twenty minutes. When they pulled into the parking lot of Hurricane O'Shea's, for that was indeed its name, Rachel was not surprised to discover that it was full to overflowing. There wasn't much nightlife in the vicinity of Tylerville to provide competition. Even the movie theaters showed the last feature at nine o'clock.

The music blasted out at them before they reached the door.

" 'You picked a fine time to leave me, Lucille!' "

" 'You bitch! You slut! You whore!' "

What? Rachel's eyes widened as the unfamiliar second line, shouted out from many throats in a gleeful chant, assaulted her ears. She, Rob, Susan, and Dave exchanged glances.

"Sounds rowdy!" Dave grinned in anticipation and pulled open the door. Rob shrugged, and they all headed inside.

The place, which Rachel realized was a converted auto repair garage, had concrete block walls that had been painted a vibrant red. Overhead, exposed electrical lines and plumbing pipes were shaded the same dark gray as the unfinished ceiling. Underfoot lay a multilevel hardwood floor. Neon signs advertising everything from Miller Lite to the Beatles flashed from the walls. Twin pianos with a pair of boisterous singers, and a long-legged blonde in a bright yellow satin parody of a cheerleader's outfit, led the action.

"'Shout! Come on, baby, shout! Come on, baby!'" The raucous melody had the crowd on its feet, singing, or rather bellowing, along. The newly arrived foursome edged along the back wall, which was on the highest level. Of the four tiers, each a foot or so lower than the previous one, three were jammed with feet-stomping, fist-waving, shouting patrons. The bottom tier was the dance floor, packed with enthusiastically gyrating bodies.

"This place is wild!" Susan said.

"Far out!" Dave concurred.

Rob caught Rachel's hand and held it tightly, as if afraid he might lose her in all the hullabaloo. Luckily they happened to pass behind a table just as its occupants were getting up to leave. Dave grabbed it with a triumphant whoop.

"What can I get you?" The waitress materialized with tray and pad as they were settling into their seats.

They ordered. Rachel, an unenthusiastic drinker even with the spur of alcohol's relative unavailability, chose a daiquiri. She found it palatable enough, and she knew from experience that she would be happy to sip on the single drink all night.

By the time their drinks arrived, Rob was visibly wincing at the unrelenting volume of the music. Rachel would have enjoyed it more if it had been a decibel or so softer, but the beat was infectious and she caught herself tapping her toes to it. Dave munched popcorn and gulped down bourbon and Coke, while Susan examined the other people present with as much interest as Rachel did. Some of the women were outlandishly dressed, in micro-miniskirts and mesh stockings and tops that glittered with sequins. Under the flashing lights that illuminated the dance floor, sequins sparkled like brilliantly colored jewels.

"Good gracious, can you imagine wearing something like that?" Susan yelled in Rachel's ear, indicating a willowy, leather-miniskirted woman with improbably red hair who swayed past them. The object of Susan's disbelief was the woman's blouse. It was black and sheer, except for a few strategically placed sequins. Clearly she wore nothing beneath. Rachel shook her head, and her gaze followed the woman down to the dance floor, where she threw herself into the music with abandon. As she watched the woman's gyrations with shocked amusement, Rachel's attention was caught by a tall, leanly muscular man and a blond-haired woman near her. The couple writhed together in a sensuous frenzy that approximated foreplay more than dancing. The light flashed again, illuminating the dance floor for seconds only.

Those few seconds were long enough. Feeling as though someone had punched her in the stomach, Rachel identified the man with the blonde as Johnny Harris. That jet-black ponytail, so out of place in Tylerville, and the wide-shouldered, lean-hipped body made him impossible to mistake. As the light flashed again, she even managed to name his companion: Glenda, the waitress from the Clock.

11

"*E*xcuse me. I need to go to the rest room." Rachel used the excuse desperately. She could not sit there and watch Johnny Harris all but making love to Glenda. Not after the fantasies she'd been having about him. Not after the way he had come on to her, and she, God help her, had responded.

Of course, she thought bitterly as she made her way toward the narrow dark corridor that led to the ladies' room, Johnny Harris had always had a way with women. Even when he was in high school, he'd never lacked for girlfriends. The ones from nice families, forbidden by their parents to so much as speak to him, had followed him with their eyes.

If she found him sexy, and honesty forced her to admit she did, she could just add her name to a long list.

The rest room was small, painted red like the corridor, with brick walls that were blessedly thick enough to mute the relentless barrage of sound. Its only other occupant left as Rachel entered. Relieved to be alone, she washed her hands, allowing the cool water to run over her wrists for a minute or so. Then she cupped her hands to take a drink. Something, the daiquiri or the noise or her own emotions, had made her feel sick to her stomach.

Another woman entered and went into a stall. Rachel dried her hands on a paper towel and left. She would go back to the table and plead illness, if that was what it would take to get away.

The men's room was directly across the hall from the women's, so Rachel was not surprised to see a man approaching. The corridor was dark except for the purple glow and occasional flash of light at its entrance and the red neon signs announcing the rest rooms. She hugged her side of the wall as she and the man prepared to pass each other. When he shot out a hand to grab her arm, she squeaked with alarm.

Her gaze flew upward to fix on Johnny Harris's face.

"Slumming?" he asked with what could only be described as a sneer.

"Obviously you're not," she responded coldly.

"No, I'm right at home," he agreed, looming closer. His left hand curled around her arm. Rachel could feel the heat and strength of his fingers clear down to her toes. In his right hand he held a beer. She would never have noticed it if he had not lifted it at that moment and taken a swig.

"I'm surprised the boyfriend brought you to a place like this. He doesn't look like the type to ever let his hair down and have a good time."

"If you'll please let go of my arm, I'll rejoin him, and we'll continue to have fun in our own dull way."

"I didn't mean that you were dull, Rachel—only him. You have immense—possibilities." The way he drew out that last word, the way his eyes glinted as they moved over her face and then down the front of her dress, made Rachel's toes curl at the same time as it angered her.

"Would you let me go, please?" Her voice was crisp.

He lifted the beer to take another swallow, then slowly shook his head. As he grinned, the pulsing purplish light made the sudden gleam of his teeth seem incredibly white.

"Not till you dance with me. You haven't danced once. I've been watching."

The notion that he had been watching her was unsettling. Rachel swallowed, then shook her head.

"Thank you for asking, but no. I have to get back to my friends, just as I'm sure you need to get back to yours."

"Glenda's a good girl, and we're with a crowd. She won't miss me for a while, or care if she does. If it's the boyfriend you're worried about, he won't see you. We'll stay to the back of the dance floor where it's nice and dark."

His hand slid down to imprison her wrist, and he was already tugging her toward the doorway as he spoke. Rachel resisted.

"Johnny, no."

He stopped, shrugging, and entwined his fingers with hers as he smiled down at her. "Okay. I guess I'll just have to take you back to your friends."

"No!" Horror sharpened her voice. The thought of what might happen should Rob get into a confrontation with Johnny over her made her shudder.

"No? Then dance with me, Rachel. Come on, it'll be fun, and then I'll let you go. Promise." His eyes gleamed down at her, teasing her, luring her. Caught between two evils and suddenly sorely tempted, Rachel was mute. Taking her silence for assent, his hand hard and warm about hers, Johnny pulled her out into the cavernous night club and toward the dance floor.

Annoyed, apprehensive, and yes, already so seduced by the notion of dancing with him that she could not have refused now even if he'd have listened, Rachel cast a wary glance toward the topmost tier, where her friends' table was. In the darkness, with about half the mob of people on their feet singing along to the strains of "You've Lost That Lovin' Feelin'," she couldn't even locate the table, much less pick out Rob.

"I don't even like to dance," Rachel protested when Johnny set his beer down on a nearby, fully occupied table and dragged her onto the floor. The Righteous Brothers' classic ended with a melodic flourish, and one of the entertainers called out, "Is it dark enough for you down there on the dance floor?"

When the response to this was a shouted "No!", the flashing overhead light changed to a glittering ball that swept the room with tiny red and purple pulse points.

"Ain't it romantic?" The entertainer sighed into his microphone, then struck up the opening bars of the Ronettes' "Be My Baby."

"If that's so, you haven't been dancing with the right man." Johnny lifted her hands to his shoulders, then grasped her waist just above her belt, pulling her close to him. Gingerly Rachel let her hands rest on the hard muscle and solid bone of his shoulders. He was wearing another of his ubiquitous white T-shirts. Through the thin cotton she could feel the ripple of his muscles as he moved and the heat of his skin. Even with the help of her heels, he was much taller than she, and she wasn't sure whether she liked or hated the feeling of vulnerability that assailed her when confronted with the difference in their sizes.

"I suppose you think you're the right man?" Rachel scoffed. He smelled faintly of sweat and beer. Held so near, Rachel found she was having trouble thinking, much less talking. She was not plastered against him. Her body only just brushed his, but the effect on her senses was electrifying.

"Could be," he said, and at the sudden huskiness of his voice she glanced up to discover that he was looking down at her, unsmiling. For an instant, no more, those smoky blue eyes were dark and intent on her face. Then he pulled her tight against him and pushed his blue-jean-clad thigh between her legs and swayed with her to the hot, sweet music.

" 'Be my—be my little baby,' " the singer crooned.

Rachel had never danced like this in her life. He shimmied with her, turned with her, dipped her back and pulled her up into his arms again. All the while the friction of his leg moving between hers stole away the last vestiges of her good sense.

After a single shocked attempt to pull away, Rachel, mesmerized, didn't even try to resist him. He was taking her with him to heaven or to hell—Rachel didn't know which—and as the explosive combination of song and man and her own longing stripped her of her reason, she didn't much care.

When the music ended, she still clung to him for a befuddled instant. Her eyes were closed, and her forehead rested against his chest. Her fingers held tightly to his shoulders. His hands were hard about her waist. His leg was between hers, pushing the demurely knee-length dress halfway up her thighs. The silky barrier of her pantyhose might as well have been nonexistent for all the good it did in protecting her skin from the abrasion of his jeans.

"See what I mean?" he murmured in her ear as the emcee said something over the loudspeaker that Rachel didn't catch. The overhead light started to flash again.

Dropped without warning straight back into reality, Rachel lifted her head from his chest and blinked into his wickedly glinting eyes. It was a moment before she realized just how intimate their entwined posture was. Yanking her hands away from his shoulders as if they had suddenly grown teeth and were snapping at her, Rachel jerked free of his hold and stepped back. Shaken, she could do nothing but stare at him. In the surreal surroundings the white T-shirt took on an otherworldly glow, accentuating the breadth of his shoulders and the swarthiness of his skin. Like his body, his face was lean and hard and possessed of a dangerous masculine beauty. He was watching her with a raptor's unblinking gaze, unsmiling, his mouth long, full-lipped, and sensuous, his eyes fixed on her face. Rachel felt breathless suddenly from just looking at him.

The pianos crashed into the opening bars of Jerry Lee Lewis's "Great Balls of Fire." All around them couples started to writhe with manic energy.

"I—I've got to go," she said, looking anywhere but into those too-knowing eyes. At her obvious discomfiture, his mouth stretched into a slow grin.

"You can run, teacher, but you can't hide." The soft words were tauntingly seductive, threatening and promising at the same time. He reached for her, clearly meaning to draw her back into his arms.

"No!"

Rachel turned away with more haste than grace, pushing through the tangle of bodies to reach the edge of the dance floor. Johnny followed her. She knew he did, though she never once glanced around. She could feel him behind her with unerring certainty, and his presence seemed to make the hairs rise on the back of her neck.

Without a word to him she made her way through the darkness back up to where she supposed her table was. As she climbed, she realized that her knees were shaky and her stomach was in knots. With unsteady hands she smoothed her skirt around her legs. It was best not to allow herself to recall how her dress had gotten so twisted in the first place. It was best to put the last incredible quarter-hour clean out of her mind.

She would never be able to put it out of her mind.

Drawn by a force impossible to resist, she looked around finally to try to catch one last glimpse of Johnny before she returned to Rob. The flashing light made identifying individuals difficult. She might have missed him altogether if he had not been wearing the white T-shirt with its strange purplish glow. Or maybe her eyes would have been drawn to him as unerringly as her body was, T-shirt or no. But for whatever reason, she found him, and when she did, the bottom seemed to drop out of her stomach.

He was on the dance floor again, performing his special brand of erotic lambada with Glenda.

At least, Rachel thought, she knew where she stood. For some reason, he got a kick out of coming on to her. He wanted her to want him. But while what she felt for him was like nothing she had ever felt before, what he felt for her was the same thing he felt for countless other women: horny.

That was the word he'd used, wasn't it? It suited him very well, she thought savagely.

Gathering up the tatters of her dignity, Rachel walked up the stairs without casting another glance at the dance floor. If he was a randy goat, why she hoped he got what he was after. But he wouldn't get it from her, ever.

She had to edge a quarter of the way around the club before she spotted their table at last. Rob and Dave were talking together, and Rob was frowning. Susan was just getting to her feet. Rachel headed toward them.

She would not think of that dance with Johnny again.

"Sorry I took so long," she murmured, sliding into her seat beside Rob. He took her hand and raised it to his lips.

"We thought you'd fallen in," Susan said with a grin as she sat back down.

"Susan was just going to look for you. We were worried about you." Rob's tone reproved Susan's levity. "Are you okay?"

Rachel leaped on the opportunity. "To tell you the truth, I'm not. I must have picked up some kind of bug." Named Johnny Harris, was the thought that popped unbidden into her mind. She bulldozed it under ruthlessly. "Would you mind terribly if we left?"

Rob looked at the others, who shook their heads. "Of course not. The music's a little loud for my taste anyway. Let's go."

As she followed him out of the club, Rachel never looked at the dance floor, and she held tightly to Rob's hand.

12

From the pulsating darkness beside the dance floor, the watcher fixed Johnny Harris with an unwavering gaze. Couldn't he somehow feel the pull of unblinking eyes? Apparently not, because he never glanced the watcher's way.

The watcher experienced wave after wave of increasing coldness even as the heat from so many energetic bodies packed into too small a space brought beads of sweat to his brow. Anger, long buried, rose to fill him like an icy gray fog.

Once again, Johnny Harris was begging to be taught a lesson.

The watcher meant to make sure that this time it was one he would never forget.

13

It was shortly after two that same night, and Johnny was in a lousy mood. He revved his motorcycle through Tylerville's deserted streets, taking perverse pleasure in the roar that told him the muffler needed some work. It was a beautiful night, warm and nearly cloudless, so that he could see the road just fine by the soft glow of the full moon. No streetlights were needed, which was just as well because Tylerville had precious few of them. The place was a backwater. That wouldn't be so bad except for the pride its most upstanding citizens took in keeping it that way. When he finally buried the baggage from his past that had haunted him for the last ten years, he would get the hell out of here before the place sucked all the juice from him, just as it had from everyone else.

The wind rushing against his face and bare arms felt good. The machine between his legs was fast and powerful, and his. His belly was full, he'd had more beer than was probably good for him, and he'd gotten laid. So why did he feel like a piece of three-week-old crap?

He knew the answer, but the knowledge didn't make him feel any better.

The woman he'd screwed hadn't been the woman he'd wanted. Glenda was an old friend, and she had a nice body, and he wasn't turning down anything thrown his way after so many years of doing without. But it wasn't Glenda who made him get hard just by looking at her.

It was Rachel. Miss Grant. Teacher. He'd had a thing for her since high school. She would have been shocked if she had been able to see inside the head of the teenage boy she'd taught English. He'd spent nearly every class period, and a good part of his nights as well, imagining what she looked like naked. What she felt like naked. What kind of sound she made when she came. If she came.

But the boy he'd been had never done more than imagine. He'd accepted as gospel the idea that she was so far above him that he was more likely to jump over the moon than get in her pants. There was the age difference, of course. At sixteen and seventeen and eighteen years old, a five-year gap had seemed more like a quarter of a century. Then there was the fact that she was the teacher, and he was one of her students—a definite taboo. But the most insurmountable obstacle between them, in his own mind at least, was their relative positions in life. Rachel and her family had money. They had a huge old house, and fancy cars, and good educations, and a gardener and a maid. That, as far as the young Johnny had been concerned, was the ultimate in class. While as for himself, as far back as he could remember, from birth it seemed, he'd known that he and his family were poor white trash. The whole town looked down on them. The other kids made fun of his drunken parents and tattered clothes and less-than-clean body and did not invite him to their birthday parties or their homes. When he grew big enough to take care of himself and mean enough to put the fear of God into them, they were respectful to his face, but still the nice ones, the ones with parents who checked their homework and gave them curfews and would one day send them off to college, gave him a wide berth. By default, he hung out with the bad crowd. And since he did, he'd taken it upon himself to be the baddest one of all.

Rachel Grant wouldn't be caught dead with someone like him.

Johnny smiled with wry inner amusement as he remembered the kid he had been. He'd had plans, big plans. He would leave Tylerville as soon as he'd graduated from high school and go off into the big world and make his fortune, though just exactly how he would accomplish that, he had never quite worked out. At the time the details hadn't mattered. What had mattered was that when he was rich, he would come back and lord it over all the country club snobs who'd looked down their noses at him and his family, and he would buy or bully his way into the affections of Miss Rachel Grant. With the confidence of youth to bolster him, he'd seen not the slightest bit of impossibility in his dreams.

But life has a way of chopping people off at the knees, and he was no exception. Ten years of his life had been stolen from him. Now he wasn't wasting another minute. He wanted to experience everything he had missed, to eat and drink and read and work and fuck as he pleased. His dreams were smaller now, but they were still dreams, and he was going after them with everything he had.

Foremost among them was to get Miss Grant into bed. If the way she clung to him tonight was any indication, sooner or later he would succeed.

He might not be good enough to sit down to dinner with her, but he was good enough to give her the best lay she had ever had.

The cycle roared down Main Street. With the hardware store in view, Johnny was just easing off on the throttle when he spotted a cop car parked in front. The engine was turned off and the lights were out, or he would have seen it sooner. His eyes narrowed, and he gave a moment's thought to pouring on the juice and racing by. But in Tylerville there was no place to go, and even if he gave them the slip for the night, they knew where to find him on the morrow.

Johnny pulled into the parking lot and braked, still straddling the idling cycle as he supported it with one leg. The cop got out of his car and walked toward him. A long metal flashlight that Johnny knew from experience could easily double as a night stick was clutched in his hand.

The cop was a big, burly dude, and as he drew close, Johnny recognized him as the police chief, Wheatley. The same guy who'd been chief when he'd been arrested for murder. Not overly bright, but basically fair. At least, Johnny thought, he didn't have to fear an unprovoked beating.

"What do you want?" Truculence sharpened Johnny's voice.

"Can you cut the engine?" A gesture imparted Wheatley's meaning since the cycle's roar all but drowned out his words.

Johnny hesitated, then turned off the ignition. In the sudden silence that followed, he dismounted, propping his bike up on its stand. Then he took his helmet off, tucked it under his arm, and turned to face the police chief.

"I broke some law I don't remember?"

"You been drinkin'?"

"Maybe. I'm not drunk. You want to give me a test, go ahead."

Wheatley shook his head. "I don't think you're that stupid, though I've been wrong before."

For a moment the two men said nothing, just eyed each other suspiciously. There was something odd about the cop's manner, something almost tentative. It gave Johnny, who was used to bluster and bullying from the strong arm of the law, the willies.

"You got something to say to me, or are you just out here stargazing tonight?"

"Smartass, aren't you?" Wheatley pursed his lips and tapped the flashlight against his leg. "I got some bad news."

"What kind of bad news?"

"There's been an accident."

"Accident?" *Rachel.* The name immediately sprang to Johnny's mind. Which was stupid. If anything had happened to Rachel, he'd be the last person they'd tell.

"Yeah. A bad one. Your dad."

"My dad?"

"Yeah."

Johnny felt as if he'd unexpectedly had all the breath knocked out of him. It was all he could do to find enough air to force out the single pertinent word.

"Dead?"

"Yeah. Dead. He got hit by a train, where the tracks cross the road not far from his house. It looks like he was drunk, though we can't be sure."

"Oh, Christ." Johnny hadn't meant to let even that much emotion escape him, not in the presence of the cop. But he couldn't help it. The news left him raw, exposed, bleeding as if an artery had been sliced. His dad, the mean old son of a bitch, dead.

Johnny clamped his lips together and forced himself to take a deep breath through his nose. He'd learned how to handle himself in a crisis because he'd had to. He'd also learned that, one way or another, if he could manage to keep breathing, the crisis would pass.

"I hate to ask you this, but we need somebody to identify the body. It's just a formality, there's no doubt about who it is. But—"

"Sure."

"I'll drive you over. Come on."

It was the first time in his life he'd ridden in a cop car and not been under arrest.

14

$\mathcal{R}$achel heard the news the next morning in church.

"I say it's God's judgment on the whole wicked family."

"Oh, no, Idell!"

"Well, I do! Those Harrises are all bad, all of 'em, and I feel God in His wisdom must be meanin' to rid the world of 'em one by one to keep decent folks safe. At least, I hope so. I'll sleep better nights when they're all gone."

"But it was such an awful way to go!"

"It's bad of me to say so, I know, but I just don't feel a bit of pity for the man! It wouldn't have happened if he hadn't been falling-down drunk. He brought his misfortune on himself, as most sinners do."

"But to be run over by a train, Idell . . ."

Rachel's blood ran cold. Regardless of the fact that Reverend Harvey was just reaching the thundering crescendo of his sermon against complacency in those who are blessed with plenty, Rachel turned in her seat to address the surprised whisperers.

"Mrs. Skaggs, who are you talking about?" The urgency of her hiss caused both ladies—Mrs. Ashton was the other one—to lift their silvery heads and gape at Rachel. Beside her, her mother gave her a sharp poke in the ribs, to which Rachel paid no heed. Above her head, the Reverend Harvey's voice continued to crash. All around her, the other worshippers gave her disapproving frowns.

"Who?" Rachel demanded in a shrill whisper.

Mrs. Skaggs blinked. "Why, Willie Harris."

At the identity of the deceased, a huge wave of relief washed over Rachel. "Is he dead?" Her voice was lower.

"Yes."

"Rachel, for goodness' sake." Elisabeth tugged at the full skirt of her daughter's silky flowered dress. Rachel turned around and did her best to resume her former posture of quiet attention to the minister's words. Truth was, she didn't hear another syllable.

Willie Harris was dead. What would that mean to Johnny? As far as she knew, he and his father had never been particularly close. But then, she really didn't know that much about his family or his early life. In any case, losing a parent, especially so suddenly and under such circumstances, was bound to be devastating. Her heart ached for him.

The service seemed interminable. Afterward, the parishioners spilled out onto the front lawn, and her mother, elegant as usual in a cobalt silk dress and tiny, matching hat, stopped to chat with her friends, as she always did. Rachel, knowing from experience that it would be impossible to budge her mother until Elisabeth had concluded the after-church visiting that was one of her favorite weekly rituals, plugged into the town gossip network to learn what she could about Willie Harris's death.

". . . and they're going to bury him in Calvary Cemetery in the morning," Kay Nelson concluded in a hushed tone. Standing beside Kay in a circle of acquaintances as she waited with what patience she could muster for her mother to go, Rachel was surprised by how many details of the death and the burial to come Kay had already learned. The telephones must have been ringing off the hooks at dawn.

"That seems awfully soon." Kay's petite sister-in-law, Amy, sounded genuinely sorry for the victim. Amy was an outsider, not having come to Tylerville until two years before, when she had married Kay's younger brother Jim. Thus she could not be expected to fully understand the intricacies of who was who and who was nobody in town. A prominent citizen who was unexpectedly lost to them might remain aboveground for as much as five or six days after death so that a large and impressive funeral could be carried out. For someone like Willie Harris, no such time period was necessary.

Jim Nelson shrugged. "He could just as well be buried today. I don't suppose there'll be anybody but Johnny going to the funeral. Unless Buck or the Harris girl shows up. Don't guess you'll make much in the way of selling funeral wreaths, Kay."

Only then, nudged by Jim's seeming familiarity with the Harrises, did Rachel remember that Jim had been a high school classmate of

Johnny's. If her memory served her correctly, she recalled that he had dated Marybeth Edwards a few times himself.

"Now you're making me feel bad. I certainly don't think of every death in town as an opportunity for profit," Kay protested, half-laughing as she punched her brother's arm. "And it's awful to think of nobody going to the poor man's funeral."

"I'm going," Rachel said abruptly. Jim Nelson glanced down at her. Like Kay, he was built along sturdy lines, and in his pinstripe suit he made an imposing figure. He looked precisely what he was, a successful small-town lawyer.

"You always did have a soft spot for Johnny Harris, didn't you, Rachel?" he said. "I remember when we were in school you let him get away with things you would have hung the rest of us out to dry for."

"Maybe I thought that his background made some excuse for his bad behavior that the rest of you didn't share," Rachel retorted, and Jim grinned in acknowledgment.

"Don't tell me you were teaching high school when Jimmy was there! Why, I don't believe it!" Amy's eyes ran over Rachel again, appraisingly this time, and Rachel could almost see the question in them: Just how old are you? But Amy was too well-bred to ask.

"She was. And she was a martinet, too." Jim was still grinning. "I hear she still is."

"Why, Jim Nelson!" Kay sounded scandalized. "What a thing to say! You know how sweet Rachel is. He's just teasing you, Rachel."

"I am not. Rachel may be sweet, but Miss Grant was a regular tartar. We were all afraid of her. Even Johnny Harris. He minded his manners with her like he did with nobody else."

"Were you friends with him? I thought . . ." Amy's voice trailed off as she looked questioningly up at her husband.

Jim shook his head. "Nah. He didn't run with our crowd. We played tennis and golf. He and his pals broke into houses."

Kay glared at her brother. Jim's eyebrows rose in surprise.

"He wasn't that bad. He used to cut our grass sometimes, when you were too busy playing tennis or golf, and he was always real polite to Mama and me. Anyway, Johnny's working for Rachel now, remember?" Kay said pointedly.

"Oh, yeah." Jim's gaze shifted to Rachel. "I don't know how you could have hired him, after what he did to poor little Marybeth. They ought to have given him the death penalty for that. Ten years is a joke for what he did. At the very least, we ought to run him out of Tylerville."

"Jim!" Kay cast an embarrassed eye at Rachel.

"I can't help what I think, and I'd feel like a hypocrite if I didn't say so."

"Everyone's entitled to his or her opinion." Rachel smiled coolly. "Mine is that Johnny Harris didn't kill her. Somebody else did."

"Oh, Rachel, I'd like to think so, too, but who?" Kay's voice was gently incredulous.

Jim spoke at the same time as his sister: "Like I said, you always had a soft spot for him. I happen to think he's guilty as hell."

"Hey, Jim-Bob, you got time for a round of golf this afternoon?" Wiley Brown, an age-mate of Jim's and the newly elected county judge, joined them, clapping Jim on the shoulder as he nodded at the rest of the group. "Or does the little woman here still have you tied to her apron strings?"

Amy turned faintly red at the teasing. Jim tweaked her ear and said to his friend, "Yeah, I got time. About two? Meet you at the club. That'll give me time to eat first."

"Sounds good."

The talk turned to golf. Seeing that her mother was between friends, Rachel excused herself and went to snatch her up before anybody else could. Sometimes serving as her mother's chauffeur was a pain.

On the short drive home, Elisabeth said reprovingly to her daughter, "Really, Rachel, what were you thinking of to talk out loud like that in church? I was never so embarrassed in all my life."

"I'm sorry, Mother. Mrs. Skaggs and Mrs. Ashton were whispering together behind us, and I overheard something that took me by surprise."

"About that Harris man's death, unless I miss my guess," Elisabeth said shrewdly. There was challenge in her voice as she continued, "I suppose you're intending to go to the funeral?"

"Yes, I am." Rachel's hands tightened around the steering wheel.

"I knew it! You always were the most obstinate child on earth! Why, pray, do you want to get yourself so heavily involved with those people? They're nothing in the world but trash." Elisabeth cast Rachel an exasperated glance.

Rachel gritted her teeth. Of its own accord her foot increased its pressure on the accelerator until they were whizzing down the narrow road. Fields dotted with herds of Black Angus beef cattle and occasional clusters of grazing horses flew past.

"For goodness' sake, Rachel, slow down!" her mother cried, grabbing at the armrest beside her as the Maxima took a curve on what felt like two wheels. Rachel, recalled to where she was and what she was doing, eased up on the accelerator. Taking a deep breath, she forced herself to concentrate on her driving. It had been years since she had argued with her mother. There wasn't any point in it as a general rule because Elisabeth never changed her mind about anything, no matter how many facts opposed her point of view. But this time, Rachel was not going to permit Elisabeth's annoying comment to pass.

"What is trash, Mother? Poor people? If Daddy had died when Becky and I were little, we would have been poor. Would we have been trash?" Despite her anger, Rachel's tone was carefully even. Her sideways glance at her mother showed her that Elisabeth looked affronted.

"You know perfectly well we would not have been trash. Money has nothing to do with it."

"Then what does? Are Tilda and J.D. trash?"

"Rachel Elisabeth Grant, Tilda and J.D. are fine people! They're Negroes, but they're clean and polite and as honest as can be and as dependable as the day is long! And you know it!"

"Well, then, what about Wiley Brown? He may be a judge, but he drinks a lot more than is good for him, as you well know. In fact, on the day he graduated from high school, he showed up at the auditorium so drunk that he fell asleep and started snoring in the middle of the ceremony. Is he trash? Or the Bowens? Mrs. Bowen ran off to Europe and left her children behind. Are they trash? Or what about the Walshes? He's a pediatrician, and she's a nurse, but she always has a black eye or a bruise somewhere from walking into doors, or so she says. Are they trash? Or how about Rob? He's divorced. Does that make him trash?"

"Rachel, I declare, God must have given you to me to drive me out of my head! You know perfectly well that none of those people are trash!"

"Then explain to me what trash is, Mother. I want to know. If being poor, or black, or drinking, or being abandoned by a parent, or spouse beating, or being divorced doesn't do it, I want to know what does."

Elisabeth spluttered, "I may not be able to describe it, but I know trash when I see trash, and what's more, so do you!"

Rachel felt herself trembling, on the brink of losing her temper with her mother, which was something she rarely did. Her voice was even as she spoke: "Listen to me, Mother. I am tired of you, and everybody else in this town for that matter, calling Johnny Harris trash. Unless you can explain to me why he is, please don't do it again!"

"Why, Rachel! What a tone to use with your mother!"

"I'm sorry, Mother. But I mean what I say."

Elisabeth's lips thinned, and her eyes narrowed as she glanced appraisingly at her daughter. "There's been talk around town about you and that boy. I didn't pay it much mind because you are my daughter and you were raised to know better. But I'm beginning to think that there may be something to it after all. When your father was a young man, before he married me, he was wild and heedless and prone to jump into trouble with both feet. It hurts me to have to tell you that you are getting to be just like him."

The combined criticism of herself and the father she loved stung. Rachel's grip on her temper slipped a little more, and she cast her mother a cold glance as she turned into their driveway.

"I hope that's so, Mother. I would certainly hate for the opposite to be true."

Elisabeth's eyes widened, and she paled as she stared at her daughter. Chin stubbornly raised, refusing to say or feel she was sorry, Rachel pulled the car under the porte cochere and stopped it with a jerk.

"You need to put the car in park." Like everyone else who knew her well, Elisabeth was aware of her daughter's erratic driving habits.

"I'm not stopping. I have an errand to run. You go on in."

"An errand! You aren't forgetting that we're having Sunday dinner at two, are you? We are having guests, as I shouldn't have to remind you."

"I'll be back by two. Please get out, Mother."

With a sound midway between a snort and a sniff, Elisabeth got out of the car and closed the door behind her with a deliberate quietness that was more eloquent than a slam. Then she leaned down and peered through the passenger-side window at Rachel.

"You are going into town to see that Harris boy, aren't you?"

"Yes, Mother, I am. And I may just bring him back to dinner."

"Rachel!"

Rachel's eyes glittered as she returned Elisabeth's look. Her hands clenched around the steering wheel so tightly that her knuckles showed white. "And if you are not polite to him, if you do not make him as welcome as any other guest in this house, then I give you my word that I will pack my bags tomorrow and move back into town."

"Rachel!"

"I mean it, Mother," Rachel said. "Now please stand back. I have to go."

"Rachel!" There was as much hurt as affront in Elisabeth's voice as she straightened and stepped back. Putting the car into reverse and then swinging it around in a wide arc, Rachel looked through the rearview mirror and saw honest bewilderment in her mother's face as the tiny, frail figure stood alone against the background of the huge white house and rolling green fields. But for once in her life she refused to let her mother make her feel guilty. This time she meant what she said.

As it happened, Rachel's confrontation with her mother served no purpose. When she arrived at the hardware store, Johnny was not in his apartment. She stopped by Long's, one of two funeral homes in town, and the one that handled services for citizens of lesser importance like Willie Harris—only to find that Johnny wasn't there, either, and that no arrangements had been made for putting Willie Harris on view, though his funeral was scheduled for ten o'clock the next morning. Rachel thanked Sam Munson, the mortician, and left. A single question burned in her mind: Where was Johnny? Rachel thought of Glenda, and her picture of Johnny alone and grief-stricken underwent a sudden change. Of course he was with Glenda. He had no need for Rachel at all.

Chest tight, Rachel gave up and drove back home. The look of relief on Elisabeth's face when she showed up alone just in time for dinner was nothing more than salt in her wound.

15

*W*hat was left of Willie Harris lay in a closed gray coffin at the front of the small paneled room. Five rows of rickety folding chairs, about forty in all, had been set up by the funeral home for the service. Afterward, the body would be cremated.

Rachel sat in the fourth row with Kay Nelson at her side. Kay, apparently stricken by guilt after the conversation at church, had crept in just as the service got under way. Besides the two women, there were five other mourners: two hard-looking, sleazily dressed young women whom Rachel didn't know; Don Gillespie, the owner of the house that the Harrises had rented for so many years; and Glenda Wright Watkins with her son, Jeremy.

Johnny did not appear. Nor did the other two surviving Harris children.

Glenda's presence without Johnny came as something of a shock to Rachel. She had called his apartment numerous times since her visit the day before and had even stopped by again late last night and this morning, all to no avail. Johnny was not there. She had assumed he was off with Glenda somewhere. But Glenda sat two rows in front of her, blond head bowed, her hand curled around that of her young son.

If Johnny was not with them, where was he?

Rachel could hardly wait for the service to conclude so that she could speak to the woman. When the final prayer was invoked and the mourners began to file out, Rachel got quickly to her feet. Beside her, Kay stood up, too.

"Isn't that the saddest thing you ever saw?" Kay whispered to Rachel. "Not one of the children here. Do you suppose he was bad to them when they were growing up?"

"I don't have any idea," Rachel answered, somewhat less than truthfully. The first year she had taught him, the sixteen-year-old Johnny had appeared at school with black eyes and split lips often enough that Rachel suspected that his father was beating him. Her concern led her to notice the other Harris children more than she otherwise would have. Big, bulky Buck, two years older than Johnny, had dropped out of school some years before and so was not available for observation. But Grady, a thin, quiet boy three years Johnny's junior, and Sue Ann, who'd still been in grade school at the time, regularly suffered injuries like Johnny's. When Rachel had tried to ask Johnny if they were being abused, he had laughed in her face and denied everything—without allaying Rachel's suspicions by one iota. She turned to her own father for advice on what to do, but Stan had been succinct: Stay out of it. What went on behind closed doors was none of her business.

That pronouncement had provoked one of the few arguments she had ever had with her father.

Despite Stan's words and Johnny's denial, Rachel decided that the next time she saw physical marks on any of the Harris children, she would report them to the county child-protective services.

But she never saw such marks again. At the time, Rachel had decided her conclusions had been too hasty. Now, looking back, she wondered if perhaps her questioning of Johnny, reported back to Willie Harris, had been enough to stop it. She hoped so.

"Who are they?" Kay, still whispering, nodded at the two young girls, one of whom had tears streaming down her face as she turned away from the coffin and walked down the aisle toward them.

"No one I know. Excuse me, please, Kay. I need to talk to someone."

Rachel caught up with Glenda just before she and Jeremy walked out the door.

"Hello, Jeremy. Hello, Mrs.—Watkins, isn't it? Do you remember me?" Rachel was unable to keep from surreptitiously looking the other woman over as she spoke. Glenda was wearing a subdued lavender suit. The outfit was inexpensive, the cloth polyester, but its modest lines were flattering to her figure while still appropriate for the occasion. Her voluminous hair was caught up at her nape by a black velvet bow. All in all, Rachel had to conclude that Glenda was nicer looking than she had at first supposed. Probably, by the standards of men, Glenda would be considered much more attractive than Rachel herself. She was tall and slim and blond and worldly looking, with breasts the size of cantaloupes. Rachel caught herself wondering if they were real and awarded herself a mental kick for cattiness.

Jeremy said nothing, just stared up at Rachel warily. He was dressed in clean but faded jeans and a well-pressed T-shirt, suggesting that, unlike Glenda, he owned no more formal clothes. Judging from his demeanor, he suspected that Rachel had waylaid his mother to tattle on him. Rachel sent him a small, reassuring smile that had no apparent effect on his look of mistrust.

"Sure I do. You're Miss Grant." Glenda nodded warmly, and her thin face broke into a smile that made her look suddenly years older as her cheeks creased into dozens of sun-caused wrinkles. "Johnny's teacher friend. I didn't know you knew Jeremy."

The glance Jeremy shot Rachel was defiant and imploring at the same time.

"We met through Johnny, didn't we, Jeremy? And got reasonably well acquainted, I think." Rachel smiled at Jeremy again before transferring her attention back to Glenda. "I was wondering, have you seen Johnny? I wanted to express my condolences, but I haven't been able to locate him."

Glenda shook her head. "Last time I saw him was Saturday night. We got to my place kinda late, both of us with a pretty good buzz on, you know, and he went straight home 'cause friend or not, I don't allow no man to spend the night when my kids are there. I had Sunday off, and I spent it with the kids, so I didn't even hear about Mr. Harris till last night. I thought I'd come today because me and Johnny, we go back a long way, and he don't have too many people in his corner right now." She shrugged. "But he ain't even here. And I cain't say I'm surprised."

"Oh? Why not?"

"Can we go, Mom?" Jeremy interrupted, tugging on Glenda's hand. "You said we could go to Burger King."

"In a minute, Jeremy. You know what I told you about interruptin'." Glenda smiled apologetically at Rachel. "Kids. Bein' a teacher, you know how they are. But about Johnny not bein' here, I don't blame him. Mr. Harris was real mean to him, to all of 'em, when they was growin' up. He whupped 'em good, more times than I can remember. Whether it's disrespectful to the dead or not," she nodded toward the coffin, "I gotta speak the truth."

Rachel's breath caught. "I suspected something of the sort at one time. But I asked Johnny about it, and he denied it."

Glenda laughed. "He would. That's Johnny for you."

"Mom . . ." There was the beginning of a whine in Jeremy's voice.

"Just a minute, Jeremy."

Kay joined them, offering Glenda an impersonal smile. "Rachel, excuse me, but could I beg a ride to my shop from you? I had Jim drop me off." There was a chasm between Kay and Glenda of which both were fully aware. Like Rachel, Kay was part of the country club crowd, while Glenda was someone whose life was considered of no account by Tylerville's more affluent citizens.

"I'll be glad to give you a ride." It was an effort, but Rachel thought she masked her impatience at the interruption very well. If Glenda had been about to make any more revelations about Johnny's early life, she wouldn't now that Kay had joined them. Rachel knew that as well as if Glenda had spelled it out. And Rachel found herself suddenly eager to learn everything she could about young Johnny Harris. "Kay, I don't believe you know Glenda Watkins and her son Jeremy. Glenda, this is Kay Nelson."

Kay nodded in acknowledgment of the introduction. "Are you a family friend of the Harrises?"

"I'm a friend of Johnny's," Glenda specified, as if she didn't care to be closely associated with Johnny's father.

"A friend, Mom?" Jeremy tittered, and his eyes sparkled teasingly up at his mother. "Is that what you call it? The other night I saw him put his hand on your—"

"Jeremy Anthony Watkins!" Clamping a hand over her son's mouth in the nick of time, Glenda turned bright red as she cast the other women embarrassed, apologetic looks. "I gotta get some food in this kid fast, before he turns into a real monster. You know how kids are when they haven't eaten. It was good to see you again, Miss Grant. And nice meetin' you, Miss Nelson."

Rachel and Kay murmured good-byes as Glenda whisked her son away.

"Put his hand on her what, I wonder?" Kay mused with lively interest as the two women started for the car.

"I have no idea," Rachel answered in as discouraging a tone as she could muster. She had no desire to discuss or even think about Johnny's relationship with Glenda Watkins.

"I could hazard a guess," Kay said with a chuckle as she climbed into the car. Casting Rachel, who was inserting a key into the ignition, an indulgent look, she added, "But I won't. Though I must say I'm surprised Johnny Harris found a local woman to take up with. Even one like that. I would have thought they'd all be too afraid of him."

"I think Johnny and Glenda have known each other for a long time," Rachel said curtly. Distracted, eager to be rid of Kay, Rachel didn't notice the concrete bump in front of the car until they jolted over it. Her lips tightening, she vowed to be more vigilant and set herself to concentrating on her driving as she pulled out into traffic.

"You know who those two girls were?" Kay was bright-eyed as she turned in her seat to relate a particularly choice bit of gossip. "Don Gillespie told me. They were hookers, Rachel. Real hookers, can you believe it?"

"Oh, Kay!" Rachel took her eyes off the road to dart a skeptical glance at her friend. "Hookers?"

"Don said Willie Harris went to Louisville twice a month, as regular as clockwork, to see one of them. He said the old man had been cavorting with the girl since she was twelve."

"Twelve! Oh, Kay! I don't believe it!"

Kay shrugged. "He said Willie Harris bragged about it. Good grief, Rachel, look out! We're running off the road!"

The Maxima's tires bumped over the gravel berm. Rachel, startled back to attention, quickly jerked the steering wheel to the left, and they were on the road again.

"Becky always said you were the most awful driver," Kay muttered, shaking her head.

"Becky is so perfect at everything she does that she tends to be critical of other people's efforts," Rachel retorted sweetly.

"Oh-ho!" Kay grinned. "Such devoted sisters! Am I glad I only have brothers. Stop, Rachel, you're driving past my shop!"

The Maxima had indeed overshot the small brick building where Kay ran her business, which was called Say It With Flowers. Gritting her teeth, Rachel turned the car around and pulled up before Kay's shop.

Kay opened the car door, then turned to glance back at Rachel. "Are you coming to the Preservation Society meeting tonight?"

"I don't think so. But Mother is, I think."

Kay smiled. "Your mother is wonderful. Did you know that she donated the rest of the money we needed to restore the gardens in the old Baptist church cemetery? I'll be able to do some pruning and plant some bulbs this fall, and then finish up in the spring. They're going to be gorgeous."

"I can't wait to see them," Rachel said politely.

Kay chuckled. "I know, I know, not everyone is as interested in flowers as I am. But it will be something to see, I promise you." Her voice turned suddenly serious. "I just love that place, and it hurts me to see it so neglected."

"The society is lucky to have such a dedicated chairwoman," Rachel said.

"It is, isn't it?" Kay grinned. "Well, I'll let you go. Thanks for the ride. Tell your mother I'll see her tonight."

Kay got out and slammed the door. Rachel drove off with a wave. Though she was in complete agreement with the sentiments behind the establishment of the First Baptist Church of Tylerville Preservation Society, she could not drum up much interest in their efforts to restore and refurbish the town's oldest church at that precise moment. She was too concerned about locating Johnny.

Her next stop was Grant's Hardware, to see if Johnny had decided to report for work rather than attend his father's funeral.

Olivia, at the counter, shook her head. "He hasn't been here at all this morning. Ben said he didn't call to say he wouldn't be in, either."

The store was empty except for one out-of-earshot customer browsing through paint charts, so Olivia's thoughtless broadcasting of yet another store problem was heard by no one except Rachel. Rachel knew that at some point she was going to have to speak to Olivia about her big mouth, but at the moment she wasn't up to delivering a gentle scolding. She was growing genuinely worried about Johnny. If he wasn't with Glenda and he wasn't at work, where was he?

"Rachel, could I speak to you a minute?" Having heard her voice, Ben stuck his head out of the storeroom. Rachel wanted to refuse, but Ben was already walking toward his office. With an inward sigh, Rachel followed.

Ben leaned against the edge of his desk, his arms crossed over his chest, as Rachel shut the door behind her and looked at him questioningly.

"Johnny Harris did not show up for work this morning."

"His father's funeral was this morning," Rachel replied defensively, without bothering to add that Johnny hadn't attended it.

"He still should have called to say he wouldn't be in, and you know it."

"I'm sure he's emotionally upset."

Ben snorted. "Nothing short of being hauled before a firing squad would get him emotionally upset. Rachel, he's bad for business. Half our customers outright refuse to let him wait on them, and the other half just stop in to gawk at him! He's rude and insubordinate, and he looks like he ought to be in that motorcycle gang, the Hell's Angels. On Saturday, I told you I was going to quit if you let that kid go without calling the police. Well, you let him go. My letter of resignation is right here."

He picked up an envelope from the desk and held it out to Rachel.

"Oh, Ben, you don't really mean it, do you?" Rachel accepted the envelope and glanced at Ben's face.

"Yes, ma'am, I mean it. That guy gets my goat every time I look at him, Rachel. I swear, just having him in the store is giving me an ulcer. The only way I'll stay is if you let him go."

"But Ben, I can't. If he doesn't have a job, they'll send him back to prison. I know he can be a bit much, but—"

"A bit much," Ben jeered.

"If you will just bear with me, I'll talk to him."

"Talking to him's about as much use as going after a tank with a fly swat. It won't do a bit of good, Rachel, and I mean what I say. If you won't, or can't, fire him, then I'm quitting. I've already gotten an offer to manage the hardware section at Wal-Mart."

Rachel stared at Ben for a moment without speaking. It was clear from the apologetic yet obstinate look on his face that he meant what he said.

"I hope you will do me the courtesy of giving me two weeks' notice," she said stiffly. Ben's lips compressed.

"You know I'll do that." His eyes shifted, then came back to her face. "I'm real sorry, Rachel."

"Yes," said Rachel, "so am I."

She turned and walked out of the office, envelope in hand. As she passed the stairs that led to Johnny's apartment, she hesitated, wondering if she should go up and knock, just to check. Ben didn't have to know that she hadn't seen Johnny at all that morning. Why, she could be going upstairs to see if he had returned after the funeral.

"Harris isn't up there," Ben said from behind her. "I practically pounded the door down not ten minutes ago. I thought he might be lazing around in bed."

"Oh. Well, I—" But before she could continue, Ben put a hand on her arm. She turned to find a frown creasing his brow.

"Look, I know it's not my place to say this, but I've seen the way Harris looks at you when you come in here, and it worries me. I'm telling you, the guy's dangerous, Rachel. For your own sake, you ought to fire him. If he gets sent back to prison, so be it. At least you'd be safe."

"Ben, it's nice of you to be concerned," Rachel said. As she patted the hand that rested on her arm, much of her rancor toward her store manager dissipated. "But I am not afraid of Johnny. He may look dangerous, but he's not, and he would never hurt me or anyone else."

"Famous last words," Rachel heard Ben mutter after she had freed herself and started to walk away.

The remark wrung a wry smile from Rachel. But she wasn't smiling some twelve hours later, when on what must have been her dozenth drive-by of the store to see if Johnny had returned, she finally saw a light in the upstairs apartment window. Then relief led to indignation, and indignation led to all-out anger. Fired with wrath, Rachel parked her car, marched up the outside stairs, and knocked.

A burst of furious barking answered her. Rachel was just recovering from her surprise when the door was pulled open. Johnny stood swaying in the doorway before her, one hand on the knob, to which he seemed to cling for balance. He was clearly well on his way to being falling-down drunk.

16

"**W**ell, if it isn't Miss Grant," Johnny said, looking her over with a jeering smile turned lopsided by drink. "Come in, come in."

Opening the door wider and stepping back from it in an exaggerated gesture of hospitality, Johnny stumbled over the carpet and almost fell. Saved by his grip on the knob, he righted himself, cursing under his breath. Behind him, a huge, dun-colored dog stopped barking, bared its teeth, and snarled ferociously at Rachel. She shrank back, her anger banished in a heartbeat by a combination of shock and fear.

"Don't mind him." Following her wide-eyed gaze, Johnny waved a dismissing hand at the slavering animal. "That's just Wolf. Sit, Wolf."

Disregarding the command as completely as if it had not been uttered, the dog continued to snarl, its beady black eyes fixed on Rachel, who retreated a pace. Johnny frowned.

"Bad dog," he said without much conviction. The animal still growled. Muttering something under his breath, Johnny let go of the doorknob, reached down to grab the beast by the scruff of its neck, and dragged it off toward the bedroom. Johnny's steps were unsteady, and he lurched occasionally to one side. It looked almost as if the dog's powerful shoulders were propping him up. It didn't require much imagination on Rachel's part to picture the animal breaking free, whirling, and leaping for her throat. She stayed pressed against the wooden rail of the outside landing until the dog was safely stowed in the bedroom with the door shut behind it. Only then did she enter the apartment.

"What was that?" she asked Johnny as, one hand on the wall to steady himself, he negotiated his way back across the living room toward her. The dog, now that it was safely incarcerated, made no sound. Rachel found that almost more unnerving than frenzied barking would have been.

"That? Oh, you mean Wolf? He's my legacy. My only legacy from my old man." Johnny started to laugh in a drunken fashion that would have sent Rachel running for cover if she had possessed the least sense at all. He collapsed onto the brown tweed couch.

"You're drunk." Rachel shut the door behind her and advanced into the room to look down at him severely. The smell of whiskey assaulted her nostrils, and she discovered a quarter-full bottle of the stuff on the lamp table by the couch.

"Yup." His head lolled back against the rolled top of the couch, and his long, bluejean-encased legs sprawled out across the beige plush carpet. He wore dirty white athletic socks with no shoes and a white T-shirt with the tail outside his jeans. His hair was loose. The jet-black strands, so long that they almost touched his shoulders, waved around his face. His blue eyes glittered restlessly up at her. From the stubble on his chin, she guessed that he had not shaved since she had seen him last. He looked like a bum, if a very sexy bum.

Strangely, Rachel was not in the least afraid of him, drunk or not. In the depths of his eyes she recognized real pain.

"You heard about my old man?" Johnny asked carelessly. He reached for the bottle, tilted it to his mouth, took a long swig, then wiped his mouth on his hand. He set the bottle with exaggerated care back on the table. "Raw hamburger. That's what he is now, raw hamburger. Made into raw hamburger by a goddamned train."

"I went to the funeral this morning," Rachel said, watching him. "It was a very nice service."

Johnny laughed again, and the sound was queer. "I bet it was. Were you the only one there?"

Rachel shook her head. "There were others. Have you had anything to eat lately?"

Johnny shrugged. "Did they sing hymns and pray?"

Rachel nodded. "Could you eat some scrambled eggs, maybe, and toast?"

Johnny made a violent gesture with one hand. "Would you quit yammering on about goddamned food? I want to know who was there. Did Buck show?"

Edging around his legs, Rachel unobtrusively picked up the whiskey bottle and headed for the kitchen. "No."

She disappeared and for the next ten minutes busied herself making scrambled eggs and toast and coffee from the groceries she knew he had on hand. On the last of her previous night's visits to his apartment, she had stifled her conscience and used her pass-key to let herself in. She had feared what she might find, but the apartment had been empty. Down to the open loaf of bread on the counter and the perishable groceries in the kitchen, it had looked as though its resident had just stepped out and would be back any minute. Only he hadn't come back for two days.

When Rachel emerged from the kitchen, carefully balancing a filled plate in one hand and a cup of black coffee in the other, Johnny was still as she had left him, sprawled on the couch with his head thrown back. But his eyes were closed. For a minute she thought he was asleep.

"I went to Detroit to tell Sue Ann," he said abruptly, opening his eyes as she set the plate down on the table where the whiskey bottle had been and handed him the cup. He took it, but his hands were so unsteady that the steaming liquid sloshed over the side to splash down on his thigh. Swearing, he brushed at the spreading wetness with his free hand. Rachel just managed to save the rest of the coffee from a similar disaster by removing the cup from his hold.

"She doesn't have a phone. Can't afford it, she said. She's on welfare, you know, with three kids. And she's pregnant, out to here." He made a gesture in front of his own flat belly to demonstrate. "In a two-room apartment with a broken toilet. Her boyfriend, the one who knocked her up, came around while I was there. He's a sleazebag, a scumball, and he treats her and the kids like shit. I wanted to beat the crap out of him. But I didn't. What the hell good would it do? Christ, she's only twenty-four." He was talking in rapid, disjointed sentences, the words just barely coherent, his head resting against the back of the couch, his eyes focused on the ceiling. Rachel made a soothing sound and lifted the cup of coffee toward his lips.

"Here. Drink this."

Johnny ignored her. "I gave her what money I had. Christ, it wasn't much. She and the kids looked so bad. They were skinny—her too, except for this huge bulging belly—and there were flies all over the place because the screen over the window had holes in it and it was hot as hell. And I thought I had it bad in stir! The place was a fucking resort compared to the rathole she lives in."

He laughed bitterly. Only dimly understanding that he was referring to his stay in prison, Rachel touched his arm. Her main concern at the moment was sobering him up as much as she could and getting some food into him. She suspected he had not eaten all day, and maybe not on Sunday either, though surely his sister had fixed him something.

"Johnny, please drink this. It's coffee, and you need it."

His gaze slewed around to her. His eyes were as turbulent as a thunderstorm. "You don't know shit about what I need. How could you? Have you ever wanted for anything? Hell, no! You and your big house and your fancy words and your la-de-da parents—what do you know about people like me?"

"I know you're hurting." Her voice was very soft, but the words seemed to sting him. He winced, his mouth twisting into a furious sneer.

"Yeah, I'm hurting. Hell, yes. Why not? I'm human, just like everybody else. I hurt."

With a curse he sprang to his feet, overturning the coffee table in front of the couch with a single furious swing. As it crashed, he turned to glare at Rachel, his eyes savage. Even the fact that he swayed slightly on his feet did not detract from his air of menace as he towered over her, his hands clenching and unclenching at his sides.

Rachel looked up at him with a calm that was only half pretense. "Feel better?"

He stared down at her, the rage in his eyes slowly turning to something else. He ran his fingers through his hair with a muttered curse.

"Christ, why aren't you afraid of me? You should be afraid of me. Everyone else is," he said. All at once, without his rage for reinforcement, his knees seemed no longer able to support his weight. He sagged forward, then almost crumpled, sitting down heavily on the floor at her feet, his back half turned to her.

"I'm not afraid of you, Johnny. I never have been," Rachel said because it was true, and because she thought it was what he needed to hear. He looked around at her then, a tired smile flickering in his eyes for no more than an instant. He dropped his head back so that it rested against her knees.

"Beats me why not," he muttered.

Staring down at that untidy black head, feeling the weight of it and the bony hardness of his skull and the silkiness of his hair as it nestled against her bare legs, she felt compassion so strong that she ached with it. Setting the cup of coffee down on the lamp table beside the plate of toast and eggs, she laid a gentle hand on his head and stroked his hair.

"I'm so sorry about your father, Johnny."

He gave another of those harsh laughs. "Sue Ann said she wouldn't come to his funeral if she lived right next door. She said she hated the old bastard. Buck hated him, too—I called Buck. And so did I. Do I, I mean. Hate him. Damn him to hell!"

A sudden catch in Johnny's voice caught at Rachel's heart. She continued to stroke his head, her fingers soothing as they smoothed the tangled strands that tumbled around her knee. If he even felt her touch, she had no idea. He talked on and on in a hoarse, creaky voice that sounded as if he were being strangled.

"Grady—Grady. He used to beat on Grady worst. Buck was too big, and I was too mean, and Sue Ann was a girl. I can still see poor little Grady—he wasn't very big, you know, just a skinny little runt with a mop of black curls—I can still see the old man yanking down Grady's pants and laying into him with his belt. I can hear Grady screaming, and then not screaming after the old man picked him up and slammed him into a wall until he shut up. He never could understand why the old man hated him worse than the rest of us. If he even saw Grady's face, he'd pop him one. Kid used to hide out in the closet if he couldn't get out the door before the old man got home."

Johnny paused to take a deep, shuddering breath. Rachel said nothing, just stroked his hair and listened. From the way he stared off into space, she wasn't even sure he remembered she was there.

"Ah, Grady. We were tight, you know? They wouldn't even let me out to go to his funeral. Drowned. I couldn't believe it." He chuckled then, the sound as harsh and full of pain as a sob. "Kid always swam like a fish. Only sport he was ever any damned good at. I think he had a death wish. I did a lot of reading in stir—hell, there wasn't much else to do—and I came across a lot of psychological stuff. Most of it wasn't worth toilet paper, but some of it made sense. Grady was always getting hurt as a kid. He had more broken bones than the rest of us put together. He even set himself on fire once, playing with a cigarette lighter, and damned near french-fried himself. Not that the old man cared. Never even took him to a doctor, and the kid had scars all over his legs and back till the day he died. I think that it hurt Grady so bad that my mom left and my dad hated him that he wanted to die. I think that's why he drowned. He wanted to die. Hell, they locked me up for murder, and they never did a thing to the old man, and he was sure as hell a lot guiltier of it than I ever was. Never. Nobody. Did nothing. Do you know that Grady was so scared of him that all the old man had to do was give him a certain look and he'd piss his pants? When he was half-grown, a teenager, even. A look, and Grady would piss like a baby. Somebody should've helped him, you know? Somebody should have taken him away from the old bastard. But nobody gave a shit."

Jaw clenching, Johnny broke off abruptly, and his eyes closed. His head was heavy against her knees. Rachel, horrified at what she had heard, sat silent, her hand frozen in his hair. She had suspected abuse, but this raw pouring-out of emotion made it so immediate, so awful, so far beyond anything she had ever imagined. Abuse was a clinical term she had learned in school. This pain was dreadfully real.

"Hell, some of it was my fault, I guess. I never told anybody. None of us ever told. Remember when you asked me if my old man was beating us up? I laughed in your face, didn't I? I laughed because I was too ashamed to admit the truth. Everybody thought we were trash. I didn't want to prove 'em right. I hated it that all the nice, Wonder Bread people looked down their noses at us. If they knew the truth, they'd just look down their noses more. He was a goddamned drunk and he beat us up, and we didn't want anybody to know. Goddamned bunch of lily-livered kids."

His breathing changed, grew harsher, and he sat up suddenly, lifting his head from her knees and turning around so that he met her eyes. Mesmerized by the sheer power of his ragged confessions, mute because she could not think of anything to say, Rachel could only look back at him, horror and pity mixed in her eyes.

"You know you were the only teacher ever even to ask about it? Hell, we had as many bruises as a Christmas tree has ornaments, and not a single other person ever even asked about them. Know why? 'Cause we were trash, that's why, and nobody gave a shit. But you asked. God, I hated for you to know that my old man beat me up! You were so—" His eyes narrowed, flickered, and he stopped abruptly, as if he just realized what he was saying. It was a second or two before he continued. "I went home that day, and when he lit into Grady, I lit into him. We had the father and mother of a fight—remember, I was out most of the next week?—and I can't say that I won. But he saw I'd fight, and he wasn't so quick with his fists or his belt after that. Just his mouth, and sometimes that hurt more. He used to call us boys damned queers, and Sue Ann a whore. There was nothing I wouldn't do to keep him from thinking I was a queer."

He stopped again, then drew in a harsh, shaking breath. His hands came up to grip her skirt on either side of her thighs, bunching the material tightly in his fists. His eyes burned into hers as if hell raged at their backs.

"He was an asshole, and a bastard, and we all hated him. Only I didn't. I thought I did, but when I saw him on that table and he was all cut up—"

He drew in another harsh, shaking breath, and Rachel realized to her dismay that it was a sob.

"I found out I loved the fucking old bastard after all, may he burn in hell!"

His teeth clenched as if at unbearable pain, his eyes glittered wildly, and then he bowed his head. His face dropped onto her lap, his fingers gripping and twisting her skirt as if he would never let her go.

The broad shoulders heaved. Desperate sounds muffled by her skirt and her legs tore at her heart. Feeling tears rise to her eyes, Rachel stroked his head, and his shoulders, and his back, and murmured inconsequential soothing words that did nothing to stem his pain.

"It's all right, now. It's all right," she said over and over again. He didn't seem to hear, but nestled his head closer into her lap, his hands clutching her with convulsive strength. The harsh, strangled sounds continued unabated. Rachel dropped her own head to rest her cheek against his hair. Her arms wrapped around his back, hugging him to her, trying to give comfort if she could.

Finally his despair eased, and he lay limply against her, his face in her lap while she stroked his hair and part of an ear and a section of bristly cheek.

For a long while he lay like that, warm and heavy against her legs, and then she felt him gather himself together. His head lifted. Without warning Rachel found herself impaled by a pair of red-rimmed, smoky blue eyes, suspiciously damp around the edges, ones that blazed into hers with all the intensity of a soul in torment. Her hands rested on his wide shoulders. Self-conscious suddenly under that burning gaze, she let her hands drop into her lap.

"You know what I used to dream about, in stir?" His voice was hoarse, the words low and fast and faintly guttural. "I used to dream about you. You were the only clean and good and decent thing left in my life, and I would dream about you. I used to dream about taking your clothes off piece by piece, and what you would look like naked, and how it would feel to fuck you really good. I used to dream about that in high school, too. In fact, I got off almost every night for the last fourteen years, dreaming about you."

Rachel's lips parted with shock. Speechless, she stared at him wide-eyed for what seemed an eternity while her heart suddenly hammered and her throat went dry.

"I'm fucking tired of dreaming," he said fiercely. Sliding his hands up her thighs beneath her skirt, he caught her hips and pulled her down onto his lap.

17

$\mathcal{H}$e was kneeling, and all at once she was straddling him, her hands splayed against his chest, her legs bent at the knee and parted all the way to her crotch as he pulled her tight against him. Her skirt, a useless flimsy thing of green cotton with huge, absurd strawberries printed all over it, was pushed almost up to her waist. Only the thin, silky nylon of her pink panties protected her from the rough denim of his jeans and the hard metal of his zipper and the swollen thickness that bulged beneath.

"So tell me no, teacher," he said when her gaze locked with his. His hands were hard with tension as they gripped her hips. His thighs were rigid beneath her bottom. She could feel the steely strength in the chest muscles beneath her hand—and the tantalizing, mesmerizing stiffness of the hillock on which she sat.

She couldn't say it. She could not. She wanted him too badly. For most of her life, it seemed, she had wanted him.

Shocking, shameful thought. But her body burned.

"Johnny," she whispered helplessly. Her eyes fell as she could no longer sustain his gaze. But in falling, they found his mouth, which was a mistake. Long and sensitive, very masculine, very beautiful, it took on a sensuous curve that stole her breath as she stared at it.

"Rachel," he whispered back. Even as she watched it, even as he leaned nearer and her arms flattened against his chest without even try-ing to hold him off, that beautiful masculine mouth came closer, blurred —then stopped, scant millimeters from her lips.

"Oh, God." She couldn't fight it. Couldn't put up even a token resistance against the fierce tide of longing that swept her. Her lips, dry and hot, parted, sucking in the suddenly scorching air in ragged pants. Beneath the pink panties, her body quaked, wept.

"Last chance." His words were low and thick, uttered as if he had trouble getting them out. He still leaned close, so close she could feel his breath against her mouth. But he didn't kiss her. Rachel's lids lifted, and of their own volition her eyes found his. His were hot, and dark, and wild, glittering with the promise of unspeakable deeds, unspeakable pleasures. Rachel could not look away as his hands slid down her lower back from her hips, down on either side of her spine to delve beneath the elastic edge of her underwear and close over her rump.

He held a cheek in each hand, palms flat, fingers spread, gently squeezing the soft, rounded flesh. Rachel thought she had never felt anything more erotic in her life than his hands on her bare behind.

His hands tightened, and he rubbed her against him, moving her back and forth over the bulge in his jeans so that the heat and the friction, separated from her quaking flesh by a single thin layer of nylon, drove her mad. Rachel gasped, her fingers digging into the front of his T-shirt, her back arching.

"You're mine, teacher," he muttered on what almost sounded like a note of triumph, but Rachel was too far gone with lust to care. If he had tried to push her away from him then, she would have clung to him, whimpering with need.

Holding her against him, he shifted his position slightly so that when he eased her backward her spine was supported by the couch behind her. He squeezed her bottom, then one hand came around, spread flat and burning hot against the quivering softness of her belly, to delve down into the hot wet darkness between her legs.

As his fingers caressed the crisp curls and tender mound and the cleft that pointed the way lower still, a funny little moan escaped her. Rachel heard the sound as if it had been made by someone else, someone she didn't know, had never known. It was almost as if she were two people and could witness what was happening to her, even as her mind clouded over with passion and her body surrendered its will to a stronger, needier, greedier force.

In her mind's eye she saw, as if from a neutral vantage point, what they must look like together: She was seated on his lap with bare knees spread wide on either side of his jean-clad hips, slender and petite, incongruously attired in a raspberry-pink T-shirt and a green golfing skirt that was pushed up to her waist. The hiked-up skirt and her semireclining position exposed her navel, and a belly with skin as smooth and white as vanilla icing—and a pair of pretty, lace-trimmed panties pulled down far enough to reveal the uppermost line of a triangle of dark auburn hair.

Inside the panties, his swarthy, long-fingered hand, concealed from view by the pink nylon, stroked and explored.

A shocking picture. Especially if she added the flush that suffused her face with color, the wanting that turned her eyes from ordinary hazel to a luminosity as burning bright as a cat's, the desire that parted her lips and arched her spine and made her quiver and squirm as he touched her where she wanted to be touched, where she had to be touched or die.

She saw him, too, his eyes hard and intent on her face, his mouth passionately aslant as he concentrated on her pleasure, on her need. The heat they generated between them hung in the air around them, setting more waves into his black hair, causing beads of sweat to pop out on his forehead, adding its own sultry perfume to the light scent of white flowers that she always wore.

He was unshaven, uneducated, uncouth. She was meticulously well groomed down to the pink polish on her toenails, bared by her brown leather sandals. Everything about her, from her simple, chin-length bob to the discreet touches of taupe eyeshadow and rose lipstick, to the pristine delicacy of the expensive pink panties, spoke of money, and breeding, and the careful maintenance of a certain position in the world. Everything about him—the overlong hair, the muscles that bulged against the white T-shirt that was really no more than a Fruit of the Loom undershirt worn as outerwear, the too-tight jeans, the damn-your-eyes belligerence that he wore like a shield—shouted hardscrabble background, ex-con, dangerous.

He was Johnny Harris, and he had his hands in her pants. Rachel wouldn't have changed anything about the situation for the world.

His hands left her panties suddenly to yank her T-shirt out of the waistband of her skirt and pull it over her head. Caught by surprise, Rachel instinctively clapped her hands over the cups of her lacy pink bra. Not from modesty but from embarrassment that he should see how skimpily she was endowed. A picture of Glenda Watkins's ripe body flitted through her head, and a sudden fierce flare of jealousy made her shake her head at him as he reached around her back to undo the clasp.

"All right," he said, surprisingly obliging. Even as Rachel wondered at it, his hands closed over her waist, and he was lifting her without any effort at all and then setting her down so that she perched clumsily on the edge of the couch. She fell backward at his gentle push, her hands dropping away from her breasts to break her fall, though it was only into the thick cushions of the old couch. Before she could reorient herself he was pulling her panties, which had gotten twisted around her upper thighs, down her legs, and tossing them aside.

"What . . . ?" she started to ask, struggling up on one elbow. But she never finished, because the intentions about which she had meant to question him were abundantly clear. He knelt before her, right in front of her knees, which she had instinctively pressed together as she fell backward, and his eyes glittered briefly at her before they dropped to the thighs he began to caress.

"I used to sit in class," he said in a raspy voice that she had to strain to hear. As he spoke he ran his hands up the tops of her thighs, under her skirt, which at least covered the most vital part of her anatomy again. "And wonder if you wore pantyhose or stockings beneath your skirt. I always liked to imagine you up there teaching in a black garter belt and black stockings and no panties."

"You didn't," she said, shocked at the very idea.

"I did," he answered, meeting her eyes. They smoldered, the smoky blue irises almost entirely overwhelmed by the black of his pupils. Rachel realized with a shaky sensation in the pit of her stomach that he spoke the absolute truth. The notion that she had figured in the teenage Johnny Harris's sexual fantasies while she'd taught him was enough to make her quiver. He must have sensed her reaction, because his gaze shifted back to her legs and his hands slid together suddenly as he drew them down her inner thighs toward her knees. When he reached her knees, he grasped them, pulling her down so that her bottom was at the edge of the couch and separating her knees at the same time.

"Johnny . . ." Slightly breathless, embarrassed by this blatant opening of her body to him, Rachel whispered his name. But even to her own ears, it did not sound remotely like a protest. She could not have protested at that point if her life had depended on it. A throbbing, building excitement held her completely in thrall.

"I used to imagine doing this to you. I used to imagine how you'd look and taste, and what kind of sounds you'd make."

"Oh, please. . . ." Rachel hardly knew what it was she asked for. His confession and the pictures it conjured up turned her muscles to mush. Eyes glazing over with desire, she watched and trembled as he pushed her skirt the rest of the way up again, baring her below the waist to her gaze and his own. His strong, long-fingered hands, bronze-skinned and sprinkled across the backs with black hair, made an incredibly erotic picture as they slid down over her stomach to rest, burning hot, on her inner thighs. The wanting they generated, and the unbearable anticipation, made Rachel draw in a deep, shaken breath. Johnny dipped his head and did what she had known he was going to do, what she wanted him to do and was on fire for him to do and was embarrassed for him to do all at the same time.

At the touch of his mouth she stiffened, gasped, then sank back against the cushions, her eyes closing, her fingers curling into the upholstery and clinging for dear life. He was gentle, so exquisitely gentle, his tongue scalding hot as it searched out the delicate nub and made its acquaintance in a way that sent tremors coursing through her whole body. When he had her mindless with excitement, her toes curling against the flat leather soles of her sandals and her bottom arching up off the couch, he put his tongue inside her, and that was the most mind-boggling act of all.

Her hands tangled in his hair, trying to pull his mouth away from her before she tumbled headlong into the bottomless black pit that yawned before her, but he would not stop. With a cry she lost the last vestige of control and fell in.

When she made it back up to the world again, it was to find that his mouth was still between her legs, his tongue still performing its intimate tricks upon her person. Sated now, the fierce hot lust having caught her up and exploded within her, leaving her wrung out, she was able to absorb more of what he was doing to her. At her vivid mental image of the picture they must present, she blushed and tried to sit up and push him away and close her legs against him. The sandpaper roughness of his unshaven cheeks scratched her tender inner thighs as he refused to be dislodged.

"Oh, no," he muttered, shooting her a brief, sensuous glance even as he caught her by her hips and held her in place for his tongue.

"But I—" she began, then broke off, her blush intensifying until it felt as if it must be suffusing her whole body as she contemplated and discarded various ways of telling him that, as far as she was concerned, there was no more need to continue.

"Came? I know," he finished for her, the words thick and slightly breathless as he lifted his head away from her at last. Rachel heard the husky timbre of his voice, saw the fierce glitter in his eyes, the wetness of his mouth, the breadth of his shoulders, and the width of his chest wedged between her thighs, holding them apart, and she felt the slightest quickening. "Do you think I can't tell? I want you to come again, and again, and again, for me."

He caught her around the waist, pulling her down into his lap and turning with her so that she lay on her back on the beige carpet, her hands clinging to his shoulders, her legs spread as he knelt between her thighs. In her surprise, she forgot about her breasts, and before she could remember, he snaked a hand under her back, deftly unhooked the clasp, and removed her bra.

"Oh, don't!" Instinctively Rachel covered her bareness with her hands, squirming to get away from him, but he would not let her go. He held her around the waist for a moment until she stopped wriggling, then turned his attention to her skirt, which was tangled around her waist. Except for that, and her sandals, and her hands over her breasts, Rachel realized that she was naked as a babe, while he was still fully clothed. Sudden embarrassment turned her cheeks as pink as the strawberries on her skirt.

"How does this damned thing come off?" He eyed her skirt with apparent bafflement while his hands felt vainly behind her for some sort of fastening.

"There's a button—in the front." Actually there were two, large, strawberry-shaped adornments on her waistband that she didn't see how he could miss.

"Show me."

Rachel reached down to comply—and realized that she had fallen into his trap even as his hands found the breasts she had left unguarded.

"No!" Her hands flew to catch his about the wrists, trying to tug them away. She was so small, scarcely more than an A cup, that his hands were almost flat as they covered her.

He let her pull his hands away, but then turned the tables on her by threading his fingers through hers and pinning them to the carpet. His eyes were on her, assessing the white swellings with their small pink nipples. Rachel almost cringed, so afraid was she that he would find her wanting.

"Shy, Rachel?" he asked, and the tender curve to his mouth made her heart turn over. Breathing suspended, she lay motionless as he bent to kiss first one stiffening nipple and then the other. The moist warmth of his mouth made her quiver, and her eyes shut of their own volition as he drew a nipple slowly into his mouth. Reaction shuddered through her. Small or not, her breasts possessed the full complement of nerve endings. Gasping, back arching with helpless pleasure, she once again gave herself into his care.

He bent over her, touching her only with his mouth on her breasts and his fingers entwined in hers, and she was as completely at his mercy as if he had tied her down. She lay spread-eagled beneath him, nothing of her hidden from his eyes or his mouth or his hands, once again so shaken with desire for him that she could deny him nothing. He touched her nipples with his tongue, sucked them, bit them lightly until she was squirming with the sheer drowning wonder of it, until she was so shameless and needful of release that she was arching her body against the denim-covered iron of his legs.

"Ah, Rachel," she heard him say, and then for the first time he lay upon her. She felt his weight crushing her into the soft carpet, and the abrasion of his clothes against her nakedness, and the rasp of his stubble against her smooth cheeks as he sought her mouth, and she dissolved once again into mindless pleasure even as she wrapped her arms around his neck and gave him back soul-shattering kiss for soul-shattering kiss.

This time she had only a few seconds of relative lucidity in which to register clearer impressions. He was heavy, a whole lot bigger than she was, and quite amazingly strong. The concrete-hard bulge in his jeans was unyielding enough to hurt as he pressed it against her. The taste of whiskey, which she normally abhorred, was dazzlingly erotic on his lips and tongue. He kissed her with a voracious hunger, his tongue filling her mouth and claiming it and encouraging her to do the same to his. She did, abandoning a lifetime of inhibitions in an instant, clinging to his neck and wrapping her legs around his back and whimpering with impatience as he unzipped his jeans and freed himself at last and plunged into her. At the feel of him, huge and hard and hot and filling her to bursting, Rachel's nails sank deep into his back, and she gasped. Then she couldn't think at all, couldn't do anything but feel as he rode her with wild abandon and she bucked and clawed and moaned like an animal in heat.

At the end it was she who was crying out, and he who merely gritted his teeth in a fiercely silent release.

He collapsed on top of her, his weight pinning her down. Even as she wrapped her arms around his shoulders and threaded her fingers through his silky black hair, Rachel fell fathoms into a deep sleep.

18

Rachel felt like a slut. Two minutes of lying beneath Johnny and listening while he snored noisily in her ear, and she felt like a slut. She was naked except for her skirt, which was hopelessly twisted about her waist and her sandals, which neither of them had ever even bothered to remove, drenched with his sweat, slick with his juices. The taste of whiskey was sour in her mouth. The air around her stank of whiskey and sex. How long she'd slept, whether fifteen minutes or several hours, she had no way of telling. All she knew was that she was bone tired, her muscles ached, and she felt unclean.

When she thought of what he'd done to her, what she'd let him do to her and gloried in the doing, she felt embarrassed. When she remembered with whom she had done such things, she wanted to die of shame.

Johnny Harris. Her former student. Years younger than she. Ex-con with an attitude. Lover of Glenda Watkins and the lord only knew how many other women as well.

He'd said himself he'd fantasized about making love to her from the time she was his English teacher in high school. She'd just helped him make an adolescent daydream come true in an interlude as steamy as it was unlikely to be repeated. Probably this one time was all he wanted of her. Certainly it was all she could expect. Anyway, what did she want—a relationship? With Johnny Harris? The very idea was a joke, a not-so-funny joke.

He had cried in her arms. At the memory Rachel felt her heart turn over. As much as she hated to admit it, there was more to her feelings for him than compassion and lust. She cared about him. And while he might see her as a shoulder to cry on—a mother figure, perhaps—he did not care about her in the same way. She knew that.

He had had the "hots" for her, he'd said. That about summed up his interest in her, Rachel feared. Now that he'd gotten what he had wanted, well . . .

He would not respect her in the morning.

That hackneyed phrase, culled from her reading, sprang into her mind. She'd been raised to be a lady—another hackneyed phrase, an anachronism even, but she couldn't help it, it was the truth. In small southern towns they still had ladies, as well as women who weren't ladies—and such ladies knew that if a girl was easy, the man would take what he could get and then move on to the next conquest like a bee flitting from flower to flower.

Easy was too mild a word to describe what she had been. *Wanton* didn't even cover it. Lover of words that she was, not even she could think of one salacious enough to fit.

Rachel was almost afraid to touch him lest he awaken and she had to face him, right then, the way she was, the way they both were. She didn't think she could bear it.

But he had to be shifted. His weight was growing increasingly unbearable, and her spine was starting to ache from being crushed into the hard floor beneath the carpet. Besides, she wanted to get away.

By dint of much wriggling and shoving at his left shoulder, Rachel was able to maneuver herself out from beneath him. He slept on, oblivious, as she got to her feet. Shaky-kneed, she stood looking down at him while she did her best to smooth out her crumpled skirt. His snoring had increased in volume, become stertorous in fact. Rachel realized that his sleep did not stem from sexual satiation. He was in a stupor from too much whiskey.

For a moment she had to fight the urge to kick him as he slept.

His arms were stretched out over his head, his fingers curling loosely down into the carpet. His long legs were close together, probably because of the constriction of the jeans and Jockey shorts, which were pushed halfway down his thighs. His buns were bare, nice, tight, round buns that were, as she now knew from firsthand experience, as hard to the touch as they looked. They were smooth and hairless and several shades paler than the muscular tops of his thighs, which were further darkened by a sprinkling of black hair. The cleft in them drew her eyes. Rachel remembered sinking her fingers into that cleft, blushed, and pulled her eyes away.

The white T-shirt was only faintly twisted at his narrow waist. Rachel speculated that its snug fit kept it from being as hopelessly dislocated as her skirt had been. Peeking from beneath one broad shoulder she spied a telltale pink strap: her bra. Bending to retrieve it, Rachel practically had to lift his shoulder off the ground to get it free. If she hadn't experienced it herself, she would never have believed that a man so lean and hard of muscle could weigh so darn much.

She discovered that her hands were unsteady as she tried twice to fasten the hooks on her bra. Finally she succeeded and, slipping the straps up over her shoulders, slid the garment into place. The thought that popped unbidden into her mind was that he had not seemed disappointed at the size of her breasts. On the contrary, he had caressed and kissed them with an enthusiasm that was, in retrospect, downright mortifying.

Rachel flinched at the memory, feeling hot color flood her neck and face. How would she ever be able to face him again, with the specter of this night between them?

The answer was, she wouldn't. Not for a while, anyway.

While it was impractical to think she could avoid him forever, and she knew it, perhaps she could for a few weeks. School started on Thursday—was that only two days away? She would be busy, too busy to stop by the hardware store for some time after that. She had to hire a new manager, but maybe Olivia could handle the job for a few weeks. Or maybe Ben could be persuaded to stay on a little longer.

Devil take Johnny Harris! Ever since he had wormed his way back into it, he had consistently fouled up her life.

Time blunted even the most excruciating memories, as Rachel knew from experience. She only hoped that it would blunt this one before she had to meet those smoky blue eyes again.

Her raspberry T-shirt lay by a corner of the couch near his feet. Rachel skirted Johnny's prone body, picked it up, and pulled it over her head. Tucking the T-shirt into her skirt as quickly as she could, she looked around for the one garment she had not yet recovered: her panties.

At the memory of how she had lost them, she wanted to hide.

They were nowhere to be found. After a careful search, Rachel decided that Johnny must be lying on them. There was simply no other place that they could be.

For a moment, she was tempted to abandon them. To all outward appearances she was decently dressed. She could just go home as she was, and no one would be the wiser.

Unless and until Johnny Harris decided to return her panties to her, which, knowing him, he was perfectly capable of doing in a very public way.

Rachel could not take that chance. The very idea made her face burn.

Kneeling beside him, she caught hold of one shoulder and heaved. Nothing much happened, except that he grunted, briefly interrupting his snoring. He was too heavy for her to shift, let alone flip over onto his back.

From somewhere behind her came a snuffle and a soft whine. The slavering beast was lurking in the bedroom with only a flimsy wooden door standing between them. Rachel was galvanized. Johnny was insensible and unlikely to be aroused even if she were to be chewed to pieces on top of him. If the dog were to get out, her fate would not be something she could consider with sanguinity.

She heaved at the shoulder again. It lifted perhaps an inch off the floor before thudding back down. Again he grunted, and the dog whined. At that Rachel gave it up for a lost cause. He was not going to be moved, not by her, not in his present state of drunken dead weight.

The snuffle came again, then a growl instead of the whine. Clearly the animal could smell her and was making his displeasure clear in no uncertain terms. Rachel decided to leave while she still could, panties or no.

Heading toward the door, she spied her panties in a ball under the lamp table. With a murmur of relief, she fished them out and pulled them on.

Then, without so much as a backward glance at Johnny, she let herself out the door.

Though the night was warm, Rachel shivered as she drove toward home. All in all, the last few hours had been some of the most physically and psychically draining of her life. First Johnny had assaulted her emotions, tearing at her heart until it bled, and then he had stormed her body. Her capitulation had been a mind-blowing surrender of body and soul. It was only natural that she should be not quite herself in its aftermath.

Tylerville at night was as dark as a graveyard. Not even the faint light from the crescent moon high overhead was enough to banish the eerie shadows that blanketed the narrow, curving road. Rachel drove toward home, past the empty fields and through the double lanes of towering pines along the route she had traveled several times a day for most of her life and tried not to let her imagination get the best of her. There were so many spooky stories about various places around Tylerville that if one dwelled on them, one would never go anywhere alone at night. The problem was, some of the tales were true, she knew. She just didn't know which ones.

Her great-aunt Virginia, for example, used to tell a story about the old Baptist church, long since abandoned, that Kay and the other members of the Preservation Society were so anxious to beautify. Its spire pointed skyward on a little hillock not far from Rachel's home. Rachel drove past it every time she went into or returned from town, and rarely did she think of the ghost of the church organist who still supposedly played there. But tonight, as she approached the church, the story retold itself in her head of its own volition. It was probably because her nerves were already so on edge, Rachel thought dismally as she pressed harder on the accelerator. But the little frame building, its white paint periodically freshened by the Preservation Society, seemed almost to glow in the dark. In all events, she could not keep her eyes from seeking out and finding it as she barreled down the road.

The story was that the church organist, a young woman whose name was forgotten in the mists of time, had been having an affair with the minister. His wife, who had originally planted the cemetery gardens that Kay was so anxious to restore, had somehow found out and had lain in wait for the two of them. Most shocking of all, the two had conducted their misbehavior in the church itself. One night the minister had been called away by sickness amongst his flock, and the pretty organist had been in the church waiting for the lover who didn't come. His wife came instead, murdered her rival by means unknown, and got rid of the body. The minister may have suspected, but no one else did.

The young woman's disappearance was one of those mysteries that enlivened the town's gossip circuit for many years to come. The minister's wife went on to lead a long and apparently blameless life with her erring spouse, and during her lifetime no one was ever the wiser about her crime. Her one error was that she had kept a diary in which she wrote faithfully every day. Recipes and church-related problems were bound up with the tale of the murder and its aftermath, so the story went. The diary, of course, later mysteriously disappeared.

The only corroborating evidence was the discovery, sometime in the nineteen thirties, of a young woman's coffinless skeleton in a partially underground crypt back behind the church. By then, the minister and his wife were long dead, and the grisly artifact with its accompanying tale of adultery and murder was excitingly scandalous rather than horrifying. That such a skeleton had actually been found the town elders had sworn. Everything else, as Rachel was aware, was pure speculation.

But the scary part was that, on a rainy night such as the one on which the murder supposedly had taken place, local wags claimed that the doomed organist could still be heard playing her instrument as she waited for her partner in sin to join her.

Aunt Vir, who had never told a lie in her life as far as Rachel knew, claimed to have heard the ghostly music herself as a young girl. She and some friends had crept into the churchyard, scared and giggly, to see the ghost for themselves—and sure enough, as they had sneaked up to one of the windows, an organist's rendition of "Amazing Grace" had swelled past their ears. The girls had run for their lives.

Years later, when Aunt Vir had retold the story for the umpteenth time for her wide-eyed nieces, it had still been frightening enough to make the back of Rachel's neck prickle.

Moonlight now touched the spire of the church, making it seem to glow. In the shadows beside the building a ghostly figure appeared to move. Rachel looked, then looked again, convinced in that hideous moment that she had actually seen something. But of course there was nothing there. She knew that as well as she knew her name. Still, she almost sideswiped a tree as she hurtled around a bend in the road.

Imagination, of course, she told herself firmly, even as the sweat dried on her palms. It was nothing but imagination.

By the time Rachel reached the gates of Walnut Grove and started up the long driveway, her heart had almost resumed its normal rhythm. That is, until she saw that the house was ablaze with light. Nearly every window in the downstairs, and most of those abovestairs, was lit up. Only the front bedroom where her father customarily slept was dark.

Something had happened. The knowledge filled Rachel with a jittery panic.

She stopped the car with a squeal of brakes, jumped out, and hurried toward the front door. It opened to meet her just as she would have put her hand on the knob.

"Where in the name of heaven have you been?" Her mother whispered fiercely, her eyes moving over Rachel and widening at what they saw.

"What's happened? Is it Daddy?" Rachel brushed by Elisabeth, her face white, her heart filled with dread as she came face to face with the unthinkable.

"Your daddy's fine." Elisabeth sounded grim as her eyes went over Rachel again. Aided by the chandelier in the front hall, she missed no detail of her daughter's appearance, from the badly wrinkled green skirt, to the mussed hair, to the slightly swollen lower lip. "It's Becky. She got home an hour ago with the girls. She's been crying to beat the band, and I can't get a lick of sense out of her to even begin to guess what's the matter. Maybe you can."

"Becky," Rachel echoed with a sense of profound relief. Whatever ailed Becky, at least no one was dead. Her blood had frozen at the possibilities. Despite the fact that she knew perfectly well that her father would never recover, would continue to decline mentally and physically until death was a merciful release, she could still shudder with dread at the thought that he had actually passed from this life.

"Where is she?" Rachel asked, shaking off the melancholy reflection.

"In the library. I started a fire and made her hot chocolate. But she won't talk to me. All she does is cry."

"I'll go to her."

"Just a minute," Elisabeth said, catching Rachel's arm. "Before you do, I want to know where you've been. It's past midnight. There's nowhere in town that's open so late, and don't tell me that you've been with Rob because he called wanting you to go to the Labor Day picnic with him."

Her eyes moved over Rachel again in a comprehensive, assessing way that stiffened Rachel's spine even as it brought hot color flooding up her neck.

"I'm a grown woman, Mother. If I want to stay out past midnight, it's strictly my own concern."

Elisabeth's face went taut, revealing the lovely bone structure and at the same time making her look far closer to her true age. "I don't understand you anymore, Rachel," she said. "You've always been so sensible, so reliable, so smart about everything. But lately, I feel I just don't know you. It's that Harris boy—since he's been back in town, you've changed. You've been with him tonight. Haven't you?"

Elisabeth looked into her daughter's eyes as if she could read the secrets hidden there.

"What if I have, Mother?" Rachel answered quietly. "Would that be so very terrible?"

Without waiting for a reply, she removed her arm from her mother's grip and went to her sister in the library.

19

*E*lisabeth had not exaggerated, Rachel saw as she paused for the briefest moment in the library doorway. Becky was huddled in a corner of the bright yellow couch, her slender legs drawn up beneath her, her curly black hair resting on the furniture's plump upholstered arm, her face turned into a small, square pillow as she sobbed. Flickering light from the fire and a soft glow from the blue-figured china lamp atop their father's massive rolltop desk provided the only illumination. The Delft blue walls and white plantation shutters that closed over the floor-to-ceiling windows gave the room a certain coziness that offset the daunting effect of the enormous crystal chandelier hanging overhead from the ten-foot ceiling. The furniture in this room that had been their father's domain was oversize, well stuffed, and designed for a big man's comfort. Against such a backdrop, thirty-one-year-old Becky, who was as petite as her mother and sister, looked tiny and almost childlike.

Watching the small body in the exotically printed silk camp shirt and walking shorts, Rachel felt a spurt of concern. Becky had always been prone to dramatize even the most mundane situation. Still, for her sister to cry so, something must be seriously amiss.

"What's the matter, Beck?" she asked as she went to place a soothing hand on her sister's heaving back.

"R-Rachel." Becky glanced up, eyes swollen and brimming with tears. To her credit, she sat up and tried for a smile. Her wavering effort had a much different effect from what she obviously intended. Alarmed by what she saw in her sister's face, Rachel sank down on the couch at

Becky's side. Their mother stood in the doorway regarding the pair of them with anxious eyes.

"Is it one of the girls?" Perhaps one of them had been diagnosed with a serious illness. But speculation was as useless as it was ridiculous. The possibilities were endless.

Becky's lovely face, so like a younger Elisabeth's that the resemblance was almost startling, crumpled anew as she shook her head.

"No." Tears poured down her cheeks. Her mouth worked.

"Michael?"

"Oh, Rachel!" Covering her face with her hands, Becky began to sob in great, tearing gulps. Appalled, Rachel put her arms around her sister and hugged her close. As aggravating as Becky could sometimes be, at times like this all Rachel could see was the curly-haired baby sister who had toddled after her from the time she could walk.

"Becky, what is it? Please tell me." Rachel rocked her sister back and forth while Becky cried on her shoulder.

"Michael—Michael wants a divorce." It was a shuddering whisper, muttered into her shoulder, so low that at first Rachel wasn't certain she had heard correctly.

"A divorce?" she repeated, stunned.

"A divorce?" From the doorway, Elisabeth pressed her hand to her throat as she echoed Rachel's words.

"He told me today. Over the phone. He's in Dayton on business, and he called me at home and said he wanted a divorce. Just like that. Can you believe it?" Becky lifted her head to glance first at her mother and then at her sister.

"But why?" Elisabeth asked faintly.

"I think he has a—a girlfriend. I guess he wants to—to marry her."

"Oh, Becky!" Becky looked so woebegone that Rachel ached for her. Becky's gaze focused on her.

"I'm just—sick. I haven't told the girls, but they know something's wrong. Oh, what am I going to do?" It was a wail, and Becky buried her face in Rachel's shoulder as she uttered it. Rachel, feeling helpless, patted her sister's back.

"You're going to stay right here with us and let us take care of you," Rachel said, while her mother, who had sunk bonelessly into Stan's wooden desk chair near the door, nodded agreement.

"Oh, Rachel, I've missed you and Mama and Daddy so much. It's been hard being away from home, trying to bring up the girls by myself. Michael's been gone so much, and I knew something was wrong, but I didn't know what. And then today—" Becky burst into fresh sobs. Rachel held her tighter.

"Sweetheart, why didn't you tell us?" Elisabeth sounded stricken.

"I didn't want to worry you. And—and I know how you feel about divorce."

Elisabeth's views on divorce—she disapproved strongly of the modern tendency to uncouple at the drop of a hat—were indeed vehement. But the vigorous shaking of her head revealed that they didn't necessarily apply to her beloved younger daughter.

"Nonsense," she said firmly, renouncing the tenets of a lifetime in the face of her child's distress. "You know that Daddy and Rachel and I will stand behind you whatever you decide to do. We only want what's best for you. And the girls."

Becky's body shook. "They adore their Daddy. I hate to tell them."

"You don't have to tell them yet," Rachel said. "Not until you and Michael have had a chance to talk some more. Maybe he didn't mean it. Maybe he was just upset about something."

"I think he meant it." There was a pathetic quiver to Becky's voice that caught at Rachel's heart. Becky took a deep, shaken breath and sat up out of her sister's arms. "Oh, Rachel, I wish he'd married you instead."

This heartfelt sigh brought a wry smile to Rachel's mouth. "Well, thanks a lot."

Becky gave a watery chuckle and mopped at her eyes with both hands. "That sounded awful, didn't it? But you know what I mean. You—you're so strong. You would have been able to handle this better than I am. I feel like such a fool. The last few years he's been traveling so much. I thought he was seeing somebody, but he kept telling me I was crazy. I—I almost believed him—that I was crazy, I mean. But I'm not. I was right all the time. He's been screwing around on me for years, and I just took it and took it and pretended I didn't know and stopped making a fuss. And now he wants a divorce, and I ruined my life over him, and he wasn't worth it, not one bit."

Tears welled again. Rachel said firmly, "Your life is not ruined. Whatever happens, you'll be just fine. You'll be happy again and find another man again—a better one this time. And you'll have lots of wonderful times. We just have to get you over this hump. And we will."

Becky smiled at Rachel. The effort was shaky but filled with affection. "Aren't you glad you escaped?"

"Yes," Rachel said, meaning it. "Yes, I am."

Without volition she thought of Johnny and the deep, dark passion he roused in her and realized with a sense almost of shock that Michael had never even touched that part of her. For the first time since Michael Hennessey had chosen Becky over her, Rachel was able to see her love for him for what it had been: a young girl's infatuation, now long in the past. She had grown up since then.

In the kitchen the schoolhouse clock that perched over the pantry struck the hour.

"My goodness, it's two in the morning. We need to go to bed!" Elisabeth exclaimed.

"Yes, we do," Rachel agreed, getting to her feet and tugging her sister up with her.

"Katie will be awake at the crack of dawn," Becky predicted gloomily, referring to her youngest daughter. "And Loren and Lisa won't be far behind."

"Tilda and Rachel and I can look after them. You need to sleep in," Elisabeth said as Rachel and Becky joined her at the door.

"I'm so glad to be home." Becky hugged her mother, then stretched out an arm to pull Rachel into her embrace. For a moment, the three women stood, united in this time of crisis, foreheads touching, arms around each other. "I love you guys."

Then, pulling away, Rachel said briskly, "Enough of this. In another minute, we'll all be crying. Mother, you and Becky go on up. I'll lock the doors and turn off the lights."

20

*T*he watcher was only occasionally present as the body in which he dwelled drove through the darkness, hands tight around the steering wheel, eyes unseeing as they stared out at the all-enveloping night. Memories that bore no connection to the watcher's present-day life flickered in and out of focus.

They brought with them pain and a growing rage, but no real understanding of what was occurring. Kaleidoscopic pictures of a time at least a hundred years in the past seemed suddenly more real than the tall oaks that guarded the winding road. The First Baptist Church appeared on the left, and the watcher's gaze was drawn irresistibly to it. Then the car swerved around the bend, and the church was out of sight. But the building triggered a burst of brain activity, and the watcher was suddenly fully present.

The watcher witnessed the unfolding of long-ago events as immediately as if they were taking place at that very moment. What he saw made him tremble with pain and rage. It was happening again—but not a hundred years in the past. He knew that. The events of the past were being repeated in the here and now.

Through the night, swiftly, silently, unseen and unknown, the watcher sped, to exact not vengeance but a terrible kind of justice. But the dwelling that was his destination was dark, deserted. No one was home.

Blood would not be spilled this night. There would be another frustration added to the watcher's rage.

But even as the watcher turned back toward town, he knew that he would return another night. Soon.

Seeking his prey.

21

The presence of her sister and three nieces kept Rachel so busy over the next two days that it was easy to hold thoughts of Johnny at bay. Mornings were spent playing with the girls, who were seven, five, and two. Lisa, the oldest, was a black-haired sprite who reminded Rachel strongly of Becky as a girl. Loren and Katie both took after Michael, who was tall and fair-haired. All three girls were thrilled to be visiting their aunt and grandparents. If they knew the reason for their visit, none of them, not even Lisa, gave the smallest sign.

Rachel, Becky, and Elisabeth lunched at the club both days, then Rachel drove over to the high school to get ready for the coming school year. The school had recently undergone extensive renovations—getting central air for the first time was one—and there was a great deal to be done to make her classroom fit for human habitation, let alone turn it into the optimum learning environment touted by the school board.

The first day of school dawned, as first days of school always did, with a rush of excitement. Rachel still felt it even after all these years. The prospect of expanding the boundaries of young minds filled her with an almost evangelical zeal. If she could just turn her students on to books, she could open the whole world to them!

Her students—she had homeroom, four English classes, and a study period—were, already well known to her. Not only did she know the teenagers themselves, she knew their sisters and brothers and parents and grandparents and cousins and even their pets. She knew which kids would have trouble and which would whiz through the year. She knew which came to school to play sports, which came to socialize, and which were actually eager to learn. These last few she treasured because they were rare.

At the end of the first day, Rachel was exhausted. She heard the final bell with a silent sigh of thanksgiving and sat at her desk for a moment methodically gathering up books and papers as, with a chorus of good-byes, the students rushed past her for the hall and freedom.

"Miss Grant, are we going to have to do a term paper on Elizabeth Browning this semester?" Allison O'Connell and her two dearest friends fell into step beside Rachel after she worked up the energy to exit the building.

Rachel shook her head. "We did Elizabeth Barrett Browning last year. We'll do somebody different this time."

"Oh, shoot!" Allison pouted.

"You like Elizabeth Barrett Browning?" Rachel looked up at Allison in some surprise. A pretty, popular girl some inches taller than herself, Allison was not a reader. In fact, Rachel found it somewhat surprising that Allison even knew who Elizabeth Barrett Browning was.

"She's got Brian Paxton's term paper from last year," Gretta Ashley explained with a devilish grin, earning an elbow in the ribs from Allison.

"I do not!" Allison, red-faced, took a single look at Rachel's face and amended, "Well, I might have seen it, but I certainly wasn't going to use it!"

"I'm sure you weren't, Allison," Rachel said straight-faced, while Gretta and Molly Fox, who completed the nearly inseparable trio, snickered.

"I'd like to do one on somebody interesting, like Michael Jackson," Molly said.

"Michael Jackson isn't a poet, or even an author," Gretta sounded scandalized.

"Yes, he is. I read his book. Remember? You borrowed it."

"What I mean is, he's not an important author. Not somebody Miss Grant would let us write a term paper on. Would you, Miss Grant?"

"Probably not," Rachel agreed with a smile.

"It'll be somebody boring," Molly said gloomily. They were walking along the emptying sidewalk past the three boxy yellow school buses that were already filled to overflowing with hooting teens. As they passed, the first bus started to pull out. The others followed.

"Do you girls have a way home?" Rachel asked.

"Allison got a car over the summer. She's driving," Gretta answered.

"How nice," Rachel said, now understanding why they were walking her all the way to the parking lots. There were two, a large one for students and a smaller one for teachers, situated side by side in front of the school.

"Yeah, I wish—" Gretta began, then broke off, her eyes widening as she glanced ahead. "Who's *that?*"

"Where?" the other two chorused, while Rachel, following the path of Gretta's eyes, faltered. It was all she could do not to turn and run the other way.

At the edge of the teachers' parking lot, wheels brushing a bright yellow curb that clearly meant no stopping, stood a large red and silver motorcycle. Leaning against it, looking very tall and muscular in his tight jeans and a black leather jacket, arms crossed over his chest, black hair pulled back into a ponytail, was Johnny. He was unsmiling. His eyes were fastened on Rachel.

Recovering her poise, conscious of the girls' widening eyes turning from Johnny to herself, Rachel clamped her teeth together and continued to put one foot in front of the other. Heartstopping memories of their last encounter rose unbidden to taunt her. Taking a quick, steadying breath, she fought to banish them. She could not face him while such searing images played themselves out across the screen of her mind.

"He's cute," Allison breathed. Gretta punched her in the ribs with an elbow.

"Don't you know who that is? That's *Johnny Harris*," Gretta hissed.

"Oh, my God!" Allison gasped.

Molly looked scared. "What's *he* doing here?"

Lagging behind, Rachel fervently hoped that Molly's question would remain forever unanswered. But she was out of luck. He uncrossed his ankles and his arms and straightened away from the motorcycle, obviously having seen his quarry. Casting him sidelong glances, the girls scuttled past him along a sidewalk that was some twenty feet away from where he stood. Rachel, after acknowledging him with an impersonal smile and wave, would have walked by behind them, but he pointed at her and crooked his finger.

"Oh, Miss Grant," he called in a dulcet tone, and beckoned. Rachel, scaldingly conscious of the girls' goggling eyes turned upon her, realized that, unless she wished to make a scene, there was no escape.

22

⚹

*S*he walked over to him.

"Hello, Johnny," she said with as much poise as she could muster. With the bright sun shining on his black hair and his blue eyes gleaming in pleasing contrast to the bronze of his skin, he looked handsome enough to knock a teenager's socks off. Fortunately, she was not a teenager. Her pantyhose stayed firmly in place—although her knees quivered. "Shouldn't you be at work?"

"I took the afternoon off. Zeigler was glad to be rid of me." His eyes narrowed at her determined nonchalance. It was all Rachel could do not to drop her eyes before that assessing gaze. Incredibly, she felt like a teenager, felt as young and idiotic as Allison and Gretta and Molly, who now had their heads together over a yellow Subaru that she could only assume was Allison's new car. They were talking a mile a minute as they watched their teacher with the town's most notorious bad guy. At that moment it was Johnny who seemed the more mature, the more in control of the situation. Rachel nervously realized that by sleeping with him, she had caused their entire relationship to change.

"Not taking phone calls lately?" he asked, his tone perfectly pleasant but something less so in his eyes.

"What?" She frowned up at him, bewildered.

"I've called you at least six times since I woke up to find that you'd flown the coop. Even at ten o'clock at night, you weren't home, which I find kind of hard to believe."

"I didn't know you'd called." That was the truth.

"I'm glad to hear that." Some of the tension around his mouth eased. "I don't think your mother likes me."

"You talked to Mother?"

"If you want to call it that. Our conversations usually went something like this: I'd say, 'This is Johnny Harris. May I speak to Rachel?' and she'd say, 'She is not here,' in a very frosty tone, and hang up the receiver. I thought maybe you'd told her to say that."

"No."

"So you haven't been deliberately avoiding me?"

Rachel glanced up into those penetrating blue eyes, hesitated, and sighed. "Well, maybe a little."

"I thought so." Johnny nodded once, crossed his arms over his chest, and stood looking down at her meditatively. "The question is, why? Because I made a total ass of myself the other night, or because we made love?"

At his plain speaking, coupled with a searching stare that seemed to see into her very soul, Rachel crimsoned. But she sensed that though his words and demeanor were almost nonchalant, his memories of sobbing his heart out to her with his head on her lap embarrassed him profoundly. And for him to be embarrassed for such a reason was something she couldn't bear.

"You did not make a—a fool of yourself," Rachel said firmly.

"Ahh." Johnny smiled a slow, warm, and sexy smile that did funny things to Rachel's insides, then reached out and took the pile of books and papers from her arms before she realized what he was about.

"What are you doing?" He placed her things on a rack behind the motorcycle's leather seat and strapped them on with thick, brightly colored bungee cords.

"Get on." With her books secure, he turned and handed her a shiny silver helmet.

"What? No!" She automatically accepted the helmet, but stared from it to him to the motorcycle as if he'd lost his mind.

"Get on, Rachel. The alternative is to finish this very interesting talk right here, with your giggly students looking on."

"There is no way that I am going to roar off with you on this—thing!"

"It's a motorcycle, not a thing. Haven't you ever ridden one?"

"Certainly not!"

He shook his head at her, reaching for his own helmet, which was hooked over a handlebar. "Poor repressed teacher. Well, just think of it as an educational experience. Get on."

"I said no, and I mean it. I'm wearing a dress, for goodness' sake."

"I noticed, and very nice, too. I think you might try shortening your skirts some, though. You've got killer legs." He pulled on his helmet as he spoke.

"Johnny—"

"Miss Grant, are you all right? Should we go get help?" Allison called. The three girls were huddled together by the side of the yellow Subaru, their expressions anxious as they alternated between watching Rachel and Johnny and conferring among themselves.

"I'm fine, Allison. You girls can go ahead. Mr. Harris is a former student of mine," Rachel called back. Her efforts at reassurance were not helped by Johnny's rather mocking smile at the trio.

"They think I'm trying to abduct you."

"Aren't you?" Rachel's reply was tart.

Johnny looked surprised, then slowly grinned. "I guess I am. Would you get on, Rachel, please? Think what you'll do for my public image when you turn up again in one piece."

"I am not going anywhere on that motorcycle. Even if I wanted to, and even if I were dressed for it, I could not possibly climb on behind you right here at school and zoom off in front of my students. The board would never get over it—to say nothing of Mr. James."

"Is he still principal?"

"Yes."

"Figures. Only the good die young. Rachel . . ."

Rachel sighed. "Okay. I accept that we need to talk. But I am not getting on that motorcycle. My car is over there. I go in my car, or I don't go at all."

Johnny looked down at her, shrugged, and pulled his helmet off. "Wheels is wheels," he said.

That wrung a wry smile out of Rachel. "For one of my best-ever students, you have dreadful grammar."

"Grammar was never my strong suit, remember? I was better at— other things."

Rachel felt a blush creep over her face at the innuendo her incorrigible mind read into that. Fortunately, he was already turning away to unfasten her belongings from the back of the motorcycle, so he did not witness her discomfiture.

"Do you still write poetry?" he asked over his shoulder, his hands busy with the bungee cords.

Rachel froze, staring at his leather-clad back. She had forgotten she had revealed so much of herself to him all those years ago, when he was her star pupil.

"I'm surprised you remember that," she said slowly.

He had her books in his arms now, and he turned back to face her. "Are you? You shouldn't be. I remember every single thing I ever knew about you, teacher."

Their gazes locked for an instant. Then Rachel, more flustered than she could ever remember being, turned and walked away from him toward her car.

She was supremely conscious of his presence as, arms laden with her books, he followed along behind her—and just as conscious of the wide-eyed gazes of the three girls, who watched every move they made. Fortunately, the teachers' parking lot was nearly as deserted as the students'. She would have hated to face the prospect of introducing censorious colleagues to Johnny.

Rachel took several deep breaths to recover her equilibrium, then started the car as Johnny set her belongings in the back. He shrugged out of his jacket and threw that in, too, to reveal one of his regulation cotton T-shirts, then slid in beside her. She would have liked a moment alone with the lipstick and powder compact in her purse, because she knew from experience that by the end of the day any makeup she might have started out with was long gone. It didn't really matter, she supposed. A little lipstick and powder would not erase so much as a day of her thirty-four years, nor would they make her one whit more beautiful to him. Her outfit, which consisted of a short-sleeved white cotton sweater with deep pink roses across the bosom and matching calf-length pleated skirt of navy cotton strewn with the same pink roses as the sweater, might not be the last word in chic, but it was eminently practical for her job. So were her low-heeled navy pumps and the small pearl studs she wore in each ear. Even her hairstyle was chosen because it required no fuss. She looked what she was, a small-town thirtysomething teacher of high school English. Johnny was as out of place beside her as his motorcycle would be parked next to her conservative blue Maxima.

They both waved at the gaping girls as they drove past them out of the parking lot.

"You shouldn't have come to school," Rachel said as she pulled out onto the road, knowing gossip would dog her every step on the morrow.

"If Muhammad won't come to the mountain . . . ," Johnny said with a shrug. In a carefully light tone that did not quite mask the seriousness of the question, he added, "Ashamed of me, Rachel?"

Rachel glanced over at him, touched by something in his voice that told her that her answer mattered very much indeed. Seen in three-quarter profile against the bright sunlight pouring in through the window, he was so handsome that he stole her breath. She had never realized before just how perfect his features were. The proud forehead, the high cheekbones, the long, straight nose with its narrow bridge, the clean, square lines of his jaw and chin were classic in their elegance. Add to that his beautifully shaped, sensuously curved mouth, the smoldering vitality of smoky blue eyes set beneath thick, straight black brows, and he was extraordinarily good-looking. And not only because she was mentally comparing him with every other man in Tylerville.

"Stop!" Johnny bellowed without warning, his eyes shifting from her face to the road ahead, his hands flying up to brace against the dashboard. The shout broke Rachel's train of thought and made her slam on the brakes so hard that only their automatically tightened seat belts kept them from being flung forward.

"What?" Rachel asked, aggrieved. She looked around to discover that they had screeched to a halt at the four-way stop in front of the 7-Eleven not far from the school. Traffic, including a school bus and a coal truck, coming from every direction zoomed past, answering her question.

"It's a miracle you haven't gotten yourself killed," Johnny said between clenched teeth. "Here, slide over. I'm driving from now on."

"This is my car, and—"

"Slide over." He was already out of the car, slamming the door behind him as he walked around the hood. Rachel, glaring at him through the windshield, bethought herself of all the watching drivers in the cars around them, bit her lip, unfastened her seat belt, and scooted over, maneuvering over the console with something less than grace. If Johnny stood in the road arguing with her while she stubbornly clung to her seat, some busybody would probably call the police.

"Want something to drink?" Johnny asked as he got in, nodding at the 7-Eleven. They had missed their turn to go, and behind them indignant cars started to honk.

"No, thanks." Rachel, resentful at being deprived of command in her own car, was determined that he should realize it.

"Well, I do." It was their turn again. Johnny shot across the road into the parking lot of the 7-Eleven and stopped. The speed of the maneuver was enough to make Rachel clutch the armrest beside her.

"Talk about my driving—" she began indignantly, but he was already getting out of the car. Seething, Rachel watched as he disappeared inside the store.

Minutes later, she saw him through the glass as he stepped up to the counter to pay. He was exchanging pleasantries with the male clerk as she watched, and a great deal of her annoyance faded as she admired his tall, athletic build and the skin-tight fit of those jeans. Then some indefinable tension in his stance appeared. Whatever he was exchanging with the clerk now, it was not pleasantries.

He threw something down onto the counter, picked up his groceries, and stalked out to the car. Rachel silently accepted the items he thrust at her through the window—a couple of cans of Coke and two packages of Twinkies—and refrained from saying anything at all until the car was in motion again, zooming backward in a wide, fast turn, then pulling out into traffic with a squeal of tires that made Rachel wince.

"What happened?" she asked when they were more or less safely rocketing down the road, which fortunately was a straight stretch at that point.

"What makes you think something happened?" This was accompanied by a glittering sideways glare from a man whose jaw was clenched so tightly, she could see the muscles bunched below his ear.

"Call it woman's intuition."

Her dry tone earned her another sideways glance, a little less fierce than the first one.

"Asshole wouldn't take my money."

"Oh." She realized suddenly that the clerk had been Jeff Skaggs. Rachel would have recognized him immediately if she had really looked at him, if all her attention hadn't been concentrated on Johnny. Not that she meant to inform Johnny that it was Jeff, if he didn't already know. Johnny was a proud man, already bitter at the townspeople, with a hot, ferocious temper that she had seen fully aroused only once or twice years ago. The treatment that was being meted out to him on all sides was atrocious, though he'd accepted it without much apparent rancor so far. But she was beginning to be afraid that he was near to reaching the limits of his tolerance. There was going to be an explosion one of these days, she feared, and she only hoped that she was nearby when it happened to undertake what damage control she could.

"I didn't kill Marybeth," Johnny said savagely, his eyes fixed on the road. "I am as innocent as that asshole in the grocery, and you know what? Whether I'm innocent or not doesn't matter a damn to anybody. Did you know I earned a college degree while I was in the can? Yep, in comparative literature, much good may it ever do me. I ran a hell of a successful business while I was inside, too. Remember I used to smoke? Well, I quit, because cigarettes are the hard currency that the joint runs on. I hoarded my cigarettes and sold 'em, and I bought some more with the proceeds and sold those, too. Pretty soon everybody was calling me the Smoke Man, and I was doing all right. I made money, and I saved it, so that when I got out I'd have something to fall back on. I survived what they did to me. But it shouldn't have happened, and it wouldn't have, except that people don't ever look any further than the ends of their noses. I am a Harris, therefore I'm no good, therefore I'm capable of murder, therefore, since I was the last person who will admit to being with Marybeth, I must have killed her. Only I didn't."

He was pulling off the road, onto a narrower lane that twisted and dipped as it cut through a thick woods. In only a few minutes they emerged from beneath the overhanging trees to park with a jerk at the edge of a small, shimmering lake with ducks paddling placidly on its surface. The cool, changeable blue of the water, the iridescent green and brown of the ducks' feathers, the bright apple-green of the sun-drenched treetops, and the deeper, mysterious pine of the shadows lower down made for a vista so lovely that it was a shame neither of them noticed it beyond the most cursory of perusals.

Johnny continued to stare straight ahead, his hands clenched around the steering wheel. Rachel, silent beside him, watched him with her heart in her eyes, but he never so much as glanced her way.

"I was nineteen years old when I went in. A boy. A cocky, scared boy, so scared that I was afraid I'd throw up the first time I walked down the block and heard all those metal doors clanging shut behind me, all those cons calling at me and whistling and stomping their feet as I passed, like I was fresh meat. Did you know I used to get fan mail while I was inside? From women. I got offered everything, including marriage. One chick who signed herself 'yours eternally' wrote me every week. Apparently they thought that being thrown in the joint for murder was glamorous. I think some of them had me confused with a goddamned rock star."

He paused and took a deep breath but continued to stare out unseeingly over the lake. Rachel bit her lip but said nothing, knowing that there was more he wanted, no, needed, to tell her.

"You know the worst thing about being inside? It was the regimentation. From the time we got up till the time they locked us in our cells and turned out the lights, there was a certain time for this and a certain time for that and some jerkoff always telling us what to do. And no privacy. Never any privacy, not for anything."

This time the pause was longer. Just as Rachel was about to reach over and lay a hand on his shoulder or knee or anywhere just so that she touched him, just so that he remembered that she was present, that she cared, he sent her a swift, shuttered look. Then he once again shifted his gaze away, focusing on the lake.

"Hell, no, that wasn't the worst thing. You want to know the worst thing? I thought I was tough when I went in. I thought nobody would mess with me. Well, I was wrong. Third day I was in, four guys cornered me in the shower. They held me down, sodomized me. Told me afterward that I was gonna be their fucking woman from then on out. I was hurt bad, because they beat the crap out of me first, you know? And I was sick, sick to my soul, in the way only a kid can be sick when something happens that knocks all the pride, all the manliness out of him. And I was scared.

"But as I healed up, I made up my mind that it wasn't going to happen again, that they'd have to kill me first. When I did that, all the fear kind of drained away. I would prevail, or I would die. It was as simple as that, and at that point I didn't much care which it was. I stole a spoon from the kitchen and sharpened it and sharpened it until I had an edge on it like a razor's. Then I waited. When they cornered me again—they were laughing, the bastards, calling me sweet thing, and dear—I was ready. I carved 'em up like jack-o'-lanterns. And those particular assholes never bothered me again."

He took another of those deep, almost shuddering breaths. Then he glanced over at Rachel, his hands still curved around the wheel.

"So now you know." He spoke simply, but what was in his eyes was not simple. They were full of pain and shame, and a kind of weary, wary pride. Rachel looked and felt her heart break for him. All her common sense, all her instincts for self-preservation, vanished in that instant.

She unfastened her seat belt, drew one knee beneath her, rose on it, and turned at the same time. With one hand on his shoulder for balance, she tilted her head and pressed her lips to his in a soft, clumsy kiss.

When his hands came up to hold her, when he would have pulled her into a deeper embrace, she lifted her head to look him squarely in the eyes.

"So now *you* know," she said.

23

So what do I know?" There was humor in his question and a certain tension, too. They were so close, they were practically nose to nose, their eyes locked, in a posture that should have felt ridiculous but didn't because what was happening between them was so serious.

"That I'm crazy about you." Rachel almost whispered the confession. The steering wheel was gouging her in the back, but she never even noticed it. The console between the seats cut into the side of her thigh, but she never felt that, either. Her entire being was focused on deciphering what was going on behind the opaque screen of Johnny's eyes.

"In spite of everything?" The slight huskiness to his voice told her that he wasn't sure what his revelation had meant to her.

"Yes."

His hands found her waist, lifted and pulled, and suddenly she was over the console, sitting on his lap, her back against the door, her arms draped loosely around his shoulders.

"I'm crazy about you, too, teacher," he said softly, then kissed her.

His mouth was very warm and tasted faintly of mint. The muscles of his upper arm, which was curled around her, cushioning her head from the door, were hard as she nestled against them. His chin felt only faintly bristly as it brushed over her cheek, and she realized with that small part of her mind that was still capable of realizing anything that he must have shaved not many hours before. His shoulders beneath her arms and hands were wide and strong. He smelled of soap, and mint, and man.

Her heart was drumming, her eyes closed as she kissed him back as thoroughly as he kissed her. Her fingers found the rubber band that bound his hair at the nape, and she tugged it free so that she could run her fingers through the crisp black strands.

"Ouch," he protested, drawing back a little when her fingers got caught in a tangle.

"You need a haircut," she told him by way of reply, already closing her eyes and tilting her mouth toward his again.

"Do I? I think you need to let yours grow. I like long hair on my women." He continued kissing her, brief, sensuous kisses pressed to the center and then to alternate corners of her mouth.

"Do you now?" This nettled her, but not enough to make her pull away from his mouth, which was running along the side of her jaw. "Are you telling me that I may now consider myself one of your women?"

"No," he answered, his voice faintly muffled as he explored the ear nearest him with his tongue, then pressed a heated kiss to the sensitive hollow just below it.

"No?" Following the gist of the conversation was growing increasingly difficult. She felt swooningly limp, dizzy almost, her limbs heavy and her body already beginning the rhythmic contractions of desire.

"You can consider yourself my woman. Singular. If you want." He kissed the sensitive cord at the side of her neck, nibbled at it really. Rachel tilted her head to one side and lifted her chin to facilitate the process.

"Johnny . . ." All the reasons why she couldn't be his woman crowded into her brain. The age difference, the lifestyle difference, her respectable profession, her family, his infamy. But just as quickly as the objections flickered through her mind, they were banished by the thought that he knew her clear down to her soul—and the return of his mouth to hers. His kiss was slow, sensual, drugging. When he slid his mouth down to nuzzle the softness beneath her chin, she was so bemused that she scarcely knew where she was.

"Yes," she murmured dreamily.

"Yes, what?" He had pulled the gentle scoop neck of her sweater aside to run his lips along her collarbone. Rachel's toes curled, and she felt one neat blue pump loosen.

"Whatever it was you asked me." Her thought processes had gone up in smoke.

"Mmmm. Let's move to the back, okay? There's not much room up here."

Before she could even process what he had said, he somehow got the door opened and was sliding out of the car with her still on his lap. Her loosened shoe fell off, but Rachel didn't care. She clung to him, her arms looped tightly around his neck. He stood up with her, one arm just

below her shoulders, one arm under her knees, lifting her with no difficulty at all. Rachel experienced a deliciously feminine sense of fragility,
of helplessness against his strength. Feeling rather self-conscious at falling prey to so atavistic an emotion, she refused to meet his gaze, looking
instead at the crow-black hair freed now to wave to his wide shoulders, at
the darkly handsome face, at the brawny upper arms that gave silent
testimony to his strength.

"I bet you don't weigh a hundred pounds," Johnny said suddenly,
jiggling her in his arms as if to test her weight.

"A hundred seven, actually."

"You need to eat more." He shut the front door with a sneakered
foot, opened the rear one by bending and feeling for the handle, while
somehow managing to hang on to her at the same time, then sat again
with her on his lap.

"Then I'd get fat, and you wouldn't like me."

Johnny tweaked her nose in teasing response and shifted her into a
more comfortable position with her back against his chest. Her head
lolled against his shoulder, and his arms hugged her waist before they
were settled to his satisfaction. Rachel, spellbound, cast a sideways
glance up and back to find that his eyes on her face were as bright and
hot as the clear August sky overhead.

"You still don't get it, do you, teacher? I'd like you any way I could
get you, any way at all. Besides, I bet you'd be cute fat. A little round
dumpling."

"How lovely." Laughing with a tiny catch in her voice at the picture
this conjured up, Rachel gave herself over for the moment to the luxury
of simply allowing him to hold her. The warmth and smell and easy
strength of him engulfed her. She felt wonderfully at home in his arms,
comfortable and familiar and happy and excited at the same time. It was
foolishness, she knew, but then judged foolishness to be a vastly under-
rated commodity. What had being sensible, as she had been all her life
until now, gotten her? Certainly not this.

The back seat was bench-style, covered with slate blue plush velour.
It was roomier than the front, but still there was not a lot of head and leg
space for a man of Johnny's height. He came to the same conclusion and
kept the door open, with one leg trailing outside. The baking heat crept
into the car as the air-conditioned coolness slipped out. With the door
open, the rustle of leaves as a slight breeze rattled the treetops, the
squawking of a pair of battling ducks, and the gentle slosh of water
against the rocky shore were as audible and immediate as if the two of
them sat entwined on the grass itself.

Johnny's hands, which had been around her waist, slid up the front of her sweater, seeking her breasts. They located their quarry, kneaded and squeezed them. Her whole body responded with an aching quiver, but her mind, her still-functioning mind, shied away.

Rachel caught his wrists. Her voice as she spoke was faintly breathless. "Johnny, I don't think this is such a good idea. It's broad daylight. Anybody could come along."

It was difficult to give voice to this objection, and it grew even more so as he kissed the eyebrow, the temple, and the cheekbone nearest him while continuing to practice his exquisite torture on her breasts. One hand finally released its prey, but before she could decide if she welcomed or regretted its departure, it slid beneath the edge of her sweater, up over her bare stomach, to find her breast again. The feeling of his warm, strong hand covering her breast with only the delicate lace of her bra between her flesh and his sent tingles of pleasure all along her nerve endings. Under the influence of that caressing touch, Rachel realized that she was rapidly losing the last vestiges of coherent thought that remained to her.

"You've got the sexiest tits," he whispered in her ear as his other hand slid under her sweater to rejoin its fellow. He ran a lazy thumb over one shy nipple, then made a sound of satisfaction deep in his throat as it suddenly stood erect. Rachel almost gasped with pleasure. She loved the way his hands on her made her feel. If only there were more of her, so she could be sure that he was as excited by what he was doing as she was.

"I—I'm not very big—" The last of this whispered confession was muffled as, unable to stand the combination of mental torture and physical bliss for another instant, she turned in his arms, burying her face in the curve between his neck and shoulder. She wrapped her arms tighter about his neck, feeling errant quivers of wanting begin somewhere in the vicinity of her midsection as the heat of those long-fingered hands slid around to the bare skin of her back.

"You're perfect. Just what I always wanted. Didn't anybody ever tell you that the best presents come in small packages?" He kissed her averted cheek, and his fingers found and unhooked her bra. Rachel felt the give in the band that told her what he had done. With a sigh she surrendered to his ministrations simply because she lacked further will to resist. There was nothing she could do to change her measurements, certainly not in the next five minutes. He would have to take her or leave her as she was.

He certainly gave no indication of wanting to leave her. Tugging at her sweater, he pulled it up to her armpits before her arms around his neck put a halt to further progress. When he gave another frustrated tug at the folds of bunched cotton, she unwound her arms and lifted them so that he could pull the garment off. With a slight shrug of her shoulders and a sensation of daring sinfulness, she let her bra drop forward until she was naked to the waist. When she dared look at him again and discovered him staring at the pink-tipped white curves of her breasts, she felt a tingling excitement that was engendered almost entirely by the sultry heat that filled his eyes and that had nothing whatsoever to do with her size, or lack of it.

Feeling her gaze on him, he glanced up. A touch of humor twinkled suddenly beneath the heat in his eyes.

"Besides, I'm an ass man, myself," he said, and grinned as her face registered shock. If his grin was a little lopsided, and his eyes returned to her breasts with unmistakable appreciation, why, his hand was delving under her skirt to squeeze the part in question, just to prove his point. "And you've got the prettiest little ass I've ever laid hands on in my life."

"Johnny!"

But her half-laughing, half-outraged protest was silenced by a shaft of pure fire as he dipped his head to capture a pink nipple and draw it into his mouth. Rachel gasped at the exquisite pleasure, and her back arched. She lay across his encircling arm as he bent over her, suckling her breasts. His hair brushed her skin, swept tantalizingly over her other breast. When he lifted his head at last, her areolas were puckered with wanting. Her nipples, the one shiny wet from his mouth, the other stiff and begging for attention, had darkened to a voluptuous rose pink and were pebble-hard.

He shifted, turned, and then they were lying along the seat with Rachel pressed tight against the velour backrest. One arm cradled her shoulders while the other made its way under her long skirt. His hand slid with exquisite friction over her legs in their sheer pantyhose. When he reached the juncture of her thighs, he delved between them, pressing and rubbing and squeezing with sensuous knowledge. Rachel made a little moaning sound deep in her throat as her thighs parted for him of their own accord.

"Rachel." His voice was low, faintly hoarse.

Rachel looked up at him almost blindly by way of answer. He was looming over her now, one arm pressed stiffly against the velour to spare her the full burden of his weight.

"I'm tired of doing all the work."

"What?" She didn't understand. Frowning, she blinked her puzzlement up into his blazing eyes.

"Unzip me."

The words, along with the guttural undertone in which they were uttered, were wildly erotic. Shocked, tantalized, Rachel caught her breath with shaky surprise. For a moment she could do nothing more than stare at him as his command percolated through her bedazzled brain along her nerve endings to her fingers. She did as he asked.

The metal button that fastened his jeans was stiff, and it took more than one try before she managed to work it free. Her fingers were clumsy as they sought for and found the tab to his zipper. The denim felt stiff and smooth beneath her hand, the small tab cool and hard. She worked it down, slowly, conscious all the while of the bulge that swelled to fill the increasing opening. His erection, burgeoning forth, fought to be free.

He wore Jockey shorts. The white cotton contained him, hiding him from her eyes, shielding him from her touch. Fascinated, Rachel stared at the thick swelling that bulged through his open fly. She stretched out a beautifully manicured finger to touch it.

The cotton was soft. Beneath it, his penis was steely hard. It jerked convulsively when she ran a pink-painted fingernail down its length.

Johnny made not a sound. But something, the tension of his body perhaps, or a sudden movement, made her glance up. Rachel took one look at his glazed eyes, the harsh intensity of his face, and she knew that her touch pleased him almost beyond bearing.

"Wait."

She was already reaching for him again when he forced the word out. Her fingers checked for just an instant, but then she would not stop, could not stop, her fingers moving of their own volition to circle him through the cotton underpants, and squeeze . . .

"For God's sake, Rachel, wait!" He jackknifed into a sitting position. Before he abruptly turned his back on her, she saw that beads of sweat had broken out along his upper lip and forehead. Bemused by his action, Rachel watched him fumble in a pocket, and then fumble some more. The faint sound of something being torn reached her ears.

"What on earth are you doing?" she asked, bewildered, struggling to sit up with his wide T-shirt-clad back all but blocking her in.

"A rubber," he answered, almost growling, turning back to her and bearing her down again into the plush seat. "What kind of bastard would I be to fuck you without a rubber? What kind of fool are you to let me? The last time I wasn't in any shape to think about it, but now . . ."

He was on top of her, kissing her as if he were ravenous for the taste of her mouth, his hands bunching her skirt up around her waist and reaching between her legs to yank at the crotch of her pantyhose until they tore. He tore her panties, too, just ripped them out of his way, and then he drove into her with a savagery that made Rachel cry out.

"Oh, Johnny. Oh, Johnny. Oh, Johnny," she sobbed. Her legs, with their delicate nylon covering still intact, were locked tight around his buttocks, and her arms were wrapped around his neck. His chest crushed her breasts. His arms were wrapped around her like iron bands. His face was buried in the curve between her neck and shoulder, and he was panting in harsh, rapid gasps as he lifted himself almost all the way out, then plunged back home, again and again and again.

"Oh, Johnny!" she cried as sensation exploded inside her. Clinging tight, she let ocean waves of ecstasy whirl her away. At her cry he gritted his teeth, drove deep one last time, and found his own release.

For a long time they lay unmoving, spent in the aftermath of passion as their breathing slowed and steadied and their bodies cooled.

Unable to be still a moment longer as his much greater weight threatened to suffocate her, Rachel wriggled to be free. Johnny's head lifted, and with his face just inches from hers he met her gaze.

Rachel looked into those knowing blue eyes and felt her cheeks grow warm. It was embarrassing, without passion for an impetus, to remember what she—and he—had done.

"Could you get off me, please?" she asked.

24

"*T*hat's not very romantic."

"I'm sorry, but you're crushing me so that I can't breathe."

A slow grin spread across his face. "So much for romance, hmmm?" he asked, and dropped a quick, possessive kiss on her mouth. Rolling to one side, he sat up. Rachel glanced at the muscular half-moons of his buns cradled by the soft plush, acknowledged that they were sexy-looking even when the sexual bloom was off her particular rose, and didn't feel one whit happier for the admission.

With his back to her, she could not see what he was doing, which was probably just as well. Harsh reality had descended, as harsh reality tends to do, and she was supremely conscious of her situation as she sat up and tried to restore her appearance as best she could. She was naked to the waist, her skirt rucked up around her hips and sadly crumpled. Her pantyhose had a great gaping hole torn in them, and her panties had been ripped so that they hung from one hip by a single piece of elastic. She was shoeless, though when the second one had dropped, she couldn't have said. Her mouth felt bruised and swollen, and her hair, when she got a glimpse of it in the rearview mirror, looked like a bird's nest. She felt dirty, sweaty, smelly, and disgruntled.

So much for romance.

He hitched up his shorts and jeans, and she heard his zipper going up. Rachel, casting about for her bra and sweater, realized that he was now perfectly decent while she was next to naked.

"Let's go skinny-dipping."

"What?" The suggestion, coupled by a devilish grin as he turned and ran his eyes over her, took Rachel aback. She clapped her hands over her breasts and scowled at him.

"Skinny-dipping. You've heard of it? You know, when people swim naked in a body of water?"

"No way!"

He laughed. It was a spontaneous, joyous burst of sound, and Rachel saw that his eyes were sparkling with humor as they surveyed her.

"Are you always this grouchy when you've just had great sex, teacher?"

Rachel's scowl deepened, although reluctantly she felt herself begin to respond to the humor in his gaze.

"I wouldn't know," she said, and stuck out her tongue at him.

"Oh, yeah?" He grinned at her.

"Yeah. Now would you please get out of here and let me put myself back together in peace? Go—go eat a Twinkie, or something."

"I think I will." Reaching a long arm between the front seats, he retrieved the Cokes and Twinkies and slid out the door. With one last glimmering grin at her, he took himself off to perch on a picnic table by the water's edge.

Rachel watched him go, silently admiring his long-legged, wide-shouldered body and graceful stride, then turned her attention to the business at hand. Her pantyhose and panties were ruined, and these she stripped off, not without some regret for the panties. Lingerie was her weakness, and she had lovely underthings. This particular pair of panties was pale blue and exactly matched the lace bra that must have gotten lost under one of the front seats. Feeling under the passenger seat, Rachel located it, pulled it out, and put it on. Her sweater was crumpled on the floorboard. She pulled that on, too. Her purse was tucked under the front seat. Squeezing through the space over the console, she caught its strap and pulled it free. Finally she had the few minutes alone with her makeup that she had craved. She ran a quick brush through her hair, glad that restoring it to shining smoothness was a simple operation, then tucked the brush back into her purse and pulled out her powder compact and lipstick. Flipping open the lid on the compact, she surveyed herself in the mirror. Despite the absence of any makeup at all—whatever had survived the day had not survived Johnny—she was surprised to see how young she looked even in the bright afternoon light. Sparkling eyes, pink cheeks, and a rosy, slightly swollen mouth definitely conveyed an illusion of youth, she reflected as she patted powder onto her nose and smoothed deep pink color on her lips. There. She looked herself again, only better: carefree, slightly mussed, happy. Snapping her compact closed and returning the items to her purse, Rachel reflected that a wild, passionate affair with Johnny Harris was the best beauty boost she had ever tried. If only she could bottle him, she thought with a wry inward smile, she could make a fortune. Her eyes strayed to where he sat with his feet on the bench and his rump on the top of the picnic table, tossing what she assumed were bits of Twinkie to the battling ducks. Great sex? Oh, yes. Not that she intended to admit it. Not to him. He was full enough of himself as it was.

One blue pump lay on its side on the floorboard, and if she remembered correctly, its mate had fallen on the gravel outside. Scooting out of the car, she picked up her shoe from the ground, balanced on one leg like a stork, and thrust her foot into it, then stood on the opposite leg as she donned the other. Wadding her ruined garments into a tight little ball, she walked over to a nearby waste can and tossed them in. Feeling absurdly self-conscious about her lack of underwear, she went to join Johnny.

" 'A loaf of bread, a jug of wine, and thou,' " he said, glancing around at her as she reached the picnic table.

"Don't you mean a package of Twinkies and a can of Coke?" Rachel climbed up beside him and sat down, accepting the aforementioned foodstuffs as he handed them over.

Johnny grinned. "Loses something in the translation, doesn't it?"

"I haven't eaten one of these since I was a little girl." Rachel pulled at the package with her nails. The plastic wrap held fast.

"Here, let me." Johnny took the package from her, put it between his teeth, and tore it open without difficulty. Passing one of the golden cakes over, he lifted the other from its wrapping and took a huge bite.

"Hey, that's mine!" Rachel frowned at him even as she delicately nibbled at the end of the cake she held.

"I'm starving. I gave half of mine to the ducks." The plaintive note to his voice made her smile. He crooked a finger beneath the ring on top of the Coke, popped it open, and passed the can over to her.

Rachel obligingly took a swallow. "I'm going to get sick if I eat this junk," she said, taking another bite out of her Twinkie.

"Danger is the spice of life."

"I thought variety was."

"That, too."

He took one more giant bite and threw the tiny end section to the ducks clustered at the water's edge. With a squawk and a great flapping of wings, three of them converged, battling for the prize. A fourth one, more cunning or luckier than his mates, grabbed the tidbit and fled.

Johnny took a gulp from his Coke, set the can back on the table, and wiped his mouth with the back of his hand.

"Rachel?"

"Yes?"

"Now what?"

Rachel finished her Twinkie, delicately brushed the corners of her mouth with her fingertips to make sure no errant crumbs lurked, and looked at him.

"What do you mean?"

"I mean us."

"Us?"

"Yeah. Assuming there is an us. I'd hate to think that you see me as just another easy lay."

A half-smile twisted his mouth, but Rachel sensed the seriousness behind his words. Nervously, she crumpled the discarded Twinkie wrappings into a compact ball.

"I haven't really thought about it."

"Maybe you should."

Rachel dug her nails into the wadded plastic wrap, not caring that its stickiness transferred to her fingertips, and turned to look at him directly.

"Are you saying that you want us to—date?"

"Date." His mouth quirked. "Now there's a word. Yeah, something like that."

"We could have dinner." The words almost stuck in her throat, so difficult were they to get out. More than anything in the world, she wanted a relationship, a real relationship, with him. But imagining any kind of mutual future for the two of them was so mind-boggling that it was almost impossible.

"Dinner would be nice. For a start." Johnny got down off the table with easy grace, turned, put his hands on her waist, and lifted her. Rachel squealed as she was unexpectedly swung high in the air and held at arms' length above him. Her hands grabbed for his brawny upper arms to steady herself. He was grinning up at her, clearly experiencing no difficulty at all in holding her aloft, and she was once again reminded of how very much stronger he was than she. The golden afternoon sunlight played over his face, lending a warm glow to the smoky blue eyes, gleaming off the swarthiness of his skin and the whiteness of his teeth as he laughed up at her. He looked so handsome in that moment that he stole her breath.

With a sickening lurch of her stomach, Rachel realized that she was falling in love.

"Put me down," she said, her voice harsh.

"Uh-unh," he said, teasing as he continued to hold her high in the air. To prove his complete power over her, he started to walk toward the car without lowering her by so much as an inch. "We're going to dinner."

"Please put me down." She was panicking, but she couldn't help it. The thought of being in love with Johnny Harris scared her to death.

"Persuade me."

"Put me down!" The sharpness in her tone made him frown. He put her down. With her feet on terra firma again, Rachel expected to feel better. But she didn't.

"What's the matter?" There was concern in his voice.

Rachel was already walking away from him toward the car. She knew she was behaving badly, but she couldn't help it.

"Rachel!"

She needed time alone, time to sort out this appalling development, time to consider her options and decide what to do. Lusting after Johnny was bad enough. Loving him, with all the complications that would ensue, was infinitely worse.

"I—my sister Becky is home. Did I tell you that? I can't go to dinner, or anywhere else. I have to go home. I forgot all about Becky." She spoke over her shoulder, her voice jerky, as she pulled the door open and got into the car.

"What does Becky being home have to do with us going to dinner?" He leaned in the open doorway, his arm on the roof preventing her from closing the door. Rachel looked up at the handsome face and frowning blue eyes and felt dazzled by the sheer force of her impulse to agree to anything he wished. She felt like an explorer who had stepped unwarily into quicksand. Now she was in way over her head and sinking fast.

"Michael, her husband, told her he wants a divorce. She's upset. I need to go home to be with her."

"The same Michael that you were in love with all those years ago?"

Rachel stared at him. "How did you know about that?"

"I remember when you brought him home with you that summer. You know why I remember? 'Cause I was jealous. The one bright spot in that whole hellish fall was when he dumped you for your sister."

"I don't believe that."

"Believe it. It's true." His lips compressed, and he studied her for a minute. "I've wanted you for a long time, Rachel. No matter how many girls I had, I was always aware of you and what you were doing. Now, how about dinner? Gino's has great catfish."

"I can't. Becky is so upset. . . ." Rachel's voice trailed off. His confession had merely served to underscore what she already knew: the situation between them was becoming far more serious than she had anticipated it would.

He stared at her for a moment longer without speaking. Then he straightened, closed her door for her, came around the car, and got in beside her.

Rachel started the car.

"Bullshit," he said as she shifted into drive and swung around in a wide arc heading back toward the highway.

"What?" she glanced over at him nervously. His lips were tight, and his brows almost met over his nose in a winged line of displeasure.

"You heard me. I said that's bullshit."

"It is not. It's the truth. Becky is home, and—"

"She may be home, and her husband may want a divorce, but that doesn't have a damned thing to do with the way you're looking—or not looking—at me." The cold, measured quality to his words was more cutting than outright fury would have been. Rachel bit her lip and concentrated on her driving. Pulling out onto the highway from the narrow road that cut through the woods, she glanced over at Johnny.

"You never did answer my question, Rachel," he said silkily before she could say anything, turning his head to meet her eyes.

"What question?"

"For God's sake, keep your eyes on the road!"

As she jerked her attention back to the road in response to this furious outburst, he was silent for a moment. He continued in a voice so soft that she had to strain to hear. "Are you ashamed of me, Rachel?"

"No!" Her gaze swung toward him again. Horrified that he should believe such a thing, she said even more forcefully, "No!"

"I don't believe you." His tone was brutal.

"It's the truth!" They were passing the 7-Eleven now, turning down the road that led toward the school. Rachel knew that she owed him an explanation, but she had to sort her feelings out for herself first. Being in love with Johnny Harris was no simple thing, especially in Tylerville. The potential repercussions were horrendous.

"Is it?"

"All right!" she burst out. "All right! This is a messy situation. You know it is. I'm a teacher. I used to be *your* teacher. Did you know my contract says I can be dismissed for moral turpitude? I'm not any too positive that having an affair with you would not constitute moral turpitude, for starters. You're five years younger than I am, for another thing. How does that look? And you—and you . . ." Her voice trailed off as she found herself quite unable to put how the townspeople saw him into words.

"And I'm an ex-con and the local pariah?" he finished for her. Rachel glanced over, stricken dumb at something in his tone, to find that his eyes were glittering savagely at her. "Good enough to hump on the side, but not quite suitable for a lady like you to be seen with in public."

Rachel bit her lip with helpless misery.

"Christ, watch the road!" he barked, grabbing the steering wheel and jerking the car back over into their lane when it would have wandered across the median line.

For a few moments after that, neither of them said anything. Rachel, recalled to the need to focus on her driving, gave her full attention to the road until she had safely turned into the school and was pulling up beside his motorcycle. She shifted into park and turned to face him, both hands still on the wheel.

"Johnny, please believe me, I am not ashamed of you. I just need a little time, a little space."

"Space." His mouth twisted as he met her look for a sizzling instant. Then his hand was on the door handle, and he pulled it down and got out of the car. Once outside, he leaned in the open door to look at her.

"You take all the time and all the space you need, teacher. Then when—if—you decide you can handle this thing between us, you give me a call, okay?" The icy anger lacing his words flicked Rachel like a whip.

"Johnny—" she began imploringly, not even knowing what she meant to say. But he didn't give her a chance to finish. He slammed the door, opened the back, pulled out his jacket, and shrugged into it. Then he turned to his motorcycle, yanked on his helmet, and straddled the machine all in less time than she would have thought possible.

She was still sitting in her car trying to think of exactly how to phrase what she wanted to say to him when he kicked the engine into life and roared away without a backward glance.

25

$\mathcal{F}$riday was one of the most miserable days Rachel had ever spent in her life. First of all, just as she had known would happen, word of her going off with Johnny was all over the school. The moment she had arrived in her homeroom, every single pair of teenage eyes was fixed on her in fascination. Her conviction that she was the object of gossip grew even stronger as the kids and even some of the teachers fell silent when she passed by various chatting groups in the hallways and teachers' lounge and monitored tables at lunch. But she didn't know for certain until just after the dismissal bell rang and Mr. James appeared in her doorway as her students streamed through it.

Rachel was gathering up the items she needed to take home with her over the holiday weekend, but she stopped to glance inquiringly at the gray-suited principal.

"Have big plans for the weekend, Rachel?" Mr. James asked, stepping into the room. He was nearing retirement age, but his stern, nononsense demeanor made him seem much older. With his thick, slicked-back iron-gray hair and stocky build and his tendency to mumble, he had always reminded Rachel of Marlon Brando's interpretation of the Godfather.

"Not really." She smiled at him as he walked over and watched her stuff compositions that needed deciphering as much as grading into a folder. "What about you?"

Mr. James shrugged. "Not really. Bess"—Bess was his wife of forty years—"and I are just going to stay home and relax. None of the children are coming in."

"That sounds nice." Rachel gathered up the last of the papers, the folder, and some books she needed to prepare for next week's lessons and stood waiting. Mr. James never engaged in small talk. He had sought her out for a purpose, and she was pretty sure she knew what that purpose was.

"We're looking forward to it." He cleared his throat, and Rachel knew that whatever he had sought her out to say was coming. "Some of the girls told Mrs. Wylie"—Mrs. Wylie was the girls' counselor—"a rather disturbing story today."

Rachel raised her eyebrows.

"They said that that Harris boy came to school to see you yesterday. That you drove off with him in your car."

"Johnny Harris used to be a student of mine," Rachel said coolly. Though she had expected to find herself engaged in such a conversation, her hackles rose nevertheless in instinctive resentment. To have her actions questioned at all did not go down well, and to hear Johnny referred to so scathingly as "that Harris boy" everywhere she went was beginning to severely irritate her.

"Then it's true?" Mr. James looked at her searchingly. His eyes gleamed at her from behind his black-framed glasses.

"That he came to school to see me and that we went for a ride in my car? Yes."

"It was a one-time thing, I hope. You must know that we can't have someone like him hanging around the school."

"What do you mean, 'someone like him'?" A hint of anger sharpened Rachel's voice. Mr. James looked surprised.

"A man who has been known to prey on teenage girls, of course. We have a duty to the parents—"

"Johnny Harris would no more prey on teenage girls than I would! I have known him since he was a teenager himself, and I am as convinced of his innocence in Marybeth Edwards's death as I am of—of yours, for want of a better comparison. He—"

"He was convicted of her murder by a court of law and duly sentenced. That he has paid his debt to society in no way abrogates our duty to our students or their parents. We must protect the children entrusted to our care. Even if it goes against how we feel about the possible lack of justice meted out to him ten years ago."

The gentleness of his tone robbed his rebuke of much of its sting. Nevertheless, Rachel grew blazingly angry.

"Is my job at risk if Johnny comes to school again, Mr. James?"

"You know as well as I do that you have tenure, Rachel. I appeal to your conscience rather than your fear of unemployment."

"My conscience is clear, I assure you. Now, if you'll excuse me."

"Certainly. I'm sorry if I upset you, but you know what they say about a word to the wise. I trust it will prove sufficient in this instance."

"Have a nice holiday, Mr. James," Rachel said tightly, and walked past the principal out the door.

Her anger had calmed somewhat by the time she got home. Mr. James's attitude was not unexpected, after all, and it was one of the reasons why she had decided she could not let her relationship with Johnny go any further without a great deal of very serious thought. She considered the restoration of her normally placid disposition a good thing as soon as she saw the sleek black Lexus parked beneath the porte cochere.

Michael had come, probably to fetch Becky and the girls back home.

"Michael's here." Her mother greeted her with a warning hiss as soon as Rachel walked in the door. From the side yard came the sounds of her nieces shrieking with laughter as they engaged in some sort of rowdy play. Glancing out the pantry window as she set her books down on the table, Rachel saw that Tilda had joined them for a lively game of badminton.

"Do the girls know?"

Elisabeth nodded. "Tilda's keeping them out of the way. I think he wants Becky to come back to him."

"What does Becky want?" Rachel opened the refrigerator and reached inside for a single-serving carton of orange juice. Bought for the girls, the drinks had instantly become a favorite of everyone in the household. Rachel inserted the little straw, then drank with appreciation.

Elisabeth shook her head. "I don't know. They've been in the library for almost an hour, and I haven't heard so much as a peep. I wanted to stay close in case Becky should need me. She gets upset so easily, you know. I just hope Michael's come to his senses. I'm sure Becky will forgive him, if so."

Rachel grimaced doubtfully and took another sip of juice. "I'm going upstairs to change and say hi to Daddy. Yell if you need me."

Elisabeth nodded. "Oh, by the way, Rob called last night, after you went up to bed. I told him you'd call him back today. And Ben called from the store."

Rachel, already on her way through the doorway, hesitated, glancing back over her shoulder. "Has anyone else called?"

Her mother shook her head. "No."

Reminded of Elisabeth's past perfidy in the matter of Johnny's calls, Rachel turned to fix her mother with a stern look.

"Are you sure?"

"Of course I'm sure."

"Johnny Harris came by to see me at school yesterday. He told me that he tried to call me several times this week, only to have you tell him that I wasn't home."

"If I said that, then I'm sure it was true." Elisabeth sounded defensive.

"You never bothered to tell me that he called, Mother."

"I probably forgot. I can forget things, you know. Especially with everything that's been going on around here lately. Why, it's a wonder that I remember anything at all." Elisabeth's hands fluttered helplessly, but Rachel, who knew her mother well, knew that she was about as helpless as a pit bull.

"You never forgot anything in your life, and you know it. I am a grown woman, Mother. Who calls me, or who I see, is my concern, not yours. I thought I'd made that clear before."

"Are you expecting that Harris boy to call you?" Elisabeth's voice was sharp.

"That's not the point, Mother."

"It is as far as I'm concerned. What kind of mother would I be if I wasn't worried about you? You're my daughter, Rachel, no matter how old you are. I hate to see you getting yourself into a difficult situation."

Rachel sighed. "I am not getting myself into a difficult situation."

"I'd call sleeping with that Harris boy a difficult situation."

"Mother!" Rachel was genuinely shocked, as much by her mother's outspokenness as by her knowledge, and it showed in her widened eyes as they met Elisabeth's determined ones.

"Did you think I didn't know, Rachel? I'm quite intelligent enough to add two and two."

Rachel could feel herself blushing as her mother's gaze bore into hers, but she refused to let her eyes drop.

"Do you deny it?" Elisabeth asked.

"I don't deny anything," Rachel replied, regaining a grip on her slipping poise. "Or admit anything, either. It's none of your business, Mother."

"None of my business when my daughter is having an affair with a murderer! I suppose you expect me to ignore it when he takes a knife to you, too?"

"Johnny never—"

"Pshaw!" her mother interrupted with robust indignation. "You can no more be sure of that than I can be that your daddy's getting better. I may believe so, but it's always possible that it's wishful thinking on my part. And so it may well be with you."

Mother and daughter were silent for several moments in which the undeniable truth of that statement hung in the air. Then Rachel's lips tightened.

"I'm going to change, Mother," she said, and turned, starting up the stairs. Before she had ascended more than a quarter of the way, the library door opened.

Rachel swung around to discover Michael framed in the doorway, with Becky, white-faced but tearless, behind him. Below her, Elisabeth too had turned to face her son-in-law.

For a moment Michael and the two women stared at each other without speaking. Michael looked far older than he had when Rachel had seen him at Christmas. He had not been able to come down at Easter or over the Fourth of July, when Becky had brought the girls to spend a week with their aunt and grandparents. Dark rings around his eyes spoke of sleepless nights, and the wings of gray behind his ears reminded her that he had celebrated his fortieth birthday this past June. His skin was pale, as befitted a man who only rarely sought the sun, and a faint suggestion of five o'clock shadow roughened his square jaw. Tall and thin, darkly handsome in his blue suit, he was the very picture of an affluent WASP lawyer. She found it hard to believe she had ever been in love with him.

Judging from his expression, it was clear that he was not pleased to find himself confronting the speculative stares of his mother- and sister-in-law.

"Hello, Rachel," he said at last, having presumably greeted Elisabeth when he had arrived. Rachel's eyes strayed past him to Becky, who looked stricken as she gazed at her husband's back, and she barely nodded in response. It was clear from Becky's demeanor that, whatever had been said between them, their differences had not been patched up.

Despite the affection she had long cherished for Michael, in this moment of crisis Rachel was fiercely on Becky's side.

"Can I get you some coffee or a sandwich, Michael?" Elisabeth asked somewhat nervously. Unlike Rachel's, her view of her younger daughter was blocked by her son-in-law's body.

"No, thank you, Elisabeth. I've got a dinner engagement. I'll say good-bye to the girls and be on my way."

"Say good-bye to the girls!" Becky laughed, the sound high-pitched and near hysterical as she clasped her hands in front of her small bosom. Michael swung around to face her. From her vantage point on the stairs, Rachel could see the look of near-hatred her sister shot him. Ten years ago, Becky had loved Michael so desperately that she had glowed whenever she so much as spoke his name. The contrast between how they had been together then and how things were between them now made Rachel angry and sad at the same time. Was nothing in life permanent?

"You say that so calmly! Don't you care what a divorce will do to them?" Becky's voice was shrill.

"Children adjust," Michael ground out. Tension radiated from his very stance. Rachel was surprised that his fists were clenched at his sides. The Michael she had known had always been so controlled—she didn't remember seeing him ever lose his temper. But then, she had only really known him over the course of one summer, in a courtship situation. Perhaps the young man she thought she had fallen in love with had been a product of her own imagination.

"You're their father!" It was a cry from Becky's heart. Michael stiffened, then turned abruptly away from his wife, strode past Elisabeth and Rachel without another word, and banged out the back door.

For a moment the three women remained frozen in place. Then Rachel recovered sufficiently to hurry toward her stricken sister. Elisabeth was ahead of her, sweeping Becky up in her arms.

"He came to see how I felt about selling the h-house!" Becky wailed. "He's going to spend the night in a hotel and come back tomorrow to talk about it. He said—he said a good night's sleep might help me put things in their proper perspective."

"That son of a bitch," Elisabeth said fiercely. Rachel, who had never heard her mother swear before, nodded in heartfelt agreement. She leaned her head against Becky's in silent sympathy as her sister burst into tears.

26

*T*ylerville's annual Labor Day picnic was held on Saturday night, and as usual almost everyone in town turned out for it. It was a festive event, beginning at six o'clock sharp with a parade and ending at twelve midnight with a dazzling burst of fireworks. A local band played everything from country to rock classics from the gazebo in the center of the town square. Teens sat cross-legged on blankets or sprawled on their stomachs in the grass in front of the gazebo, shouting requests at the band. With nearby streets closed to traffic, younger children ran wild, chasing one another and evading their exasperated parents with practiced ease. Adults filled up on the potluck supper in the garage of the new fire station adjacent to the square. Highlights of the evening included the Tylerville Civic Club–sponsored chasing of a greased pig, and a hot-air balloon ride for the bargain price of one dollar. By the time Rachel arrived, at a quarter to seven, the line for the balloon ride was easily a hundred and fifty strong. Apparently no one was deterred by the fact that the tethered balloon went up for only about twenty feet before it was hauled back in again for the next group of riders.

Rachel's party included Rob, Becky, the girls, and her mother. She had been of two minds about whether to accept Rob's invitation, but when he had very decently included the rest of her family in his offer of escort, she saw no reason to turn him down. Becky needed the distraction of an outing, and her daughters, wilder than usual in the crisis that was engulfing their young lives, needed an outlet for their excessive energy. If Rachel's heart ached for Johnny, she refused to dwell on the pain. It would go away—it had to. Her mother's words about wishful thinking—extrapolated to include not just the subject of Johnny's guilt or innocence but the long-term prospects of any relationship they might attempt—had fallen on fertile ground.

"Aunt Rachel, can we go on the balloon ride?" Loren, age five, tugged on Rachel's hand excitedly.

"After we eat," Becky interposed before Rachel could answer in the affirmative. Rachel had taken the older girls to a movie earlier in the afternoon while Becky and Michael had talked further. Elisabeth, who had kept two-year-old Katie, gave Rachel to understand that the visit had not been a success. Becky had run up to her room in tears not fifteen minutes after it began, and Michael had icily promised to return again the next day. But by the time Rob came to collect them for the picnic, Becky had herself under control, and except for a slight redness around her eyes, a stranger would have found no indication that anything was amiss with her. Rob, apprised of the situation by Rachel, obviously found Becky's courage commendable, and he spent much of the drive to town and the subsequent walk to the square telling foolish, corny jokes in an attempt to lift her spirits. By the time they joined the throng around the supper tables, Rachel thought that if she had to listen to one more such idiocy, she would dump her paper cup of iced tea over his head.

But Becky was relaxing and even smiling a little under his verbal nonsense. It occurred to Rachel that she might be in danger of losing yet another man to her sister. It also occurred to her that this time, with this man, she didn't really care.

"Katie, no! That's hot!" Rachel grabbed for her youngest niece, who was lunging for the silver coffee dispenser set up at the end of a long, heavily laden table. Barely catching the toddler in time, she hauled the struggling Katie onto her hip and pacified her with a brownie purloined from the dessert table. They were twenty-five cents each, but the line to pay was long, and she decided to let Katie eat the treat there and then, and confess and pay for it when she paid for her own plate.

"Let me take her, Rache," Becky murmured when Rachel rejoined the group. Katie, her face wreathed in chocolate icing and smiles, shook her head vigorously at her mother.

"Katie stay with Aunt Wachel," she said firmly. Rachel laughed and hugged her niece, not even minding when Katie patted her cheek with a gooey hand. Becky, with an exasperated cluck, used her paper napkin to remove the worst of the mess from the vicinity of the child's mouth. By then, the napkin was so dirty that to attempt to wipe Rachel's cheek with it would only have made the problem worse.

"She's got chocolate on your face," Rob whispered to Rachel when Becky's attention was claimed by their mother.

"That's all right. It'll wash off."

Rob used his own napkin to rub the icing from Rachel's face, and she smiled at him for his trouble.

"Your sister's children are real cute," he told her.

"Aren't they?" Rachel kissed Katie's plump baby cheek to prove it and picked up a plate to serve herself from the buffet. Around her, friends and neighbors called greetings to the three Grant women, and there was much exclaiming over Becky, who didn't get back to Tylerville that often, and her children. Becky looked very pretty in her ankle-length green sundress with its bare shoulders and back. Rachel, who had chosen to wear navy shorts and a bright yellow T-shirt, could not help but notice the male attention that Becky attracted on all sides. If Michael was no longer interested in his wife, she would not be left to wither on the vine. Rachel was glad to discover that her sister's appeal to men pleased rather than pricked her, as it might once have done.

Rachel chatted to all and sundry and obligingly turned when requested so that Katie could be viewed and admired. Katie, bless her, had decided for some unknown reason to be good. She laughed and clapped her hands and said "Hi!" to everyone who spoke to her. "Little angel," "What a poppet!" and "Look at that sweet child!" were some of the comments that came Katie's way. Rachel, fielding compliments and diverting grabby little fingers as best she could, discovered that balancing a squirming two-year-old on one hip while trying to fill a plate at the same time was no easy feat. Fortunately, Rob, seeing her dilemma, took her plate and filled it at her direction. Lisa and Loren were old enough to manage on their own, with a little help from their mother and grandmother, and eventually the whole group was able to retire to one of the dozens of tables set up under the trees.

Rachel relinquished Katie and sat down with an inner sigh of relief. The child seemed to weigh a ton, despite her diminutive size. It was still daylight, as it would be until almost nine o'clock, but the fierce heat of the day had gentled into a comfortable warmth, and a soft breeze fanned Rachel's hair back from her face. It was pleasant to relax with family and friends, pleasant to listen to the music that was just the right distance away, pleasant to watch the children laughing and playing tag and hide-and-go-seek across the square. Pleasant even to cut up food for the delectation of her smallest niece.

"I want another bownie," Katie said, eyeing the plenty before her with disfavor.

"After you eat," Rachel told her, reducing the child's ham to bite-size pieces.

"No, now!"

"Katie, behave." That was Becky, intervening from across the table.

"Mom, she's not going to have a fit, is she?" Lisa asked in an undertone, sounding disgusted. Like the rest of the family, she was well aware of her youngest sister's propensity for tantrums when life did not please her.

"Bownie!"

"Mom . . ."

"Aunt Rachel, I've finished. Can we go ride in the balloon now?" Loren bounded up from the table and came around to Rachel's side.

"Let Aunt Rachel eat first, dear," Becky said.

"Aunt Rachel—"

"We will, sweetheart, I promise. But I am starving, and if I don't eat, I'll probably just dry up and blow away."

"Will not!"

"Loren, run and play." There was a slightly harassed note to Becky's voice.

"Bownie!"

"Katie, dear, won't you eat up your nice ham for Grandma? Or how about a bite of macaroni and cheese?" Elisabeth held a forkful of her own macaroni and cheese across the table.

"Bownie!" said Katie, scowling ferociously at her grandmother.

"Katie, hush and eat!" Becky sounded tense as she frowned at her youngest. Seated between Rachel and Rob, Katie looked adorable with her blond pigtails and blue gingham pinafore, even with her lower lip thrust out and her small arms crossed defiantly over her chest. Lisa, seated between her mother and grandmother opposite Katie, and Loren, still dancing around the table, gave their little sister identical disgusted looks.

"Bownie! Bownie, bownie, bownie!" It was a piercing shriek. Heads turned at surrounding tables.

"Mom, can't you do something?" Lisa asked in a low voice, scrunching down in her seat. Loren stood still to watch the fun.

"Katie Lynn Hennessey, that is quite enough! Young ladies do not behave that way." Elisabeth tried to quell her headstrong granddaughter with a stern tone and a shake of her head.

"Please, Mom? Before she has a fit?" Lisa's plea was urgent.

"What do you want me to do?" Becky said to Lisa through her teeth. Then, "Rachel, look out!"

But Becky's warning came too late. Katie, screaming, "Bownie, bownie, bownie!" at the top of her lungs, knocked her filled plate to one side. It skittered along the side of the table and overturned in Rob's lap.

"Oh, no!" Rachel gasped.

"Oh, dear!" Elisabeth moaned.

"Katie Hennessey!" Becky hissed.

"Damn it!" Rob bellowed.

The cries of distress were simultaneous. Rob jumped up and brushed as much of the mess as he could from his perfectly pressed khaki slacks. Rachel, grabbing a screaming, kicking Katie before she could cause more chaos, looked at the damage to Rob's trousers and was appalled. Ham, mashed potatoes, gravy, macaroni and cheese, cherry Jell-O, and bits of fruit salad all clung to the expensive twill.

"For shame!" Becky said, coming around the table to claim her bellowing youngest. For an instant, just an instant, Rob glared at Katie with real fury in his eyes. Rachel saw his expression and was taken aback. Katie was just a baby, after all, and her action was nothing more and nothing less than babies do every day. It had certainly not been deliberate. Was this the man she had thought would be a good, patient father?

"I'm so sorry," Becky apologized to Rob, while at the same time doing everything she could to hang on to her child, who was caught up in the throes of a full-blown tantrum. Elisabeth, attempting to come to Becky's aid, whispered, "Naughty, naughty!" and shook her finger at Katie. The older girls, transparently embarrassed by their sister's lapse, slunk out of sight.

"Don't worry about it. It wasn't your fault." Rob had recovered his suave good manners and was ruefully dabbing a napkin at the mess on his pants. Rachel, wetting her napkin in Katie's glass of water, bent to help him.

The roar of an engine drew her eyes past Rob's leg to the barricades that closed off the street at the edge of the firehouse parking lot. That she had heard the sound at all over Katie's blubbering, the caterwauling of the band, the hiss of the hot-air balloon, and the chattering of her neighbors at the surrounding tables surprised her. She must be somehow attuned to the sound . . .

. . . of Johnny's motorcycle. Because, of course, that was what it was. He turned the machine in a wide arc at the barricade and headed back down the open street away from the convivial gathering of friends. A woman was mounted behind him. Her helmet hid her face, but from her build and the strands of curly, blond hair that blew in the wind, Rachel concluded that Johnny's companion was Glenda Watkins.

At the knowledge that it could have been herself, Rachel felt heartsick.

27

"**Y**ou got any more beer?" Johnny, sprawled out on the dilapidated couch in the living room of Glenda's trailer, felt restless. The TV was on, blaringly loud as it broadcast a *Wild Kingdom* special on poisonous butterflies of the Amazon or some such thing. Stretched out on the floor, his head propped on his hands, Jeremy watched, transfixed. Jake, four, sat contentedly in Johnny's lap and stared at the TV, though Johnny was pretty sure the kid had about as much idea of what was happening on the screen as he did.

"In the fridge." Glenda was in the bathroom giving her two girls a bath. Their every splash and giggle could be heard in the living room— the trailer was that small. It boggled Johnny's mind how Glenda could live in a space consisting of two tiny bedrooms, a living room barely big enough for a couch, an easy chair, and a TV, a minuscule kitchen, and an equally minuscule bathroom, with four kids and not go insane.

"Jeremy, would you do me a favor and get me a beer?"

Silence greeted this request. Jeremy was too caught up in his program to hear. Johnny thought about trying again, at a greatly increased volume, but then decided against it. Let the kid watch TV in peace.

"Come on, pardner, got to scoot," he said to Jake, who obligingly permitted himself to be set down on the couch. Johnny got up, stretched, and walked into the kitchen in his socks to get himself a beer. His sneakers had been lost somewhere beneath the couch, removed earlier by Jake, who was developing a fascination with shoe strings.

Opening the refrigerator door, Johnny saw one intact six-pack with some surprise. He could have sworn there had been two. How many beers had he drunk?

Did it matter anyway? Johnny mused as he pulled one free of the rings and popped the top.

"Hey, Johnny, throw me a Coke!" Jeremy called over his shoulder.

"No Coke!" Glenda shouted from the bathroom.

Jeremy shrugged. Johnny poured the kid a glass of milk and took it over to him. It was really touching how Glenda tried so hard to be a good mother to her kids. Making them drink milk instead of pop, for instance. Giving every one of them a bath every night. Reading books to the younger ones, though Glenda had never read anything more complicated than a cookbook herself, to Johnny's knowledge. Making sure that Jeremy and Ashley, at six the older girl, did their homework on school nights. Glenda hadn't been raised with such care. Johnny knew that her childhood had been almost as rough as his own, and he thought a lot of her for trying to give her kids better.

At least, since they'd started going out, he'd made sure there was always food in the refrigerator. He'd gone hungry himself enough times to be unable to stand the idea of kids not having enough to eat.

"Ugh," Jeremy said without looking up as Johnny set the glass on the floor beside him.

"You're welcome," Johnny answered dryly, and settled back down on the couch to drink his beer. Jake immediately climbed onto his lap again, resting his curly blond head against Johnny's chest. Poor kid, he didn't see much of his dad, and he was clearly hungry for a man's attention.

"Tell us a story, tell us a story!" Ashley and her sister erupted from the bathroom, galloped the few feet down the hall to the living room, and leaped on Johnny. Freshly bathed, with their blond hair pinned on top of their heads and wearing sweet little ruffled nightgowns, they were so cute that he forgave them for spilling his beer.

"Not a scary one," three-year-old Lindsay said solemnly as she claimed the knee that Jake wasn't using. Jake, jealous of his prerogatives, pushed his sister. Lindsay pushed back.

"One about monsters," Ashley said wickedly. Ashley was curled up as close to Johnny's side as she could get.

"No scary ones!" Lindsay screamed, pushing at her sister.

"Could you guys please shut up?" This request was made by Jeremy in a loud tone.

"All right, bedtime!" Glenda came into the room, clapping her hands. Her T-shirt was soaked, and so was the front of her jeans. She wasn't wearing a bra. Johnny noticed that fact without the interest it should have provoked, though Glenda was a voluptuous woman. Damn it to hell anyway, what was wrong with him? But he knew the answer, and it didn't make him happy: Glenda wasn't the woman he wanted.

The woman he wanted had been at that damned town picnic—the picnic that probably would have run him out on a rail if he had dared show his face at it—with another man. The respectable, solid citizen type. The prick.

Johnny took another swig of beer.

"Aw, Mom!" four voices said in chorus.

"I mean it! Hit the beds! I'm gonna count to three—and the last kid in has to sit in the middle of the back seat tomorrow when we go to church."

That produced immediate results. The trio on the couch scrambled for their beds, and even Jeremy got up and turned off the TV.

"It's just a trick, Mom. You know I always gotta sit in the middle to keep the little kids from fighting," he said gloomily.

"You're always the last kid in bed," Glenda retorted, ruffling his hair as she walked by him toward the bedroom that opened directly off the living room, the larger one that she shared with the two girls.

From down the hall, Jake called plaintively, "Mommy, I'm scared!"

"Go on to him, Jeremy," Glenda said over her shoulder.

"Do I have to?"

"Yes!"

"Shit!" Jeremy said under his breath. Fortunately for him, his mother didn't hear.

Johnny finished his beer and started on another to the sound of Glenda's voice reading her girls a bedtime story. From the opposite end of the trailer, he could hear Jeremy reading to Jake. Ever since he'd been coming around, that was how they'd done it: Glenda had read to the girls, and Jeremy had read to Jake.

When Glenda finally emerged from the bedroom, she smiled at him and put a finger to her lips as she closed the door. Then she walked past the silent TV and down the hall to say good night to the boys.

Johnny drained the last drops from his can and walked into the kitchen to get a replacement. It was getting harder and harder to get the cans free of the damned little plastic rings, he discovered as he yanked at one. The remaining three, still looped together, dropped off the refrigerator shelf right onto his toe.

"Ouch! Goddamn it to hell!" The beer he held in his hand crashed to the floor alongside the others and rolled away. Johnny hopped about on one foot cursing as Glenda emerged from the back bedroom to glare at him.

"Hush!"

"Hurt my damned toe!"

"Shhh!"

Johnny picked up the half-empty six-pack. It hung by a loop from one finger as he gingerly tried to set his foot on the ground.

"Want to watch a tape?" Glenda, callously unsympathetic to his pain, stood in front of the TV holding up a videocassette.

Johnny grunted, stuck the beers back on the shelf, and retrieved his fallen one, which had rolled partway under a cabinet. He shut the refrigerator door and limped over to collapse on the couch. He massaged his big toe through the thick white athletic sock. Damned thing was probably broken. Glenda, meanwhile, slid the tape into the VCR and curled up beside him.

The movie was one he'd already seen, and Glenda, tenderly rubbing her hand along his thigh as she stared at the screen, was building up to something he didn't particularly feel like doing. With one foot, he probed unobtrusively beneath the couch for his sneakers. There they were!

"Gotta go, babe," he said, bending to retrieve his shoes and slide them back on. He tied the laces, then took a final swig from his beer before setting it down on the floor.

"Now?" She was frowning.

"Wolf's home alone. If I don't go let him out, he'll do a horse pile in the living room."

"You ought to house-train that dog."

Johnny grunted and stood up. Surprisingly, the movement made him feel kind of woozy, and he staggered.

"How many beers have you had?" Glenda stood up, too, and steadied him with a hand on his arm.

Johnny shrugged and, stepping away from her touch, fished in his pocket for his keys.

Glenda walked over to the refrigerator and looked inside, then came back to Johnny, shaking her head.

"Uh-unh, you ain't goin' nowhere, friend," she said, deftly removing the keys he had just extracted from his pocket.

"Give me back my keys!"

"I won't!" Glenda retreated, holding the keys behind her back. "You know, you drink too much."

"I don't either. Give me those keys." Johnny walked over to her, wrapped his arms around her in a bear hug, and tried to wrestle the keys from her fingers.

"You get caught for drunken driving, they'll send you back to jail." That gave him pause. "I'm not drunk."

"Yes you are."

He let go of her and collapsed again onto the couch. "So I'll spend the night," he said, knowing what she would think of that idea.

"You cain't! Tom"—Tom was her almost ex-husband—"might find out and use it against me in the divorce."

"So give me my keys."

Glenda stood there for a moment, undecided. She was chewing on a fingernail, his keys dangling from her other hand. He could lunge and get them, but he didn't feel like lunging, and besides, he didn't want to hurt Glenda. As unfocused as he was feeling, he just might miscalculate his own strength.

"I'll call you a ride," she said after a minute. Johnny pondered this surprisingly sensible suggestion. A taxi would be a good idea, he thought. He really had quite a buzz going.

Glenda disappeared into her bedroom to use the phone.

Johnny leaned back against the cushions. The couch had a broken leg—it was propped up at that end with a dictionary and a paperback romance—and a green chenille bedspread was spread over it as a kind of makeshift slipcover, but it was surprisingly comfortable. If he wasn't careful, he just might fall asleep.

"Don't go to sleep," Glenda said, plopping back down beside him and staring at the TV again. "It'd take a bulldozer to move you."

"I won't."

For a moment neither of them said anything as Glenda watched the TV and Johnny stared at nothing. Then Glenda glanced sideways at him.

"How come you don't wanna do it?"

"Do what?"

"You know."

Johnny did. He shrugged and slid his arm around her. "What makes you think I don't?"

"I can tell." Her hand slid over his crotch in a way that was more matter-of-fact than suggestive.

Stung, Johnny caught her hand, removed it to her own lap, and dropped his arm from around her shoulders.

"Maybe I've had too much to drink, like you said."

"That never slowed you down before."

"Glenda, I was eleven years younger back then. Nothing slowed me down."

For a few minutes neither of them said anything. Johnny thought maybe she'd gotten engrossed in her movie and hoped that he'd heard all he was going to hear on the subject.

"Johnny?"

"What?"

"Can I ask you somethin'?"

"Short of putting a pillow over your face, I don't guess I can stop you." His reply was sour because he guessed the question had to do with why he wasn't hard, which was something he didn't feel like talking about. It was embarrassing not to be able to get it up instantly. Last week, before he'd gotten so tangled up with Miss High and Mighty Schoolteacher that he didn't know which end of him was which, he hadn't had to work at bedding Glenda. The urge had just come naturally, as it should.

"You got somethin' goin' with Miss Grant?"

"What?" he almost yelped as his eyes swung around to Glenda's face. Eleven years ago, she hadn't been able to read minds.

"You heard me."

It took a minute for Johnny to recover his poise. "What in the world makes you ask a question like that?"

"Somethin' in her voice."

"Something in her voice?" He must have had too much to drink, because the conversation was befuddling him.

"Yeah. I could tell she didn't much like the idea of you bein' with me. She sounded real stiff-like. Not friendly, like she usually is."

"When did she sound real stiff-like?"

"When I talked to her."

Johnny almost ground his teeth. A hideous suspicion occurred to him, so hideous that he was almost afraid to give it voice.

"When did you talk to her?"

"A little while ago. When I asked her to come get you."

"Goddamn!" Johnny bounded up off the couch and glared down at Glenda. The room swayed again, but he stayed on his feet. "What the hell did you call her for? I thought you were calling a cab!"

"There's only two taxis in Tylerville, and both drivers are liable to still be at the picnic. You know that."

He'd forgotten. "Goddamn!" he said bitterly. Turning, he walked to the TV, snatched his keys off the top where Glenda had left them, and headed out the front door.

"Johnny, stop! You cain't just leave!"

"The hell I can't!"

Glenda followed him outside. She was almost wringing her hands, she was so upset. "But she's coming! She'll be here any minute! What'll she think if you're gone? And anyway, you're still drunk. You cain't ride that motorcycle drunk."

"I don't give a damn what Miss Goody Two-Shoes thinks. And I'm not drunk."

He reached his motorcycle and pulled it down from its center stand. For a minute he had to brace himself against the weight of it, which normally wouldn't have bothered him.

"You are so. Give me those keys!"

She had followed him down to the gravel drive that ran past her trailer. Hers was closest to the road, and a sickly yellow lamp at the gate of the development shed a meager amount of illumination on the scene. By its light, he was able to see that she was really upset.

He put his bike on its kickstand and caught her by the shoulders.

"Hey, I'll be all right," he said, his voice gentling.

Glenda stared up at him for a minute. Without bright daylight to point out her flaws, she looked almost as young as she had all those years ago, when they'd been friends more than lovers. Kind of like now, Johnny thought, and felt a rush of affection for her.

"You really like her, don't you? Miss Grant."

Johnny thought about lying, but he was too on edge and too buzzed and too sick of playing the whole stupid game. "Yeah, I really like her."

"She's real classy, I know. But isn't she—well, like, old?"

Johnny shrugged. "We're both adults."

"Are you sleeping with her?"

Johnny released Glenda's shoulders and turned away. "You don't think I'm going to answer that, do you?" Grabbing the motorcycle's handlebars, he kicked the stand up and straddled the seat.

"Johnny, wait!" Glenda pressed up against him and threw her arms around his neck. Johnny looked down at her with more than a hint of irritation.

"Let go, Glenda."

"You're just gonna get hurt, messin' around with her. She's not your kind. Not our kind."

"That's my problem, isn't it? Would you please let go of my neck?"

"But—" Glenda's eyes shifted briefly, staring out into the night, and when they returned to his, there was resignation in her face. "Yeah, I guess it is your problem. You be careful, you hear? I'd hate to wake up in the mornin' and hear that you'd been arrested—or had a bad wreck."

"I'll be careful." Surprised by her easy capitulation, Johnny dropped a quick kiss onto her cheek and inserted the key into the ignition. Turning it, he gunned the throttle and kicked the engine into life.

Maybe he had a buzz on—okay, he did have a buzz on—but he

could ride this baby through hell in the dark blindfolded. He'd get home all right.

With a wave to Glenda and a shower of gravel he was gone, roaring into the night.

28

*G*lenda watched him go, a kind of sadness on her face as she wrapped her arms around herself. He hadn't seen what she'd seen—the blue car coming around the bend, past the light at the other end of the trailer park. It was Rachel Grant's. That kind of foreign car was unique enough in Tylerville that it was instantly recognizable.

Johnny had been mad as hell at her for calling Miss Grant to come fetch him, but who else could she have called? Not many people she knew around town wanted to let Johnny Harris into a car with them. A lot of them thought he'd killed that girl. Glenda didn't. She'd known him all her life, and she'd never seen him lift a hand to a woman in violence. A man who didn't hit, to her way of thinking, didn't kill. Maybe another man in a drunken fight, but not a woman, and not the way that girl was killed. It took somebody vicious mean, or crazy, for violence like that.

Johnny was going to be mad when he found out that he hadn't succeeded in avoiding Miss Grant after all. The lane leading back to the trailer park was wide enough for only one vehicle to traverse at a time. Glenda didn't see the schoolteacher politely pulling over to let Johnny by. Glenda had told Rachel that he was drunk as a skunk and liable to kill himself before he went a mile.

Johnny and Miss Grant, getting it on. Now that she thought about it, Glenda wondered why she hadn't suspected it before. He'd always had a soft spot for the schoolteacher, reading books and writing things to impress her and being real polite when she was around. And since he'd come back, the two of them had hung out together a lot. Why, she'd even given Johnny a job in her daddy's hardware store.

And Miss Grant was kind of pretty, in a well-scrubbed sort of way. Her clothes were all wrong—really frumpy, with none of the style on which Glenda prided herself—and she had no chest at all. But her complexion was good, very good, for a woman her age, and she had a snooty air about her that a man from a background like Johnny's might find kind of sexy. A challenge and all that.

Still, it put paid to her budding hopes that she could grab him for herself. Not that she was crazy in love with him or anything, but he was good with the kids.

"Glenda!" The whisper startled her out of her reverie. Stiffening, eyes widening, she turned and peered around. On three sides there was nothing but darkness. Behind her now was the dim glow of the light.

"Who is it?" For some unknown reason, she was afraid. Which was silly. There was nothing to be afraid of in Tylerville. No crime at all, except an occasional silly teenager shooting out some lights or knocking over a mailbox with a bat. Nothing violent, not even a mugging, in eleven years.

"Could you give me a hand with this?"

The whisper must belong to Mr. Janusky, the frail octogenarian who lived in the trailer just behind hers. Mr. Janusky had been suffering from the flu, and that was why his voice sounded odd. But what on earth was the old man doing outside at this time of night? It must be close to twelve, and he was usually in bed at nine.

"Is that you, Mr. Janusky?"

"Yes. Hurry, Glenda."

The voice was coming out of the darkness to the left of the trailer, over where the Dumpster stood. Maybe the old fellow had come outside to throw out some trash and discovered he couldn't lift it high enough to get it in the bin.

"Where are you?" Having reasoned away the shivers, Glenda walked in the direction of the voice.

"Over here."

Glenda moved out of the pool of light, took a few steps into the enveloping darkness, and stopped dead. A feeling of dread washed over her like a shower of icy rain. But before she could act on it, before she could run or scream or even move, something hard crashed into the side of her head, hitting her with such blinding force that she was thrown to the ground and blacked out for a minute and saw stars.

When she came to, it was to pain, and fear, and the realization that she was being stabbed. And stabbed and stabbed again, in a frenzy of fury. Whimpering, half lifting an arm in a futile attempt to ward off her attacker, she had just an instant to register the unbelievable fact that she was being murdered.

In that instant, her only coherent thought was a frantic prayer: "Oh, please, God—I don't want to leave my kids! Oh, no! Oh, please! Oh, please!"

Then the darkness descended again like a heavy velvet stage curtain.

29

*B*etter. The watcher felt better, cleansed almost, now that justice had been done. Blood was everywhere, and he drank in the remembered scent with growing pleasure, rubbing red-coated hands together, relishing the warm, wet sliminess of the liquid of life. Like the other woman eleven years before, this one had deserved to die. The watcher stared down at the woman on the ground gloatingly. She lay motionless, her flesh torn and bleeding, silent now, past trying to fight. He felt no pity for her.

The watcher slowly bent to retrieve the dark red roses that would be his tribute to the departing soul. With quick movements, hands still coated with blood scattered velvety petals over the still-warm body.

Summersweet for the first one, who had been young if not innocent. Roses slightly past their prime for this one.

How fitting, the watcher thought, and finished the task before vanishing into the night.

30

❧

*R*achel slammed on her brakes, and not a moment too soon. There, in the bright beam of her headlights, hurtling toward her like a bat out of hell, roared Johnny's motorcycle. He must have seen her at approximately the same time, because the cycle checked, then swerved violently to the left and almost seemed to fly off the road.

When Rachel got out of the car, the cycle was lying on its side in the grass, wheels still spinning. Johnny was pulling himself into a sitting position beside it, cursing furiously under his breath.

"Dear God, are you all right?" Rachel ran to him, leaning over him with one hand on his shoulder as she peered at the face beneath the silver helmet.

"No thanks to you," he grunted, and clambered rather shakily to his feet. For a moment he stood there swaying, his fingers fumbling with the clasp under his ear. Then it clicked free, and he pulled the helmet off.

"You *are* drunk," Rachel said, taking a step back as the beer fumes hit her in the face. "When your friend called me, I had a hard time believing that you would actually do something as dumb as drive after drinking nine beers. But obviously you're stupider than I thought."

"I couldn't have had more than six—or maybe seven," Johnny said, scowling. "I'm not drunk. I've just got a little buzz going."

"Oh, yes?" Rachel asked furiously. "Then how come you wrecked your motorcycle?"

"Because you damned near ran me off the road!"

"I had my headlights on, and I was driving within the speed limit! If you didn't see me until too late, it's because you're drunk!"

"I am not!"

"You are too!"

For a moment they stood almost nose to nose. Rachel, with her head thrown back and her hands on her hips, glared up at him. His answering look was just as unfriendly. Then his eyes slid sideways to his downed bike.

"Look what you did." His tone was faintly plaintive as he turned away to bend over the machine.

"You did it, not me! You're lucky to still be alive."

"I might not be, if I hadn't laid it over on its side. See that big oak over there? I was headed right toward it."

Rachel looked and shuddered. Johnny caught the cycle by its handlebars and hauled it upright, heaving it up on its center stand as he examined it with obvious anxiety. The stench of spilled gas was even stronger than the smell of beer.

"Blew a tire." Obviously disgusted, Johnny straightened up from where he had crouched by the rear of the bike.

"Too bad."

Johnny hesitated, looking at her truculently. "You'll have to give me a ride home."

"That's what I came for."

"I'll come back for my bike tomorrow."

"Fine."

Rachel was already heading back toward her car, which was parked in the middle of the road, lights on, still running, its driver's side door wide open. She didn't even look behind her to see if Johnny followed as she got in.

Seconds later he slid in beside her, tossing his helmet and the spare into the back seat.

Rachel backed up, pulled out, and drove off toward town without a word. The knowledge that Johnny was fresh from the arms of Glenda Watkins ate at her. Jealous—that's what she was, jealous. But what else had she expected from Johnny Harris? Catting around was in his blood.

Rachel caught herself up. She was as guilty of stereotyping as the rest of the town. He wouldn't have turned to Glenda—or at least she didn't think so, anyway, not so soon—if Rachel hadn't sent him away herself. The thought rankled.

Johnny reached over and flipped the radio on. The Rolling Stones in a golden oldie revival were wailing about not getting any satisfaction. Johnny scowled and turned the dial, settling on a country station that at the moment featured the Judds.

"Have a good time at the picnic?" His remark out of the blue earned him an unfriendly sidelong glance.

"Yes."

Silence.

"I apologize if I interrupted your evening."

"You should. And you did."

"Hope the boyfriend wasn't inconvenienced."

"No."

"You still sleeping with him?"

At that Rachel cast him a furious glare. "I never said I was in the first place. You know why? Because it's none of your business."

"Isn't it?"

"No!"

Silence.

"You catch any flak at school about me coming around?"

"Do you care?"

"Yes."

Rachel shot him a quick, surprised look. She had expected some smart-alecky comeback, not that quiet affirmative.

"A little."

"Sorry."

The worst of her anger cooled. "It's not your fault."

They had reached the outskirts of town, and Rachel turned right on Main. The hardware store was three blocks down on the left.

"Do you have your key?" she asked as she pulled into the parking lot and stopped the car.

"Yeah." Johnny dangled a jingling key ring from one finger to demonstrate.

"Then good night."

He was looking at her, but in the darkness she could not read his expression. She had not even put the transmission into park, the engine still ran, and it was obvious that she was only waiting for him to get out before driving off.

"Rachel," he said quietly, "come up?"

"No."

"Still need space?"

Rachel's lips compressed, her eyes flashed, and she turned on him.

"Yes, I do. Any woman with a grain of sense would! Look at you! You're drunk, and this isn't the first time either! You zoom around on that motorcycle like an overgrown adolescent bent on suicide! You sleep around, your hair's too long, your manners are dreadful, and you've got a chip on your shoulder the size of Hong Kong! You say you've got a college degree. Are you using it? No! Do you have any plans to use it? Not as far as I can tell. You just spent this evening with your girlfriend, who at least cares enough about you not to let you drive home drunk. Then you have the nerve to ask me to come upstairs with you? What in the name of heaven do you suppose you have to offer me? Can you tell me that?"

There was a long, tense pause. Rachel felt as much as saw Johnny's slow stiffening.

"Great sex?" he drawled.

The question hung in the air between them. Rachel felt anger build inside her, turning in just a matter of seconds into a hot, fierce fury of which she would have never suspected herself capable.

"Get out!" she said softly, so angry her voice trembled. Then, as red rage rolled over her in a boiling tide, her voice rose until she was shouting at him. "Get out! Get out of my car! Get out of my life! Get out, get out, get out!"

She slammed the car into park and shoved at his shoulder, doing her best to force him out the door, without making the least headway. She was so furious that she was sobbing with it, so furious that she wanted to kick and scream and yell like Katie in a tantrum. What she might have done if he hadn't opened the door and climbed out at that moment, she couldn't say.

"Anything to make you happy, baby," he said with an insolent curl of his lip. He slammed the door and swaggered across the parking lot. He was climbing the stairs as Rachel, trembling from reaction, threw the transmission into reverse and careened out of the lot

31

They were getting ready for church when the telephone rang. Rachel, already dressed except for the pink linen suit she meant to wear, tied a perky blue ribbon in Loren's hair while Becky wrestled Katie into her shoes. Lisa hogged the upstairs bathroom. Elisabeth was still in Stan's bedroom, helping him dress and talking to J.D., who, with Tilda, had come in to watch over him while the rest of the family attended the Sunday morning worship service.

"Telephone, Rachel," Tilda called up the stairs.

"Rob?" Becky inquired with a lift of her eyebrows.

Rachel shrugged and ran down the stairs to take the call. When she put down the receiver she was frowning.

"Who was that, honey?" Tilda asked, looking up from loading the breakfast dishes to catch Rachel's expression.

"I have to go down to the police station."

"What?" Becky, coming downstairs with Katie in her arms, overheard Rachel's remark.

"They need me to come right away. They wouldn't say why." But she knew, she knew as well as she knew her name, that it had something to do with Johnny. Her lips tightened. He must be in some sort of trouble. Had he gone out again last night?

"On Sunday morning?" Becky was disbelieving. "What about church?"

"I should be able to make it." Rachel glanced up at the clock. There was still a good hour before the service began.

"You can always go with J.D. and me this evening," Tilda said, pouring detergent into the dishwasher and closing the door. Tilda went to a different church from the Grants, but Rachel and Becky had accompanied her on many occasions in the past. Though the congregation was mostly black, anyone was welcome, and everybody knew that the Grant girls were almost as much Tilda's family as her own children. "Tanya's singin' lead in the choir now, you know."

"Is she?" Tanya was Tilda's youngest. "I'd like to hear her. But I hope to be able to meet Mother and Becky at church."

"Do you think it's something about the store—or that Harris man?" Becky, having set Katie on the floor, was looking at her with troubled eyes.

Rachel stared at her sister for a moment, then sighed. "Has Mother been talking to you?"

"Of course."

"Of course." Rachel should have known that Elisabeth would confide all to Becky. "It's probably the store. Maybe a kid threw a rock through a window or something."

"Maybe."

Rachel could tell from Becky's tone that she was skeptical. What had Elisabeth told her about Johnny and Rachel's relationship with him? Rachel hated to speculate.

"I'd better get down there and see what they want."

Becky and Tilda were exchanging significant looks even as Rachel fled the room.

Minutes later, fully dressed and with her car keys in her hand, Rachel poked her head into the kitchen on her way out the door. Elisabeth was still upstairs, for which small mercy Rachel was thankful. Becky and Tilda, who'd had their heads together near the dishwasher, immediately stopped talking when they saw Rachel.

"Beck, tell Mother where I've gone, would you? Tell her I'll try to make church, but if it's not possible, I'll be home as soon as I can. And try to keep her from coming down to the police station if this takes a while, please?"

"I'll do my best." Becky shook her head sympathetically at her sister. "But you know how she is."

"I know." The two exchanged rueful, affectionate smiles, and then Rachel left.

The police station was a small brick building located on Madison Street, about half a mile south of the hardware store on the very edge of downtown. Rachel had been inside only a few times, usually to sell or buy tickets for some school or civic function. The parking lot was unusually full for Sunday, and as she entered the front reception area with its linoleum floors and hard plastic chairs, she noticed that there seemed to be a lot of officers on duty. She didn't really think about such details, just noticed them and tucked them away somewhere in her mind to be recalled later.

"Hello, did you need to see me?" she said to the young officer at the desk a moment later. His face wasn't familiar, and she assumed he was a newcomer to the town.

"Miss Grant?"

"Yes."

"Just a minute." He picked up the receiver of the telephone on one side of the metal desk, punched a button, and said, "Miss Grant is here."

"Can you tell me what this is about?" she asked as he put the receiver back in its cradle.

He shook his head. "You'll have to ask the chief."

Surprised, Rachel was about to ask what Chief Wheatley was doing working on Sunday—he was a member of her church, and he and his wife never missed a service—when the chief himself came through a door that led to the rear offices and prisoner holding area.

"Rachel." He smiled as he greeted her, but Rachel, her perceptions sharpened by a growing alarm, thought he looked tired and a little grim. There were bags under his eyes that weren't usually there, and his skin, normally ruddy, had taken on a tinge of gray.

"What's happened?" she asked sharply.

"Come into the back, Rachel. We can talk there."

He held the door for her. Rachel, increasingly nervous as she considered and discarded various hideous possibilities, walked through the door and along the short corridor, then allowed him to seat her in a hard gray chair before the desk in his small office.

Chief Wheatley closed the door, then walked around the desk to sit down. The only window was tiny, permitting very little natural light to enter. The bright glow from the fluorescent fixture overhead was unflattering to everything—the dingy linoleum floor, the brownish metal of the desk, the tired, drawn face of the chief. Rachel could only imagine what she must look like under its unrelenting glare.

"What's happened?" she asked again, her hands clasping in her lap.

"I need to ask you a few questions first," he said. "Mind if I tape-record this?"

"Why, no."

"I appreciate it. Helps prevent confusion later." Opening the bottom left drawer of his desk, Chief Wheatley pulled out a small portable tape recorder and clicked it on. Then he leaned back in his chair and peered at her through half-lowered lids. His hands were folded over his belly. Rachel noticed that he was beginning to develop a slight paunch. He must be sixty or near it, as his grayish, thinning hair and slack jaw muscles attested.

"You went to the Labor Day picnic yesterday, right?" he asked.

Rachel nodded. Then, remembering the tape recorder, she said, "Yes."

"Afterward, what did you do?"

"I went home. Why?"

"Is that all?"

"No. I went out later. To pick up—a friend who'd had too much to drink and had no business driving."

"What friend?"

Rachel wasn't going to be able to keep Johnny's name out of it.

"Johnny Harris."

"You went to pick up Johnny Harris because he'd had too much to drink and had no business driving. Is that right?"

"That's what I said."

"Where did you pick him up?"

"At that trailer park out by the river—I forget its name."

"Appleby Estates?"

Rachel nodded, then remembering the tape recorder again, said, "Yes."

"Did Harris call you to come and get him?"

"No. Glenda Watkins did."

"Ah." The fingers that had been resting on his stomach steepled. "What time was that?"

"About eleven, I guess. Maybe a little after. Why?"

"We'll get to that in a minute. First I need to know a few more details. Did she seem upset, or in any way—uh, emotional, when she called?"

"No."

"Did you actually pick Harris up?"

"Yes."

"What time would you say that was?"

Rachel thought a minute. "It probably took me half an hour to get over there, because I had to get dressed. Around eleven thirty, I guess."

"Tell me exactly what happened, Rachel. This is important, so be as accurate as you can. Start from when Mrs. Watkins called you. What exactly did she say?"

Rachel told him, then went on to describe getting dressed, driving to the trailer park, and then, rather reluctantly, her encounter with Johnny. If this was about drunken driving, as she half-suspected, she did not want to get him into more trouble than he was already in, richly though the wretch deserved it.

"So he wrecked his motorcycle."

"Yes."

"Was he drunk?"

Rachel pursed her lips. "He had been drinking, yes."

"But was he out-of-his-head drunk? Did he know what he was doing? Did he seem—normal?"

Rachel's brows rose. "Entirely normal. Just a little tipsy."

"What was he wearing?"

Rachel looked her surprise. "Blue jeans, a T-shirt, tennis shoes."

"Were they—did you notice any stains or discolorations on them, or anything like that?"

"No. I suppose there were probably grass stains on his jeans from the wreck, but I didn't notice them."

"So you noticed nothing unusual about either his demeanor or his clothes?"

"That's right."

"Okay. After you picked him up, what happened?"

"Why, I drove him to his apartment."

"What time did you arrive, do you think?"

"About midnight, probably."

"And what happened then?"

"He went inside. And I went home."

"He went inside his apartment at about midnight? Did you actually see him enter?"

"I saw him climb the stairs."

"All right. Let me go over this to see if I understand it correctly. Stop me if I get anything wrong. Mrs. Watkins called you at eleven to pick Harris up because she thought he was too drunk to drive his motorcycle home. You drove out there, arriving about eleven thirty, and ran Harris off the road in front of the trailer park. He left his motorcycle there, got in the car with you, and you drove him to his apartment, arriving about midnight. Is that essentially accurate?"

"Yes."

"Then I have just one more question for you. When you were picking Harris up, did you actually set eyes on Glenda Watkins?"

"Why, yes. I did. Not to speak to, but I saw her from a distance, standing out in front of what I assumed was her trailer, as I first approached the trailer park. When I came around the bend in Manslick Road."

"You saw her? Are you sure?" He sat abruptly upright, his eyes sharpening on her face, his hands moving to rest palms down on the desk.

"Why, yes."

"You're sure it was her?"

Rachel nodded, surprised at his sudden intensity, then said, "Yes. I'm sure."

"What was she doing? Was she—did she seem—all right?"

"From what I could see, she seemed fine. She was standing in front of the trailer, staring off down the road in the direction I was coming from."

"How soon after that did you almost hit Harris's motorcycle?"

"Why, right away. Less than a minute, I'd say."

"Rachel, think. This is important. Did Harris ever, at any time after his motorcycle ran off the road, get out of your sight?"

Rachel thought, then shook her head. "No. Why? What's happened? Is it—has something happened to Johnny?" A straightforward charge like drunken driving wouldn't merit the game of twenty questions the chief and she were playing, or his humorless demeanor, Rachel realized. It was something else, she very much feared. Something very bad.

Chief Wheatley sighed, and some of the stiffness went out of his spine. He reached over and clicked off the tape recorder.

"Mrs. Watkins was murdered last night."

Rachel gasped. "What?"

The chief nodded grimly. "And that's not the worst of it. The crime is almost an exact replica of the Edwards case, down to the flowers strewn over the body. Only in this case, they were roses, not summersweet blossoms. Taken from a garden nearby."

"Glenda Watkins was *murdered*?" Disbelief and shock combined to make Rachel's voice crack on the last word.

"Stabbed thirteen times. Sometime between eleven forty-five and ten after twelve, which is when her son went out to look for her. He said he saw something moving in the dark, so he got scared and ran back inside and locked the door and called a neighbor. The neighbor went to check and found the body."

"Oh, my God!" Rachel felt sick with horror.

"Just like the last time. Johnny Harris was seeing both women, and he was the last person to see the victim alive."

Rachel, still in shock, absorbed this, then shook her head. "No, he wasn't—I was. I saw her standing there, and he had just left. On his motorcycle. I saw her after Johnny had already left, do you understand? He could not have killed her."

Chief Wheatley slowly nodded. "That's right. If you are absolutely sure it was Glenda Watkins you saw."

"I'm sure."

"Sure enough to testify to it under oath, in court?"

"Yes. I am absolutely sure. She was standing in a pool of lamplight, and I saw her clearly."

Chief Wheatley pursed his lips, steepled his hands, and looked down at them, then up at her again, his eyes penetrating.

"Rachel—Harris didn't somehow get in touch with you, ask you to say this, did he? If he did, tell me now, and it'll stay between the two of us."

Rachel stared at him, her eyes widening. "No!" she said, outraged. "No!"

"If that sounded insulting, then I'm sorry," he said heavily. "But we've got a real nasty incident here, an incident that looks identical to the one that Harris was convicted of eleven years ago. Only this time he has an airtight alibi: you. So where does that leave us?"

"Johnny didn't murder Marybeth Edwards! I knew it! I knew it all along!" Rachel was suddenly, fiercely exultant as her eyes met the chief's.

He held up a hand. "Now, that's just one possibility we have to consider. Another is that this is a copycat killing, designed to place the blame on Harris. There are three possible rationales with that theory. One, someone—like maybe her husband—wanted to get rid of Mrs. Watkins real bad and, with Harris out of prison, decided the easy thing to do would be to kill her and make it look like Harris did it. The second possibility is that someone hates Harris so much that they killed the woman he was dating so he would get sent back to prison, or worse. That would seem to point to one of Marybeth Edwards's family or friends as the perpetrator. The third possibility—well, it's a tough one."

"Which means?"

"Which means that there's a wild card out there. Someone out-of-his-head crazy, or with a motive that we haven't latched on to yet. But we will. We definitely will." There was bleak determination in the chief's voice.

He stood up abruptly, looked at Rachel, hesitated, then leaned toward her, putting both his hands flat on the desk in front of him to support his weight.

"Rachel, I don't mean to accuse you of lying. I've known you since you were a baby toddlin' after your mama, and I've never known you to be anything but one hundred percent honest and morally upright. But I've got two girls of my own, as you know. And I've seen what happens to young women when they fall under the spell of a man."

Rachel, guessing where this was leading, opened her mouth to refute it with some indignation. The chief held up his hand to silence her.

"I wouldn't even say this, except to warn you. You do realize that, if —just if—you should happen to be lying, you've placed yourself in the gravest possible danger. You are all that stands between Harris spending the rest of his life in prison, or maybe this time, without youth for a mitigating factor, the electric chair. I wouldn't want to be in that position. Not with a man who could commit crimes like these."

"I am not lying, chief," Rachel said firmly.

The chief straightened. "All right. I certainly take you at your word, and we'll start looking further afield for the perp. We've had some tests run on Mrs. Watkins that we'll be comparing to Marybeth Edwards's results. They've already been sent off to the lab, and we should know within a week to ten days whether we're dealing with the same killer in both cases, or a copycat. I'll keep you posted."

"Thank you."

The chief came around his desk, heading toward the door. Rachel stood up and realized that the interview was at an end.

"Where are the children—Glenda Watkins's children?" she asked. A lump formed in her throat at the idea of four little ones motherless. Jeremy and his mother had seemed so close.

"We called their dad first thing. He came and got 'em while we were still there investigating the crime scene. Oldest boy was plenty shook up. He kept saying he saw something in the dark. But he couldn't tell us who, or what." The chief shook his head. "This is bad business, damned bad business. We're going to find whoever did this. I gave that kid, and I give you, my word on it."

He held the door open for Rachel.

"Will you be wanting to collect Harris while you're here, or should I tell him to walk home?"

Rachel, passing through the door in front of him, heard that with disbelief. She turned to face him.

"Are you telling me that Johnny is here?"

The chief nodded. "Yes, ma'am, I am. We picked him up about two this morning. He told the same story you did, but I wasn't letting him go until I checked it out."

"Well, you can just let him go! He did not kill Glenda Watkins!"

"So it seems," the chief said heavily. "Wait out front, Rachel. I'll see that he's brought out."

32

Johnny walked through the door that led from the back of the police station into the waiting area some fifteen minutes later. Rachel, who'd been leafing sightlessly through an old copy of *Field and Stream*, stood up. Johnny needed a shave, his hair was rumpled, and his face was haggard. From the jerkiness of his movements and the glitter in his eyes, it was clear that he was furious. A bruise was purpling on his left cheekbone, and a trickle of dried blood curled like a comma at the corner of his mouth.

"He's been hurt," she said in some surprise to Kerry Yates, who had followed him out and was keeping a cautious eye on Johnny's taut back.

"Yeah, well, he resisted arrest. He's lucky we're not charging him with assault. He hit Skaggs pretty good."

"Let's go, Rachel," Johnny said. A muscle worked in his jaw as he cast Kerry Yates a single murderous glance.

"But they hit you! You should file a complaint," she said indignantly as he pulled her toward the door.

Johnny snorted. "Yeah, right. Just keep on living in the land of Oz, teacher. Out here in the real world, I'm lucky they didn't shoot me and ask questions later."

He opened the door for her, waited impatiently for her to walk through it, then followed her outside.

"But you didn't do anything! They know that now! At the very least they owe you an apology!"

Johnny stopped and looked down into Rachel's face, which was flushed with righteous anger on his behalf. They were standing in the parking lot at the foot of the shallow flight of concrete steps that led up to the door. The September sun was bright and hot, the sky an endless blue, and a lazy breeze just stirred the air.

"You're so damned naive sometimes, I can't believe it," he said harshly. Releasing her arm, he strode off without her. For a moment Rachel wondered if he meant to head out for his apartment on foot. But he stopped at the car and got in.

When she got in, too, he was lying back in the seat with his eyes closed.

"They tell you about Glenda?" he asked as she started the car.

"Yes. It's terrible. That poor woman. Those poor children."

"Yeah." He was silent. Pulling out into the street, Rachel glanced at him but said nothing. He looked utterly drained.

"She was a good girl. A good friend. I hate to think of her dying like that."

"I'm so sorry."

"So am I. Damned sorry. But it doesn't do Glenda a hell of a lot of good." His fists clenched, and suddenly he sat up, his eyes alive with anger and pain. "God, it must have happened right after I left! If I'd gone back instead of going off with you, I could have prevented it! At the very least, I might have caught the bastard in the act."

"And maybe been killed yourself," Rachel said quietly.

He shook his head. "Whoever this is, he's into women. I doubt he's got the nerve to tackle somebody big enough and strong enough to fight back."

"So you think it's the same person who killed Marybeth?"

"Yeah. I don't put much stock in copycats. In a town the size of Tylerville, what are the odds on there being two people that sick?"

"You have a point."

They had reached the hardware store, and Rachel turned in and parked. Johnny reached for the door handle, looked over at Rachel, and hesitated. When he spoke, there was a gentleness to his voice that hadn't been there before.

"You look real pretty. You going to church?"

"I was."

"There's still time. If you hurry."

Rachel met the smoky blue eyes, saw the loneliness and hurting and need there, and gave a delicate little shrug. "I haven't missed church in nearly ten years. I suppose one time can't hurt."

"Spend the day with me?"

"I'd like that."

Johnny smiled, a slow, sweet smile that pierced Rachel clear through to the heart. She realized something then, something that had been hovering on the edges of her consciousness but which just at that moment took on concrete shape. Even though she had defended him, even though she had been positive in her own mind that Johnny had not killed Marybeth Edwards, she had always harbored just the tiniest sliver of doubt. Now that doubt had gone, vanished completely. He was innocent, as innocent as she.

Rachel felt as if her heart had suddenly been set free.

They spent the day together and by unspoken, mutual agreement refused to talk or even think of the hideous event that had occurred so near them the night before. Rachel went in with him and was reluctantly reintroduced to Wolf, who didn't seem a bit more disposed to like her on this occasion than the last. With Wolf watching her with wary disapproval, Rachel waited while Johnny took a shower. When he emerged from the bathroom with a towel wrapped around his waist, she went into his arms. It was the first time they'd ever made love with both of them naked, in a bed.

"I've missed you," he said a long time afterward as she lay with her head on his chest, threading her fingers through the crisp black curls that grew there.

"I've missed you, too." She lifted her head, propping her chin on his chest to smile at him. They were stretched out side by side, with her leg thrown over his and his arm around her shoulders as he idly stroked her skin. The bedclothes had been lost somewhere at the foot of the bed.

"I thought about what you said last night. About my being drunk, and having a chip on my shoulder, and all that."

"I was mad."

"I know." He smiled a little. "You look cute mad."

Rachel tweaked a chest hair so hard he yelped. Removing her fingers, he rubbed the injured spot and gave her a reproachful glance.

"That hurt."

"It was meant to. I hate to be called cute."

"But you are cute. The cutest thing I ever saw in my life. Especially your cute little a—"

He started to say "ass," but Rachel clapped her hand over his mouth in the nick of time.

"Don't swear," she said.

He cocked an eyebrow at her and removed her hand, placing it back on his chest.

"Trying to reform me?"

"Yes."

"Okay. I probably need it. Which brings me back to what I wanted to say in the first place."

"Which is?"

"You were right. I was drunk last night. It won't happen again."

"Won't it?"

She hardly dared believe what she was hearing. He shook his head.

"Nope. Behold a newly converted teetotaler." He looked over at Wolf, who was jealously regarding his master while sprawled panting on his stomach in the hall, then back at Rachel. "I was starting to remind myself of my old man. He drank from morning to night for as long as I can remember. I'm not going to let myself end up like that."

"I'm glad to hear it."

"Life's too short."

"Yes."

For a moment they were silent as they both, without wanting to, remembered Glenda. Johnny looked at Rachel.

"You really want me to get my hair cut?"

Rachel laughed, glad to shake off the somber mood that had threatened. "Not if you don't want to. You've got beautiful hair."

"Why, thank you, ma'am." He hesitated, then a wry smile curved his mouth. "I wear it this way basically because it annoys the hell—oh, sorry, what should I say? heck?—out of people."

"I know."

"So I'll get it cut if you want."

"Thank you. But I don't want you to make too many sacrifices. Staying sober's plenty."

"So you're not going to make me give up my motorcycle?"

Rachel looked up at him with sudden interest.

"Would you, if I asked?"

He caught her hand and carried it to his mouth, where he pressed his lips to the palm. "There's not much I wouldn't do if you asked, Rachel."

The phone beside the bed rang. Its shrill summons was so unexpected, Rachel jumped.

Johnny stretched out a hand and lifted the receiver to his ear. "Hello?"

He listened, frowning, as his eyes traveled over Rachel's face.

"Why, yes, ma'am, she is."

Rachel's eyes widened as he handed the phone to her.

"Your mother," he mouthed.

Rachel grimaced but accepted the receiver. "Hello, Mother," she said with resignation.

"Rachel Elisabeth Grant, what are you doing with that Harris boy in his apartment?"

Rachel almost told her, but before she could, Elisabeth continued in an urgent near-whisper that Rachel supposed was meant to keep Johnny from overhearing.

"Did you hear about the Watkins woman?"

"Yes, I did."

"That she was murdered? Just like Marybeth Edwards? Last night?"

"Yes, Mother. It's a terrible tragedy."

"And you're in his apartment?" Elisabeth's voice said plainly that she couldn't believe her daughter was guilty of such stupidity.

"Johnny didn't kill her, Mother."

"For goodness' sake, Rachel, can he hear you?"

"Yes, he certainly can."

"Oh, my God! Is he holding you hostage? Should I call the police?"

"No, he is not holding me hostage, and you should not call the police." Rachel was exasperated, but Johnny's face broke into a broad grin. "He did not kill Glenda Watkins, Mother. I know he didn't, because he was with me last night when it happened."

"With you! But you were home in bed!"

"No, I wasn't." Rachel sighed. "Listen, I'll tell you all about it when I get home, okay? Please don't worry about me. I'm fine. I probably won't be home until sometime tonight. We're going to go out and get something to eat. Unless—"

She lifted her brows questioningly at Johnny and covered the mouthpiece so her mother couldn't hear. "Do you want to go to my house for Sunday dinner? My mother is a fantastic cook."

Johnny shook his head in comical alarm. Rachel had to smile.

"We're going out to eat," she repeated, uncovering the mouthpiece. Then, with a teasing look at Johnny, she added, "But guess who's coming to dinner next Sunday?"

"Rachel, you wouldn't!" Elisabeth sounded horrified.

"Yes, I would, Mother. Don't worry, he doesn't look any more eager than you sound. But I want you two to get to know each other."

"Oh, Rachel, why?" Elisabeth moaned.

"Because I'm madly in love with him, Mother," Rachel said, her eyes locking with Johnny's as she spoke. On the other end of the line, Elisabeth gave a little choked cry.

To Rachel's surprise, Johnny reached down and took the receiver from her hand.

"Rachel will call you back, Mrs. Grant," he said into the receiver, then put it gently in its cradle.

Rachel lay very still as he slowly turned back to her. He was frowning as he hitched himself up some, then folded both hands beneath his head, propping his head higher on the pillow so that he could better see her face.

"Did you mean that, or did you just say it to make her mad?"

Rachel met his eyes. "I meant it."

"Oh, yeah?" The beginnings of a smile curved his lips.

"Yeah."

"Yeah?"

"Yeah."

The smile broadened into a grin of pure delight. Johnny reached for her and pulled her across his chest and down onto her back on the mattress. He leaned over her, propped on one elbow.

"Care to repeat it? To me this time."

Rachel looked up at him, at the darkly handsome face, the smoky blue eyes, the long, sensuous mouth with the small cut in its corner. She lifted a tender finger to trace the bruise on his cheekbone.

"I'm in love with you," she said softly.

"You left out the 'madly,' " he chided. "I want to hear the whole thing, said right to my face."

"I'm *madly* in love with you." Her lips curved in a tender smile as happiness bloomed and swelled inside her. There, she'd said it. Her secret was out, revealed, secret no more. She'd cast her cap over the windmill, and she was glad.

"Rachel." There was wonder in his eyes, and passion, too, as he cupped her face with his hands and bent to seek her mouth. His kiss was exquisitely gentle, exquisitely intimate, saying things that he had not yet put into words. Rachel, enraptured, wrapped her arms around his neck and gave herself up to the sheer glory of his lovemaking.

Later, when she lay wrapped in his arms in a supremely contented, half-dozing state, she heard a sound that made her frown. For a moment she couldn't imagine what on earth it could be.

"Your stomach's growling!" she said, looking up at him wide-eyed. Johnny grimaced at her.

"I'm starving," he confessed. "I haven't eaten since about six o'clock last night."

"You should have said something!"

"I had to choose between food for the body or food for the soul, and the soul won."

The crooked grin on his face dazzled her with its charm. She reached up, put a hand behind his head, and drew his mouth down for a warm, lingering kiss.

"Christ." He pulled her higher up on his chest, wrapping his arms around her and turning with her so that she once again lay beneath him. His intentions were very clear.

"None of that now," she said, poking him in the ribs. "We're going to get up, and we're going to get something to eat. We can't stay in bed all day."

"I'd like to." But his stomach growled again, and Johnny reluctantly released her and got to his feet. For a moment, as he stood naked beside the bed, Rachel allowed herself the luxury of just looking at him. He was really the most beautiful man, she thought. Long and lean, his shoulders and arms corded with muscle, his stomach ridged with it, he looked better than any *Playgirl* centerfold that she and Becky had snickered over as teenagers. A V of thick black curls covered his chest, tapering to a narrow line that ran over his navel and farther down to widen again at his genitals. For a moment her eyes focused there with pure pleasure. He was watching her look at him, his eyes intent. Rachel, meeting his gaze and recalling that she was lying stark naked atop the mussed bottom sheet, stretched slowly, deliberately, like a lazy cat. As his eyes heated, traveling the length of her arching body, she felt deliciously sinful. And desirable. So desirable.

His stomach growled again.

"All right. That's it. In the shower with you, before I faint from lack of nourishment."

He reached down, scooped her up in his arms, and stepping over Wolf, who looked disdainful at such goings-on, carried her into the bathroom, where he dumped her on her feet in the tub. He turned on both faucets, tested the temperature of the water, pulled the little peg that activated the shower, and stepped in beside her, closing the curtain behind him.

33

$\mathcal{S}$he was thirty-four years old, and she had never in her life showered with a man. As Johnny soaped her back, then ran sensuous hands beneath her arms to cup and lave her breasts, Rachel realized just what she had been missing. There was a whole world out there, a wonderful world of the senses between a man and a woman, that she had barely glimpsed. The small affairs she had been party to in the past were nothing like this. As his soapy hands slid down over her stomach, over her hips and thighs and around to her behind, she figured out why. Because this time, the love in the word *lovemaking* was the most important component. She was so in love with him that she was giddy with it.

She, Rachel Grant, was in love with Johnny Harris. The notion was so ridiculous that she giggled.

"What's so funny?" he asked, growling—her response to his questing fingers was something other than he had expected. He turned her in his arms and looked down into her face with mock sternness while the steaming needles of water soaked them both.

"You are. I am. *We* are. Whoever would have thought it?"

He ran his fingers through her soaked hair, separating the strands so that the rushing water could wash away the last of the shampoo. His hands slid down to rest on her slim waist.

"I've been thinking of it for years. Almost half my life, in fact."

Rachel stared up at him, suddenly serious. She'd been in the midst of the enjoyable process of soaping his chest, but her fingers stilled as her task was forgotten. With his hair as wet as hers and sleeked back from his face, he looked very different from the Johnny to whom she was accustomed. He was just as handsome, just as sexy, but older, more mature. In that moment, not the smallest hint of the overgrown adolescent remained. He was an adult, just as she was. The difference in their ages seemed no more an obstacle between them than the dissimilarity in their hair color.

"Now that you've got what you wanted from me, how long till the honeymoon's over?" Rachel asked in a jocular way, because she didn't want him to suspect how very, very much she needed a particular answer. Johnny had said nothing about love, only a great deal about need and lust. If all he wanted was to fulfill a teenage sex fantasy, he'd done that in spades. Her fingers started to move again, but rather jerkily, rubbing the soap in circles over his chest.

"Teacher, I haven't even scratched the surface of what I want from you." He was smiling, but something at the back of his eyes made Rachel's heart speed up. His hands came up to catch and cover hers, stopping their half-hearted movements and trapping the soap against his chest.

"It's going to take me years to get what I want from you. It may take the rest of my life. Maybe even longer than that."

"Oh, yeah?" She smiled rather mistily up at him through the relentless curtain of water.

"Yeah."

He bent to kiss her, and the soap skittered away unnoticed into the pooled water at their feet.

They stayed in the shower until the water ran cold and Johnny's stomach had started its rumbling again.

"How about if I cook, instead of us going out?" Johnny asked after they had both stumbled out of the tub and stood shivering on the cold tile floor drying themselves. The question was faintly muffled because he was vigorously toweling his hair.

"You?" Rachel, who had wrapped a towel around her body, stopped running a wide-toothed comb through her towel-dried hair for a moment to stare with some disbelief at him through the mirror.

"Yeah, me. Why not? I can cook." He finished with his hair and wrapped the towel around his waist.

"*You* can cook?" Her disbelief was so transparent that he grinned.

"Rachel, sweetheart, I hate to tell you this, but your stereotypes are showing. Good God, what is it about me that makes people assume the worst? Of course I can cook. Growing up in a family like mine, if you can't cook, you starve."

"*You* can cook." Still faintly disbelieving because she couldn't help it, she ran her gaze down that long, strong, quintessentially masculine body. In her family, her mother had cooked, and the girls had learned from Elisabeth. If Stan had ever so much as stirred a pot of soup, Rachel had never seen it. But Johnny was right, of course. Just because he was so very, very male was no reason that he couldn't prepare a meal. She was stereotyping him, just as everybody else did.

"Well?" His eyes met hers through the mirror.

"By all means, cook. I can't wait."

He grinned and left the bathroom. Rachel heard him rummaging around in the bedroom and assumed he was getting dressed. She went into the living room to fetch her purse, gingerly stepping over Wolf, who sprawled in the hall watching Johnny in the bedroom with slavish devotion. The huge animal rolled an eye at her as she almost hopped over his prone form, but Wolf didn't so much as offer up a growl.

Applying the few cosmetics she habitually carried in her purse— lipstick, powder, hand lotion for moisturizer—she fluffed out her already drying hair and headed for the bedroom to dress. In the kitchen, she could hear Johnny banging around with pots and pans. The idea of his cooking her a meal was so endearingly ridiculous that she smiled as she stepped into her clothes.

A short time later, wearing most of the outfit she had arrived in— the slim skirt of the pink suit, her short-sleeved white silk blouse, a single strand of pearls, and beige pumps—but leaving off the fitted jacket, she headed toward the kitchen to see if she could assist the chef.

Wolf, lying by the door that led down to the store, watched her with a brooding look that made Rachel a little nervous. She cast him a wary look, then stepped into the kitchen.

It was empty. Pots bubbled on the stove, and a delicious, garlicky smell emanated from the oven, but of Johnny there was no sign.

"Johnny?" she called, turning back to seek him. He must have gone into the bathroom without her noticing. There was noplace else in the small apartment where he could possibly be.

Wolf stood in the doorway, staring at her.

Rachel stared back, not knowing what else to do. The dog blocked the only exit.

"Johnny!" A hint of panic edged her voice. The animal was enormous, tall and stocky and obviously battle scarred. If he was any particular breed, Rachel couldn't identify it. But then, she had had very little experience with dogs. Her aunt Lorraine had once had a toy poodle, and that was the extent of it. Her mother would never tolerate dogs in her immaculately kept house.

Johnny, wherever he was, did not answer. Wolf's eyes appeared to sharpen, and the look he focused on Rachel seemed almost greedy. Dear God, did the creature mean to eat her? Would he actually attack?

Rachel stepped back a pace. Wolf, to her horror, advanced one.

"Johnny!" It was a full-throated yell. Wolf's ears pricked up at the cry, and he took another step forward.

Rachel, cautiously retreating, found herself with her back against the counter. Moving as nonchalantly as she could, so as not to provoke the dog, she braced both arms against the countertop behind her and eased herself into a sitting position atop it. Wolf took another step forward. He was all the way inside the kitchen now, not more than a yard from her dangling feet.

"Johnny!" This time it was a despairing wail. Wolf's head came up, his eyes gleamed, and Rachel hastily tucked her feet beneath her, then scrambled to her feet. Crouched on the counter, she grabbed a long-handled wooden spoon that rested near the sink and held it out before her as a very inadequate shield.

"What the—" At Johnny's voice from the doorway, Rachel practically sagged with relief, so glad to see him that she didn't even mind the amusement evident on his face.

"Help," she said weakly.

Johnny grinned.

"Where were you?"

He walked into the kitchen, still grinning, brushed by Wolf, who flattened his ears and wagged his tail for his master, and opened the refrigerator door.

"Down in the store. I needed some salt for the spaghetti sauce, and I remembered that Zeigler keeps little packets from Burger King in his desk."

Extracting something from the depths of the refrigerator, he tossed it to Wolf, who gulped it down eagerly and wagged his tail for more.

"Go lie down," Johnny said, waving the animal away. To Rachel's relief and amazement, the animal turned and went.

"He wanted a hot dog." Johnny came over to lift Rachel down from the counter and remove the spoon from her grasp.

"A hot dog? Are you sure?" Still shaken, Rachel leaned her forehead against Johnny's chest.

"I'm sure. What did you think he wanted?"

"To eat me," Rachel said with conviction.

Johnny burst out laughing. He laughed until Rachel, disgusted, brushed by him, meaning to return to the bedroom.

Wolf, sprawled on his stomach just outside the kitchen door, stopped her in her tracks. She eyed him with dislike. He looked back at her with what she was ready to swear was mockery.

"Here. Give him one."

Johnny, coming up behind her—and wisely no longer laughing—tried to put a slimy-looking hot dog into her hand.

"No! I'd sooner try to feed a barracuda!" Rachel folded her arms over her chest so as not to be persuaded.

"I want you two to be friends. Come on. Please."

Johnny in a coaxing mode was enough to weaken her knees—but not her fear. Rachel shook her head.

He sighed. "I'll make a deal with you. You try to make friends with Wolf, and I'll try to make friends with your mother."

Rachel stared at him disbelievingly. "Are you actually comparing my mother to an ill-trained, ferocious, gargantuan monster of a dog?"

Johnny shrugged. "She scares the hell out of me."

Rachel looked up at him for a moment, considering. "All right," she said grudgingly, and held out her hand for the hot dog.

By the time Johnny's spaghetti dinner was ready, Rachel felt that if she and Wolf were not exactly friends, they had at least called an armed truce. The cost of peace had been one and a half packages of hot dogs.

For the rest of the day, they did very little. They ate, walked Wolf in the vacant lot across the street from the store, went for a drive to nowhere really, then returned to sprawl on the couch with Johnny's head in Rachel's lap, watching TV and talking about nothing. The topic of Glenda they both deliberately avoided. Fortunately, the joy of new love proved a potent anesthetic against their sorrow.

At six, Rachel reluctantly began thinking about going home. When she broached that notion to Johnny after a quick meal of bacon and eggs that she threw together before she left because she couldn't bear the thought of him eating alone, his eyes clouded, but he nodded.

"Yeah, it's getting late."

"I'll stay the night, if you don't want to be alone."

They were in the kitchen, unloading the dishwasher. The ease with which they performed simple domestic chores such as cooking and cleaning up together surprised Rachel. It was as if she had known him all her life—which, when she thought about it, she nearly had. The realization made Rachel smile a little.

"You don't need to do that."

She put away the skillet that she had been returning from dishwasher to cabinet and turned to face him. He was leaning against the counter, watching her. His face was perfectly expressionless, but she knew, without knowing how she knew, how much he hated the idea of her going.

"I know I don't need to stay. The question is, do you want me to stay?" Her words were direct, cutting through the smokescreen of his self-sufficient maleness. She waited. He had been without anyone to lean on for so long that admitting to needing her, or indeed anyone, was hard for him.

He grimaced. "Your mother will probably come after me with a shotgun if you stay. If anyone else finds out, you'll be branded a scarlet woman by the whole town. The school board might invoke your—what was it?—moral turpitude clause, and you'll get fired. Do I want to put you through that? No."

"None of that matters, if you need me."

"I want you to stay, but I don't need you to, not enough to put you in that kind of position. No, you go home tonight, and sleep in your own bed, and come spend the evening with me tomorrow."

"Will you cook?" Rachel asked, smiling.

"Spoiled you already, have I?" He grinned and held out his arms to her. Rachel walked into them, and they closed around her as if he never meant to let her go, for all his fine words.

By the time she left his apartment, it was nearly eight o'clock. He saw her into her car, then stood on the pavement, watching her drive away.

Leaving him alone with his ghosts was the hardest thing Rachel had ever done in her life.

34

The following few days were at the same time the best and worst that Rachel had ever experienced. On the plus side, she spent her evenings with Johnny, sneaking up the back way to his apartment after the store closed so that she wouldn't be seen and staying until eleven or eleven thirty each night. They walked the dog, slow-danced around the living room to a collection of oldies that Johnny had put together as a teenager and had just lately retrieved from his father's house, cleaned the apartment, cooked, made love. All the while they talked, about anything and everything, and Rachel rediscovered the sensitive, intelligent, knowledge-hungry mind that had once so attracted her. That that mind now resided in the body of a man, not a boy, a man with whom, moreover, she was deeply, passionately in love, seemed like a gift from the gods. To be able to discuss such widely divergent topics as life after death and the intricacies of spaghetti sauce with a man who both quoted Henry Wadsworth Longfellow and drove her out of her senses with lust was more than she had ever thought to ask from life.

On the debit side, Tylerville was agog with Glenda Watkins's murder —and most of the townspeople were convinced that the killer was Johnny Harris. The town's propensity for gossip had turned ugly, and rumors abounded. Tales ranged from a cult of devil worshippers (with Johnny as the head demon) to Johnny as homicidal sex maniac. The more ridiculous tales would have been easy to laugh off, except that they concerned the man she loved.

Even her own mother, despite Rachel's assurances that Johnny could not possibly have done it, outspokenly considered him a psychopath. As she told her daughter, she hoped he would not undergo a Dr. Jekyll–Mr. Hyde–style personality change while Rachel was with him.

Only Becky was in the slightest degree sympathetic to Rachel in love, and that was because she was experiencing her own tumult. Michael had gone back to Louisville without Becky's signature on the papers that would permit him to sell the house, but he had threatened to return the coming weekend. Becky, sick at heart, put aside her grief to champion her sister to their mother. Rachel in turn listened to Becky's outpourings whenever her sister felt the need to talk. Devoted to each other as children, only slightly estranged by the upheavals of adolescence and Becky's subsequent marriage, the two now grew close again. Rachel discovered that having her sister as friend and ally was an enormous source of comfort, and Becky seemed to feel the same.

Glenda's funeral was scheduled for Saturday morning, a week to the day after her death. The additional time was needed to allow authorities to run more tests on the body. On Thursday preliminary word had come back from the state crime lab that her killer and the murderer of Marybeth Edwards appeared to be one and the same. In the eyes of the law, Johnny was beginning to look like an innocent man. But gossip had branded him guilty, and the town sizzled with discontent because so obvious a suspect remained free.

Chief Wheatley had warned him not to come, and he had promised Rachel that he would heed that warning, but Johnny showed up at Glenda's funeral. Rachel nearly fell out of her chair when she saw him walk in the door of the same small paneled room in Long's funeral home where the service for Willie Harris had been held. A good portion of the town had turned out for this one, although most were curiosity-seekers drawn by the sensational nature of Glenda's demise rather than family or personal friends. Even a reporter for the *Tylerville Times* was present, along with a photographer. When the photographer began snapping pictures, Sam Munson hurried up and asked him to stop. A loud argument ensued, the upshot of which was that both reporter and photographer were summarily evicted from the proceedings.

Things quieted down for a few minutes after that. More flowers arrived. Taped funeral music blared forth unexpectedly over the loudspeaker, causing the nervous to jump before the volume was hastily adjusted to a suitable level. The eyes of many in the overflowing crowd focused on the closed coffin as someone wondered too loudly just how disfigured the corpse was. The room seethed with morbid speculation on the exact details of the murder. Everyone, it seemed, agreed on just one thing: the most likely suspect. The name Johnny Harris was bandied about freely, though it was never spoken above a whisper.

More flowers were carried in, to be placed with the banks of chrysanthemums and lilies and carnations that surrounded the coffin. There were no roses. If any had been sent, Sam Munson had tastefully hidden them from sight.

By the time the minister arrived to begin the service, the funeral had taken on more the atmosphere of a macabre circus than a religious ritual.

Seated between Kay Nelson on her left and Becky on her right, watching the minister walk up the aisle, Rachel suddenly realized that the whispering had increased and changed in character, taking on an ugly overtone. Looking around for the cause—had the family entered?—she spied Johnny, clad in the same style jeans and T-shirt that he always wore, propping a shoulder against the wall at the rear. Exactly when he had entered she didn't know, though probably, judging from the volume of talk, only a few seconds earlier.

Rachel's face paled, but before she could rise to go to him, there was another surge of whispering. The four Watkins children, accompanied by a gaunt-faced, fortyish man whom Rachel assumed was their father, a young woman (the "whore" Jeremy had mentioned?), and an older couple, walked up the aisle and sat in the front row. Then the minister, who in his black robes had been impatiently waiting, advanced to the podium and began.

"Dear friends, we are gathered together today to mourn the passing of our loved one, Glenda Denice Wright Watkins. . . ."

There was no way Rachel could reach Johnny now, seated in the middle of a row as she was, without drawing more attention to herself and him than she cared to. Becky and Kay, alerted by her obvious agitation, glanced around and saw him, too. So did Chief Wheatley, who was present with several of his men. Though the chief didn't look any too happy about the necessity, he unobtrusively rose from his seat at the back and went to stand beside Johnny. The two exchanged measuring glances, but more than that Rachel could not see. She was forced to turn her face to the front as the minister exhorted them all to pray.

The service was short and, to Rachel at least, extremely moving. Tears flowed down her cheeks as she listened to the eulogy, the hymns, and the prayers and thought of Jeremy and his brother and sisters. The loss of a mother was perhaps the worst thing that could happen to a child, and Rachel grieved for the children as well as for Glenda.

Afterward, when everyone was standing and getting ready to file out, Rachel, trapped in a sea of people, watched Johnny skirt the crowd by moving around the perimeter of the room. He headed toward the front, where the coffin sat amid the massive display of flowers. Chief Wheatley trailed him doggedly, as did Kerry Yates and Greg Skaggs. The two younger officers' expressions were carefully wooden, as if they were doing their job but didn't particularly like it.

"I thought you said he wasn't coming," Becky whispered to Rachel as she caught sight of Johnny and his police contingent. Becky had only been two grades ahead of Johnny in school, and so she had known him— or rather, known of him—fairly well for most of her life. Rachel watched her sister study the man Rachel loved but could read nothing in Becky's face.

"Look, there's Johnny Harris," said Kay in a rather louder whisper from behind Rachel. "I can't believe he had the gall to come! Oh, look, he's actually going to talk to the family!"

Rachel—distracted from her intention to assert very firmly that Johnny had come because he was innocent, because he had cared for Glenda and grieved for her—watched as he reached Jeremy, whose back was turned, and laid a gentle hand on the boy's shoulder. Jeremy glanced around, gave a glad cry, and suddenly all four kids came swarming, huddling around Johnny. Their arms circled his thighs and hips and wherever else they could reach. Johnny, visibly moved, dropped down on one knee to envelop them in a hug.

"Can you believe that?" Kay asked as if she couldn't, while all around them similar sentiments were being aired. Rachel finally reached the end of the aisle and hurried toward Johnny. Though he was intent on the kids and Chief Wheatley and his officers formed a wary guard behind him, there was no one to protect him from the vicious murmurs and hate-filled stares that suddenly electrified the atmosphere.

The smell of the flowers was so strong it was sickening, Rachel thought as she reached the little group so near the casket. Then she noticed that something, perhaps a fluke in the air-conditioning, made this section of the room icy cold. With a nod to Chief Wheatley, Rachel knelt beside Johnny. She said nothing to him, though the look she shot him spoke of her reproach. Still, at the sight of his set face and the obvious affection the clinging children felt for him—Jeremy whispered in his ear, while the smaller boy hugged his bent knee and the two girls, one about six and the other maybe Katie's age, rested their heads on his chest —she forgave him for risking a snub or worse. The children clearly took comfort from his presence, and she understood that that was why he had come.

Only the older girl, a pretty blond sylph in a tucked and ruffled white dress that had obviously been purchased new for her mother's funeral, was crying. The rest of the children were pale but dry-eyed.

"Guys," Johnny said in a tone much nearer normal than anything

Rachel could have managed at the moment, "this is Miss Grant. She and your mother were pretty good friends. Rachel, this fellow here is Jake—this is Lindsay, this is Ashley, and you know Jeremy."

"My mom's dead," three-year-old Lindsay offered, sticking her thumb in her mouth and regarding Rachel out of huge blue eyes.

Rachel felt a lump rise to her throat that choked all utterance. The only thing she could do was pat the child's soft cheek.

"She knows that, dumbo. It's why she's here." Jake, the sturdy little boy whose arm was hooked around Johnny's leg, scowled at his sister.

"Would you just stop talking about it?" Ashley whirled away from Johnny with a sob and ran across the room. She cast herself against the older woman who had entered with them and who now stood chatting with a crowd of well-wishers. The woman, who Rachel assumed was the children's grandmother, put her arms around the weeping little girl and looked over her head to find the others, who still surrounded Johnny. She turned her head and said something to the children's father beside her.

Mr. Watkins's face turned lobster red as he looked around.

35

$\mathcal{J}$ake tugged on Rachel's hand. She smiled at him, taking his chubby baby fingers and rubbing them gently between hers, and he smiled guilelessly back.

"How are you doing, Jeremy?" Rachel asked, still holding Jake's hand as she looked up at the older boy with compassion. Jeremy had stopped whispering in Johnny's ear to stare after his sister.

Jeremy glanced at Rachel. The strain and sadness of the last few days showed in his wan face. The look in his eyes was the saddest thing Rachel had ever seen in her life.

"I'm okay. And so's Jake." He paused, and his lower lip trembled before he pressed both lips firmly together. "But with my mom gone there's nobody to read to the girls, or fix their hair. My dad doesn't know how to braid."

"Oh, Jeremy, I'm so sorry about your mom." The very fact that he wasn't bawling made Rachel want to.

"Miss Grant, I—" Jeremy began in a quick undertone, only to break off abruptly as Becky, standing behind her, touched Rachel on the shoulder.

"Rache, look out," Becky murmured, but before she could say more, Jeremy's father stormed across the room. Unaware or uncaring that he was suddenly the cynosure of all eyes, he snatched Jake away from Johnny's knee with one hand and shoved Johnny backward with the other.

"Damn you, you stay away from my kids!" Mr. Watkins roared. He grabbed Lindsay by her arm and jerked his head at Jeremy in a silent order to him to move away. Rachel shot upright in instinctive defense of Johnny, took one look at him as he scrambled to his feet, and held her breath in anticipation of the brawl she expected to follow. Chief Wheatley, obviously laboring under the same assumption, grabbed one of Johnny's arms, and Greg Skaggs latched on to the other. Johnny, to his credit, didn't struggle at being thus restrained but stood motionless, regarding the bellicose Mr. Watkins with a smoldering anger that was nonetheless potent for being held carefully in check.

"That's enough, Watkins!" Chief Wheatley's voice was sharp.

"Why don't you arrest him instead of protecting him? My kids have lost their ma, and you take the side of the man who did it!"

"From the way it looks right now, Harris isn't any more guilty than you are, Mr. Watkins. I told you that."

"He killed her! He had to have done it! First that other one, and now Glenda!"

"Dad, Johnny wouldn't ever hurt Mom! They—they kissed and stuff! Besides, I saw—I saw—" Jeremy rushed to Johnny's defense, only to break off abruptly, clamping his mouth shut. His eyes were wide as he glanced at the ring of people assembled around him.

"What did you see, son?" The chief's voice was gentle.

"I saw something in the dark. Something—I don't know," he muttered, looking at the gray-carpeted floor. Then his eyes flashed up, and he said with a resumption of spirit, "But it wasn't Johnny! I know it wasn't Johnny!"

"You go on to your grandma, Jeremy, and take Jake with you," Mr. Watkins ordered. Jeremy threw his father a partly scared, partly resentful glance, then took the softly blubbering Jake by the hand and led the little boy away.

Mr. Watkins, holding a thumb-sucking Lindsay in his arms, said to Johnny after Jeremy was out of earshot, "I see you near my kids again, I'll kill you. I swear to God I will."

Then he spat at Johnny's feet and walked away. The shiny globule of saliva trembled on the carpet. Rachel glanced at it, then looked quickly up as her stomach churned.

"Are you going to let him get away with that? And he threatened Johnny—that was a threat if I ever heard one!" Rachel turned on the chief with trembling outrage before anybody else could say a word.

"Let him be. He's the kids' father, for God's sake. They don't need any more to worry about right now." Johnny sounded tired. He shrugged free of the men holding him. First the chief, and then, more slowly, Greg Skaggs stepped away from him. Rachel, offering silent comfort without thinking about how it might look, took Johnny's hand, entwining her fingers with his. His hand linked with hers felt warm and strong and right.

Becky, Kay Nelson, who had followed the sisters when they moved toward the front, and Susan Henley, who had just joined the group, presumably to speak to Rachel, stood mute, having watched the unfolding drama wide-eyed. Rachel looked beyond Susan to Rob, who had just walked up with Dave Henley, and inwardly winced. But she did not release Johnny's hand.

Rob said nothing, but his eyes were angry and shocked as they traveled from the linked hands to Rachel's face.

"Rachel," Susan said, "we're going to lunch, and we thought you and Becky—and Kay if she wants—might like to join us. And—and . . ." Susan's voice trailed off as she, too, noticed the whereabouts of Rachel's hand.

Johnny looked sardonic. Rachel, clinging tightly to his hand when he would have withdrawn it, shook her head.

"Thank you, Susan, but Johnny and I have other plans. You do know Johnny Harris?"

"Yes. Oh, yes." Susan looked unhappy.

"Rachel, could I see you a minute?" Rob's voice was as cold as his face. Rachel glanced at Johnny, uncertain how he would react to this, only to find his hand freeing itself from hers. His body had stiffened at Rob's words, and his eyes gleamed at Rob in a way that was a good deal less than friendly. But he said nothing to deter Rachel.

Feeling that another unpleasant scene might well be imminent if she allowed the two men to remain in close proximity for very many more seconds, Rachel cast Becky a pleading look. She allowed Rob to take her arm and pull her away into a corner where a large silk ficus provided a measure of privacy. Before the foliage blocked her view, she was relieved to see her sister move closer to Johnny. Becky, fiercely loyal in a crisis, would spread the mantle of her good name and sterling reputation over Johnny while Rachel was otherwise occupied.

"I couldn't believe my eyes," Rob began in a furious undertone, turning to face her. "You were actually holding hands with that murderer in front of all these people! At the funeral of the woman he probably stabbed to death! Have you lost your mind?" He took a deep breath and held up a hand for silence when she would have replied. When he continued, his tone was more conciliatory. "Rachel, I've ignored the gossip, and I've marked down your interest in Harris to a kind heart and your instincts as a teacher. But this is taking things too far! Either you agree right now to stop having anything to do with him, or we're history."

"Then I guess we're history." To Rachel's surprise, she almost enjoyed saying it.

"What?" Rob sounded stunned. Clearly that was far from the response he had expected. "Rachel, you have to be nuts! You told me he couldn't possibly have killed Glenda Watkins because you were with him, but I think that's horse crap! Somehow he found a way! It's too much of a coincidence otherwise! Even if I didn't care about you, I'd point out to you what is just as plain as the nose on your face: you're putting your life in danger every time you're with him! Who knows what it takes to make him go off?"

"Johnny does not 'go off.' And he would never hurt me."

"Johnny," Rob said bitterly. "Rachel, you fool! I was going to marry you!"

Rachel ran her eyes over him from the top of his neatly groomed head to the bottom of his shined wingtips. Her gaze missed nothing on the way. Without regret, she absorbed the maturely attractive face, the conservative suit, the correct tie, the aura of affluence that he emanated. Rob was the very embodiment of the husband she had made up her mind she wanted. Only now it seemed her dreams had changed.

"I don't think we would have suited each other very well, Rob," Rachel said, with more gentleness than he perhaps deserved after all his unkind remarks about Johnny. But it was not Rob's fault that under Johnny's tutelage she had discovered a wild, hedonistic, uninhibited side of herself that she had never suspected existed. It was not Rob's fault that he talked of golf and the stock market and his day at the drugstore, when what she wanted to talk about was the meaning of life and the writings of William Blake. It was not Rob's fault that his idea of a fun evening at home was a sweet little woman to cook his meals and clean up the kitchen afterward while he sat and watched football on TV. It was not Rob's fault that they were fundamentally incompatible. Indeed, he had had no reason to even suspect such a thing, when she had never let him see beneath the conventional veneer she showed the world to the dream-filled romantic that she truly was underneath.

"Apparently not." There was anger in Rob's voice now, anger in his controlled stance and his narrowed eyes. "I've been mistaken about you, Rachel, and I can only say I'm glad I discovered your true nature before it was too late."

"So am I," she agreed, perhaps too cordially for his taste.

Her reply seemed to infuriate him. His face reddened, and she could almost hear him grinding his teeth. (It was a habit of his when he was annoyed that she was just now discovering she truly despised.)

"You've changed," he said. "It's Harris who's changed you. You are having an affair with him, aren't you?"

"We're soulmates," Rachel said, meaning to be flippant. Only as her words reached her own ears did she realize they were true.

Rob snorted.

"Ready to go, Rachel?"

Rachel almost jumped at Johnny's quiet voice behind her. She turned to discover that he was looking at Rob, his gaze hard and steady. Johnny's hand, as it took her arm, was proprietary. Feeling it grip the soft flesh just above her elbow, Rachel was conscious of a sudden rush of joy so strong, she nearly smiled. She loved the idea that he was staking a public claim. She had had enough of creeping around backstairs to last her a lifetime.

"You're crazy, Rachel," Rob said harshly, his gaze moving from Johnny to fix on her face for a single sizzling instant. His lips tightened when she didn't reply, and he brushed past them. Rachel, watching him go, saw Dave and Susan Henley fall in behind him. Left with her and Johnny were Becky, Kay, Chief Wheatley, and the two young police officers who had watched this byplay impassively from a few feet away.

Fortunately the room had emptied. Sam Munson and his men were the only ones who remained, hovering discreetly around the coffin, which would only be removed to the waiting hearse for transportation to the cemetery after everyone was gone. The family still had the burial to endure, but for everyone else the funeral was over.

Rachel, ashamed of her own sudden happiness in this place of grief, bowed her head and allowed Johnny to steer her from the building.

36

⚜

At Glenda Watkins's funeral, the watcher went through the motions of normalcy, but underneath a tumult of emotions struggled for supremacy. For the first time, the dominant surface personality beneath which the watcher dwelled had begun to sense, inside its own body, the presence of the monstrous soul that was the watcher. The surface personality, the everyday personality that knew everyone and was known to all, was as different from the watcher's as it was possible to be. The everyday personality was pleasant and likable, concerning itself with the thousand and one small tasks that make up day-to-day life. The watcher was ageless, genderless, and pure evil. He seethed with rage and hatred, and those emotions drove him to kill.

Until this past hour, the everyday personality had had no inkling that it had had a hand in the killings of Marybeth Edwards and Glenda Watkins. But the sight of those four bereaved children—particularly the older boy, whom the watcher had glimpsed on the night of the Watkins murder—triggered a memory of that night in the surface personality. The memory seemed so real: blood everywhere, the look and feel of it— and the smell. The surface personality grew dizzy with horror and fear. But the surface personality did not want to remember. It fought against remembering. Confronted with a kaleidoscope of the sights, sounds, and smells of that night, it rejected them utterly.

The watcher and the surface personality became allies in inducing sweet amnesia. The watcher, wary of what might happen once the surface personality became aware of his existence, shut down. For a brief period, it was as if the watcher's independent thoughts and feelings and memories ceased to exist.

The surface personality concentrated on reality: the sharp edge of the seat against the backs of tensed legs, the comforting cadence of the preacher's voice, the warmth of the bodies of the friends who sat on either side. The hideous, whirling images that must have been conjured up from some long-forgotten horror movie receded. Thankfully, reality won.

Moments later, with the surface personality lulled, the watcher once again, very carefully, came to life. Peering out through the body's eyes, the watcher experienced with satisfaction the funeral service of the woman he had murdered. But before the mourners filed out the door, the watcher was once again filled with rage. Because it seemed that the Watkins woman's killing, like the one before that, had been in vain.

Johnny Harris had found a new paramour. And the watcher was now presented with a new quarry to hunt down and destroy.

He seethed with the need to do that.

But first, the surface personality must be given time to lock that errant memory of the Watkins murder firmly away. Then the small threat that had so unexpectedly reared its head had to be removed.

The boy had seen something in the dark, had he? The watcher was suddenly filled with black humor.

Wait till he got a closer look.

37

---

*D*espite Rachel's obvious reluctance to leave him, Johnny sent her off with her sister and their friend for the afternoon. Then he took off on his motorcycle, which now sported a new set of tires. There were things he had to do and think about. Glenda's face and the faces of her kids haunted him. He kept thinking that he could have done, should have done, something to prevent what had happened. He had not killed Glenda, just as he had not killed Marybeth, but somehow he felt guilty, as if the deaths were in some way his fault.

The why of it he had not yet figured out, or the who of it, as in who had done it. But he felt, with a deep, dark instinct that he could not properly explain, that the murders were linked in some inexplicable fashion to him.

He thought back, way back, all those years ago to Marybeth. She'd been a pretty little thing, slender and blond and petite, as he had always preferred his women to be. Her folks were affluent members of the country club and pillars of the community. Marybeth, as their youngest child, had been spoiled to death. Anything she had wanted, Marybeth had gotten—until she wanted Johnny Harris.

For the first time in her life, he guessed, her parents had told her no. Marybeth had refused to take no for an answer.

She'd been a sweet girl, very young and silly, her head full of dreams of becoming an actress or a model or even an airline hostess (which to her way of thinking was almost as glamorous as the other two). At the time, Johnny had been overwhelmed by her prettiness, her willingness to sneak around behind her parents' back to see him, and her innocent, ardent sexuality, of which he had taken full advantage with the utter self-centeredness of youth.

Looking back, it was easy to see that he'd been her first rebellion against her parents' velvet-gloved control. Such a typical adolescent rite of passage should not have cost her her life—but for some reason it had.

Glenda, now, was different. He had never at any time fancied himself in love with Glenda, nor had she been in love with him. They'd been friends, playmates as kids, buddies through grade school and early high school, casual lovers in their junior and senior year when both of them got an itch and there was no one else available to scratch it. When he got out of prison, they'd been friends and casual lovers again. She'd been as lusty as he was himself, but there had never been any delusions of love between them. Still, he had cared for her in his own way, and she for him.

Like Marybeth, Glenda had not deserved to die. Those children had not deserved to be robbed of a mother.

So what were the facts? There were two dead women, murdered by the same killer. A killer who'd struck twice in eleven years. The years in between the murders were the years he had spent enjoying the hospitality of the state. What had the two women had in common that he knew of? He had been sleeping with both at the time of their deaths. At the thought Johnny's blood ran cold.

Because now there was Rachel. Rachel, for whom he would have raked the moon from the sky and bagged up the stars and harnessed the sun. Rachel, who was more than he had ever dreamed she would be. His adolescent sex fantasy about making it with his pretty teacher had been a fantasy, but Rachel was real, a kind, gentle, courageous, loyal-to-a-fault woman who enchanted him even as her love unlocked the cold prison of his heart.

Rachel loved him. Those three words were the most beautiful poetry he had ever heard.

Was she in danger now because of that? Was there a loony-tune out there who killed the women he cared for? Or was there some other link between the victims, of which he was unaware? The whole thing was so impossible, so nightmare-crazy, he couldn't figure it out.

But at the thought of Rachel in danger he nearly turned his motorcycle around and hightailed it back to her side like a buck deer who has heard the hunter's gun in the woods.

Logic alone stopped him. It had been eleven years between murders. Another one was not likely to occur within a week of the second. Perhaps there would never be another one. Perhaps Marybeth had been killed by a wandering psychopath (Rachel's pet theory) and Glenda's was just a good copy of the first. Maybe Tom Watkins was smarter than he looked. Or perhaps—God, who knew? The possibilities were endless.

No, he did not *really* think Rachel was in danger. But he had been wrong before. And life had taught him to be wary.

If he was the link, who outside of her family knew about himself and Rachel? There was Rachel's mother, whom he knew basically as a disembodied, disapproving voice on the other end of the phone, and her sister, Becky, who'd been the most popular girl in her class at school. Becky was little, like Rachel, but more vivacious, more sure of her own attractiveness, more the kind of woman who would appeal to a cross-section of men. He'd always admired Becky from afar—her physical attributes, which she shared with her sister, were of the type that had always appealed to him—but it had been Rachel he'd lusted after even then. Between himself and Rachel, there had always been an awareness, an indescribable spark.

Soulmates. That's what they were. Johnny's lips lifted wryly as he considered that. How hopelessly romantic—and stupid—that sounded. He'd always heard that love brought strong men to their knees and turned their brains to mush. Maybe he'd better think twice about getting his hair cut.

He acquitted her mother and sister of wishing harm to Rachel. They were a thousand times more likely to murder him than her.

Besides, Glenda had been tall and strong for a woman. To murder her so quickly and viciously would have required an enormous amount of strength.

A man's strength.

Was there a man out there who hated him enough to kill the women in his life so he would be blamed?

Johnny almost smiled at that. Hell, that was most of the town.

It was a conundrum. He'd puzzled over it and turned it every which way he could and yet no solution suggested itself. All he could see was that two women he had cared for had been hideously murdered. Was he the link between them that had brought about their deaths?

If that particular theory was true—and there were lots of theories— then Rachel was in danger. He could stop seeing her—to protect her he was willing to do anything—but as he considered it, it occurred to him that the damage had already been done. That very public hand-holding at the funeral had been witnessed by at least a third of the town.

The other two-thirds would know about it by suppertime tonight. Tylerville's gossip network was ruthlessly efficient.

If for no other reason than to quiet his own fears, Johnny decided to go to Wheatley, point out Rachel's possible danger, and see what the police chief thought. Wheatley, for all that he was engaged in a profession that Johnny despised, was basically all right. He could be trusted, and he had access to a lot of information that Johnny didn't. Maybe he knew of another link between the dead women that would leave Rachel entirely out of the picture. Or maybe he did not.

Maybe, just maybe, there *was* someone out there who wanted to kill the women in his life.

Rachel was with her sister and their friend this afternoon. She would be perfectly safe. Johnny decided to rush his business so that he could be back by nightfall. Darkness brought danger with it, and until dawn cracked, he wouldn't let her out of his sight. If necessary, he would never again in his life let Rachel out of his sight.

The next day would be Sunday, with that infernal lunch that meant so much to her. Johnny grimaced. He'd have to face her mother across a tableful of silver and china and crystal. He suspected that Elisabeth Grant would take pleasure in making the meal as elaborate as possible just to rattle him.

Well, she could do her darnedest. Though he would never have admitted it to another living soul, not even to Rachel, he had prepared himself for this eventuality. Emily Post had been his late-night reading almost since Rachel had come back into his life.

He meant to do his best not to embarrass her, and his best was usually pretty darned good.

He also meant to do his best to keep her alive.

When this was over, if it was ever over, he'd have a second chance. The cops now believed he was innocent, not only of Glenda's murder but of Marybeth's. He needed to talk to his lawyer, which was one reason why he was headed for Louisville now. He wanted the stain of that earlier conviction erased from his life.

It was as if fate, having seen how much that was good in life it could snatch away, was now starting to hand things back.

38

$\mathcal{R}$achel was still feeling slightly affronted by Johnny when she and Becky dropped Kay off at her apartment. Grieving as he was in the aftermath of Glenda's funeral, she would have supposed that he would need her to comfort him. Instead, he had sent her off with Becky with an absent-minded squeeze of her hand and the excuse that he had business to take care of that afternoon. Rachel couldn't imagine what kind of business, as he worked for her and the hardware store was closed for the day because of the funeral. He hadn't even kissed her good-bye.

Rachel was surprised and ashamed to find herself minding that.

She knew he loved her, knew it with her heart and mind and soul, though he had never actually said it in so many words. But their love was so new, so unbelievably, excitingly wonderful, that she regretted every minute that they spent apart.

Clearly he did not feel the same regret.

"Sure you all don't want to come in for a few minutes? I have some great herbal tea." Kay climbed out of the car and turned to smile at Rachel and Becky. Rachel really looked at her for the first time in years and noticed with surprise that Kay, who'd been something of a wallflower through most of her youth and young adulthood, was now blossoming. There was color in her normally pale face, as though she'd been exercising or spending time outdoors or something. She wore makeup, which she usually didn't, and a sultry floral perfume. She'd tinted her naturally mousy brown hair to a sort of burnished auburn, and her apple green suit was smart. Her figure, always inclined toward plumpness, was still round, but more attractively so, and Rachel wondered if she had lost weight. She had been so caught up in her own concerns lately that such changes had happened without her being aware of them.

"No, thanks," both sisters chorused, mutually repulsed by the idea of herbal tea. Then they looked at each other and grinned. Kay shook her head at them, waved, and disappeared into the vestibule of her building.

"Kay's looking good, isn't she? I wonder if she's in love?" Becky asked idly as she pulled out of the parking lot and headed for Walnut Grove. She was driving Rachel's car, having had too much experience with her sister's driving to be a contented passenger.

"I was just wondering the same thing."

Becky laughed. "Who could it possibly be? The only two bachelors in town that I can think of are feuding over you."

"You mean Johnny and Rob?" Rachel glanced at Becky. "There have to be more single men in Tylerville than just those two."

Becky shook her head. "I've been keeping my eye out, and I haven't seen any. You probably haven't noticed, but I've been away long enough that I see things that are different when I come back. Young men with any ambition at all tend to leave Tylerville early, and if they return, it's with a wife and kiddies in tow." Becky smiled rather sadly, and Rachel was reminded of why her sister was checking out bachelors.

"Do you think you'll stay in Tylerville, Beck? After—after it's over?"

"The divorce, you mean? Go ahead and say it—I've got to learn to live with it. I will soon be a divorcée. Can you believe it?" She gave an unamused chuckle.

Rachel shook her head. "Life takes strange turns, doesn't it?"

"Like you staying home, when you always planned to travel everywhere and see the world and have wonderful adventures? While I—I thought I'd fall in love and get married and have babies and raise them here in Tylerville and never leave home at all. We neither of us got what we expected, did we?"

"You had the marriage and the babies."

"But it didn't turn out like I thought it would. Even when things between Michael and me were good, it—oh, it wasn't enough! Everything was always about *him*. His career, his clothes, his social life. I kept thinking, what about me?"

"I didn't know you felt that way. I always thought you were deliriously happy."

"I know. I wanted you all to think so, you and Mother and Daddy. I wanted everyone to think my marriage was a big success. I felt so bad about taking him away from you, Rachel. Did you love him very much?"

"Not nearly as much as I thought I did at the time."

They were silent for a few minutes, remembering. Then Becky threw Rachel a teasing look.

"I will say this for you—you know how to pick 'em. Johnny Harris is a hunk."

"A *hunk*?" Rachel had to laugh. Becky sounded like one of her teenage students.

"He is," Becky insisted. "I hadn't seen him in so long, I'd forgotten. He was two years behind us, but my friends and I always did think he was the handsomest boy in school. If only he hadn't been so wild! Anyway, he's a man now, and he's absolutely drop-dead gorgeous! All damn-your-eyes sexy, and the way he looks at you—wow! I wouldn't mind having an affair with him myself."

Rachel glanced at Becky and clasped her hands in her lap. "This may be more than an affair, Beck. In fact, I think it is."

"How much more?" Becky sounded suddenly serious.

"A lot more. I'm so in love with him, I make myself sick."

"You're not thinking marriage, are you, Rache?"

Rachel shrugged. "He hasn't asked me, so I can't say."

"Come off it, Rachel Elisabeth, I know you too well. You are thinking marriage, aren't you?"

"Maybe."

"You know all the obstacles as well as I do."

"Yes."

"Then I won't say anything more. Except that marriage is hard enough when people have everything going for them—like I thought Michael and I did. I'd hate to have two strikes against me from the start."

"I know."

There was a pause.

"Rachel?"

"Yes?"

"To answer your earlier question, I think I will stay home in Tylerville for a while. It's good for Mother to have the girls, and it's good for the girls to have Mother. And it's good for me, too. So—if you're thinking you might want to move away, you can consider yourself free to go. I'll keep the home fires burning till you decide to come back."

Rachel glanced at Becky, surprised. "You do know me too well, Beck."

"How else could you marry Johnny Harris? He's not the type to stay here, and I don't see how he could even if he were. Whether he's guilty or not will never matter to most of these people. They think he is guilty, and nothing and nobody will ever change their minds."

"I know. I was thinking about that."

"So if you're bound and determined to do it, don't let any worries about Mother and Daddy stop you. You've done your part. It's my turn to do mine."

"The question may never arise. But thank you."

"Anytime." Becky smiled at Rachel, then returned her attention to the road. Seconds later, she gave her sister a sideways glance. "Rachel?"

"Yes?"

"You *are* sure he is not a psychopathic lady-killer with a Dr. Jekyll–Mr. Hyde complex who likes to turn his women into hamburger, aren't you?"

Despite Becky's attempt at levity, Rachel sensed seriousness behind the question.

"I'm sure," she said quietly.

Becky said nothing more.

When they arrived back at Walnut Grove, Rachel was suddenly, fiercely glad that she hadn't gone with Johnny after all. Michael's black Lexus was in the driveway with Michael standing beside it. The girls, with Tilda behind them, swarmed all over their father.

Becky, her eyes fixed on Michael, stopped the Maxima with a jerk worthy of Rachel at her worst. For a moment, a moment only, Becky sat staring out the windshield at her family without saying a word.

"Just looking at him makes me feel sick," she said. Before Rachel could do anything but glance at her sister with compassion, Becky clamped her lips together and got out of the car.

As soon as she did, Loren and Lisa left Michael and came running toward her. Katie, caught up against Michael's chest, stayed put.

"Mom, Dad says you two are getting a divorce!" Loren stopped dead in front of Becky to fix her mother with accusing eyes.

"He says that we should enroll in school here because we're going to be staying with Grandma and Aunt Rachel for a while!" Lisa sounded as upset as Loren.

Rachel, coming around the car to Becky's side, watched Becky whiten and felt helpless. There was nothing she could do to make this blow easier for either her sister or her nieces to bear.

"Darlings, Dad and I are talking about getting a divorce." Becky reached out to place a hand on each of her older daughters' shoulders. "But we haven't one hundred percent decided yet." She cast a burningly angry glance at Michael, who was walking toward her with Katie in his arms.

"It's best to tell them the truth, Becky," Michael said.

Becky's lips tightened and her eyes flashed, but after one glaring glance at her husband, she turned her attention back to her daughters.

"At this point, it looks very likely that Dad and I will get a divorce, so we'd probably better go ahead and get you enrolled in school here. That will be fun, won't it? To stay here with Grandma and Aunt Rachel and go to school right next to where Aunt Rachel teaches?"

"You mean we're not ever going to go home again?" Loren asked, wide-eyed.

"What about our friends?" Lisa looked on the verge of tears.

"And our toys!"

"And Rumsley!" Rumsley was the girls' cat, presumably left behind with Michael in the house.

"We'll get Rumsley, of course. And all your things. And you can still be friends with your friends from home and make new friends here at the same time." Becky tried desperately to put a positive face on the situation.

"I want to go home!"

"I don't want you and Dad to get a divorce!"

"Don't you care about us at all?"

"I hate you!"

Lisa burst into tears and ran for the woods behind the house. Loren started to cry, too, and ran after her sister.

"You handled that well," Michael said sarcastically, coming up to Becky and handing her Katie.

Becky stiffened. Rachel bristled on her sister's behalf, but she bit down hard on her tongue rather than say anything. This was her sister's life, her sister's business, and the best thing she could do for Becky was to keep her mouth shut and be there to support her when she needed it.

"*I* handled that well? How could you tell them, just like that? I was going to wait until we were sure—"

"We are sure." Michael was brusque.

Becky whitened. Wordlessly Rachel reached out and lifted Katie from her sister's arms and carried the toddler a few paces away to watch a pair of squirrels playfully frisking around a tree trunk. Rachel was still close enough to hear and see what was going on. It was her intention to keep a discreet eye on her sister in case Becky should need rescuing. Michael in this mood was a stranger, and Rachel had no idea what he was capable of.

Becky wrapped her arms around herself and stared up at her husband.

"How can you just throw the four of us away?" Becky's voice cracked as she spoke. Rachel felt her stomach clench in sympathy.

Michael looked impatient. "You're being melodramatic, as usual. I'm not throwing anything away. My daughters will always be my daughters, and I am sure we can work out a reasonable schedule of visitation. You know as well as I do that our marriage was a mistake. It quit working years ago. Now I've found somebody else I want to be married to. Why the hell won't you just let go before you hurt the girls any more?"

"Before *I* hurt the girls—!" Becky was speechless.

"This could be quite painless if you would just stop behaving so damned hysterically. I've already got a buyer for the house, at a premium price that's hard to come by in this tight market, I might add. Add that to what I'm prepared to give you to put a quick end to this nonsense, and you'll come into a nice little windfall if you'll just be sensible. And I'll continue to support the girls, of course."

"I've been asking myself if I ever really knew you," Becky whispered, her face as white as Rachel's silk blouse. "I don't think I ever did. Please don't come here anymore. If you have something to say to me, talk to my lawyer. I'll call your office on Monday and give you his name."

"I thought we both agreed that we would use mine."

"You agreed. I didn't. I don't think it's such a good idea."

"Becky—" Michael sounded impatient.

"Go away, please," Becky said in a stifled tone that Rachel knew meant that she was on the verge of tears. Becky turned away from her husband as she spoke. Rachel saw her sister's white face and desperate eyes as she walked blindly toward the house, and she felt her temper heat.

"See if you can talk some sense into her, would you, Rachel?" Michael asked in a harassed tone as he came to stand beside Rachel and stare after Becky. Rachel, her arms tightening around Katie, who was contentedly sucking her thumb, looked up at Michael in disbelief.

"You are a son of a bitch," said the woman who hardly ever swore, while Michael's eyes suddenly focused on her and widened with surprise. "And my sister is well rid of you. Now, please get off our land, or I will call the police."

Then she, too, turned her back on Michael and walked away.

A few minutes later, still seething, she watched from the front window as the black Lexus roared down the driveway and out of sight.

Rachel had meant to join Johnny that evening at his apartment, as had become their custom, but by seven o'clock it was evident that she was not going to be able to get away. Becky and the girls were still so upset that she couldn't leave them with their grief. Predictably enough, Loren and Lisa blamed their mother for the whole mess and could not speak to her without the discussion degenerating into shouted accusations and outbursts of hysterical tears. Rachel was left to try to explain the situation and comfort her older nieces and distract Katie, while Elisabeth provided a shoulder for Becky to cry on.

In the midst of this turmoil, the telephone rang.

Rachel picked it up. In the hallway beside the kitchen, Katie took one of the crayons Rachel had given her and began scribbling big red circles on the gold moiré wallpaper. Rachel grabbed the crayon, and Katie immediately began to howl. Sighing, Rachel spoke into the telephone as Katie ran off.

"Where are you?" said the voice on the other end without preamble as soon as she said hello.

As she recognized the peremptory growl, Rachel immediately felt better. Just hearing Johnny's voice soothed her.

"I can't come tonight," she said quietly, not wanting her older nieces, who sat around the kitchen table having brownies and milk, or her mother, who was in the library with Becky, to overhear. "There's been a crisis."

"What kind of crisis?" Johnny's voice sharpened.

"Michael told the girls that he and Becky are getting a divorce. Everyone's all upset. I really need to be here tonight."

"Oh." There was a pause. Then, on a slightly hopeful note, he continued, "Does this mean I can forget about coming to Sunday lunch?"

Rachel had to laugh. "No, it does not."

"I was afraid of that," he said gloomily. "Two o'clock, right?"

"About a quarter till. And Johnny—"

"Yes?"

"Don't worry. Mother can't eat you."

"Easy for you to say." But there was humor in his voice, and Rachel smiled.

"I love you," she said into the receiver.

"Hmmm." That was the closest he'd gotten to answering in kind. Then, in a slightly different tone, he added, "Rachel?"

"Yes?"

"Do me a favor?"

"Anything, except cancel lunch."

"Not that." He was smiling. She could tell even over the phone. "But don't go outside tonight, okay?"

"Why not?"

She could hear him hesitate. "I did a lot of thinking today. And it occurred to me that Marybeth and Glenda had at least one thing in common: me."

"So?"

"So—so do you. I don't know if they were killed because of something to do with me. I hate to even think it. But where you're concerned, I don't want to take any chances. So stay inside tonight, would you please?"

"All right." Rachel spoke slowly as her mind grappled with what he suggested. It was so obvious, and yet it had never occurred to her. If—and it was a big if—the murders had been aimed at Johnny in some way, she was now a likely target. The realization scared her silly.

"Promise?"

"Absolutely." She meant it. Wild horses couldn't have dragged her out of the house at night now.

"That's my girl." He sounded satisfied. "See you tomorrow for lunch then. Take good care of Becky and the girls—and yourself."

"I will. 'Bye."

"'Bye."

He was the first to hang up. Rachel held on to the phone a little longer. She loved him so much, she ached with it, and more than anything on earth she wished she were in his apartment, eating spaghetti or dancing or talking or . . .

"Rachel, who was that?" Elisabeth popped her head out of the library.

"Johnny, Mother. He said he's looking forward to lunch tomorrow."

"Is he?" Elisabeth looked as if she had tasted something sour, but after a glance at Rachel's face, she said nothing more on that subject. "Do you think the girls can talk to their mother like sensible human beings now instead of throwing tantrums right and left?"

Rachel shrugged. "Who knows?" she said, and waited for Elisabeth to notice Katie's embellishment to the wallpaper. But Elisabeth merely cast a harried eye over the thick red lines and withdrew. Rachel went into the kitchen to coax the girls into the library.

39

Back at his apartment, Johnny found himself missing Rachel sharply. He ate his solitary supper—a bologna sandwich, since he didn't feel like cooking—and tried to distract himself with a talk show on TV. But after watching for twenty minutes without even realizing until the end that the program was an infomercial, he switched the TV set off in disgust. Next he tried to read, but that, too, was a waste of effort. He couldn't concentrate on the printed page.

He should've been tired. He had had a hard day. Three hours on the cycle to Louisville and back, and another three spent taking care of the business that had taken him there. His visit with his lawyer left him feeling as if a weight he had been dragging for years had suddenly lightened. The attorney was readying the paperwork required to petition the court to overturn his conviction. If the petition was successful, and the lawyer expected it to be, he could expect to have the record of his conviction expunged. The next step in attaining full redress was to sue the state —but Johnny didn't even care that much about the money. What he cared about was that he would no longer be a marked man. He would be free to start his life anew.

That thought alone should have made it possible for him to sleep. But every time Johnny closed his eyes he kept picturing Glenda as he had last seen her and what had happened to her next.

And he thought of Rachel.

He could not escape the conviction that someone was out there in the night stalking Rachel. Call it morbid, call it paranoid, call it anything he would, the feeling would not be shaken.

At last, around eleven, Johnny gave up trying to distract himself. Pulling on his boots, patting Wolf an affectionate good night, he gathered up blanket and pillow and headed out the door.

Stupid as he would feel if he were discovered, he was going to camp out in Rachel's backyard. If there was someone out there, this time he was not going to confront a lone woman in the dark.

This time Johnny meant to be there, too. He would sleep outside Rachel's house until she was free to spend her nights safely in his arms. For as long as it took, until he was sure she was safe.

It would not be the first time he had slept out under the stars.

40

"*J*eremy." The soft voice cut through the misery that cloaked the boy. Seated on the back stoop of his father's small frame house, his head cradled in his arms and his arms resting on his bent knees, Jeremy heard it and looked up. He could see nothing through the moonlit darkness but the shed and the few small trees that dotted the field behind the house.

Sam whined pitiably from somewhere. Sam was his puppy. His dad had bought the dog to make up for what had happened to his mom. Oh, his dad hadn't come right out and said so. But Jeremy knew. He wasn't stupid. He'd never been allowed to have a dog before. Then Mom got murdered, and two days later he and Jake and the girls had a new puppy. It didn't take a genius to figure it out.

He was never going to see his mom again. That was what death meant. He knew it, even if the littler kids didn't.

Tears coursed down his cheeks. He brushed them away with an angry swipe of his arm.

"Jeremy. Could you help me please? Your dog's got all tangled up in this wire."

Sam, whose nightly business was the reason Jeremy was sitting on the stoop in the first place, whined loudly. Jeremy had just seen the pup scant moments before, when he'd been frisking about in front of the shed. He got to his feet and started down the steps. There was all kinds of barbed wire back behind the shed, and it could really hurt a little puppy like Sam if he got caught up in it. It was nice of Heather to be so concerned. His mom had always called Heather "the whore," but since his mom had died, she'd been real nice to Jeremy.

Only as Jeremy walked across the yard toward the shed did he remember that Heather was giving the girls a bath in the house.

But by then it was too late to run.

41

*E*lisabeth, with a big white apron wrapped around her church dress, was in the kitchen pulling the rolls from the oven and making the gravy. Rachel was taking Stan for a before-lunch walk in his wheelchair outside while the girls frisked around their aunt and grandpa in the backyard. Since Tilda and J.D. customarily had Sunday afternoon and evening off, it was left to Becky to answer the doorbell.

She put ice into the last crystal tumbler, then went to get it. She knew who it was before she even opened the door. Elisabeth usually had anywhere from four to six guests every Sunday afternoon. Today they were having just one.

Johnny Harris.

With a welcoming smile pinned to her face, Becky pulled the door wide. Then she stood gaping, the forgotten smile fading.

"My goodness!" she gasped, her eyes running over him again in disbelief. He wore a suit, an expensive-looking navy blue business suit that fit him like a glove, a crisp white button-down shirt, and a maroon silk tie. He'd had his hair cut. It waved crisply back from his face in a sexy businessman's cut that covered the tips of his ears and just brushed his shirt collar in the back.

"Am I early?" he asked. Her eyes traveled to meet his. It was Johnny Harris, all right. The blue eyes and the lean, dark, sinfully good-looking face hadn't changed much since high school days. She had thought him the handsomest man in Tylerville since she'd seen him at Glenda's funeral yesterday, but with his jeans and long hair, he hadn't been quite the type she fancied for herself. Now he was, and Becky was conscious of a stab of envy that her sister had nabbed a man who looked like that. Hunks were more her style than Rachel's, as a general rule. Though, of course, this one came with some major drawbacks.

"Becky?" He was looking down at her a little quizzically as she continued to stare at him without speaking.

"You look wonderful," she said with a burst of candor. Her instinctive pang of sister-envy was replaced by a tingle of anticipation at how pleased Rachel was going to be at his transformation. She smiled up at him. "Rachel is going to be shocked."

"Thank you—I think." In response to her gesture, he stepped into the huge entrance hall with its bronze busts and antique landscapes and the ancient oriental runner over the polished hardwood floor, looking just slightly ill at ease as he glanced around. "Where is Rachel?"

"She's outside with Daddy and the girls. Come into the living room. I'll get you a drink while you wait for her to come in." Becky shut the door, then led the way through the mahogany pocket doors that separated the living room from the front hall. "Won't you sit down? What can I get you to drink?"

"I'll have iced tea, please," Johnny said. Ignoring her invitation to sit, he walked to the huge bow window at the far end of the room. Through it he could clearly see Rachel pushing her father in his wheelchair along a stone walk that connected the patio to a paved area in front of what had once been a barn but was now a garage.

"Thank you," he said, accepting the glass from Becky as she rejoined him. "Are those your children?" He indicated the three girls who were playing in the grass.

"Yes. The one with black hair is Lisa, the younger fair-haired one is Loren, and the baby is Katie. I hope you don't mind dining with children. They always join us for Sunday lunch."

"I like children."

"Do you?" It seemed to Becky that she had endowed the question with a shade too much meaning—she immediately pictured him dandling Rachel's children on his knee and did not know quite what to make of the prospect—so she spoke again at random to cover up any awkwardness. "Rachel tells me you also like dogs."

"Does she?" A slow smile crossed his face, and he took a sip of tea.

"Rachel tells me that you and her mother don't."

"Why no, we don't. At least, we've never had one. My girls have a cat."

"That's nice."

The conversation faltered. Becky, who had never in her life felt uncomfortable talking to a man, floundered about searching for something to say and finally gave up. He did not look at her, but stood sipping his tea and watching Rachel through the window with an unreadable expression on his face. Becky thought of the wild, rebellious youth he'd been in school, of his time in prison, of the murders Rachel was so sure he had not committed, and shivered inwardly. He was a gorgeous man, no doubt about it, but there was an aura of danger about him that made it almost impossible for her to picture him with Rachel. Sweet, dreamy Rachel, who had always been so perfect, never behaving badly, never taking a wrong step. Rachel, who always knew the right thing to do and did it with inborn grace. To imagine her with a rebel like Johnny Harris, even in his present clean-cut incarnation, was mind-boggling.

"Rachel is—very fond of you," Becky said abruptly, wanting to discover just how he would answer. Rachel had never been as popular with men as Becky, and it was possible that her head had been turned by the raw sexuality that this particular man possessed in spades. If he spoke of Rachel with affectionate contempt, or dismissed her lightly . . .

"Did she tell you that?" His eyes slid around to Becky's face. She felt uncomfortable beneath their unblinking regard. What was it about him that made her so uncharacteristically nervous? His reputation? His looks? The suit, which made her think of him as a wolf in sheep's clothing?

"Yes. Yes, she did."

He smiled, and to her amazement Becky realized that, in addition to his devastating looks, he also possessed a large degree of charm. No wonder Rachel had fallen for him, and fallen hard. If it were not for Rachel, Becky thought, she might be tempted to indulge in a little flirtation with him herself. Nothing serious, of course, and certainly, under no conditions would she ever consider marrying a man like Johnny Harris. But for a short-term relationship, a fling, he would be wonderfully exciting. Unless it turned out that he was a Dr. Jekyll–Mr. Hyde type after all, as Elisabeth feared.

"Your sister is an amazing person."

Becky shook off the sudden attack of nervous shivers that threatened her. "I know. I'm glad you realize it."

Johnny looked out the window again almost meditatively, took a sip of tea, and glanced again at Becky.

"Rachel tells me you're getting a divorce. I'm sorry."

"Thank you." Becky gathered up her resolve. If she was going to learn anything about the real Johnny Harris, then she would have to be bold. Politely fencing with him would get her nowhere. "I hope you won't think me terribly rude for butting in, but my sister is very dear to me. You

—she"—despite her best efforts Becky was floundering again—"you're a very unlikely couple."

"I suppose we are, on the face of it. But your sister has a rare ability to see beneath the surface."

"There is a gap of several years between you."

"I don't let it worry me. She's of age."

The flickering smile that accompanied this silenced Becky for the moment. Like him, she sipped tea and looked through the window at Rachel, who was now pushing their father back toward the house. With the wind blowing her chin-length brown hair away from her face and whipping the full skirt of her lemon yellow shirtwaist dress around her slim legs, Rachel looked much younger than her thirty-four years. Love softened her face as she leaned forward to talk to their father, though Becky knew he probably didn't understand a word of what Rachel said or even realize that he was being spoken to. As she watched, Becky's heart swelled with affection for her sister, and she felt a fierce protectiveness as well.

"I just want her to be happy. She deserves to be happy," Becky said suddenly, intensely.

"We want the same thing, then."

"Rob—the man she was seeing—is a very nice man. He's a pharmacist, and he owns a lovely house, and he's forty years old. He'd make her a good husband." This abrupt speech was imbued with far more meaning than the words themselves indicated.

"I disagree with you there. I think she would have been quietly miserable within a year if she'd been foolish enough to marry him."

That startled Becky into looking up at him. "Why would you think that?"

"Because Rachel's a dreamer. Only a very few people realize it because of that practical exterior of hers. She experiences life differently from most people. Her loves are deeper, her loyalties are deeper, and her capacity for hurt is deeper. She deserves more than to be some Neanderthal's little housewife, and she wouldn't be happy in that role."

Becky's jaw sagged slightly as she listened to this eloquent, thoughtful, and totally on-target assessment of Rachel. She wouldn't have thought Johnny Harris possessed so much insight. In fact, before today she would have doubted that he possessed any insight at all.

Maybe Rachel's regard for him was based on more than Becky had supposed.

"Since you know all that, I suppose you know, too, that you could hurt her very badly."

"I would sooner cut off my hand than hurt Rachel." That flat, quiet statement rang with such truth that Becky felt the bulk of her fears slowly melt away. There were still many obstacles in the way of Rachel finding happiness with Johnny Harris, but the man's feelings for her weren't one of them.

"Becky, where are you? I need you to—" Elisabeth's voice arrived seconds before she herself did, and it broke off when she saw that her daughter was not alone.

"Oh," she said, and was silent for an instant as her eyes swept their guest from head to toe. From the faint shock that passed over her mother's features, Becky was confident that his appearance was as much a surprise to Elisabeth as it had been to herself. But Elisabeth, schooled in the social graces by years of acting as her husband's hostess for all manner of business and political functions, recovered almost at once. Becky did not think that anyone who did not know her intimately would even have recognized the slight hesitation before she continued, "I didn't realize you had arrived. How do you do? It's very kind of you to join us for lunch."

"It's kind of you to ask me."

Becky's nervousness over being the referee at this initial meeting began to dissipate. Her mother was being very formal but gracious enough. Clearly she had absorbed a sufficient understanding of Rachel's feelings for this man to avoid saying anything overtly impolite, though there was a certain stiffness to her bearing that Becky knew stemmed from disapproval. Johnny Harris could not know that, however, and what he did not know could not offend him.

Elisabeth, however, surprised and embarrassed Becky by being very direct.

"Rachel tells me she is in love with you. That fact alone dictates that we should become acquainted, don't you think?"

"Absolutely, ma'am." Johnny smiled at her. Elisabeth was made of sterner stuff than Becky—or perhaps she was past the age of being bowled over by a man's attractiveness. She did not appear visibly moved by his charm.

"I am glad you agree with me. That will make what I have to say much easier." Elisabeth moved forward, but she stopped walking when she stood directly in front of the fireplace, perhaps six feet away. She folded her arms over her chest. Becky, having listened to her mother's opening salvo with dismay, wished futilely for her sister's instant presence. Her wish was in vain.

"You must know that I have strong misgivings about your relationship with Rachel. She is convinced that you are not a murderer, and at this point I feel that I have no choice but to go along with her admittedly better-informed view of you." Elisabeth's chin came up, her eyes flashed, and she took a few purposeful steps forward, pointing a menacing index finger straight at Johnny Harris's nose. "But let me warn you, sirrah, that should harm befall my daughter while she is seeing you, I will hold you responsible, no matter what the police or the courts or anyone else might say. And I will get my husband's gun and seek you out and shoot you myself. I'm an old woman, my life is almost done, and I have very little to lose by doing so. So you may believe that I mean precisely what I say. Is that perfectly clear?"

"Yes, ma'am." Becky was relieved to see that Johnny looked slightly amused. She'd been afraid, listening to her mother, that he would take offense and stalk out, and she would be left to explain everything to Rachel, including why she had not intervened. But then, when had anyone ever been able to stop their mother when she was hell-bent on doing or saying something?

"Good. Then perhaps you would be so good as to step along to the backyard and fetch Rachel and the girls. Ordinarily I would not ask a guest to do so, but she's been on tenterhooks all morning waiting for you to get here. She meant to be inside when you arrived so that I wouldn't have a chance to speak my piece. But I fancy you were a little early."

"A little." Johnny regarded Elisabeth steadily. "I'm glad I was, though. Because now I have a chance to speak my piece as well. You don't have to fear that I'll murder Rachel, because of course I won't. But the rest of our relationship is strictly her concern, and mine. No one else's."

Elisabeth met Johnny's eyes in a measuring glance that reminded Becky of nothing so much as two opponents weighing each other's worth and recognizing the foe as formidable. Then Johnny smiled at Elisabeth, and Becky got the impression that the foils, having saluted, were now sheathed.

"I think I will go fetch Rachel. Excuse me."

With a nod at both women, he left the room, and seconds later they heard the front door open and close. Elisabeth glanced at Becky.

"He's not what I expected."

"No." Becky drew in a quick breath. "Mother, how could you say that to him? It was so rude."

"Better rude than to have your sister end up like the other women he's dated. Not that I sense that kind of viciousness in him, but how can anyone really tell? He's a handsome boy, and not afraid to stand up for himself. I like that in a man. But it's early yet to form an opinion of him. We'll see how this thing between him and Rachel goes."

"Mother—"

"Oh, hush, Becky, and come into the kitchen. I need you to fill the glasses while I serve the soup."

42

*W*hen Jeremy opened his eyes, he still couldn't see anything. For a moment he was frightened, thinking he must have somehow gone blind. Then he realized that wherever he was was very dark. So dark, he could see nothing. Absolutely nothing, not even his knees, which were drawn up right in front of his nose as he lay on his side on something very hard and cold.

Everything around him was cold, and musty-smelling, like an old basement. No place in his father's house was as dark and cold and bad smelling as this place, whatever it was. They didn't even have a basement. Or a cave, which was kind of what this felt like.

He was not in his father's house. Jeremy shivered as he realized that. Was he dead, then? Was this hell, or purgatory? Was his mom somewhere around? But no, she would be in heaven. If anyone deserved to go to heaven, it was his mom.

He lifted his head, meaning to look around. The sharp pain that ricocheted through his skull made him dizzy and nauseous. His head hurt. How had he hurt his head? Had he fallen?

Then, slowly, memory returned. He'd been sitting on the stoop, and someone—not Heather—had called him to come help free Sam. It occurred to Jeremy in a hideous flash of insight that that someone must have been whoever had killed his mom. The thing he'd seen in the dark —it had come back for him.

Jeremy whimpered. The sound scared him, and he shut up. What if he was in the thing's hideout—what if it was nearby, listening for him to wake up? Would it kill him, like it had killed his mom?

Very carefully, very quietly, he laid his head back down on the hard, cold surface beneath him, drew his knees closer into his body, and wrapped his arms around them. Curled up in a little ball, he closed his eyes again.

Silent tears seeped down his cheeks.

43

❧

"*A*unt Rachel, look!" Coming upright from where she had been turning cartwheels alongside the stone path, Loren pointed toward the house. Rachel, looking, frowned. Who was the man walking down the path toward her?

Johnny! She almost gaped as her eyes ran over him from the top of his shorn head to the polished tips of his cordovan dress shoes. He was still the handsomest man she had ever seen, but the elegant clothes gave him an aura of polish and easy power that she had never before associated with him. He looked like a young, handsome, and very sexy CEO. Who he didn't look like was Johnny Harris.

"Well?" He was grinning as he got near enough to speak, probably because of her expression. Rachel closed her mouth and shook her head at him.

"You got a haircut!"

"You told me I needed one."

"But you didn't have to—I hope you didn't do it for *me*."

"No, I did it for Wolf. Of course I did it for you! And for me, too. I'm getting too old to play James Dean."

She looked up, met his eyes, and in the silent exchange read the message he was giving her: He was ready to grow up, to give up his bad-boy persona, to move away from the past. The realization both touched and excited her. Maybe a future for the two of them was less impossible than she had thought.

"You look fantastic."

"Thank you. You look pretty good yourself." He glanced down at

Stan, who was staring blankly off into space, walked around the wheel-chair, put his hand under Rachel's chin, and turned her face up for his kiss. It was brief and hard and possessive. Rachel, dazzled by its effect, turned, tiptoeing, to wrap her arms around his neck and return the favor. A chorus of giggles stopped her in her tracks. She looked around, her face crimsoning.

Johnny grinned down at her as she sank back on her heels. Loren and Lisa, with Katie between them, stood close by watching and snickering.

"Is he your new boyfriend, Aunt Rachel?" Loren asked, wide-eyed.

Rachel had thought that it was not possible for her blush to get any hotter, but she discovered she was wrong.

"Yes, I am," Johnny answered for her, smiling at the girls. "And you must be Lisa," he pointed, "and Loren, and Katie."

"How'd you know our names? Aunt Rachel, did you tell him?"

Rachel, recovering her poise, shook her head. "This is Mr. Harris, girls."

Johnny's sidelong glance held a degree of amused surprise. "I'm not used to being called Mister. They can call me Johnny if they want."

Rachel shook her head. "Mr. Harris," she said firmly to her nieces. Then, to Johnny, "It's a mark of respect. They call all adults Mr. or Mrs., except for relatives."

"I see." He grinned at her. "I'll try to get used to it. But don't be surprised if I don't answer the first few times they speak to me."

"That's okay. As long as you answer when I do."

"Depends on what you call me."

Rachel made a face at him. Taking him by the hand, she walked around in front of the wheelchair. Johnny glanced at her questioningly, but she was looking down at her father and did not notice.

"Daddy, this is Johnny Harris," Rachel said in a quiet voice that was nonetheless insistent.

Stan continued to stare at nothing. His face was pale and expressionless, and his hands rested without moving on the blanket that covered his lap.

"Hello, Mr. Grant."

But Johnny's words had no more effect than Rachel's. Rachel stared down at her father as hope turned to resignation. He had not heard her. He would never know Johnny, and the realization brought with it a sense of loss.

"He used to be so—funny," she said over her shoulder to Johnny, who squeezed her hand with silent sympathy. "Bigger than life, always on the go, cracking jokes and cutting up, and—" Her voice faltered.

"Actually, I remember him from when I was a little kid," Johnny said to Rachel's surprise. "I was always afraid of him. He was such a big man, with his deep, booming voice. I remember one time I was in your hardware store cramming bubblegum into my pockets, and he said something behind me. Boomed it out. Just the sound of his voice scared me silly. I looked around, ready to run, certain I'd been caught red-handed, and discovered that he wasn't even talking to me. Boy, was that a relief! And did I hightail it out of there! And I never stole another thing from Mr. Grant's store, either."

Rachel knew her face must have been a study as she stared up at him. "*You* shoplifted from our store?"

Johnny grinned down at her. "I shoplifted from every store in town. Your dad coming up behind me was the closest I ever got to being caught."

"You're kidding!" Rachel pulled her hand from his.

He laughed. Amusement danced in his blue eyes. "No, Rachel, I am not kidding. You didn't think I was a choirboy, did you? As far as I know, the only thing I'm rumored to have done that I'm innocent of is murder. I never killed anybody. But the rest—yeah, it's pretty much true."

"Johnny Harris! No wonder you were so sympathetic to Jeremy!"

"Why'd you think?"

"Because you are a kind, caring human being who couldn't bear to see a child turned over to the police?"

"That, too. But I kept thinking that it could have been me sitting there, a long time ago."

Rachel spluttered wordlessly.

"Of course, I'm totally reformed," Johnny continued. His grin faded and he added in a more serious voice, "I talked to my lawyer yesterday. He said that with the evidence the police have, he can get the murder conviction expunged from my record. If he's right, I won't be a felon anymore."

"Really?" Rachel started to smile.

"Yeah, really." He grinned back at her. "Good news, huh? But you don't know the best of it yet."

"What's the best of it?"

Johnny shook his head. "I'll tell you after we eat. Your mother sent me out to round you and your nieces up."

"You've talked to Mother?"

"Oh, yeah. And Becky, too. And I drank some tea."

Rachel glanced down at her watch. "It's just now two o'clock. What time did you get here?"

"A little early," he said with a rueful grimace.

"Was Mother—did you and she—?"

"Your mother," Johnny said, "is a remarkable woman. And that's all I'm going to say."

"Oh, lord. Was she rude?"

"Not at all. Just—forceful. I think I could grow to like your mother."

Rachel, pushing the wheelchair, eyed him askance. "What does that mean?"

"It means that I now know from whence you got your spunk, Rachel the lion-hearted. I don't think either you or your mother realizes that you're just about five foot nothing and that a strong puff of wind—to say nothing of a full-grown man—could carry you off without even trying."

Rachel started to reply, but Becky appeared just then on the patio, beckoning impatiently.

"Mother's got lunch ready! Come on!"

The girls scampered toward their mother. Johnny insisted on pushing Stan up the elaborate system of ramps that led to the house, and he and Rachel were not far behind.

Lunch was served at the table so Rachel had ample opportunity to observe Johnny interacting with her family during the meal. Thanks to Becky, there were only water and wine glasses on the table, and the silverware had been kept to the bare minimum of salad and dinner forks, soup and dessert spoons, and steak and butter knives. Rachel had discarded the notion of trying to educate Johnny in the delicate art of table manners in preparation for today's lunch, so she was surprised and relieved when he unfolded his napkin and placed it on his lap when he sat down and passed the food to the rest of them without a hitch. When he used the correct plate for his roll, broke the warm puff in two with his fingers, and even removed a pat of butter from the communal dish to his bread plate before spreading it, she was impressed. When he flawlessly chose the correct utensil for each course, she was amazed. It was all she could do not to goggle at him as he managed course after course as if he'd sat down to such meals every day of his life. Her mother, who'd been watching him like a hawk at the start, was so reassured by his performance that she actually took her eyes off him for long periods of time as she lovingly fed Stan, who sat in his wheelchair beside her.

"Do you enjoy working at the hardware store?" Elisabeth asked Johnny as she expertly spooned a little soup into Stan's mouth.

"Not really," he answered. "Though I don't imagine I'll be there much longer."

"Oh?" It was Elisabeth who asked the question, though Rachel and Becky both looked at him in surprise.

"I've been thinking about going back to school."

"Really?" Rachel asked, while Elisabeth said at the same time, "Going *back* to school? Oh, you must mean attending college."

"Actually, I meant law school." Johnny consumed a bite of steak Diane as casually as if he hadn't made an announcement that Rachel, for one, considered momentous.

"Law school?" All three women spoke at the same time, with the same intonation. They glanced at each other, then focused as one on Johnny. He continued eating his steak, unconcerned. The girls, schooled to silence when eating with adults in the dining room, looked up from their own meal, their attention caught by the sound of their elders' amazement.

"Yeah." Johnny took a sip of wine and grinned directly at Rachel. "Don't you think I'd make a good lawyer?"

"But, Johnny—" she began, then broke off as she realized that this was something better discussed between the two of them in private. But he seemed to have no such reservations.

"That's many years down the road, surely? First you must get through college—and they don't allow convicted felons in any of the law schools I ever heard of." Elisabeth stopped feeding Stan to frown at Johnny.

"I have a college degree," Johnny said, his expression serene as he cut another bite of steak. "I earned a bachelor of arts in comparative literature while I was in prison. Besides working on a state road crew, taking college correspondence courses was how I passed the time. And if my lawyer is correct, I won't be a convicted felon much longer."

"What?" Elisabeth sounded stunned.

"The police are convinced that whoever killed Glenda Watkins also killed Marybeth Edwards. Everything about the murders, from the depth and severity of the wounds, which point to the same murder weapon, to the flowers strewn over the bodies, are virtually identical. I was with Rachel when Glenda was killed. So that lets me off the hook on the other rap as well. My lawyer says that with that kind of evidence, coupled with the fact that they never had any physical evidence on me to begin with, it should be fairly easy to get the record expunged."

Elisabeth looked first at Rachel and then at Johnny. "I see," she said slowly.

Rachel could see her mother turning the news over in her mind.

"May I be excused, Mom?" Loren piped up, pushing back her chair without waiting for an answer.

"Me, too, Mom," Lisa said, following suit.

"Don't you two want dessert?" Elisabeth, roused from her thoughts, smiled approvingly at her granddaughters. She had good reason, Rachel thought. They'd really been very well behaved, and with Katie upstairs napping, the meal had been as calm as any they'd enjoyed for some time. Since Becky and her brood's advent, to be exact.

"I'm too full," Loren complained.

"We'll have some later." Lisa looked at her mother. "Please, Mom?"

"It's fine with me," Becky said, while Elisabeth nodded. The girls left the room. Rachel could hear them running up the stairs. Their Nintendo had arrived along with boxes of other possessions, and Becky had had a man hook it up just the day before. Undoubtedly the girls planned to play video games to work off their lunch.

"That was delicious, Mrs. Grant," Johnny said, sitting back in his chair and placing his napkin beside his plate. Rachel, reminded of how impressed she was with his table manners, smiled at him.

"Thank you." Elisabeth smiled at him, too. Rachel noticed how much more cordial she was to Johnny now than at the beginning of the meal and was amused. Her mother was a sucker for two things: ambition and education. By laying claim to both, Johnny had gained a bushelful of stature in Elisabeth's eyes.

"Dessert?" Rachel asked. "Mother made cherry cobbler."

"Like your nieces, I think I'm going to have to wait till later."

"Coffee?"

Johnny shook his head.

"Rachel, if you all are done, why don't you take Johnny outside and show him around? I'll help Mother clean up."

"Thanks, Beck," Rachel said with real gratitude, and stood up. She was dying to get Johnny alone. She was holding back a question so hot that it was practically burning a hole in her tongue.

Johnny stood up too, complimented Elisabeth again on the meal, and followed Rachel from the room.

44

*"D*id you mean it, or did you just say it to shock Mother?" Rachel asked without preamble as soon as she was sure she had him alone. They were outside, walking down the same path along which she had pushed Stan earlier. Her hand clung tightly to Johnny's. Just how it had gotten there, or when, she couldn't have said.

"Mean what?"

"About law school."

"Oh." There was a pause. "Yeah. I meant it."

"Really?" Pleasure colored her voice.

"Can't you see me as a lawyer?" He laughed. "Don't answer that. But it's not so farfetched, you know. I got to know a lot about the law, and lawyers, while I was in the joint. I think I'd make a hell of a good public defender."

Rachel was dazzled. "Oh, so do I!"

"Like the idea, do you?" His eyes gleamed at her.

Rachel floundered. She had no reason, no concrete reason, to think that his future plans would have any impact on her. But her heart still beat faster as she contemplated life as Mrs. Johnny—no, Mrs. John Harris, Esquire.

"What *is* your middle name?" she asked, frowning.

He cast her a quick glance. "W. Why?"

"The letter W is not a name."

"If I tell you what the W stands for, you'll laugh."

"I won't. Anyway, I probably already know it. I'm sure it was on your school records, only I can't quite remember."

"Wayne."

Rachel's forehead knit. "Wayne? Why, that's a perfectly good name. What's wrong with John Wayne—" She broke off, and started to smile. Recollecting his warning abruptly, she turned her head away.

"Told you you'd laugh."

"I'm not laughing. Cowboy."

"There you go. That's what always happens. That's why I keep it to myself."

"I think it's charming. John Wayne Harris." She giggled, then covered her mouth with her hand as he shot her a mock-warning look. He pulled her off the path toward the woods that marched alongside the yard.

"I'm glad you like it." He was ahead of her, dragging her along behind him as he entered the woods via a well-worn path that she and Becky, and now her nieces, had used in their games. It led clear to the other side of the woods, a distance of perhaps two miles. But Johnny only went perhaps two hundred yards to the big climbing tree where, long ago, Stan had built his daughters a treehouse. It was scarcely more than a platform with sides, accessible by one-by-fours nailed ladderlike into the trunk of the huge oak. As children, Rachel and Becky had played there endlessly, and as a teenager Rachel had spent many a summer afternoon lying on the wooden floor, lost in a book. Now the leafy canopy that spread overhead was just beginning to turn gold. As Rachel looked up, a single yellow leaf floated slowly down to earth, twisting hither and yon with the whims of the wind.

"How did you know about our climbing tree?" Rachel asked as it became clear that this was the destination he had had in mind all along.

"Do you think I never explored these woods? Heck, Grady and I even watched you and Becky playing here once or twice. Sometimes, when no one was around, we played pirates conquering an enemy ship, and your treehouse was the ship."

"I didn't know that."

"You were too old for us to play with then, so we left you alone."

"I'm probably still too old for you to play with." Rachel's voice was rueful. Johnny glanced at her, leaned back against the tree, and pulled her against his chest.

"You're just perfect for me. If it was the other way around, if I were five years older, people would think that the difference in our ages was just right. How old is your pharmacist friend? Forty, isn't he? That's even more of a difference than between you and me, but did you ever think that he was too old for you? No, you didn't. You're guilty of sexism, Miss Grant."

His arms were around her, her body was pressed against his, and his voice poured over her with the seductive sweetness of warm honey. Rachel listened to the rumbling timbre of it with her eyes half closed and a small smile curving her mouth. When he wanted to, Johnny could charm the quills off a porcupine.

"Besides, I'm mature for my age," he whispered in her ear when it became clear that she wasn't really listening, and kissed the side of her neck.

"You were great with Mother," Rachel murmured as he kissed his way down her neck to the open collar of her dress.

"She still scares me to death, but I guess I'll get over it." Johnny tipped her chin back and kissed the hollow of her throat. Rachel, clinging to his shoulders beneath the sophisticated suit coat, closed her eyes and gave herself over to the pleasure of being made love to. The smoothness of the expensive dress shirt covering his muscles felt different enough beneath her fingers to act as a mild aphrodisiac. Rachel pressed closer against him as her toes curled in her Sunday pumps.

"Rachel."

"Hmmm?"

"Do you suppose you can climb this tree in that dress and those shoes?"

"Climb the tree?" Bewildered at his request, which was rather different from what she had expected, Rachel opened her eyes to frown at him. He dropped a soothing kiss on her turned-down lips.

"You heard me. Do you?"

Rachel looked at the makeshift ladder that led high into the tree. She followed its path with her eyes to the small hole in the floor of the platform that she would have to wriggle through. She glanced down at her pristine yellow dress with its tiny waist and full skirt, and the champagne-colored pumps below it.

"If you'll go first," she said.

"Surely you don't think I'd be so crude as to look up your dress?" Johnny set her on her own two feet and clapped his hands to his cheeks in mock distress.

"Yes, I do."

"You know me so well," he said, and grinned. As Rachel watched, he turned, reached up, grabbed a one-by-four, and headed upward with the agility of a teenager. Rachel followed, though a little more carefully. She really did not want to ruin her dress.

"Drat, I forgot about my pantyhose." She was frowning as she levered herself through the opening to sit with legs dangling down the hole. A large rip in the nylon was already sending half a dozen runners snaking out in both directions.

"You could always take them off," Johnny said with a suggestive gleam. Rachel turned to look at him. He was sitting with his back against the opposite wall, watching her with a wicked expression that told her more clearly than words could have what he had in mind. The entire platform couldn't have been larger than eight by ten feet, and the walls surrounding it were perhaps three feet high. There was no roof except the twining branches overhead and the thick canopy of leaves that blocked out most of the bright blue sky. Up so high—they were perhaps twenty feet off the ground—the breeze was stronger. Though the walls of the treehouse provided wind protection for its interior, branches swayed and creaked and leaves rustled, then gave up their tenuous hold on summer one by one to be borne whirling to the ground. The effect reminded Rachel of being caught inside a snow globe, only with golden leaves instead of crystalline flakes. Though the temperature was warm, the indefinable scent of approaching fall was in the air.

Rachel's eyes wandered over Johnny. He was watching her, his eyes a brighter blue than the barely glimpsed sky, a half-smile curling his mouth. The walls of the treehouse rose no higher than his shoulders, and behind him leafy green-gold branches made a backdrop so lovely, it was slightly unreal. The wind ruffled the blue-black waves of his hair. Rachel thought how much the more conservative cut became him. Now the planes and angles of his face, with its firm chin and high cheekbones and intelligent forehead, were more readily apparent, making him handsomer than ever. He looked a far different creature from the hard-bitten man who had stepped from the bus just a few short weeks before.

If she had known then how he would change her world, she would have run straight into his arms—and probably scared him right back into prison.

At the thought of how he would have reacted to such a greeting, Rachel smiled.

"Something funny?" he asked, cocking an eyebrow at her.

Rachel shook her head. "It's just that I'm happy."

"Are you? So am I. But I'd be happier if you'd come over here and sit beside me. I think we need to talk."

"Talk?"

"Why, did you think I had something else in mind?"

"I hoped."

Johnny laughed and held out his hand to her. "Come here, Rachel, and feel in my pocket. I brought you a present."

"Really?" She smiled at him in delight. The idea that Johnny had brought her something pleased her enormously. His first gift to her—besides himself. She would treasure it.

"Feel in my pockets," he said again when she was sitting beside him.

"I feel silly," she protested, laughing as she obeyed. The first pocket she checked was empty, but the second contained a tiny wrapped box. Drawing it forth, Rachel stared at it for a long time as it rested in the palm of her hand. Wrapped in silver foil and done up with white ribbons, it was exquisite. She glanced at Johnny.

"It's lovely."

"Open it."

He sounded slightly tense, and Rachel felt her heartbeat speed up as she slid the ribbons off and began to unwrap the box. She was almost sure she knew what it contained, but still, she might be wrong. She didn't want to get her hopes up too high.

The box was of shiny red cardboard, perfectly plain. Pulling off the lid, she discovered a jeweler's box inside.

Her hands were shaking as she withdrew the hard plastic case from the cardboard box and flipped back the lid.

Inside was a diamond ring, a gorgeous solitaire that was at least a half-carat in weight, set in white gold.

"Johnny! Wherever did you get the money?"

"Is that all you can say? I didn't steal it, if that's what's worrying you. The railway company offered Sue Ann and Buck and me seventy-five thousand dollars as compensation for my dad's death. They wanted to take it, so I agreed." The merest flicker of humor touched his eyes as he nodded at the ring. "There sits approximately one-fifth of my share."

"You shouldn't have! It's beautiful!"

"Would you please look at the damned thing?"

The edginess of his voice surprised her, but then she took a closer look at the ring. A tiny gift enclosure card was tied to the shank with a slender strip of white ribbon. Johnny's flowing black handwriting was on the card. Tilting the box so that she could see the words, Rachel read the inscription: "Marry me?"

She looked up at Johnny, who was regarding her with an odd, endearing mix of tenderness and anxiety.

"Well?" he said when she said nothing.

Rachel withdrew the ring from the box, slipped it, tag and all, on the ring finger of her left hand, then wrapped her arms around his neck.

"Maybe." She kissed his mouth.

"Maybe?" He sounded affronted, but as he was kissing her back very thoroughly at the same time, she couldn't be sure.

"You don't think you're going to get away with that measly excuse for a proposal, do you? If you want me to marry you, then you're going to have to ask me properly."

Johnny groaned. "I should have said it with flowers. I knew it."

Rachel punched him in the arm. "Quit joking. I'm serious."

He caught her by the shoulders and pushed her a little away from him so that he could see her face. She was kneeling beside his sprawled legs, her skirt spread out around her like the petals of a daffodil. Her hands came up to grasp his forearms as he gazed at her with some exasperation.

"So am I," he said.

"Then . . . ?"

He sighed. "Okay. Okay. Rachel, will you marry me?"

"No."

"No!"

"Try again. That was unsatisfactory."

"Good God. Do you expect me to get down on one knee?"

"That would be nice."

"You're kidding, right?"

Rachel shook her head. He stared at her for a moment, very hard. Then he gave her a wry smile of surrender, moved so that he was on one knee, and took her hand.

"Rachel, will you marry me?"

"Better, but no cigar. Or bride, in this case."

"Damn it, Rachel!" He glared at her in a distinctly unloverlike manner. His grip, which had tenderly cradled her fingers, grew hard.

The look she gave him was very bright and direct. "Johnny, do you love me?"

He met her eyes, and his gaze softened and warmed, though she did not miss the dark blood that crept up to stain his cheekbones. Clearly admitting to such a thing embarrassed him.

"Of course I do. You can kind of take that for granted when a man asks you to marry him."

Rachel shook her head. "I don't want to take anything for granted. I expect that this is going to be the last proposal I ever receive in my life, and I want it done right. If you love me, say so. Tell me, for goodness' sake."

"Rachel . . ." he began, with no small degree of wrath. He appeared to think better of whatever he had been going to say, because he closed his mouth and met her deliberately limpid gaze with narrowed eyes. Then, to her mingled surprise and amusement, the hand that was not holding hers moved to cover his heart. He looked for all the world like a surly boy getting ready to recite the Pledge of Allegiance under duress.

"Johnny—"

"Hush. Can't you see I'm about to bare my soul?" He frowned her into silence and took a deep breath. " 'My love is like a red, red rose that's newly sprung in June. My love is like the melody that's sweetly played in tune. So fair art thou, my bonny lass, so deep in love am I, an' I will love thee still, my dear, till all the seas gang dry.' "

Johnny's deep, low voice gave the poetry a haunting resonance that touched Rachel's heart. He no longer looked surly, no longer looked like a schoolboy reciting against his will, but like a man humbled and strengthened by the love he was confessing. Rachel met those smoky blue eyes, and at what she saw in them, tears rose to her own. Her fingers tightened on his as he continued softly.

" 'Till all the seas gang dry, my dear, and the rocks melt with the sun. And I will love thee still, my dear, while the sands of life shall run. And fare thee weel, my only love, and fare thee weel awhile. And I will come again, my love, though it were ten thousand mile.' "

For a moment after the last words died away, they were both silent. Rachel looked deeply into Johnny's eyes and thought she saw the true and good and shining thing that was his soul. Her eyes were so teary that they threatened to overflow—and then, suddenly, he grinned.

"Robert Burns must've had his pick of chicks. That poem of his is one hell of a line."

"Johnny Harris!" Shocked out of her weepy sentimentality, Rachel shoved him hard. He didn't fall on his backside, as she had intended, but he did lose the smirk and grab for her.

"Let me go!"

"Christ, Rachel, I was joking! I didn't mean it!"

"That lovely poem—I almost cried—and you were joking! I could kill you! I said let me go!"

She was struggling to get free. He managed to hold on to her as he sat again and dragged her across his lap, but the glare he got for his efforts was hot enough to singe his eyebrows.

"Take your hands off me!"

"Rachel, you misunderstood! I—"

"If you don't take your hands off me, I'll—I'll—" Rachel, furious, was unable to think of a dire enough threat. While she sputtered, tugging at his ring to remove it and throw it in his grinning face, he pulled her closer against his chest, locked her hands in place with one long arm around her waist, and tilted her face up to his with his free hand.

"I wasn't joking about the poem."

"You said—"

"I know what I said. I didn't mean it. I mean, I meant the poem. Every word. I swear."

Rachel stopped wriggling and stared up at him with transparent suspicion.

"You knew that that poem is my very favorite in the whole world, didn't you? You deliberately used it to manipulate me."

He kissed her temple, his expression blatantly unrepentant. "I knew —I had a poetry-spouting tartar for a high school English teacher, remember? She fascinated me so that I remember practically every word she said. But I still meant it."

"Liar."

"I'm not lying," he said, and kissed the tip of her nose. "And what's more, you know it. You know how I feel about you. Just like I know how you feel about me. Rachel, sometimes when I'm feeling really sickeningly maudlin, I think that we were meant to be."

Rachel looked up at him, up at the dark, handsome face and twinkling blue eyes and sexy, smiling mouth, and gave it up. If she wanted Johnny Harris, then she was going to have to take Johnny Harris on his own terms.

What good was a bullied confession of love, anyway? As he said, she knew how he felt. Knew it with the combined power of her mind and heart and soul.

45

"Yes," she said.

"Yes?"

"You heard me."

"Good," he said, and grinned. "I'd hate to have to return the ring. I didn't keep my receipt."

"Aren't you funny today!"

"I try." But when he looked at her, his eyes were suddenly grave. "Rachel, I can't stay in Tylerville."

"I know."

"I thought we would get married as soon as possible, quietly, and go someplace, maybe out west."

"How soon did you have in mind?"

"The sooner the better. This week. Rachel—" he hesitated. "I don't think you're safe here. I've thought and thought about this, and the only thing I can come up with is that there is a nut out there who hates me enough to kill the women in my life. If it's true, the next logical target is you."

"Do you really think so?" Her voice was very small.

"I hope not. But we have to act as if it were true. Guess where I spent last night?"

"Where?"

"Standing guard. In your backyard."

"You're kidding, right?"

"I'm not kidding. I've even got the mosquito bites to prove it." Johnny pushed up one arm of his jacket and unbuttoned his shirt-sleeve to exhibit his forearm, which besides being brawny, and nicely covered with dark hair, also sported perhaps half a dozen red, swollen-looking insect bites. "I've got more on my other arm, and still more on the back of my neck. Anywhere they found a bare patch of skin, those little blood-suckers attacked. The bites itch like hell, too."

Rachel was both surprised and touched. "You didn't have to do that."

"Didn't I?" Johnny gave her a level look. "I don't mean to lose you, teacher. If the cost of keeping you alive is nights spent offering up my carcass to a swarm of mini-vampires, then I'll pay it. The other women I've been involved with have ended up *dead*, Rachel."

Rachel shivered. "That scares me to death."

"It scares me, too. But nothing's going to happen to you because we're going to make sure that it doesn't. You're going to stay in your house at night, and I'm going to camp out in your backyard just in case you should forget. And we get married quick and get the hell out of Dodge. Right?"

"Right." A smile trembled on Rachel's lips. "Cowboy."

Johnny groaned. "I knew I should never have told you my middle name."

Despite the seriousness of the topic under discussion, Rachel had to laugh. He looked down at her for a minute, eyes gleaming, then silenced her by the simple expedient of kissing her. Rachel gave herself over to that kiss, to the hands that stroked over her back and smoothed her dress along the curve of her bottom, to the possessiveness of the arms that held her. She was his now, just as he was hers. With all the disparity in their backgrounds, they belonged together like two halves of a whole.

"Rachel?" He was dropping kisses along the line of her jaw while his hands fumbled with the tiny buttons at the front of her dress and then unfastened her belt.

"Yes?" She was tugging, without much success, at the knot in his silk tie. How on earth had he tied it? The thing seemed destined to stay in place for the next hundred years.

"Do you want children?"

Her mind, which was in the process of fogging over with passion, cleared for a minute at that.

"Yes, very much. Why?"

"Good." He straightened to flash a quick smile at her as he tugged her dress down over her arms. "I hate rubbers."

He pulled her dress the rest of the way off, tossing it carelessly aside. Rachel knew a momentary pang of distress for the fate of the discarded frock, but he was already stripping her most efficiently of her shoes and ruined pantyhose. At the glint in his eyes as he took a very slow, very thorough look at her sitting on his lap in nothing but pristine white bra and panties, she forgot everything but him and the way he made her feel.

"Nice underwear."

"Thank you."

"Lace and silk and pearls. Better than anything I ever imagined."

"I thought you imagined me in no underwear at all."

"Well," he said with a slow grin, "not better than that. But close."

His hand covered one lace- and silk- and pearl-clad breast while he bent his mouth to hers. Rachel felt a shaft of excitement shoot clear through her body to curl her bare toes as his tongue staked a leisurely claim to her mouth. Her nipples stood at quivering attention under the ministrations of his kneading hands. The now-familiar quickening in her loins made her pull her mouth from his.

"Just a minute," she said when he would have recaptured his prey.

"Mmm." He was looking down at her bare legs, which were draped across the dark blue wool of his suit. The contrast between the slim feminine curves and silky tanned skin of her legs and the masculine propriety of his trousers was enough to make his eyes darken. He ran an admiring hand along the inside of her thigh to her knee and back. Rachel's legs parted instinctively, but then she snapped them shut and wriggled off his lap and out of his reach.

"Behave yourself," she told him even as he grabbed for her. Fending him off, she knelt in front of him and worked his zipper down.

"Rachel—" He broke off when her delving fingers found him and pulled him out, wincing only a little as she worked him free of underwear and trousers without doing more than unzipping his pants.

"Shh." She leaned over and touched her tongue to the tip of his penis. It was a light, almost teasing gesture, but it made him gasp.

"Oh, yeah," he muttered when her hair puddled in his lap and her mouth swallowed him up. His entire body stiffened, his head was thrown back to rest against the top of the wall, and his hands were threaded through her hair, caressing her skull, guiding her motions.

"Aunt Rachel!"

It took a moment and another shout for this to sink in.

"Oh, Christ!" Johnny groaned, his fingers tightening on her scalp in protest. "Not now!"

"What . . . ?" Rachel looked up. She felt slightly dazed, her senses were disoriented, and the taste of him was in her mouth.

"Aunt Rachel!"

"Loren!" she gasped, dropping him as if he'd suddenly turned red hot. For an instant only they stared at each other in consternation. Then

Rachel was crawling across the platform in a frantic scramble for her clothes.

When she looked around, it was to find Johnny, who had had much less to do to restore himself to respectability, leering at her.

"Nice ass," he said.

"Aunt Rachel!" The cry was close at hand, perhaps just below the treehouse. Rachel, trying frantically to pull on her twisted and torn pantyhose, gave Johnny a hunted look.

"Go down and stall her," she hissed.

"Right." Fully dressed and grinning, he left her to her task and disappeared down the hole. Rachel, buttoning her dress, heard him greet Loren with commendable casualness. She fastened her belt, listening to the low hum of their voices as they talked.

Rachel was just pulling on her shoes when Johnny's head appeared in the opening.

"Dressed?" he asked, but there was something about his expression that gave her pause.

"Is something wrong?"

"Put your other shoe on and come down."

"Johnny—" But he was gone, back down the tree. Rachel knew without knowing how she knew it that something bad had happened and jammed her foot into her shoe and hurried in his wake. Near the bottom, she felt his hands close on her waist to lift her the rest of the way down. When she was on her feet, she turned to face him. What she saw in his eyes frightened her.

"What is it?" she asked quietly.

"It's your father. He's apparently had a heart attack. An ambulance is on its way."

His arm was around her, supporting her, as she partly stumbled, partly ran to the house. That was the only thing that kept her on her feet.

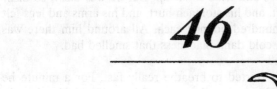

46

*"J*eremy."

There it was again—the voice. The soft, terrifying voice, calling him. Jeremy, huddled in his cold dark prison, shivered. He'd been in there for hours, days, he couldn't tell. Most of the time he thought he'd been asleep. But always, always, he'd heard that voice, whispering in his mind.

"Jeremy."

There it was again. He wanted to scream, wanted to cry, but he was too scared to do either. He was hungry and thirsty, and he had to pee, but all that was secondary to the fear that possessed him.

Something evil lurked in the dark.

"Move, Jeremy. You have to move."

"Mom?" It was a croak, and even as he forgot himself enough to say it aloud, Jeremy cringed in anticipation of being attacked. His mom was dead. The voice he heard could not belong to her. The evil thing was tricking him again, just as it had done the first time.

"Move, Jeremy."

But it sounded like his mom. Jeremy's lip quivered. He wanted it to be his mom so bad. Maybe she'd come to be with him, to keep him company while he died.

He didn't want to die. He was too scared.

"Get up, Jeremy."

The voice was insistent, and for the first time he began to wonder if it was maybe inside his own head. His head ached and throbbed and felt as if it had swollen as big as a pumpkin. Was his mom talking to him inside his head?

He opened his eyes and tried to sit up. But he was dizzy, so dizzy and sick. His head hurt, and his stomach hurt, and his arms and legs felt as if they weighed a hundred pounds each. All around him there was nothing but blackness, cold dank blackness that smelled bad.

Was he in a grave?

At the thought he started to breathe really fast. For a minute he almost panicked. Then he managed to control himself with the thought that wherever he was, it was too big to be a grave. He hadn't been buried alive.

At least he didn't think so. But his head hurt when he tried to use his brain.

"Hide, Jeremy!" The voice, whatever its source, screamed inside his head. He wanted to scream back in terrified answer, but a scratching sound, a real scratching sound, shut him up. The sound scared him more than anything else so far had done.

He got up on his hands and knees and, feeling in front of him, found a wall of what felt like some sort of very smooth stone right next to where he was. It wasn't the outer wall but an inner wall, and he'd been lying maybe two inches from it. It was gritty with dust and cold to the touch, yet he kept his hand on it for direction as he crawled as fast as he could away from the scratching sound.

A shaft of light—no, not light, but lessened darkness—allowed him to see that the stone wall was four feet tall and perhaps three feet wide—and that he could conceal himself from the revealing slice of grayness by ducking behind it.

He did, cowering, barely daring to peep around the edge to see what threatened him.

At once he recognized it as the thing he had seen lurking in the shadows the night his mom was killed. A solid, dark presence was towering in a doorway that led from the place where he was imprisoned to the night beyond the door. A rush of fresh air, warmer than that which he breathed, fluttered the hem of the cloak that concealed the outlines of the creature itself from his view.

He could not see it, not properly, but Jeremy sensed the presence of evil. It was as tangible as a smell. He made himself very small, fighting the urge to whimper, resisting the impulse to run.

There was no place to go—except straight at the thing.

"Jeremy."

It was the voice he'd heard in his backyard. It was different from the whisper that had awakened him and told him to move, which he now knew was a beneficent entity. This whisper made the hair rise on the back of his neck.

"Come here, boy."

The thing moved, and he saw a glint of something silver clutched before it like a shield. Jeremy stared and realized what it was that he was seeing: a knife, long and glittering sharp.

The knife that had killed his mom, probably. The knife that the thing meant to use on him.

Jeremy felt a rush of warmth between his legs and realized that he'd wet his pants like a baby. Humiliation mingled with his terror. It was all he could do not to sob out loud.

In the doorway the thing sniffed once, twice, audibly, as if it could smell him. Then, from somewhere outside came a flash of light. Twin lights. Headlights from a car. Jeremy opened his mouth to scream.

"Be quiet," the good voice warned him. He shut his mouth.

The thing seemed to hesitate, then as quickly as a bird taking wing, it melted away. The door shut. Jeremy found himself once again alone in the dark.

Only this time, he welcomed the dark as his friend.

47

The next few days passed in a blur for Rachel. She spent nearly every waking moment at her father's hospital bedside, holding his hand and talking to him and praying for his recovery, though she knew that it was wrong to want to hold him back from the release that death was to him now. But she couldn't help it. She could not bring herself to let him go. Not yet, not this way.

Elisabeth, who even slept on the floor beside Stan's bed, felt as bad. She was white-faced and shrunken-looking as she watched over her husband, and she could hardly speak coherently even to the doctors. It fell to Rachel to talk to them and to try to make sense of what they were telling her. Then she had to report the situation as she understood it to Elisabeth and Becky.

Becky, torn between her daughters at home and her father at the hospital, kept watch with her mother whenever Rachel caved in to exhaustion and let Johnny drag her away for a few hours of sleep. His intention to keep a nightly vigil in her backyard was forgotten, because she no longer spent her nights at home. Rachel now went to Johnny's apartment as naturally as she would have to Walnut Grove, because it was close to the hospital and because Johnny was there. His arms held her as she slept, he dried her tears when she cried, and he made her eat when she didn't feel like it. It was Johnny who took care of the small things that made such an exhaustive vigil bearable. He drove the women back and forth when they were too tired to even think coherently, much less operate a motor vehicle. He carried food and snacks up to them when he couldn't persuade them to visit the cafeteria for a meal. He bought personal necessities such as face soap and toothbrushes and toothpaste at the hospital pharmacy for them when they awoke feeling grubby and disoriented after spending that first terrifying night with Stan. Most important of all, he provided a strong male shoulder to lean on for whichever woman was feeling lowest at any particular moment. Even Elisabeth came to rely on him during those terrible days. She said more than once that she didn't know how they would manage without him. In the shock following Stan's hospitalization, she had even accepted the news of Rachel's engagement without a murmur. Not that Rachel would have chosen that time to tell her, but with the glittering ring on her finger —tag still attached—when she arrived at the hospital, the fact was hard for even Elisabeth, distraught as she was, to miss.

Life outside the hospital went on while Stan lay hooked up to what seemed like the dozens of machines that kept him (just barely) alive. Friends poured into the waiting room, but only family members were allowed to see Stan. Kay was a frequent visitor, as were Susan Henley and all of Elisabeth's cronies from church. Even Rob sent flowers, which gesture Rachel appreciated. At such a trying time, she found that she and Elisabeth and Becky needed people. The visitors even went out of their way to be civil to Johnny, whose status as an almost family member had quickly become the talk of the town. For once, Rachel was thankful for the efficiency of the gossip network that had trumpeted their engagement. At the moment, Stan's crisis was all she could cope with. She didn't think she could summon the energy to explain Johnny's almost constant presence to her friends and neighbors as well.

A substitute had replaced Rachel at school for as long as she was needed at the hospital. Michael came once from Louisville to visit Stan, but he got so frosty a reception from Elisabeth and Rachel that he didn't stay for more than ten minutes. Becky, coming in a little later with swollen eyes, reported that he had stopped by to see the girls at Walnut Grove, and that after he had left, Loren had asked her how long divorce lasted anyway, because she was getting tired of it. The question had made Becky cry.

The hardware store was once again being managed capably by Ben, who had agreed to stay on under a hastily worked-out deal that gave him profit-sharing as well as a nice raise and included the proviso that Johnny would no longer work at the store. Johnny didn't mind being out of a job, since he was only awaiting a resolution to Stan's health crisis before leaving Tylerville forever with Rachel.

Chief Wheatley was one of the dozens of Stan's friends who stopped by the hospital to see him. Unlike the others, he was permitted, because of his official status, to visit the patient's room. He said he had no real progress on the murder investigations to report, but he brought with him disturbing news: Jeremy Watkins had apparently run away from home. At any rate, he had disappeared, and his father and grandparents were distraught. No, the chief did not really suspect foul play—little boys were not the murder victims of choice in Tylerville lately—but still it was worrisome. After Rachel and Johnny assured him that neither of them had seen Jeremy since his mother's funeral, Chief Wheatley pursed his lips and nodded. The kid had been still adjusting to his new home situation, which was less than ideal and in the chief's opinion gave him a reason to run away, but still they were checking out every possibility.

The only thing that bothered him, he declared, was the way Jeremy had kept insisting that, on the night of his mother's murder, he had seen something in the dark. If the murderer had gotten wind of that, perhaps he had felt the need to get Jeremy out of the way. That was why he was interviewing Johnny and Rachel, and everyone else who had heard Jeremy's remark. Of course, the way Tylerville worked, it was hard to find anyone who did not know what the kid had said, so the list of potential suspects was by no means limited to the few who had heard it from Jeremy directly.

Rachel gasped in horror at the suggestion, but the chief told her that it was only one of many possibilities, and not even a very likely one, since if the boy had been killed, his body would surely have been found by now. Whoever had murdered Marybeth Edwards and Glenda Watkins had not been shy about leaving their victims on view.

No, the most likely scenario was that the boy, distraught over his mother's death, unhappy in his new home with his father's girlfriend on the premises, had simply run away. He had been reported missing across the country, and the chief expected to receive a call announcing that the boy had been picked up almost any time.

Rachel hoped so, but the news that Jeremy was missing made her uneasy. Glancing up at Johnny as the chief left, she could tell he felt the same way.

But there was nothing they could do to locate the boy, and Rachel was so caught up in the heartbreak of her father's situation that she pushed the mystery of Jeremy's whereabouts to the back of her mind. As Chief Wheatley had said, the poor little boy had very likely simply run away.

Johnny made an excuse to leave the room a few minutes after the chief left. Rachel had not seen the curt jerk of the head with which

Wheatley had summoned him, so she just waved in an absent-minded way when Johnny said he'd be back in a minute.

Wheatley was no longer in the corridor when Johnny stepped out of Stan's room. Johnny hoped that he had not stopped by the waiting room, where usually one or more of the Grants' friends could be found—that was a gauntlet that he avoided whenever possible. One of the white-clad nurses, pushing a squeaky-wheeled cart that held lunch for those patients who could eat, told Johnny in response to his terse query that the chief had just stepped into the elevator. Taking the stairs two at a time, Johnny caught up with Wheatley in the lobby.

"Chief." His voice stopped the older man just before he would have pushed through the revolving doors in the center of the vast glass wall that fronted the entrance of the hospital.

Wheatley glanced back, saw Johnny, and made a motion to him to follow him through the doors. Johnny did, impatiently. Outside the hospital, in the still-warm September air, the two men stood side by side on the walk in front of the tall brick building. The chief, a burly figure in his blue uniform and hat, had his arms folded across his chest. Johnny, leaner in his jeans and white T-shirt, his new, shorter haircut making him much less likely to attract conservative Tylerville's negative attention, stood with his hands thrust into his pants pockets.

"You wanted to see me?"

Wheatley nodded once, curtly. "I didn't know if you'd gotten the message."

"What is it?" Johnny was terse.

"It's not good news."

"Never is."

"Okay. There's a lot of bad feeling against you in town."

Johnny relaxed slightly. He'd been afraid that Wheatley was going to tell him something had happened to Jeremy that he hadn't cared to mention in front of the ladies when they were already so upset. Hearing more of the same crap he'd heard all his life was a relief. "So what else is new?"

The chief shook his head. "This is different. The talk's real ugly, uglier than I've ever heard it. People think you're guilty as hell, no matter what I tell 'em to the contrary, and it's making 'em mad that you're still running around free."

"Are you trying to tell me that I should keep one eye open for a lynch mob?"

The chief pursed his lips. "Now, I never said that. These people here in Tylerville, they're good people, by and large. But the Watkins woman's killing and her boy going missing have got everybody real upset. People are wondering if the kid's been killed to shut him up, and Tom Watkins says for his money you're the one that did it. Other people have put two and two together to identify Rachel as the killer's next target, if there is one. Most folks hereabouts have got kids of their own, so the boy worries 'em. And everybody's got a real respect for Rachel, so they don't much like the idea of her ending up like the other two."

Johnny looked hard at the chief. "You still think I did it, don't you?"

"You're putting words in my mouth again. I'm not saying that I think you did it. If Rachel's telling the truth—and I've never known her to lie —you couldn't have. All I'm saying is, if something happens to Rachel, or the boy turns up dead, your life isn't gonna be worth a nickel around here. It's not worth much more than a quarter as it is."

Johnny started to speak, but the chief held up a silencing hand.

"Now, you let me finish. There's two ways that I've been looking at it. One, Rachel's telling the truth, and you couldn't have killed Mrs. Watkins. Still, you were seeing her, just like you were seeing Marybeth Edwards. They're both dead. Looks to me like Rachel's a prime candidate to make a third, because the only thing that makes a lick of real sense with that theory is that somebody's killing off your women. Or number two, you're a maniac who killed Marybeth Edwards and Mrs. Watkins yourself, for unknown reasons, and Rachel's lying to protect you. That's the word that's going around town. Either way, Rachel's in a heck of a lot of trouble—because of you."

Johnny's lips tightened. "You need to put police protection on her. I've been meaning to talk to you about that."

The chief nodded. "I have considered it. But we've got a six-man force, and all the other crime in Tylerville is not going to cease because we've got an ongoing murder investigation. The last two killings were eleven years apart. I can't assign a man to Rachel full time for the next eleven years."

"So you called me out here to tell me that I'm still a suspect, and that any way it goes down, Rachel's in danger. Is that it?"

The chief slowly shook his head. "You got it wrong. I called you out here to tell you to get the hell out of town. We'll all sleep easier with you gone."

"What about Rachel?" Anger sharpened Johnny's voice.

Wheatley shrugged. "She can't be worse off with you out of here, and she may be a heck of a lot safer. And I don't much fancy the prospect of cutting you down from a tall tree one of these days."

Johnny's mouth twisted. "Okay, you've said your piece. Now let me say mine. Much as I want to, I'm not leaving this one-horse town unless

Rachel comes with me, and Rachel can't leave right now because of her father. So Tylerville's fucking stuck with me."

The chief didn't even blink at the biting profanity. "Can't force you to leave."

"No," Johnny said, meeting his eyes dead on, "you can't."

"Fair enough. Just thought I'd pass my thoughts along." Wheatley started to move away, then glanced back at Johnny. "For the record, I personally don't think you're guilty. But I've been wrong before."

Johnny didn't say anything. The chief shrugged and headed toward where his gray Taurus was parked against the curb not far away. He opened the driver's door while Johnny watched him. Then Wheatley looked at Johnny across the car's roof.

"By the way, you got any old girlfriends left around here?" he asked.

"None living," Johnny replied tightly. The chief appeared to consider that, nodded once, and got into his car.

Johnny stood there for a long time before he went back inside.

48

It took a long time to die. Jeremy discovered that, as the hours blended into each other with seamless horror. No food, no water, no light, no end to the awful stabbing pain that shot through his head every time he moved, but still he lived. How many hours, or days, or weeks had passed he didn't know, but it seemed longer than a year that he had been locked in the cold smelly darkness, alone except for his mom's voice.

He knew now that the voice was hers, and it comforted him. His fingertips were raw and bloody from where he had tried to claw his way out through the stone walls or through the iron door where the thing had stood. He knew now that there was no way out, and hopelessness increased his misery. He lay curled on the stone floor while his head pounded and colored spots flickered against the screen of his closed lids and his body shivered with chill. He drifted in and out of awareness, and when the pain or fear got bad, his mom talked to him. Jeremy pretended that he was safe in his own bed with Jake curled next to him and his mom in the rocking chair in the corner of the room where she always sat.

"Jeremy, do you remember when I let you play hooky from school and we went fishing in the creek?"

Yeah, mom.

"Remember two Christmases ago, when Santa brought you that new bike?"

Yeah, Mom.

"Remember Halloween . . . Thanksgiving . . . your birthday?"

Yeah, Mom.

Sometimes she recited the nursery rhymes he remembered from

earliest childhood, sometimes she sang to him, nonsense songs that he liked and lullabies for Jake, and sometimes she just told him that she was present. When thirst parched his throat, it was his mom who made him get up despite his aching head and feel around the walls of his prison for trickles of moisture that would keep him alive. When he found one, he licked greedily at the slimy stone wall and as the water soothed his dry tongue and burning throat he felt her jubilation. Though more and more he yearned to go to her, he felt that she did not want him to cross over to where she was. She wanted him to live.

Hunger was a gnawing pain inside him at first, but gradually it subsided into a dull emptiness that didn't hurt anymore. He lay all curled up next to where the water trickled down the wall, licking it when he needed to, and listened to his mom. That was the best way to keep the terror at bay.

Because he knew that sooner or later, the thing would come back for him. And this time he was afraid that it wasn't going to go away.

At the thought of that shiny silver knife, he sobbed aloud. And he kept on sobbing, even though his mom talked to him through the blackness to try to take away his fear.

"Be brave, son. Be brave."

49

*O*n Friday, Stan improved slightly, enough that both Elisabeth and Rachel felt that they could leave him at the same time. Becky stayed at the hospital—none of them would even consider leaving Stan alone—while Johnny drove Rachel and her mother to Walnut Grove in Rachel's car. Elisabeth, sitting in the front seat with Johnny, was little more than a pale shadow of the woman she had been the Sunday before. She leaned her head back against the seat, eyes closed, hands resting quietly in her lap. For one of the very few times in her life, Rachel realized that she was seeing her mother less than perfectly groomed.

None of the three in the car spoke. Rachel and Elisabeth were worn out, and Johnny was quiet because he sensed that they needed to be. But the silence was comfortable. For the first time, Rachel was able to take stock of all that had happened since Stan had been stricken. She realized that one good thing had resulted from the nightmare: the last disorienting days in the hospital had done much to reconcile Elisabeth to Johnny. Crisis had forced her mother to rely on him, and Johnny had responded even better than Rachel could have hoped. He'd been there when he was needed, and in the process he had done much to endear himself to her family. By that odd alchemy that sometimes occurs in times of stress, Johnny had become one of them.

As they pulled in the gates of Walnut Grove, Rachel felt a lightening of her spirits for the first time since Stan had been stricken. The sun was shining, the air was warm, the foliage that was changing into its autumn colors was beautiful. Even the house seemed especially welcoming as they entered. Katie was singing a silly song with Tilda in the kitchen, and the child's gaiety touched a chord in Rachel's heart. A big pot of what smelled like vegetable soup bubbled on the stove.

"Just in time for lunch," Tilda said, looking up with a wide smile as they entered. Katie ran with a screech straight for Rachel. Rachel scooped the child up, kissing her and never minding that her little hands were sticky from the candy stick that she had abandoned on the floor in her excitement.

"Where is everybody, Tilda?" Elisabeth asked. It was obviously an effort for her to speak at all. She was so tired that her words were faintly slurred.

"J.D.'s gone to fetch Loren from kindergarten, Lisa's at school till three, and Katie-did and I are right here in the kitchen, aren't we, Katie-did?"

"In the kitchen," Katie corroborated with a nod.

"Why don't you go upstairs and lie down for a while, Mother?" Rachel asked with some concern.

"I think I will. I am bone tired." Elisabeth kissed Katie, who giggled, then left the kitchen, moving like a very old woman. Never before had Rachel thought of her mother as old, and the notion frightened her.

"I think I'll go help Mother get settled," she said, and passed Katie to Tilda. The child protested, but Tilda distracted her with a pan and a spoon to bang it with. The noise followed Rachel up the stairs.

When she returned to the kitchen some fifteen minutes later, after having run her mother's bath and laid out her robe and nightgown, she discovered Katie standing on a chair playing happily in the sink, Johnny leaning against the counter talking to Tilda, who treated him much like one of her own four sons, and Tilda slicing ham for sandwiches. That done, Tilda dished up two bowls of soup. She placed those and the lunch plates, which included potato salad and pickles and big glasses of milk as well as the sandwiches, on the round, polished oak kitchen table, then bore a protesting Katie out of the kitchen so that Rachel and Johnny could eat in peace.

Johnny tucked into his food with relish, but after a couple of sips of soup, Rachel pushed hers away.

"Something wrong with it?" Johnny inquired with a truculent look that told Rachel he knew very well there wasn't. He had become very particular about how much and what she ate over the last few days, telling her that it was no wonder she was so tiny because a good-size mouse consumed more than she did. Rachel, in no mood to be force-fed, made a face at him. But in a compromise response to his hard-eyed stare, she ate the rest of her soup. More than that she simply could not do.

"It won't help your father if you make yourself sick from not eating," Johnny said as he downed the last morsel on his plate. Rachel watched him drain the last of his milk with loving repugnance. While stress made her stomach churn whenever she tried to eat, Johnny had never, in her experience of him, failed to enjoy his food, and his appetite was enormous.

"I have a headache," Rachel replied with dignity.

"Do you indeed?" Johnny eyed her speculatively. Then he grinned. "Run upstairs like a good girl and put on a pair of jeans and some sneakers. What you need is fresh air."

"You're probably right."

A walk did sound good, and Rachel did as he said. When she returned to the kitchen, he was just polishing off a brownie.

"If you keep eating the way you are, you're going to be a fat old man." She grinned teasingly at him.

"No way. My metabolism's too high." He wiped his fingers on his jeans and walked toward her.

"That's what they all say."

"Oh, yeah?"

"Yeah."

"Come on. It's a beautiful day outside."

Johnny grabbed her hand, and Rachel gladly went with him out the door and across the patio and down the path to the garage. His motorcycle was parked there, along with her mother's car and the car Tilda used for errands. Breathing deeply, Rachel drank in the fresh scents of early autumn. Someone, somewhere, was burning leaves. The acrid odor of smoke was faint but detectable.

It was still warm enough that one didn't need a jacket or sweater, but it was appreciably cooler than it had been in August. A rising wind rippled through Rachel's hair and set the dark branches, clad in their autumn finery of rust and gold, moving high overhead like uplifted, swaying arms. Rachel drank in the sights and sounds and smells with a sense of renewal. Early fall was her favorite time of year.

"Here," Johnny said, handing her a helmet. Rachel had been so caught up in her own thoughts that she hadn't noticed that their walk had ended beside his motorcycle or that he had released her hand.

"Oh, I don't think—" Rachel shook her head at what he obviously intended, backing away at the same time. With an admonishing cluck, Johnny came after her. He took the helmet from her hands and held it over her head as he looked down at her with a lurking grin.

"Don't you trust me?"

"Yes, but—"

"Good." He pushed the helmet down over her head and fastened the chin strap. Then he silenced her protests with a quick, hard kiss.

"You'll love it. I promise." He pulled her against him by the simple expedient of hooking his fingers into the belt loops of her jeans. Her head tipped back as she looked up at him, and he kissed her again.

"Give it a chance?"

"What do I do?" Rachel capitulated with a sigh. Resisting him when he chose to exert that coaxing charm was impossible, she thought. Besides, she really did trust him, implicitly. She might not love riding with him on his motorcycle, but she could pretty much take for granted that she wasn't going to come to any harm.

"Hop on." Johnny, grinning, pulled on his own helmet, threw one leg over the seat, rocked the bike off its stand, and kicked the engine to life, all in less time than it took Rachel to adjust her helmet so that it felt reasonably comfortable and secure.

"How?" Rachel had to shout to be heard over the roar. The seat was a good way off the ground, and somehow it didn't seem dignified to straddle it. It was all very well for him, but he was over six feet tall.

"Pretend the bike's a horse!" he yelled back.

Rachel did, stepping awkwardly up on one foot peg while he braced the bike with both legs on the ground, then throwing a leg over at his instruction. All at once she found herself seated behind him, wedged in between his tall, broad back and the leather backrest, her thighs gripping his, her crotch pressed against his buttocks.

"Hang on!" he called over his shoulder.

Rachel gritted her teeth and locked her arms around his hard waist. He released the throttle and lifted his feet, and off they shot. As they flew down the driveway, kicking up tiny pebbles, Rachel thought that riding a rocket would be tame in comparison.

But Johnny clearly loved it. She could feel his exhilaration in his body as she pressed close against his back. She could see it in glimpses of his averted face. She could hear it in his voice as he shouted remarks back to her. So she clung to him without protest as they flew over bumps and careened around curves, even though she felt as if she were on the roller-coaster ride of her life. For Johnny, she would learn to enjoy this form of transportation if it killed her. He had made such an effort to fit into her world that she would do this one thing for him.

By the time he pulled into the garage again an hour and a half later, Rachel had even opened her screwed-shut eyes.

"Wasn't it great?" He was grinning widely as he stopped the bike. Rachel, thankful to be alive, smiled and nodded as she removed her helmet, handed it to him, and slid to the ground. Then something funny happened. Her knees, in mutinous collaboration with her thighs, were shaky. Her bottom frankly ached. She rubbed it, wincing, as Johnny turned off the engine, put his beloved machine up on its stand, and balanced the helmets on the rearview mirrors.

"What's the matter?" He turned to catch her rubbing her behind. Frowning, he looked her over. Rachel summoned a smile for him as her hand dropped to her side.

"I'm saddlesore," she said, determined to make light of an affliction much worse than anything she had ever suffered on horseback.

"I kept you out too long your first time." He sounded remorseful.

"First time?" she thought with an inward shudder but continued to smile as she turned to head toward the house. But she couldn't control her instinctive wince as she took a step forward.

"Baby, I am sorry." Johnny came up behind her and scooped her up in his arms before she had any inkling that he meant to do so. For an instant she stiffened, surprised, but then she relaxed as he walked off with her held high against his chest. This was the man she loved, and he could carry her off if he wanted to. She smiled at the sheer luxury of it and curled her arms around his neck.

"Forgive me?" He really did sound contrite. Rachel tweaked a curl that grew low on his nape.

"Yes, silly."

"You'll toughen up to it in time."

"I'm sure I will."

"You don't have to ride if you don't want to."

"I know."

Johnny stopped walking for just long enough to kiss her. When he finally lifted his head and got under way again, Rachel was surprised to find that he was heading for the woods.

"Where are we going?"

"Someplace where I can make the bad hurt all better."

"Sounds exciting." She smiled up at him.

"Does, doesn't it?"

They were at the edge of the woods. Johnny carried her along the path to the foot of the climbing tree, then set Rachel on her feet. Her bottom still ached and her thighs still quivered, but she managed to climb up with no more than an occasional inward wince. When Johnny appeared through the opening, she was stretched flat on her back on the wooden floor, her arms flung over her head as she admired the fluttering orange-gold canopy overhead. Dressed in faded jeans and a rose-pink T-shirt, her hair tangled and her eyes bright and her cheeks abloom with color, she looked and felt about eighteen years old. When Johnny loomed over her, she grinned at him with gay abandon. He stood looking down at her for a moment, brushing back an errant lock of black hair from his forehead, then dropped to his knees beside her.

"Turn over."

"Why?"

"I told you I was going to make the bad hurt go away. The cure for what ails you is a good massage."

"Is it?"

"Uh-huh."

Rachel turned over, folding her hands beneath her cheek to pillow her head. She felt the sure strength of Johnny's hands as he began to knead her abused buttocks through the worn denim and gave herself over to sensation. He was right—what he was doing was definitely easing the ache in her muscles. Or at least, transferring it to another location.

It was funny, when she thought about it, how swiftly and hotly he could awaken her need for him. No other man had ever had that effect on her. But when Johnny touched her, she wanted sex.

She was getting up the energy to turn back over and tell him so when his hands slid beneath her to seek and find the fastening of her jeans.

"What are you doing?" she asked lazily as he unzipped her fly and began pulling her jeans down over her hips.

"I think the massage would be more effective if there weren't so many barriers between my hands and your skin."

"Oh, really?"

"Yep."

He slid her sneakers from her feet, then pulled her jeans off after them. Rachel still lay on her stomach, her head on her hands, dressed in her T-shirt and peach nylon panties and pink ankle socks with their delicate lace trim. The air felt just faintly cool against her bare legs. The titillating chill was quickly dissipated by the warmth of his hands as he ran them up her thighs to resume their task.

Rachel had to admit that his ministrations were infinitely more effective without her jeans. She arched her back like a cat being stroked when his hands slid beneath her panties, and for a moment she enjoyed the slightly rough abrasion of his fingertips against the soft skin of her behind. Then, summoning what determination she had left, she rolled over and sat up.

"Feeling better?" he asked, sinking back on his heels, his hands sliding around to rest on the front of her bare thighs.

"Infinitely." Rachel smiled at him, looped her arms around his neck, and pressed her mouth to his in a sensuous, seductive kiss, which he returned with enthusiasm.

"I owe you one," she said at last, pushing him away and shaking her head at him when he would have maneuvered her down onto her back on the floor.

"Oh, yeah?" He sounded interested as she reached for his zipper and worked it down. Leaning against the wall, he watched her efforts with a quirky smile.

"Yeah," she answered, reaching through the opening she had made. His smile vanished and his breathing quickened as her hand burrowed beneath his underpants to locate its prey. He was already hard by the time her fingers closed over him and pulled him out into the open air. His erection was enormous, throbbing, burning hot and quivering in her hand, though she had done no more than hold it. Rachel squeezed experimentally and was rewarded by the sudden hot flare of Johnny's eyes and the rush of dark blood to his cheeks. As she bent her head to him, he shut his eyes and clenched his fists. Then her mouth found him and took him inside, sucking. Johnny groaned.

Rachel liked the sound so much that she did it again.

50

*U*nbeknownst to the two in the treehouse, there was someone else in the woods behind Walnut Grove that afternoon. The watcher was there, too.

The tan car, with the watcher's everyday personality at the wheel, had been traveling down Main Street on an errand when Johnny Harris's motorcycle whizzed past. The sight of the woman snuggled up behind him, her arms locked around his waist, had infuriated the watcher so much that, in no more than that one instant of recognition, he had wrenched control of the body from the everyday personality. Following a safe distance behind the big bike, the watcher had done battle with a vicious urge to simply accelerate and run the traitorous pair down. But he had managed to resist. Killing Johnny Harris was not part of the plan.

But the watcher could not resist following them into the woods. Standing beneath the tree, he listened to the sounds of lovemaking overhead. His worst suspicions were confirmed: they were lovers. Though the watcher made no sound, inside was raging with fury, transformed by jealousy into a howling, hungry beast maddened with bloodlust. He had killed twice already, but never had the urge for bloody vengeance been as strong as it was now. The woman had to die. The woman would die. And soon. Soon.

But not immediately. The watcher was too clever for that. He could wait until he got the woman alone.

It would be worth the wait.

Because this time, the woman who died would be the right one. The first two killings had not accomplished the watcher's goal, and now the watcher knew why. This woman, Rachel Grant, was The One. The watcher, with full knowledge of his own identity as a reincarnated spirit, was seeking one specific other reincarnated soul. Rejoicing, he realized that he had finally located his quarry, his true quarry, the quarry that had been his nemesis through eternity. The watcher knew that the memories and emotions and thought patterns that made up the everyday personality of Rachel Grant were as superficial as those that made up the watcher's own everyday personality. Beneath those unremarkable surfaces lurked far more: genderless souls bound to each other by destiny, whose fate it was to be reborn together again and again to play out a never-ending cycle of betrayal and murder and redemption. Along with the watcher himself, and the soul of Johnny Harris, the woman's soul formed the third point of the eternal triangle.

The watcher knew that his destiny was to destroy that triangle. Only when that was accomplished would the watcher find peace.

What made it easier, from the watcher's viewpoint, was that Rachel Grant, like Johnny Harris and indeed most other individuals, had no idea of the existence of any part of themselves besides their surface personalities. The notion of reincarnation, of destiny and redemption, which the watcher embraced and knew to be the ultimate, universal truth, was beyond their understanding. Only a few enlightened souls, of which the watcher knew himself to be one, were permitted the full spectrum of divine knowledge. Most would never see any deeper than their surface personalities, which were only tiny facets of the vast gem that was the complete soul.

The watcher thought of the matter this way. From the air, islands dotting the ocean seemed complete in themselves. Only when one delved beneath the surface of the sea did one discover that islands were no more than the tips of gigantic mountains that the water concealed from view.

Everyday personalities, the watcher considered, were like islands. But only the most perceptive were permitted to see what lay beneath.

The sounds of lovemaking suddenly ceased overhead, distracting the watcher from his ruminations. Briefly he glanced upward, yearning to complete his preordained mission of murder at that very moment. Hate, furious biting hate for the betraying soul that lived in Rachel Grant, warred with instinctive cunning.

Cunning won. Moments later, the watcher turned and walked quickly away.

There would be another, better day for vengeance.

51

It was around four o'clock when Johnny drove Rachel and her mother back to the hospital in her car, and he was beat. Rachel had worn him out. He grinned to himself as he thought how unlikely he once would have considered that. She'd called the shots this time, and he had loved every minute of it. But now she seemed revitalized, while he felt as if he'd been worked over with a baseball bat. Muscles he hadn't realized he had ached. He needed a hot shower and a change of clothes and something to eat. He would see Rachel safely up to her father's room and then make a quick trip to his apartment. He would be back within the hour, and it didn't get dark until nearly six. She would be safe in the hospital room with her mother and sister and a dozen doctors and nurses within call. It was still daylight out, after all. He'd been with her nearly every waking and sleeping minute for the last week. He could leave her for an hour without fear.

Rachel was perfectly agreeable to being left. She leaned in through the window to kiss him while her mother walked ahead toward the hospital entrance.

"No talking to strangers, okay?" He was only half-joking, but she grinned as she straightened.

"I won't." She flicked his nose with a finger and turned to follow her mother into the hospital. Johnny, stopped illegally in the patient pickup lane, watched her go. She was wearing a simple skirt and blouse of bright turquoise silk with a silver-studded leather belt around her waist and silver earrings. Her ass swayed sassily as she walked in her modest high heels. Johnny ogled it with appreciation. All he had to do was watch her walk away from him, and he got the hots for her all over again.

On the way to his apartment, a few fat drops of rain splattered against the windshield. Johnny turned on the wipers and peered up at the sky. It had not rained in weeks, but from the looks of the clouds that were blowing up in the east, that was about to change. Good—they needed the rain.

He parked the car behind the hardware store, climbed up the outside steps to his apartment so as not to have to deal with any crap from anybody in the store who might feel like dishing it out, fished his mail out of the box by the door, and went in. Wolf greeted him with an exuberance that nearly knocked Johnny back down the steps.

"I missed you, too," he told the ecstatic animal, rubbing him fondly behind the ears. Cocking a wary eye at the sky, he decided that it would be best to take Wolf for a quick walk now before it really began to pour. Accordingly, he put a leash on the dog and headed down the steps with him. More drops splattered on the asphalt as he trailed Wolf over to the grass.

By the time Johnny returned with Wolf to the apartment, big wet blotches dotted his shirt and jeans. If the size of the drops were any indication, the impending storm would be a doozy.

Back inside, he stripped and jumped in the shower, then emerged to towel himself dry and pull on clean clothes. The temperature had dropped considerably since his and Rachel's afternoon idyll, so he shrugged into a long-sleeve denim shirt and started to button it up. As he did he cast his eye over the mail scattered on the table. Mostly junk, with a few bills thrown in. A large manila envelope had been forwarded from the prison. Seeing the name of the place stamped onto the upper-lefthand corner of the envelope was enough to give him the willies.

But all that was behind him now, and he meant never to look back. The stain would be expunged from his record, just as he meant to expunge the memory from his mind. Those years belonged to another Johnny Harris. Rachel and her love, and the promise of a new life together, had made him a different man.

Just thinking of Rachel mellowed him out. With a puff of his cheeks he blew away his tension and concentrated on the good things his life now held. First and foremost was Rachel. He'd take his leather jacket back to the hospital with him for her to wear when she left for the night. The turquoise silk had been pretty, but he doubted that it was very warm.

For no real reason at all except that he wanted to throw the offending envelope away, Johnny ripped open the communication from the prison. His stomach tightened as he did so—what did he expect, a summons to return? he asked himself sarcastically—but it was no more than his forwarded mail. The groupies had no way of knowing that he'd been released. He wondered how long they would continue to write.

His most faithful correspondent had written again, Johnny saw as he dumped the six or so letters out onto the table. She always used purple ink on pink stationery, and she always perfumed her letters. The scent she used was a sultry floral, and Johnny wrinkled his nose at the potency of it as it reached his nostrils. He didn't remember the smell being this strong when he'd read her letters in prison. Maybe being confined in the manila envelope had somehow intensified it.

The smell continued to tease him as he slitted the envelope with his thumb and glanced over what she had to say. For courtesy's sake, he supposed he should drop her a note advising her that penning further love epistles to him was a waste of time, but he knew even as he entertained the thought that he wouldn't do it. He would never glance at his prison mail again, either. It brought back old memories, bad memories that made him angry. He would throw it away unopened, like the rest of the junk mail, and get on with his life.

He wondered, as he perused the letter more from habit than any real interest, what kind of woman became infatuated with a stranger, and an imprisoned murderer who never once wrote back to boot. This one had written to him without fail every single week for the ten years he had been inside, and she had assumed from the very first an intimacy that he found ludicrous. Hell, he didn't even know her name because she never signed her romantic outpourings with anything other than "eternally yours." She never addressed him by name, either. Her letters invariably began, "My very dear." From her tone, she might almost have considered them husband and wife.

Weird. Johnny grimaced and tossed the letter back onto the pile. Then he went into the kitchen to wash his hands to rid them of the cloying smell, picked up his jacket, and headed out the door.

He was halfway down the stairs, moving fast because of the splattering raindrops, when realization hit him and he froze. He had smelled that perfume before and not just on those letters. It had been recently. Since he had returned to Tylerville. On some woman. He knew it as well as he knew that rain was falling on his head, but he couldn't for the life of him immediately match a face to the memory of the smell.

Wheatley had asked him if he had any old girlfriends living around here, and his answer had been, at least to his knowledge, no. But Johnny, his mind working at lightning speed, suddenly came face to face with a harrowing possibility.

Whoever had written him those wacky prison letters might well be here in Tylerville. Maybe she had always been here. Maybe she—not he, but *she*—had killed Glenda and Marybeth. Because she fancied herself in love with him.

Whoever she was, he had been in her company more than once in the few weeks since his release from prison. The memory of the smell tantalized him as he tried to recall exactly when. But the scary thing was, he could not. It could have been almost anybody, almost any woman in town. Any store clerk. Any of the hardware store customers he had waited on. Any of the Grants' friends.

Maybe the letters could be traced. Johnny pivoted, running back up the stairs, fumbling to fit his key in the lock before he finally succeeded in getting the door open. Leaving it ajar behind him, he rushed to the table and picked up the letter and its matching envelope.

The return address was a Louisville post office box. That shouldn't be too hard to check out.

Letter in hand, Johnny went for the phone. Picking it up, he dialed, and when a bored female voice at the other end answered, he said, "Give me Chief Wheatley."

52

✦

"**R**achel!"

Rachel was heading for the elevators when she heard her name called. Looking around, she saw Kay emerging from the glass doors behind her. With a welcoming smile and a little wave, she stopped, waiting for her friend to catch up.

Kay did not smile back. As she drew closer and Rachel was able to discern the expression on her face, she started to feel alarmed.

"Is something the matter?" she asked sharply.

"Oh, Rachel, I hate to be the one to tell you." Kay looked unhappy. "There's been some trouble. Johnny—Johnny's been arrested."

"Arrested? For what?"

"I'm so sorry, Rachel. Apparently they've found some new evidence that he really did kill those women."

"But—he just left me to go to his apartment."

"They stopped him right around the corner, handcuffed him, and took him to jail. I happened to be driving by and saw the whole thing."

"That's not possible!"

"I'm really sorry, Rachel. But you know, maybe they're wrong. I know you think he's innocent. Maybe he is."

"I have to go to him. Oh, no, I don't have a car. Johnny was driving mine. Kay, I hate to ask you, but—"

Kay smiled and curled a hand around Rachel's arm. "Don't be silly! What are friends for? I'll be glad to drive you over. Come on."

Rachel never even noticed being splattered by the first raindrops Tylerville had seen in a month as she hurried with Kay out the door.

Rachel pulled her seat belt around her as Kay maneuvered her tan Ford Escort out of the parking lot. The wind had picked up and the sky had darkened over the course of the last hour, presaging a much needed storm. The swish of the wipers and the steady plop-plop of enormous raindrops self-destructing on the windshield made a soothing background noise for the conversation in the car. From the back seat, the spicy scent of a bouquet of pink carnations filled the air. Rachel assumed Kay had a delivery to make after she dropped her off.

"They've made a mistake," Rachel said impatiently. "Johnny did not kill either of those women! I've told Chief Wheatley time and time again that he was with me when Glenda Watkins was killed."

"I believe you," Kay said, shooting Rachel a sidelong glance.

"I thought the chief did, too. I can't believe he thinks I would lie about something like this—even to protect Johnny! I wouldn't. I'm not."

"I never thought Johnny killed the first girl. And I don't think he killed the second one, either."

"Then you're one of the few . . ." Rachel's voice trailed off, as she noticed their direction for the first time. "Kay, where are you going? You're headed out of town."

"I know."

"But the police station's just a few blocks from the hospital! You'll have to turn around."

"I can't do that," Kay said in an odd apologetic tone that made Rachel look at her, really look at her, for the first time since she had encountered her in the hospital lobby. Kay was casually but attractively dressed in a pair of khaki pants and a matching sweater over a white blouse. Her hair was pinned up into a chic chignon, and her only makeup was a touch of lipstick and mascara. But the overall effect was to make her look different. Uncannily different, almost like another person.

Faint tremors of unease stirred inside Rachel.

"Are you all right?" There was concern in Rachel's voice.

"It depends on what you mean by all right." Kay sounded almost sad as she glanced over at Rachel. "Do you believe in reincarnation?"

"What?" Kay's question was so unexpected that it threw Rachel for a minute.

"Do you believe in reincarnation?"

"No, I don't. Why?"

"I do. I got interested in the subject years ago, you know. While I was still in high school."

"You're entitled to believe anything you want, just like everyone else. That's why they call America the land of the free." Rachel was impatient at the pointless turn the conversation had taken. "Kay, could you turn the car around and drive me back to the police station? If not, pull over and I'll walk back."

Kay smiled regretfully. "You still don't get it, do you, Rachel?"

"Get what?"

"Johnny wasn't really arrested, silly."

"Then why did you say he was?" This was growing curiouser and curiouser, as Alice had said when she found herself in Wonderland. Rachel took another careful look at Kay. Had she been drinking? Was she on drugs? Whatever was wrong with her was starting to cause Rachel real concern.

"To get you to come with me."

"Why do you want me to come with you?"

"Did you know that my grandfather served on the city council in the thirties? When they found that woman's body in the crypt? The diary was in there, too—her killer's diary. My grandfather kept it—that's how it disappeared—and I read it the first time when I was about ten. It fascinated me, and I kept reading it, over and over again. Then I started dreaming about what I had read—vivid dreams, so vivid, as if I were *her,* living *her* life. I was really scared—until I started reading about reincarnation. Then I realized that we are all reborn again and again and again. My dreams were so real because I had once been that woman. I had experienced everything that *she* had experienced."

"Kay, forgive me, but what on earth does any of this have to do with Johnny?" In her impatience, it was all Rachel could do not to shriek the words at her friend.

"Oh, Rachel. I'm really sorry," Kay said in a faint, die-away voice. Her hands tightened on the steering wheel, she stiffened, and Rachel had a sudden horrifying impression that the woman she was now looking at was not the woman who had been there the instant before.

"Do you know who you are?" Kay asked then, glancing at Rachel. Her voice was lower than normal and deeper. Her pupils had dilated so that they had taken over almost all of her irises, leaving only a soft blue rim around the black.

"Kay—"

"No," Kay said, and smiled. "I'm not Kay. My name is Sylvia. Sylvia Baumgardner."

There was such evil, such menace, in that smile and in those eyes as they glanced again at Rachel that a chill ran down Rachel's spine. Had Kay gone mad?

"Pull over, please. I want out."

It was a long reach to attain the note of crisp authority with which she had ruled countless classrooms, but Rachel made it. Whatever ailed

Kay, she was suddenly downright scary. Rachel wasn't going to sit there and play spectator while her friend lost her grip on reality with a vengeance. She was getting out of that car.

Kay laughed. "You don't have a clue, do you, you poor, stupid creature? You're Ann Smythe, the organist. Sweet little Ann. Butter wouldn't melt in your mouth, would it, dear? Always so pretty, so demure. Nobody would have guessed you were a whore, would they? Nobody but me. I knew, you see. I knew him so well. I knew the minute you started throwing out lures to him, the minute he responded. I knew the minute he broke his marriage vows with you. He was mine. He *is* mine."

Rachel's eyes widened as she listened to this guttural speech. Kay was almost spooky. She looked different, and she sounded different. Could she be a split personality? Rachel felt a tingle of fear at the possibility. She released her seat belt while holding it in place with her arm, and her fingers fumbled unobtrusively for the door handle. She would jump if she had to. Anything to get out of this car.

"Ah-ah. It's locked," Kay said, wagging a finger at Rachel as Rachel pulled on the handle, to no avail. Kay's eyes were wide open, but Rachel got the impression that they did not really see. She felt that something—not Kay, but *something*—was looking at her through those eyes like a creature peering out of a hole.

"Kay. You're not making any sense." Rachel kept her voice quiet and even. Common sense told her that Kay could not keep her a prisoner in the car forever. Rachel had only to stay calm, and she would be fine. What she was witnessing was horrifying, true, but it was surely some sort of nervous breakdown. Perhaps Kay had been under a great deal of stress lately. Rachel was ashamed to admit that she had been so caught up in her own concerns that she didn't know.

"You want sense?" Kay smiled nastily. "You want to understand what's happening, Rachel? You could ask Ann—but you don't even know Ann, do you? At least, not consciously. So I'll tell you. You—as Ann—stole my husband. Enticed him into adultery. Fornicated with him. You and he both thought I didn't know. But I did. I did, and I put a stop to it. Then. But he is weak, you know, weak in that way. He lusts after women. I put the fear of God back into him when he found out what I had done to you, and he was never again tempted to stray. Not in that lifetime. But when I found him again, he was up to his old tricks. Bedding cheap little tarts while ignoring the good woman whose love was his destiny. Because I was plain, you know. And you were pretty. All his women were pretty."

"You're very attractive, Kay," Rachel said uneasily.

Kay glanced at her with such hatred that Rachel shrank back. "I thought they were you, you know. But they weren't. You've been hiding, haven't you? While you schemed how to get him for yourself. But I've found you at last."

Rachel looked into the nearly black eyes and saw a real and terrible threat. Kay, for whatever reason, believed what she was saying with all her heart. Rachel fought down a sudden surge of panic. At all costs she had to stay calm.

"Kay, you're not well. Why don't you turn around, and we'll go back to the hospital and get you some help? Please, Kay." For all her good intentions, Rachel's voice trembled. Her every instinct screamed that she was in danger, but her mind still refused to accept that this woman who had been her lifelong friend could pose a threat. The thought that kept running through her head was, "This cannot be happening. Not to me."

"I am not Kay. I am Sylvia Baumgardner, wife of Reverend Thomas Baumgardner, minister of this church. You know Thomas as your precious Johnny." On the last three words, Kay's voice took on a terrible mockery. The car slowed as it turned off the main road, and Kay gestured out the window as she spoke. Rachel, scarcely daring to look at anything other than Kay now, saw that they were not far from Walnut Grove, pulling down the narrow dirt road that led to the First Baptist Church. As Rachel stared at the small frame building, Kay's meaning suddenly became all too clear.

Like everyone else in Tylerville, Kay had grown up with the tale of the minister who had cheated on his wife with the organist, and the wife's terrible revenge. Somehow Kay imagined herself as the wronged wife and had cast Rachel as the organist.

Rachel went cold as she considered the implications.

53

It was after five o'clock, and dusk was darkening the small patch of outdoors that Johnny could see from where he sat in Wheatley's office. He watched the sky and grew increasingly restive. He did not like the idea of Rachel being out of his sight once night fell.

"I need to make a phone call," he told the chief finally.

Wheatley, who'd already put a call into the Louisville postmaster to find out who owned that drop box, grunted. He had been probing Johnny unmercifully for every scrap of memory he could summon concerning the previous missives—all five hundred or so of them—from "eternally yours." So far he had not gotten the answers he sought.

"You sure you threw away every single one?" Wheatley sounded disgusted as he peered at Johnny from beneath lowered brows.

Johnny nodded. "I'm sure. There didn't seem to be any point in keeping them. Did you hear what I said? I need to make a phone call."

The chief pursed his lips, and his eyes narrowed. "Who to?"

"Rachel. It's getting dark. I want to tell her to stay put till I get there. Do I need you to sign a permission slip or something before I can use the phone?"

The chief smiled sourly at this and shoved his phone across the desk. "Go ahead."

"Thanks." Johnny picked up the receiver and dialed the hospital. On the third ring Elisabeth answered.

"Hello, Mrs. Grant. This is Johnny. Could I speak to Rachel a minute, please?"

He listened for an instant and went cold. His eyes rose to lock with the chief's, and he placed a suddenly sweaty palm over the mouthpiece. "She's not there," he said in a hoarse voice. "I dropped her off at the hospital more than an hour ago, and she's not there. She's never even been up to the room."

54

"*A*re you saying that you think Johnny is the reincarnation of Reverend Baumgardner?" The idea would have been ludicrous if the situation had not been so deadly serious.

"I don't *think* so. I know so. His soul is there in his eyes. Just as yours is. I don't know why I didn't recognize you sooner." The car bumped to a stop behind the church. They had driven the last few dozen yards over thick grass and were now parked next to the black iron fence that encircled the church's small graveyard. Nearly all the tombstones dated from the mid-nineteenth century, and the three side-by-side crypts at the very back were older than that. The cemetery was scrupulously maintained by the Preservation Society.

Rachel stifled a near-hysterical giggle as she remembered that Kay had lavished loving work on the restoration of the flower beds that the long-ago minister's supposedly murderous wife had planted. Had she been imagining herself as the minister's long-dead wife even then?

"The other two were a mistake." Kay was glaring at Rachel now that she was free to turn her attention from the road. Rachel was suddenly conscious of how much larger Kay was than herself. Kay was at least five feet seven or eight, built on queenly lines. If the matter were to degenerate to hand-to-hand fighting, Rachel realized she wouldn't have a prayer. Then Kay's words, and the meaning that had to lie beneath them, penetrated her distracted brain. All at once, with a sensation like a blow to the gut, she realized precisely with whom she was dealing.

"You—*you* killed Marybeth Edwards and Glenda Watkins, didn't you?" Rachel shrank as close to the door as she could get as she waited for the locks to be released. Once that happened, she would be out that door and across the grass like a hare with the hounds at its heels. Walnut Grove, the nearest residence, was only about three miles away. She just had to make it across the field and through the woods, and she would be safe.

"Like I said, they were a mistake." Kay shrugged. "Sometimes it is hard to see clearly. But now I've found you, and I *know*. The other two were no more than fool's gold. You're the one. When you are gone, he will be mine."

Rachel felt almost faint with horror. "But, Kay, you and Johnny— you've never seemed interested in him, or he in you. What makes you think that killing me will make him turn to you?" She didn't really hope to make Kay see reason. It was clear that Kay was beyond that. But she was willing to try anything, anything at all that might increase her chances of staying alive. Because she had just figured out that Kay had brought her out to this deserted cemetery to kill her.

"With you gone, he will no longer have any reason to struggle against his destiny. We are the eternal triangle, he and I and you. Sometimes you and I are men, and he is the woman. But you are always my friend, and my betrayer. You must always be destroyed before we can be happy together. He would have responded to me before now if it had not been for you. I know that. He has sensed your presence for years. Just as I have. Only you and he didn't know what you sought, and I didn't know who."

"Kay, this is crazy." As soon as she said it, Rachel knew she had made a mistake.

The smile Kay gave her was terrifying.

"Get out of the car," she said, and fumbled between her seat and the door for something. Rachel, poised to take advantage of the first instant the locks were released, was shaken to see that Kay was suddenly clutching a gun. It was large and black and businesslike, and it was pointed right at Rachel's chest.

"Kay . . ." It was a whispered appeal to her childhood friend, as Rachel truly faced the fact that she was about to die. Her appeal did no good at all. Kay's eyes glowed with satisfaction at this evidence of her rival's weakness.

"Be very careful," Kay warned her, her voice menacing. "I don't want to shoot you. But I will if I have to. Now get out of the car."

55

"*S*he's coming."

The words roused Jeremy from semiconsciousness.

Who, Mom? But then he knew. Not "it" but "she." The thing was a she, then. He trembled in terror.

"Get up. Stand over by the door."

Jeremy whimpered. The thing was coming, coming to kill him. If only he could die now, right now, and get it over with. He was so scared. He wanted to die. Mom, Mom! Take me to where you are!

"Get over by the door! Hurry!"

When his mom used that voice, she meant to be obeyed. Gasping, shaking, Jeremy managed to get on his hands and knees. He was dizzy, sick and dizzy, and his head pounded so, he thought it might explode. But his mom was relentless. He had to stand up. He pushed against the wall with his feet while his shoulder scooted up the cold stone. When he was upright, he was sweating. But he gritted his teeth and moved near the door.

"She will open the door. When she does, run! Run as fast as you can! Remember how you always won the hundred-yard dash at school? Run like that. You can do it, Jeremy."

I'm sick, Mom. And I'm scared.

"I'll be with you, son. Just run."

56

"*W*ait."

Rachel was out of the car, having slid out on Kay's side at Kay's command. It was raining now, sullenly. Rachel hardly felt the drops that pelted her. Her eyes were glued to Kay. The pistol never wavered as Kay walked around to the car trunk—it stayed pointed squarely at the center of Rachel's chest.

Kay slid a key into the trunk, opened it just a little so that it would not block her view of Rachel, and felt around inside. She pulled out a bundle of moldy-looking black cloth. Rachel, watching helplessly while her heart banged like a jackhammer, felt physically ill as Kay grasped the cloth with one hand, shook it out, and swirled it around her shoulders.

It was a cloak, a hooded black cloak that looked as if it dated to the nineteenth century. Wearing it, Kay seemed to have stepped into the present from another time. Looking her over with disbelief, Rachel frantically tried to think of some way she might escape. But she could come up with nothing.

"The flowers are for you, you know. For—later. Pink carnations. Pink is your color, don't you think?" The calm, eerily sane-sounding question was terrifying. Rachel was speechless.

Kay felt in the trunk again and withdrew a knife. It was a butcher knife, the kind found in many kitchens, including the one at Walnut Grove. But in Kay's grasp it took on a hideous menace. Rachel knew that she was looking at the weapon that had murdered Glenda, and possibly Marybeth as well, and she wanted to throw up.

Would she be number three? The possibility seemed unreal, so unreal that as she contemplated it, Rachel almost moved beyond fear. Surely she would not die in such a way. Her life was so sweet! She wasn't ready yet. She couldn't leave Johnny, or her mother, or Becky, or—

But such reflections led to panic, and panic was the one thing she couldn't afford. She must think like a rational being because that was the one thing Kay no longer was.

Kay could not stab her and hold the gun on her at the same time. That was one point in Rachel's favor, and she grabbed onto it like a drowning person to a branch.

Then a niggling little voice added a caveat. Maybe this time, Kay meant to use the gun. Maybe the knife was for stabbing her body after it was already dead.

Kay was insane. Hysterical sobs bubbled up in Rachel's throat as she faced the fact. Swallowing, she forced them back. If she was to have any chance at all, she had to stay calm.

Kay shut the trunk. Then she waved the gun at Rachel.

"All right. Walk."

"Where to?"

Rachel toyed with the idea of running, just taking off that very minute as fast as she could go and gambling that Kay would not shoot or would miss if she did.

"Toward the back of the cemetery! Now!"

At the last minute Rachel found she could not risk running. The idea of being shot in the back made her knees threaten to buckle. She turned and walked. Glancing about, she sought desperately for anything that might aid her. If only someone, anyone, would come! But the church was little more than a relic now, visited only on Memorial Day and when the Preservation Society came to plant flowers or pull weeds or do whatever it was they did. The building itself hid the graveyard from the road. About half a mile to her right, across an expanse of tall, golden grass, was the beginning of the woods through which she would need to run to reach home. To her left was a copse of trees that ended at an abandoned rock quarry. No hope for succor there. Ahead of her was the graveyard, and beyond it more fields.

If she was going to do anything to save herself, it had to be done in the next few minutes. She could sense Kay's growing agitation as the other woman walked some six paces behind her, and she feared that it might explode at any second into murderous rage. When that happened, unless a miracle occurred, her life would be over.

"Toward the vaults back there. That's right, the one on the end."

As Rachel slowly complied with Kay's orders, her eyes fell on a stout branch on the ground next to the partially buried crypt that was her destination. As weapons went, it was likely to prove pathetic against a gun and a knife. But it was all that offered itself to her, and perhaps if she grabbed it at the last minute and whirled about, swinging it—

She would be shot, or even stabbed. But it was better to die fighting than just to die.

Rachel felt terrified sobs rise up in her throat. She choked them back, clenched her fists, and fought to remain clear-headed. If she were to have any chance at all, she had to be able to think.

At that moment she began to pray.

57

"$\mathcal{R}$eady, Jeremy?"

I'm ready, Mom.

But he was so scared. At least his fear was making him feel stronger. At the idea that the thing would soon appear in the doorway with its knife, his heart pounded and his breathing quickened, and the awful, blinding pain seemed to leave his head.

"As soon as the door opens, son. Run."

Jeremy flattened himself against the damp moldy stone as he heard the scratching sound for the second time. He knew what it was now — the sound of a key scrabbling in search of a lock.

He braced himself to shoot forward like a bat out of hell.

His only chance lay in catching her by surprise and barreling past her before she recovered. If he couldn't do that, he would die.

The lock creaked as it turned in its cylinder.

"I'm with you, Jeremy. On your mark . . ."

58

When Rachel stopped on Kay's orders, the branch was about eighteen inches from her feet. Kay smiled continually now, only the smile was a grimace. It was the most terrifying thing Rachel had ever seen. The ancient stone burial vault to which Kay had herded her was partially buried and overgrown with vines and moss, with the name *Chasen* carved into the rusty iron door.

Chasen. Rachel felt a new wave of horror as she realized that this was the crypt where the organist's remains were reputed to have been found. Kay, as a part of her mad fantasy, was going to kill her in the vault.

"Don't move." Kay stepped around her carefully to assault the lock with a long, ornate iron key that she pulled from a pocket of the cloak. It was slow work, as the lock was old and Kay couldn't take her eyes off Rachel. Rachel, fighting panic, knew that when the door opened, the fight for her life would begin.

"You didn't bring the others here." Rachel strove to keep her voice calm. She hoped to distract Kay from her task long enough to sidle closer to the branch.

"There's too much hue and cry now. If you were found like the others, I might put myself at risk. Certainly I would put Thomas at risk. I don't want him to go back to jail."

"I'll be missed, Kay. My family will look for me everywhere."

"But they won't find you." The lock clicked audibly, and Kay smiled with satisfaction. "The police will look, but they'll end up saying you ran away. Just like they did when I killed you before. Just like they did with that boy."

"That boy—" Rachel stiffened with horror. "You mean Jeremy Watkins? Did you do something to him, too?"

"He saw me." Kay pulled the key from the lock and pocketed it. "He's in here. Dead, by now. Or near enough to make no difference."

"You killed him?" Rachel felt faint again at the thought of poor little Jeremy suffering the same slashing blows as his mother. The same ones that would shortly rain down upon her.

"Not like the others." For a moment Kay looked almost confused. "I didn't hate him. He just got in the way. So I hit him and brought him here. I was going to kill him, but I was interrupted. Some fool out-of-towner saw my car parked by the church and pulled in to ask directions." She chuckled, and the sound was horrible. "It was almost as if God didn't want me to kill him that night. So then I decided, I'll let God take him in His own good time. By now, He's probably done so."

"How can you talk so calmly of God?" It was a cry from the heart, and as soon as it left her lips, Rachel wanted to recall it. The confusion vanished from Kay's eyes to be replaced by the same icy intent that had dwelled there since that moment in the car.

"This is all part of a divine plan," Kay said almost primly, and took hold of the hoop-shaped handle. The hinges must have been oiled sometime in the not-too-recent past, because the door swung open easily and without a sound.

59

o!"

Jeremy burst shrieking from that nightmare cave, his arms held out before him to shove the thing with all his strength if need be. She was there all right, huge and hideous, with her face in shadow and her black cloak billowing on the wind, but his screaming advent took her so by surprise that she fell back a pace. Jeremy, with his mom shouting encouragement in his ear, exploded past her into the blinding light of a world he hadn't seen in what seemed like forever. The fresh smell of the earth, the vitality of the wind, the life-giving shower of rain on his face all assaulted his senses at the same time as the light. He could barely see, but he didn't need to see. He only needed to fly, fly, fly into the light.

60

$\mathcal{R}$achel screamed, too, as Jeremy erupted from the cave. Her heart cheered to know that he was still alive, still able to flee, but then she had no more time to think. Kay stumbled back as Jeremy bolted past her and almost dropped the gun. Rachel, acting solely on instinct now, dived for the branch and came up swinging like Ted Williams at his best. The branch caught Kay full in the chest and knocked her down, back into the crypt.

Quick as a flash, Rachel slammed the door. Kay had the key. Kay was bellowing, and Rachel knew she wouldn't be able to hold the door closed for long against the other woman's greater strength. Still acting on instinct, she wedged one end of the branch into the door and the other into the soft earth.

It wouldn't hold for long, but it might give Rachel and Jeremy time to get away.

Kay was on her feet now. Rachel could hear the solid slam of her body against the door as she tried to force it open. Rachel kicked off her shoes and, feeling as if her feet had grown wings, fled toward the car. If she wasn't mistaken, Kay had left the car keys in the trunk.

"Jeremy!" She tried to call him, but he was already far ahead of her, flying down the dirt road toward the paved one, his arms outstretched in front of him, screams so high-pitched as to sound almost unworldly tearing from his throat.

Rachel had time only to glance after him before she was at the car. She dragged the keys from the lock—thank God they were there!—then jumped into the driver's seat and thrust them, with nary a fumble, into the ignition. Even as the engine turned over, the door to the crypt flew open and Kay stumbled out.

Rachel saw her with horror as she shifted into drive. Pressing the accelerator to the floor, she sprayed mud and grass in every direction as she made a wild, bucking semicircle and shot down the dirt road toward the highway.

In the rearview mirror, she could see Kay running after her, her face contorted, the black cloak flapping behind her in the wind so that she looked like Zorro, or an enormous crow.

Jeremy had almost reached the highway. Rachel swerved in front of him, blocking his escape, and leaned across the seat to throw open the passenger door.

"Get in!" she shrieked. For a moment she thought he meant to swerve and keep on running, but then he dove for the open car door and somersaulted headfirst into the seat.

Rachel glanced behind her in the rearview mirror, saw neither hide nor hair of Kay, and stomped on the accelerator for all she was worth. The passenger door flapped in the breeze.

"Jeremy. Jeremy, shut the door!"

At first she thought he was too overwrought to understand. But after no more than an instant, he reached out to slam the door shut. Rachel jammed the automatic lock button down, and the locks clicked shut.

They were at the junction of the dirt road and the highway when Kay exploded from the copse of trees to the left like an oncoming army. Rachel screamed, Jeremy screamed, and the car slithered as Rachel floored it. To Rachel's horror, it did a doughnut in the rain-slick mud and grass—and suddenly Kay was no more than five feet away, planted squarely between the car and the highway.

She was smiling that wicked smile. Her eyes glowed like twin pits of hell. Her arms came up, and she pointed the pistol right at Rachel's face.

Jeremy shrieked, cowering. Rachel shrieked too—and hit the gas.

Kay flew straight up in the air like the enormous crow she resembled as the Escort plowed into her and she landed on the hood with her face pressed to the glass of the windshield. Keening with horror, Rachel glimpsed the glazed-over eyes and the blood that trickled from Kay's nose and mouth before instinct kicked in again. She jerked the steering wheel sharply, sending the car careening to the left, and the body flew off the hood to land facedown on the road.

61

As nervous as she was, as fast as she was going, it was only moments before Rachel skidded off the rain-slick pavement. The Escort slid into a ditch, and she and Jeremy were flung violently forward. Jeremy landed in a heap in the passenger side footwell, while Rachel, slamming into the steering wheel, had the breath knocked out of her. For a moment she could only lie motionless, draped over the steering wheel like a rag doll. Then, slowly, painfully, she eased back from the steering wheel to look down at Jeremy. But first she glanced fearfully into the rearview mirror. She knew the road behind them would be clear. Still, she had to look, just to be sure. It was clear.

The car was almost on its side, tilted into the ditch at a crazy angle. It was indubitably stuck.

"Jeremy, are you all right?"

"Mom?"

"No, dear. It's Rachel. Rachel Grant."

"Oh." He was silent for a moment, and then he lifted his head and looked at her. "Is she dead?"

"Yes. Yes, I think so."

He started to cry soundlessly. "My head hurts. And I want my mom."

Rachel wanted to cry with him, for him and for herself, but first she wanted to be in a place that she knew beyond a shadow of a doubt was safe, surrounded by lots and lots of people.

"Jeremy, we're stuck, and I think we need to get out of here. Just—

just in case. My house is just a little way up the road. Do you think you can walk that far?"

He stopped crying and wiped his eyes on his forearm. "Yeah. If I have to."

"Come on."

Rachel forced her door open with some difficulty and climbed out. It was really raining now, hard enough to plaster her hair to her skull in just a few seconds. Jeremy, slithering out behind her, shivered as the rain struck him. He was wearing incredibly filthy shorts and a T-shirt, and blood was caked in a gaping wound perhaps three inches long just above his left temple. No wonder his head hurt!

"Let's go," Rachel said, looking fearfully back the way they had come. The downpour limited visibility, but she saw nothing to fear. Still, she clutched Jeremy's hand as they started off down the road.

It was less than a quarter mile to Walnut Grove's driveway. As they reached it, Jeremy, drenched like herself, his pale face awash in rain, glanced up at her.

"Is this your house?"

"Yes."

"Let's run."

They did, arriving at the front door just as a clap of thunder shook the sky and the heavens opened.

It was locked. Rachel pounded, put a finger to the bell and left it there, but no one came.

There was no one home.

That was odd, but Rachel wasn't about to stand out on the porch and try to figure it out. She was going to go inside and lock the doors and phone for help.

Luckily, they kept a spare key under the flower pot beside the steps.

"Is anything wrong?" Jeremy looked around nervously as Rachel opened the door. He had been a small boy before, but now he was wraithlike, nothing but skin and bone and huge sunken eyes. His ordeal had been much worse than hers. Rachel put an arm around his shoulders.

"No, nothing at all," she lied, and walked him into the house. With great care, she locked the door behind them, then reached for the switch to illuminate the front hall.

It worked. Rachel breathed a sigh of relief. She had not realized how much she had dreaded the dark or how frightened she still was.

"Come on, Jeremy. Let's go into the kitchen and call the police. Then we can get warm and dry and eat something, and—"

"You got any hot dogs?" he asked with faint interest.

Rachel laughed, hugged him, and sat him in a kitchen chair. "I'm sure we do," she said. "You can check for yourself while I make this one call."

He availed himself of her invitation, opening the refrigerator door and rummaging inside while she picked up the phone. Her fingers were shaking as she dialed the police. When the woman answered, she said, "This is Rachel Grant. I need to speak to Chief Wheatley immediately, please."

"He's out on a call and—did you say you were Miss Grant?"

"Yes."

"Oh, my land, the whole police department is out looking for you! We thought you'd been kidnapped! Where are you?"

"I'm at my home now. I *was* kidnapped. I have Jeremy Watkins with me, and we just ran over Kay Nelson with a car, and—"

Rachel broke off as she saw a shadow darken the glass window in the back door. Her eyes widening with horror, she recognized the wild-eyed, blood-streaked face with its hideous grin as it peered inside. With the overhead fixture turned on, there was no chance of them escaping Kay's detection.

"Send someone out here as quickly as you can! She's at the door!" she hissed into the phone. She dropped the receiver without bothering to hang up.

Kay rattled the doorknob. Thank God the door was locked! If they could only keep her out until the police arrived. . . .

Jeremy looked around, saw Kay at the door, and shrieked. Kay started laughing, wiggling her fingers at the boy in a taunting wave. Rachel flew to his side.

"Come on," she said urgently, pausing only to pull a butcher knife from the block on the counter before fleeing with Jeremy up the stairs. "The police are coming. She can't get in. We're safe. We're safe."

"Please don't let her get me again! Mom! Mom, where are you? I need my mom!"

"Come on, Jeremy!"

As they reached the second-floor landing, Rachel was horrified to hear the crash of breaking glass.

"She's coming!" Jeremy sounded near hysteria. Rachel felt the same way herself. But this time help was on the way, and she knew where there was a gun.

It was her father's, and to Rachel's knowledge it had been fired exactly once in the last ten years, to make sure it worked. It was on top of the tape storage cabinet in the third-floor ballroom. The bullets were kept beside it.

There was another crash of glass, and then a high-pitched, triumphant giggle made Rachel's blood run cold.

"Miss Grant—"

"Hush!" she said fiercely to the boy. For an instant, just an instant, she thought about running into one of the upstairs bathrooms and locking the door. But the locks were flimsy, and if Kay broke through them, she and Jeremy would be trapped. No, it was better to go all the way up to the top of the house and get the gun. Kay would have to search for them.

Kay was inside now. Rachel heard her grunting, heard the crunch of footsteps on broken glass, and felt sick. Jeremy moaned with terror. Rachel clapped her hand over his mouth and urged him up, up the narrow stairs to the third floor.

Down below she could hear Kay's voice calling, "Rachel!" Only it was not Kay's any longer. It was eerie, high-pitched, and evil.

Jeremy was shaking. Rachel snuggled him against her as they rushed toward the ballroom, praying that the police would get to them in time.

"Rachel!"

Kay was coming up the stairs! They had left wet, muddy footprints that she could follow. She must be hurt, or she would be upon them by now.

Cling to that thought, Rachel told herself fiercely as she ran around the corner into the ballroom with Jeremy in tow. The room was dark, a thick gray kind of dark because of the vast windows opening onto the rainy dusk. The ballroom was shrouded with shadows, but Rachel had no time to be afraid of them. She pushed Jeremy down behind the old couch and flew silently across the hard wooden floor to the tape cabinet. Running her hand along the top of it, frantic now as she expected to hear Kay behind her at any minute, she discovered to her horror that the gun was missing.

"Rachel!" The taunting cry was close now, and Rachel realized in despair that Kay was on the third floor coming swiftly toward the ballroom.

"Hide!" she hissed to Jeremy, who cowered behind the couch. He curled up in a little ball, his arms covering his head.

Downstairs she could faintly hear the clock chiming six o'clock.

Rachel barely had time to duck behind the tape cabinet when Kay appeared in the doorway. Kay was stooped over and seemed to list to one side. Her cloak dragged the ground, leaving a great muddy path in its wake. With her hair plastered to her skull and the hideous grin splitting her face, she resembled nothing human. Rachel's heart stopped as Kay's eyes found her in the shadows. Her hand tightened on the hilt of the knife she still clutched. If she could only hold Kay off, the police would come. . . .

Then Kay lifted her hand, and Rachel saw to her horror that she still had the gun.

From behind the couch Jeremy began to sob.

Kay's eyes swung around to seek him out. She took a step toward the boy's hiding place.

The sound of running feet pounding up the stairs and along the hallway arrested Kay in midmotion. Rachel felt a wave of relief so intense that she was light-headed with it. It had to be the police. Thank God, thank God! Kay shifted her attention from the terrified boy to the door, pointing the gun at the open doorway and taking a few steps backward to be able to cover Rachel and Jeremy as well as their rescuers.

Silent as a mouse now, Jeremy took advantage of the respite to slither on his belly all the way underneath the couch. There was no other cover in the room.

Rachel prayed he wouldn't need it.

Johnny burst through the open doorway, grabbing the frame and sliding to an ungraceful stop as his wet sneakers slid on the shiny wood floor. He was soaked to the skin, so wet that water ran off him to form puddles around his feet. He was wild-eyed and breathing hard as he glanced around the room.

"Johnny." Rachel's lips formed his name, but no sound came out. Horror closed her throat even as his eyes found her and some of the stark fear left his face. Except for Johnny's panting and the crashing of the storm outside, the big house was silent. It was obvious that he had come alone.

That meant that they were all three at Kay's mercy—and Kay had a gun.

"Thomas." Kay blinked once and took a step toward him. The gun wavered and lowered a degree. A smile curved her lips. Her eyes glowed. The effect was nightmarish.

"My God," Johnny said, his eyes widening as they fastened on Kay at last, absorbing the state she was in—and the gun.

"Johnny, I mean. You don't know you're Thomas, do you? But you are. And you're mine. Just as I am yours. Eternally yours."

Johnny cast a lightning glance at Rachel, who dared not risk drawing Kay's attention by uttering so much as a syllable. Given Kay's infatuation with Johnny, it was possible that he would be able to keep her talking until the police arrived, as they must surely do soon.

"I got your letters while I was in prison," Johnny said. Totally focused on Kay now, his voice was soothing, though he could not quite disguise the watchful gleam in his eyes. "They *were* from you, weren't they? They were beautifully written."

"How clever of you to guess." Kay giggled, a high-pitched, girlish sound that made Rachel's skin crawl. "You were always so clever, Thomas."

"My name's Johnny, you know." He smiled, stuck his hands in his jeans pockets, and leaned a shoulder against the jamb. Water dripped from the ends of his hair, and his drenched T-shirt was plastered against the hard muscles of his chest.

"Don't move!" The gun came up a degree, and Kay's warning was sharp. When Johnny showed no sign of disobeying, Kay again lowered the gun that small fraction and gave a tiny shrug. "It doesn't matter what you call yourself. I know who you are."

"How do you know?" Johnny's easy, lazy manner showed no sign of the tension he must be feeling. Rachel herself, still crouched behind the tape cabinet, peering out around the side, was gripping the hilt of the butcher knife so hard that her knuckles showed white.

"I recognized you the first time you kissed me."

"The first time I *kissed* you?" Bewilderment was plain in Johnny's voice. He straightened away from the jamb.

"I said don't move!" The hand holding the gun wavered alarmingly. Then Kay's voice changed, gentled. "It was my first grown-up kiss. You remember: It was at that Christmas party, when we were in high school. I was a senior, and you were a sophomore. I was with a girlfriend—I didn't have a date—and you were with a group of your friends. You were so cute. I couldn't keep from watching you, but I didn't think you even noticed me. I walked through a doorway—mistletoe was over my head—and you were standing there. You grabbed me and kissed me. Then you did it again. I knew you'd been aware of me all night just as I had been aware of you—and I knew who you were from the first kiss. My man. Mine."

"Hell, the only school Christmas party I ever went to, I was so drunk I could barely stand up. I don't remember a thing about it." It was an unguarded utterance, prompted by surprise, and it was a mistake.

"You don't remember?" Hurt was plain in Kay's voice. Her eyes narrowed. "No, I guess you wouldn't. I've been faithful to you, but you—you've been with so many girls since then that you probably don't remember the half of them."

"I do remember, now. . . ." But Johnny's valiant effort to save the situation was swept aside. Kay stood straighter, her face contorting with hate as she cast a venomous glance at Rachel before focusing on Johnny again.

"You've always been a philanderer, haven't you? I hope you're proud of yourself. Do you see what you've driven me to? Ann Smythe, Marybeth Edwards, Glenda Watkins, all dead because of you. And more, so many more over the centuries we've been together. Do you think I *wanted* to kill them? Do you think I *want* to kill Rachel now? It's you, you, *you*."

The wail of approaching police sirens cut through the noise of the storm. Kay broke off, listening. Rachel listened, too, frozen in place. Neither she nor Johnny dared move their eyes from Kay.

"The police are coming. They'll take me to jail. And *she'll* have you." Kay was babbling now, her voice growing increasingly shrill. "I have to kill her— No. I'll kill us. You and I. We'll be together in eternity and *she'll* never have you! Not in this lifetime!"

Kay gave a crazed giggle that raised the hairs on the back of Rachel's neck. The hand holding the gun jerked up, aiming squarely at Johnny's head. Johnny took an instinctive step backward, holding up a hand to ward off the forthcoming bullet. . . .

"Die, my darling," Kay said, giggling.

"No!" Rachel shouted, leaping to her feet. Outside, thunder boomed. Rain rattled at the windows. The sirens grew louder. . . .

Kay glanced at Rachel for no more than a split second. In that tiny fraction of time, Johnny launched himself toward the woman in a low, fast dive reminiscent of pro football at its best.

Kay shrieked, leaped back—and the gun fired with a sound like an explosion.

Johnny screamed and hit the floor just short of his target, rolling over and over in Rachel's direction, his hand clutching the side of his neck. Rachel was horrified to see bright red blood well out between his fingers.

"Don't be afraid, Thomas. Death doesn't hurt," Kay whispered as she came after him, pointing the gun toward Johnny's prone form, clearly intent on finishing the job.

"No!" Rachel screamed again, hurling herself at Kay with the butcher knife raised high.

"Slut!" Kay's gaze shot up, and the gun fired a second time. The impact was like being kicked in the shoulder by a horse. It sent Rachel tumbling back while the knife went flying from her hands to land with a clatter some six feet away.

Kay turned her attention back to Johnny, who lay unmoving while blood poured from a jagged wound in the side of his neck, and aimed the gun at his head.

From out of nowhere came a huge flash of lightning and an ear-splitting crack. A large branch blew against the wall-to-ceiling windows that lined the far end of the room, shattering them.

Kay, who was closest, was showered with exploding glass. She cried out and swung around to face the windows. With Johnny lying forgotten behind her, she took a step toward them, then another, as if drawn by something she saw in the blustery, rain-filled night.

In that instant, Stan's wheelchair, which stood not many feet from Rachel, must have been caught in the current of cold, wet air that suddenly blew through the room, because it moved.

With a certainty that defied all explanation, Rachel knew what she had to do.

Ignoring the pain in her shoulder, she lunged toward the chair, grasped the handles, and ran toward Kay as hard as she could. The chair caught Kay squarely behind the knees. Kay fell hard into the leather seat, but her weight only seemed to make the chair move faster. Rachel barely had time to release the handles before the chair hit what remained of the window frame and tipped violently forward. Kay screamed once as she was pitched through the broken window, and then she vanished into the night.

Rachel turned, made it to Johnny's side, and collapsed. She was still on her knees, trembling, desperately pressing the wadded hem of her skirt against the oozing wound in his neck, when the whole six-man Tylerville police force burst into the room.

62

On the following day, in a hospital in Louisville, a small group of people clustered in a corridor just outside a closed door. Tom Watkins and his children, Tom's girlfriend Heather, and Chief Wheatley were among those talking quietly to a white-coated doctor.

"Ready?" the doctor broke off his conversation to look down at Jeremy when the boy shuffled his feet impatiently.

Jeremy nodded.

"Come on, then." The doctor walked over to the closed door, opened it, and stood back. Tom and Jeremy approached the door hand in hand. Then Tom stepped back.

"You go on," he said to his son, letting go of his hand.

"You sure, Dad?"

"Yeah. Get in there."

Jeremy stepped past the doctor and hesitated. The room was very dark and quiet compared to the hallway outside, and he couldn't really see the figure in the bed clearly. What if someone had made a horrible mistake? He didn't think he could stand it if they had.

"Are you Jeremy?" A nurse had been sitting beside the bed. She stood up and smiled at him.

Jeremy nodded.

"She's been asking for you." The nurse beckoned him closer.

Jeremy was almost afraid to move, but he forced himself to take a few steps. The nurse looked down at the motionless figure in the bed.

"Your son's here, Mrs. Watkins," the woman said softly.

Jeremy felt his heart begin to pound as the figure stirred.

"Jeremy?" It was a weak whisper, so weak that Jeremy could scarcely hear it. But he knew that voice.

"Mom?" He took another step forward, and then he was running. He would have flung himself upon the bed had the nurse not caught him around the waist with both arms and held him off with a gentle, "Easy, now. We don't want to hurt her, do we?"

"Mom!" It was she. She turned her head, and the greenish light from the bedside monitor illuminated her features.

"Jeremy." She smiled lovingly at him, and her hand emerged from the bedcoverings to grope toward his. The nurse let him go with a warning squeeze. Jeremy caught her groping hand in both of his and leaned over the frail body of his mother. Tears—of happiness, of relief, of thanksgiving—rose to fill his eyes, then overflowed to trickle down his cheeks.

"I thought you were dead." He choked the words out.

"Not yet." Glenda managed another weak smile. "I'm harder to kill than a polecat. They say I'm gonna be all right. Don't worry."

Jeremy leaned closer to press his cheek against his mother's.

"It was the worst nightmare." His voice broke and, sobbing, he buried his face against Glenda's thin shoulder.

"I've been having nightmares, too," she whispered. "Horrible nightmares, about you being trapped in a dark cave and calling to me. I tried and tried to go to you."

"I was in a kind of cave, and I did call you." Jeremy lifted his head to stare at his mother.

"Yeah? I kept dreaming you were in danger."

"I was. You saved me. That bad woman was gonna kill me—"

"That's enough," said the nurse. "We don't want to upset your mother, do we? You can tell her about your adventures later. For right now, she needs to be quiet and rest." The nurse put a silencing hand on his shoulder.

Jeremy bit his lip. Glenda reached up and pulled him close. Mother and son clung to each other as the nightmare slowly went away.

Outside in the corridor, Tom Watkins scowled at Chief Wheatley.

"You had no right to let these kids think she was dead. They've been through pure hell."

Wheatley sighed. "I told you how it was, Tom. My primary goal was to keep Glenda alive. We couldn't protect her from everybody in Tylerville, twenty-four hours a day for what might've been weeks. She was in a coma when we found her, and she stayed in a coma till yesterday, when I'm told she started hollering Jeremy's name and woke up. If we'd told anybody, especially the kids, that she was alive, the whole town would've found out. You know how people are. And there wasn't anybody, including you, who I wasn't a hundred percent sure was not a suspect. We had a guard outside her room, but one slipup, and she could've been dead for real. Don't forget she saw the killer."

"Yeah, yeah."

"Seemed like the best thing to do was let the killer think she was dead until Glenda woke up enough to tell us who stabbed her."

"And did she? Tell you, I mean."

"Oh, yeah. About this time yesterday. By the time she gave us Kay Nelson's name, the woman was already attacking Miss Grant and Harris and your boy."

"Thank God they're all alive."

"Amen to that."

The door to Glenda's hospital room opened, and Jeremy came out. The nurse waited in the doorway.

"She wants to see the girls and Jake." Jeremy was beaming even as he dashed tears from his cheeks.

"Mama! Mama!" The three children rushed toward the open door.

"One at a time," the nurse said good-humoredly. Ashley pushed forward, and the door closed behind her.

"Mama," Jake said pitifully as he and his sister turned away from the door. His lower lip quivered in ominous warning.

"You'll both get a chance," the doctor told them, placing a consoling hand on each small shoulder.

"Mom's alive, Jake," Jeremy told his brother. He looked at Lindsay. "Mom's alive, Lin!"

"That's pretty great, ain't it?" Tom Watkins said, smiling.

"Yeah, Dad. Pretty great," Jeremy answered, and grinned.

Epilogue

"*K*ay *was* crazy, wasn't she?"

"Of course she was." Johnny took her hand and squeezed it reassuringly. Since he'd come zooming to her rescue on his motorcycle, rocketing through the storm at speeds of well over a hundred miles an hour and leaving the police far behind, he had seemed to need to touch her. Even in the hospital under heavy sedation as he was that first night, he had tossed restlessly, calling for her, until Rachel, whose flesh wound had required only outpatient treatment, had come to sit with him. He'd quieted as soon as she'd taken his hand.

The time was two months later, and Rachel stood with Johnny beside her father's grave. Stan Grant had died that horrible night when Kay had tried to kill them, and the urgent summons of all family members to his bedside was why Rachel had found no one at the house. His passing had occurred at exactly five minutes past six o'clock.

Rachel, at first haunted by the fact that she had not been with him when he died, gradually became possessed of a notion that gave her comfort and would not leave her.

The clock had chimed six only minutes before the branch had blown through the windows and the wheelchair had moved. If that had not happened, Kay would most likely have killed Johnny, and possibly Rachel and Jeremy, too, before the police arrived. Rachel was certain in her own heart that they had been saved by the spirit of her father, who had passed from this life at almost the precise moment of his daughter's greatest need. Had he paused on the road of his final journey to save his daughter's life?

Rachel felt certain that at the end his spirit had been in that room with her.

It was a lovely thought, and Rachel embraced it. It helped her to let go of her father with love rather than grief and turn her focus forward to the remaining days of her own life.

"We can stay in Tylerville a little longer if you want," Johnny said softly. It was November now, and a definite chill hung in the air. Johnny wore his leather jacket zipped up around his chin, and Rachel's coat was of heavy wool and skimmed her ankles. The only reminder of his wound —a jagged scar midway up the left side of his neck where Kay's bullet had gouged his flesh—was hidden beneath his leather collar. Rachel's own wound was no more than a graze, across the top of her shoulder near where her bra strap rested. It ached faintly in the cold, and she wondered if that ache would stay with her for the rest of her life as a reminder of what she'd almost lost.

"No, I'm ready to go. I just wanted to say good-bye to Daddy first."

"I wish I could have known him better."

"I wish he could have known you. I wish he could have been at our wedding."

They had married quietly, in the living room at Walnut Grove, only the day before. Jeremy was best man, and the rest of the Watkins family, with Glenda in a wheelchair, had been in attendance. When they left the cemetery, they would be heading straight for Colorado, which Johnny had always wanted to see, for a combination driving tour–honeymoon. Rachel's only stipulation was that the journey be undertaken by car, not motorcycle. Johnny's only stipulation was that he drive.

"Johnny, do you think it's possible Daddy's spirit saved us?"

Johnny lifted the hand he held to his lips. They had talked about this before, and he knew the idea gave her comfort.

"It's possible," he said. "Why not? Certainly something of us survives death, and your father loved you devotedly." He smiled down into her upturned face, and quoted softly:

" 'The countless generations like autumn leaves go by: Love only is eternal, love only does not die.' "

"That's beautiful," Rachel breathed, turning into his arms, which closed tightly around her. Briefly she was reminded of Kay's obsession, and she shivered.

"Henry Kemp." Johnny identified the poet with satisfaction. "Like Robert Burns, he had a hell of a line."

"Oh, you!" Rachel pulled away from him, but she was laughing. His words had banished the sudden chill.

"I love you," he said, suddenly fierce.

"I love you, too," she answered.

Johnny bent his head to kiss her. Then, fingers entwined, they walked together out from beneath the trees overhanging the graveyard into the bright sunshine of a new life.